The Painted Canoe

Other Phoenix Fiction titles from Chicago

The Great Fire of London by Peter Ackroyd
The Bridge on the Drina by Ivo Andrić
Concrete by Thomas Bernhard
Gargoyles by Thomas Bernhard
The Lime Works by Thomas Bernhard
Woodcutters by Thomas Bernhard
The Department by Gerald Warner Brace
Lord Dismiss Us by Michael Campbell
The Last, Long Journey by Roger Cleeve
Acts of Theft by Arthur A. Cohen
A Hero in His Time by Arthur A. Cohen
In the Days of Simon Stern by Arthur A. Cohen
Solomon's Folly by Leslie Croxford
The Old Man and the Bureaucrats by Mircea Eliade
Fish by Monroe Engel
In the Time of Greenbloom by Gabriel Fielding
The Birthday King by Gabriel Fielding
Through Streets Broad and Narrow by Gabriel Fielding
Concluding by Henry Green
Pictures from an Institution by Randall Jarrell
The Survival of the Fittest by Pamela Hansford Johnson
The Bachelor of Arts by R. K. Narayan
The English Teacher by R. K. Narayan
Swami and Friends by R. K. Narayan
Bright Day by J. B. Priestley
Angel Pavement by J. B. Priestley
The Good Companions by J. B. Priestley
Golk by Richard Stern
A Use of Riches by J. I. M. Stewart

The Painted Canoe

Anthony Winkler

The University of Chicago Press

The University of Chicago Press, Chicago 60637
The University of Chicago Press, Ltd., London

© 1983 by Anthony C. Winkler
All rights reserved. Originally published 1985
University of Chicago Press edition 1989
Printed in the United States of America

98 97 96 95 94 93 92 91 90 89   5 4 3 2 1

Published by arrangement with Lyle Stuart, Inc.

Library of Congress Cataloging in Publication Data

Winkler, Anthony C.
   The painted canoe / Anthony Winkler.   *11.95*
      p.   cm.—(Phoenix fiction)
   I. Title. II. Series.
PR9265.9.W54P35   1989   88-28738
813'.54—dc19   CIP
ISBN 0-226-90206-4 (pbk.)

For Roy Porter, who believed.
For Cathy, who went home with me.

Chapter 1

His name was Zachariah Pelsie. He was unspeakably ugly. When he was a child he contracted a disease that left him horribly disfigured. His jawbone was swollen and elongated, giving his face the truculent underbite of a barracuda. His hands were huge and dangling. He walked with the stooping, shuffling gait of a seafarer and squinted at everything about him as though even the grasslands and the trees sparkled with the painful scintillation of the open sea. Yet he was a man of unyielding pride, who insisted that men call him his rightful name given him by his mother. He would not endure being demeaned by some frivolous nickname, such as fishermen are fond of calling one another.

It was such a trivial thing as a nickname, for instance, that had driven him from the parish of his childhood. When he was still a youth, his fish traps caught so many goatfish that the other fishermen began to call him "goatfish". Men passing on bicycles hollered out "goatfish" and were insulted if he did not acknowledge them. Women higgling fish along the roadside carolled "goatfish" when he walked past. Nothing he did or said could erase that foolish name. Had he not been so hideously ugly, he would have endured this nickname; but in his shame and sensitivity over his ugliness, he forgot the original incident that had brought on the name, and took it, instead, as an insulting reference to his horrible looks. Then living in the parish of Westmoreland, Zachariah made up his mind to move.

He sold his canoe, packed his few possessions, and moved away from the parish. Wandering from one district to another, he fished and foraged among wild fruit trees for food. Sometimes he worked as a day labourer for the Public Works Department, spreading white marl stones on unpaved roadways, drawing water from springs for use in the steam rollers. As soon as he earned enough money to buy food, he would wander into another parish.

Bristling with promontories, Jamaica, the island of his birth, swims on the edge of the Greater Antilles, its dorsal side sheltered by the spine of Cuba, its rocky underbelly raked by seas driven off the Yucatan peninsula. Here Zachariah was born the descendant of African slaves, and here he wandered trying to escape his ugliness.

He went from one village to another, through the interior of the island where the cane waved shiny and green in the morning breezes; through coastal villages where white combers roared over reefs and shattered against sea walls; through the plainland parishes where cotton trees loomed majestically over the small plots of cultivators and the sun scorched the earth with a vengeful heat.

He slept in the bush, curled up against the trunks of **trees for shelter against** the dewfall. He bathed in warm streams that tumble over every part of the island. And when it rained, he slept shivering and wet under a tree, his head covered by a banana leaf.

He was attacked by village dogs, accosted by suspicious constables, and roughed up by gangs of unruly country youths. He came across lunatics in the bushland, some who shrieked their madness, others who sat by the wayside peering out gloomily through the thicket. He passed couples fornicating on the ground, heard them grunting their passion, and saw the bushes tremble where they lay. He ate fruit

2

growing wild on trees, caught small shore fish and ate them raw. Once, as he was fishing from a rock, he saw a pelican floating on a nearby swell, and killed it with a stone. Wading into the roaring breakers, he retrieved the dead bird from the sea, cut its throat, plucked it, and roasted it on a spit. But the flesh tasted so raw and bitter that he had to throw the carcass away after only one bite.

Eventually he came to a village he liked and settled in the bushland as a squatter. He met a woman who took him in to live with her in a small wooden house on the edge of the bay. She was the first woman in his life.

The woman bore him three children, the first of whom — a daughter — died in infancy. His children grew up calling him "Papa" and "sah", which is Jamaican for "sir". His neighbours called him by his rightful name. The new village, in the parish of Portland, was Charity Bay.

Here Zachariah made his living as a fisherman, and here he continued in his stubborn ways. Once he had made up his mind that a thing was so, or that a thing should be so, nothing could shake his belief. And even when he was proven wrong, he still persisted in the wrongful belief out of sheer obduracy.

Because of this flaw in his character, he lost money on bets he should never have made. He would wrongly remember the outcome of a cricket match, or something that had happened long ago, and insist that it was so. Someone would maintain that it was not so, and in the heat of argument and rum drinking, a bet would be made, which Zachariah would lose. But even when he lost and was forced to pay his debt, he would leave muttering to himself that a dreadful mistake had been made, still holding vehemently to wrong opinion.

Zachariah was, in the words of Parson Mortimer, "uglier

dan sin and stupider dan fowl!" For, as the Parson told Mr. Wilson once in a fit of temper, "When ugly man wrong, him worse wrong dan when pretty woman wrong, dan when criminal wrong, dan when Clerk o' de Court wrong. For when a man uglier dan sin and stupider dan fowl, and him wrong, and you prove dat him wrong, and you show him on paper in black and white where him wrong, and him still to him dying day swear dat him right and you wrong, when de whole world know dat *him* wrong and *you* right, dat man suffer from perversity o' sin, excess o' pride and boastiness, and woe unto him one o' dese days!"

So the Parson fumed to Mr. Wilson, the oldest fisherman in the village, one Sunday morning on the steps of the stone church. Mr. Wilson listened dourly and refused to take sides. Zachariah was his friend who fished beside him at nights on the deep side of the reef, their canoes separated by the lunging black sea. When the fishing was bad, they called to each other across the ocean to pass the long night.

The quarrel between the Parson and Zachariah was over religious doctrine. Although he could neither read nor write, Zachariah had his own definite ideas about the ways of God, which he had explained one day to the Parson. And nothing would have come of the explanation, if the Parson had not laughed so hard that spittle ran down the corners of his mouth. For the Parson was vain about his American university education, and could not stand to be contradicted. He was constantly bragging about the books he had had to read at the university, books with such unsayable titles that the mere mention of them brought stares of awe from the illiterate villagers. Whenever anyone disputed an opinion of the Parson, he would glare at the offender and rattle off some of the titles of these books, defying the contradictor to pronounce them correctly.

4

"You ever read de Apocrypha?" the Parson would demand. "How you say 'Apocrypha'? You ever hear o' de Elysium Mystery? How you say it? Make me hear you say it right!"

When the flustered, cornered heretic would stammer over these strange words, the Parson would fix him with a piercing stare and say scornfully,

"Him can't even say de word let alone read de book! So don't tell me 'bout religion, man! 'Cause me read dat book from start to finish and you can't even say it proper!"

The argument began when Zachariah told the Parson that he thought he understood why God did not come more often to the aid of suffering men. God did not help, Zachariah solemnly said, because men called on him too often, over every little foolish trouble that only required human effort and persistence to solve. So when real trouble came, and the sufferer called out to God, the Almighty turned a deaf ear, for he was constantly being badgered to help over foolishness. This was what Zachariah believed and what he explained to the Parson one day in idle conversation on the stone steps of the church.

At least, it was what Zachariah thought he believed. It had occurred to him one night during a rain squall, when his canoe rolled perilously on the deep side of the reef. There was lightning that arched into the turbulent ocean, and thunder so loud that it sent a shiver running through the seamless hull of the canoe. Zachariah was huddled down in the bottom of the canoe, holding on to its gunwales, and wincing with fear over every peal of thunder. He was about to call out to God to come to his rescue, when the idea dawned on him.

The rain roared against the sea and pelted him on the back of his neck as he cowered in the bottom of the canoe

5

and tried to think about why he was calling to God. For he was in no real danger from the squall so long as his anchor held the canoe fast against the reef. The canoe pitched and rolled terrifyingly, but with her prow swung into the seas, she was riding out the squall as she was built to do. There was a howling wind off the open sea, and the rain had doused the kerosene light of the cresset, leaving him in darkness, but no man had ever died from the noise made by the wind, or from the blackness of the turbulent sea. Yet here he was bawling out to God as though he were at death's door.

"When me go to de Almighty again," he muttered, wiping the dripping rain off his face, "you know me on death doorstep."

For the rest of the night, he was comforted by this idea as he clung to the gunwales of the canoe and watched the lights of Charity Bay tossing against the dark, wind-swept shoreline.

"You think God Almighty, who make and care for de sparrow, is like a stingy landlord?" the Parson guffawed, when Zachariah told him about his idea. "If you ask him to fix de toilet, him won't come fix de running pipe. And if you bodder him 'bout de pipe, when de roof leak him let you bed get wet. You think God is so hardhearted?"

"But," Zachariah protested, "God have plenty on him brain, and when you run to him over every little thing, soon him don't know when you truly need him or when you just bawling over little fool-fool hardship."

The Parson chuckled.

"You ever hear o' de Apocrypha, Pelsie?" the Parson asked, giving off a rumbling belly-laugh.

Zachariah scowled at the mention of this big word.

"You ever catch a mackerel, Parson?" he replied angrily.

The Parson pounced immediately on this.

6

"Dat's exactly what me mean," he said triumphantly. "Me will leave de fishing to you. You leave God Almighty to me."

Trapped by his own words, Zachariah stalked gloomily down the pathway that led from the church, the laughter of the Parson ringing in his ears.

And there the quarrel would have ended once and for all with a less obdurate man.

But it began all over again the following Sunday. The Parson had chosen Zachariah's idea for the theme of his weekly sermon. Without saying where the idea had come from, the Parson informed the congregation that last week a man had approached him with a comparison between God Almighty and a hardhearted landlord. This man, said the Parson with a wheeze, believed that God should only be asked for help when the trouble was especially severe, but never if the trouble was minor or the kind that one might meet in daily living. Wrinkling up his brow, the Parson lifted a finger of reproof and took a deep breath, intending to excoriate this mistaken doctrine. But before the Parson could say another word, Zachariah stood up and walked out of the church, drawing the stares of the congregation.

The Parson could not believe his eyes. Never before had any of these villagers walked out in the middle of his sermon. When service was over, he drove to the Pelsie house to ask about Zachariah's health, certain that the ugly fisherman must have taken dreadfully ill to do such a rash thing. He was met at the gate by Zachariah, who leaned against a wooden fence post and smoked a plug of donkey-hemp tobacco.

"Pelsie," the Parson said severely, going over to where the fisherman stood, "what sick you today, man? How you leave de church so sudden? De gripe take you belly?"

7

"Wrongful doctrine sick me," Zachariah replied coolly.

The Parson was too stunned to answer for a second or two. Then he got very vexed. Better, he told Zachariah sternly, that a sinner not come to church at all, rather than leave in the middle of God's word. They had a terrible row right at the fence. Zachariah obdurately maintained that he would walk out of the service from now on whenever he heard anything said in the sermon that he disagreed with. The Parson got livid with rage. His black face swelled up like a puffer fish and looked as though it might explode.

For who had read the Apocrypha? the Parson wanted to know. And who had studied Elysium Mysteries? And who had been trained at the university in the United States of America, and excelled in polemics and hagiography? When Zachariah was unmoved by all this boasting, the Parson demanded to know further whose face was so ugly that one glimpse of it was enough to kill any fish? And whose jawbone was so huge that Samson could have used it to smite a Philistine? These insults the Parson screamed at Zachariah, until Carina, Zachariah's woman who was known to have a fiery temper, came out of the house and swore that she would beat the Parson with a switch if she heard one more insult out of him.

And so the trouble began between Zachariah and the Parson. Three years later, the quarrel was still going on. True to his word, whenever Zachariah heard anything in the sermon that he disagreed with, he walked out of the church. It did not matter how many faces turned and scowled at him as he walked down the aisle. It did not matter how many feet he had to step over to get out of the pew. It did not matter how much the Parson was screaming and jumping up and down in the pulpit. Carina would glare at him and hiss like a mad fowl. His two sons would hang their heads

8

in embarrassment and fidget. Nevertheless, Zachariah always walked out of the church if he disagreed with the sermon.

The Parson was vexed beyond reason at this defiance of his authority by an illiterate fisherman.

"All de years o' educashion in de United States of America," the Parson ranted to his mistress, a paunchy half-Chinese shopkeeper who lived in Port Antonio, "all de years I study doctrine, creed, biblical conundrum and scriptural enigma, and I come back to dis God-forsaken country only to have one ugly, illiterate brute tell me what I can preach and what I can't preach — Lawd God Almighty in celestial Kingdom of adamantine boulder, how much more temptation can mortal flesh and blood withstand?"

No man was more stubborn or set in his ways than Zachariah of Charity Bay. Nor was any man, woman, child, and some said even any beast, uglier.

Because of his stubborn, foolish pride, Zachariah also had a falling out with Carina, his common-law wife of twelve years.

When she had first laid eyes on him in the bushland, she thought he was the ugliest man she had ever seen. But his manner was gentle and shy and she felt sorry for him because he was ragged and poor and slept under a tree. She took him into the house she had lived in alone since the death of her mother, and she fed him and gave him a place to sleep on the floor.

During that first week, she watched him out of the corners of her eyes and wondered why he ignored her as a woman, why he shied away from touching her. Then she realized that his ugliness had driven women away from him, that he was as innocent as a child about such things. So she went to him one night and led him into her bedroom and taught him what most men learn in their boyhood, and showed him how he could please her in lovemaking.

She did this by lying on top of him where she could better teach him and show how it was to be done.

Many years later, they were still making love the same way, with Carina being on top. But this way of lovemaking became a bone of contention between them.

For the Jamaican countryman, and no one really knows why, is scornful of the man who will allow a woman to mount him during lovemaking. Some say that the Jamaican countryman has no sense, and that is why he mocks the man who is mounted by a woman. In Kingston, the capital, they say that the countryside Jamaican is a bush baby, a butu, a fool-fool from Back o' Wall — meaning that he is a lout from nowhere with no sense. He lives by superstitions and legends brought from Africa; he is haunted by ghosts he calls 'duppies', and terrified of voodoo, which he calls 'obeah'. The idea of being mounted by a woman drives him to speechless vexation.

Nevertheless, none of this would have troubled Zachariah. He had had only one woman in his life; she had taught him all that he knew about lovemaking. And he saw nothing wrong or demeaning in what she had taught him. Then Sparrow, a calypso singer from Trinidad, had a hit record called, "She Pon Top, Him On De Bottom", and the song was played over the radio stations and at all the dances. The way Sparrow sang the song, and the way the words went, told Zachariah that it was demeaning to a man who allowed a woman to mount him in lovemaking. Such was his obduracy and pride, that once he got this idea into his head, he could not let it go.

The next time that Carina felt in the mood for lovemaking, he tried to push her over and get on top. She flew into a temper and pushed him back down on the bed so that he was on the bottom. Zachariah got mad and threw her down and mounted her. But this made her so infuriated that she grabbed him in a private place, which she wrung as though she were killing a chicken for supper. Zachariah made a loud outcry, which woke up the two sons in the next room. Carina, however, was so enraged that she would not let go of the private part, but continued to wring it vigorously as though she intended to pop it off between her fingers.

And so they had a falling out over who should be on top and who should be on the bottom during lovemaking.

For the truth was that Carina could not stand the idea of being mounted by a man. When she was a child, she had been beaten and abused by her mother's lovers. In her heart, she was distrustful of men. She did not like to be dominated by them. She could not endure having a man tell her what to do. She would not put up with being mounted by one, as though she were a donkey to be ridden. Zachariah had not known any of this until he had tried to mount her.

Because Zachariah was so stubborn and proud, they had made no love for over a month. Each would look hungrily at the other in the flickering light of the kerosene lamp after the sons had gone to sleep, but neither would consent to being mounted by the other.

It was a fool-fool argument — so Carina told Zachariah one night — an argument that should never come between a man and a woman.

"Nobody lay atop o' de odder, Zach," Carina whispered to him. "Me lie on me side and you lie on you side and no one have to mount de odder."

He frowned as he considered this.

11

"But all dem years when you was on top!" he muttered complainingly like a man who finally realized after many years that he had been tricked all along.

"Dem years pass and gone, Zach. Now is de new time. Now we learn it fresh."

It was a Sunday night, the one night of the week when the canoes did not go to sea. The kerosene lantern on the small wooden table threw shuddering shadows against the walls of the small house. Outside, a freshening breeze lifted off the sea, and the cries of a patou – a night bird – drifted through the open window.

"All right," Zachariah said with decision, looking very grave and solemn and ugly. "Make me go on top twenty times, starting dis night, den after dat we do it 'pon de side."

"Me don't want no damn man riding me like me is a damn mule!" Carina snapped, her eyes flashing fire.

"Aha!" Zachariah exclaimed, spotting the insult. "But is all right for you to ride me like me is de mule! Zach is de mule and Carina is de rider, eh? Is so it go? Is so?"

She flew into a rage at his taunting tone.

"Who look more like mule?" she spat angrily, "you or me?"

There was no answering such an insult. Stooped over in the shoulders from all the years of rowing the cottonwood canoe, he stood up and left the room. She watched him go through the door while she cast around quickly for some object to hurl at the back of his head.

He went down to the beach. Working by the light of the moon, he readied the canoe for tomorrow night's fishing. From the window of the house, Carina watched him bending over the canoe, arranging the nets and the lines and the fish traps. She could see him inspecting the sail and the paddle and the oarlocks made of rope. As she watched, he took off his clothes and went into the sea for a bath as he usually did on a Sunday night before going to sleep.

When he came back into the small house, he walked silently into the bedroom and crawled over to his side of the bed on the far side against the wooden wall.

She was in such a temper that she thought of going out and cutting a switch and beating him.

The sons, however, were fast asleep. If she beat their father, he would no doubt raise an outcry that would wake them. There would be an uproar tonight and tomorrow, a scandal. She decided against beating him, telling herself that a woman should not beat her husband on the Sabbath.

Instead, she went down to the standpipe, drew water for breakfast and returned to the house with the pitcher balanced on her head. Then she lay down quietly beside him on the bed. He was already snoring.

But he did not sleep long. An hour later he woke and sat up quickly in bed. He had been dreaming that he was at sea and that he had fallen asleep. He looked around the dark room and felt the bed under his fingertips and saw the shadowy form of Carina sleeping next to him. He peered out the window and saw fireflies dancing in the darkness. In the distance, the calm harbour-locked ocean glistened under the glow of a new moon. He stayed awake almost all night, listening to the whispers of the sea against the shoreline.

Chapter 2

This was the month of September, the beginning of the rainy season. During the months ahead, the sea would be squally and dangerous. Northers would howl off the Florida peninsula and whip across the Antillean islands. And before the rainy season was over, one or two canoes would be blown out to sea by fickle, veering winds. Two years ago, a fisherman by the name of Obediah was killed when the land breeze blew his canoe out into the open sea. Last year, Ezekial Smith, who had only one eye and who had spent his boyhood in the nearby district of Cashew Ridge, perished in a squall.

So when Zachariah arose this morning, he stepped out into his yard and put his nose into the wind like a dog and sniffed the air to determine what kind of weather was brewing. He smelled the morning breeze from the step that led into his bedroom and then he circled the coconut tree growing beside the wattle-and-daub outhouse and sniffed the wind that came off the ocean.

His nose told him that the wind was freshening out of the east, which meant afternoon rain. After the rain, the sea would be flat and glassy, making it easy for the canoes to pass through the harbour breakwater and out into open sea. But by nightfall, a freshening land breeze would spring off the mountain range behind Charity Bay, a land breeze that would threaten to push the canoes off their anchorages on the fishing shoal. He told himself, as he made his way to the outhouse, that tonight he would be watchful for the land breeze. He would carry extra ballast in the bottom of the canoe so that she would ride heavy and stable in the wind.

The rest of the morning he was busy weaving a net from skeins of cotton lines. He hung the woven end of the net on the limb of a sea grape tree and he stretched the cotton lines over the beach and tied the unwoven ends to a stake driven in the sand. Sitting cross-legged on the beach, puffing a donkey-hemp cigar, he wove the net, knotting the lines into the webbing that would snare the fish by the gills.

The morning passed quickly, he was so engrossed in this labour. He would weave a few inches of net, then wade into the sea and splash water down the back of his neck, and rub sand between his toes, which gave him a pleasurable sensation. Once he had cooled himself off, he would return to his sitting position on the beach and resume the weaving.

In the afternoon, when he was weary with weaving, he turned the canoe over and ran his fingers across the bottom of her hull, searching for soft spots in the cottonwood. Then he turned the canoe right side up and swabbed the smell of dead fish and stale bait from her insides, and loaded the smooth, riverbed rocks in the bow and the stern for ballast.

He filled the water bottles from the standpipe. The cresset that hung from the prow of the canoe and gave him light to fish by, he filled with kerosene oil. Then he checked the calabash bowls that served as bailers during heavy seas and counted the number of lines which were stored in a small box and wedged under the rear thwart.

Walking around the canoe, humming a careless air to himself, Zachariah next examined the harpoon — a bamboo shaft fitted with a filed-down, barbed machete blade — which he used against the sharks that often circled the canoe with malevolent curiosity. After he had satisfied himself about

15

the condition of the harpoon, he took out the gaff, which he had made himself by lashing an enormous fish hook to a branch from a lignum vitae tree, and he filed down the point of the hook until it glittered in the sun.

The name of the canoe was the "Lucky P". Its hull was painted black and its boomless mast flew a yellow triangular sail, which enabled the canoe to run with the wind astern. But because she had no keel, the canoe could neither beat nor reach. So when the wind was contrary, Zachariah would row the canoe with the oars. But when the wind was astern, he sailed the canoe and steered her from the rear thwart with a paddle.

Soon he was satisfied with the gear loaded in the canoe, so he repacked everything in its proper place. Under the rear thwart he loaded the water bottles along with a bag of salt. Here he also placed a cork-handled knife.

When this was done, he inspected the anchor rope, and found a frayed length. He cut out the frayed piece and retied the rope to the anchor. With the land breeze blowing tonight, he would depend on the rope and the anchor to hold the canoe firmly against the fishing shoal.

"Ole rope," he muttered to himself, coiling it up again and placing the anchor in the canoe. He would replace the rope the next time he had a good catch, he told himself, staring at the sleek black canoe that was now ready for sea.

Next, he crossed the street and went into his house to prepare the bait for the night's fishing. Usually, he fished with four lines. He held two in either hand, and ran the other two down between his toes, his feet propped up on the gunwales. Two lines he baited with squid and ran down above the shelf of the reef, fishing for snappers. The other two lines he baited with fries — small fish taken with a throw net — and ran down to the bottom of the reef, where the alewife, the grunt, and the parrot fish lurked in the dark.

When everything was ready for the night's fishing, he went down into the village to the small shop owned by

16

Mr. Lewis where the fishermen could usually be found playing dominoes during the daylight hours.

The shop reeked of salted fish, cornmeal, and rancid oil. There were holes and fissures in the creaking wooden floor. Swarms of flies settled around the small glass case in which the cheeses and sugar buns were stored. Outside, under the shade of the shop's awning, the fishermen sat on wooden boxes and played dominoes.

Zachariah entered the dingy interior of the shop, said "good afternoon" to Mr. Lewis behind the counter, and bought some donkey-hemp tobacco. Mr. Lewis laid out the donkey-hemp, which was curled up like a long rope, and measured out a yard for Zachariah, who paid him with a coin. Mrs. Lewis, meanwhile, was fussing behind the counter with a broom, sweeping the floor. Whenever she came near, Mr. Lewis cringed and eyed the broom furtively. It was well known throughout the village that Mrs. Lewis was a terrible husband-beater.

"De wind goin' blow tonight, Zach," Mr. Lewis whispered, keeping a cautious eye on the broom. "You still goin' out to sea?"

"Wind never stop me yet," Zachariah replied, cutting off a piece of the donkey-hemp tobacco and chewing on it.

"See here, Missah Zachariah," Mrs. Lewis said, bad-temperedly glaring, "no spit no tobacco on me clean floor."

Zachariah bristled at this remark, which he took as an insult.

"You ever see me spit tobacco on dis floor?" he demanded, scowling.

"No," Mrs. Lewis said waspishly, with vigorous sweeps of the broom, "but dere's always a first time."

"But you never see me spit on you floor?" Zachariah persisted, fixing her with a dark stare.

"No, I never see you, but I also say dere's always a first time."

"Now see here, now." Zachariah raised his voice angrily

17

to recite his grievances to all onlookers within earshot. "Dis woman never see me spit on de floor. In all de years I come to dis shop, nobody ever see me spit on de floor. Now all o' de sudden, she giving me lesson in manners like me is a little boy, telling me dat me mustn't spit, when nobody ever see me spit on de floor. Now, sah, Mr. Lewis, is dat proper and correct?"

Mr Lewis squirmed and stroked his face with a nervous hand.

"Well," he muttered, looking cautiously at his wife.

A few higglers poked their heads inside the shop to see what the row was about. A fisherman loitering against the far counter, drinking a bottle of aerated water, listened attentively. Faces peered inquisitively through the open window.

Mrs. Lewis became very vexed and approached the counter with the broom, moving to assault range. Zachariah laid one huge fist on the counter, and measured the distance he would have to swing to get in a good thump if she clouted him with the broom.

Seeing that the ugly brute would not back down, Mrs. Lewis waved her hands placatingly and said, "I don't mean nothing by it, Missah Zachariah. I know you never spit on me floor."

"Den don't say nuthin' to me, den, until you see me spit on de floor. For you is out o' order to do dat! Right, sah?" Zachariah appealed to the fisherman at the end of the counter.

The fisherman nodded gravely.

"Completely out of order," he ruled with a solemn nod.

"Me say me sorry!" Mrs. Lewis said surlily. "Body can't do no more dan say it sorry. Me sorry. Me don't mean no offense. What you goin' do wid me? Take de ole body and push it inna hole? Beat me 'pon me head wid stick? Drown me in ocean waters? Body can't say nuthin' more dan sorry. Me sorry!"

Arms akimbo, not looking in the least sorry, she glared at Zachariah.

"A-hoa," Zachariah grunted, which was the triumphant sound of one who has won an argument, a sound that galled Mrs. Lewis so much that she very nearly let fly with the broom, but for the huge gnarled fist bristling with wicked looking knuckles that curled menacingly nearby on the dirty counter. For country people are always arguing about manners and custom and properness. And when one has clearly won, he says "A-hoa," to signify the victory.

"What you looking at, you ugly brute, you?" she challenged her husband, as Zachariah walked out of the shop. She was in such a bad mood that she felt impelled to clout her husband with the broom.

"Me? Me looking? Who see me looking at anything?" Mr. Lewis said, trying to shrink out of her reach. Nevertheless, she banged him sharply on the head with the broom handle, sending him scurrying into the backroom, before she returned to her sweeping.

Zachariah stood in the shade of the shop awning and watched the game of dominoes being played. The fishermen slammed the bone cards down on the wooden table, making loud noises, for the banging of the cards is part of the game. They argued about the plays and laughed boisterously when one of the players made a bad move.

Half an hour later, one of the players left to look to his canoe for tonight, and Zachariah sat down in his place.

Zachariah was not a good domino player. The game is one of subtlety and skill, requiring above everything else, a good memory. But Zachariah had no mind for numbers, and he had no skill for counting the cards to see which had been played and which were still in the hands of the players. Nor was he skilful at deducing who was holding onto what cards, for that required a cunning mind and sharp watchfulness. But Zachariah had no such gifts when it came to dominoes.

19

So he usually played either by luck or by hiding two or three cards of a suit that had almost been played out. And when he hid these cards, and the game was at its end, he would sometimes achieve a block and get a pass on the player under him. "Zachariah the dodger" was how his style of play was known to the other fishermen, who were very familiar with it.

He was sitting at the wooden table under the shade of the shop awning, hiding two cards from the six suit, when a country bus, crammed to the brim with higglers and animals, came to a stop across the street. Holding onto goat kids, chickens, and wicker baskets heavy with fruit, higglers streamed out of the bus.

The remaining passengers stuck their heads out of the windows to get some air, for the inside of the bus was stuffy and smelled of sweat and diesel fuel. A few higglers even rode on top of the luggage rack, clinging to the boxes and baskets when the bus swayed around corners.

The fishermen continued their play, ignoring the throbbing of the diesel engine and the jabber and confusion of the unloading passengers. Suddenly, a woman whose head was stuck out of the rear window, pointed at the domino players and shrieked, "Look here, me God, 'pon dis here ugly man!"

Zachariah winced but ignored the cry. Others in the crowded bus, having nothing better to do, took up the cry, and soon many of the higglers were chorusing about the ugliness of the fisherman playing dominoes.

"Where dat jawbone come from?" one shrieking voice jeered.

"De man look more like goat dan goat itself!" yelled another.

"Even me Mumma dog no ugly so!" cried a third, with a piercing laugh.

Zachariah played on, staunchly ignoring these taunts. But in his nervousness he made a bad play, which caused his team to lose.

20

"When God make a goat, and him make dat man, him mix up de jawbone o' de goat wid de man jawbone. Someplace, me say, someplace in Jamaica, you bound to find a goat wid a man jawbone 'pon him face!"

This was what one old higgler shrieked, baring her toothless gums when she laughed.

The others guffawed and carried on mischievously as they mocked Zachariah.

Finally, Mr. Wilson, who was standing nearby, could stand it no longer.

"Where you learn you manners," he cried in a loud voice, "You dutty negar, you?"

Which was a dreadful insult, meaning "dirty nigger", an expression that country people find very provoking.

The jibing higglers became nasty and hurled curses and insults at Mr. Wilson.

One screamed at Mr. Wilson that she saw his mother fornicating with a mongrel bulldog.

Another shrieked that he saw Mr. Wilson's "daddy" gormandizing on goat turds in the bush.

Among this general laughing and jeering, the bus pulled swayingly away, trailing behind an enormous, choking plume of black smoke.

The game was over. Zachariah stood up and said that he had to sleep in preparation for the night's fishing. Then he left the fishermen and went down the road towards his house.

Dogs wagged their tails as he approached. Small children playing in the dirt waved at him and cried, "Good afternoon, Missah Pelsie!" For their mothers had taught them with a switch to greet neighbours with well wishes and respect.

But Zachariah heard none of these greetings. His feelings hurt, he trudged down the village street wearing a hangdog look.

He was cursing silently to himself, muttering the patois obscenities of "Rass" and "Rass claat" under his breath,

21

paying no heed to the dogs who wagged their tails as he passed, or to the children who did as their mothers had taught and greeted him with good wishes.

He was brooding over his ugliness and pining for the day when his face had been normal looking. For he dimly remembered a time before the disease and the incessant headaches, when he had the normal face of any other grubby country boy, when his jawbone had looked as plain and comely as any other. In those long gone days, his mother even used to tell him that he was handsome.

Forgotten was his triumph over Mrs. Lewis, or the game of dominoes, or the quarrel with Carina about who should be on top of whom. All he could think of was the jeering and mocking over his ugliness.

"Rass," he whispered, glancing out to sea where clouds hung low over the horizon and white caps rolled in the afternoon sun.

When he got to bed, he was so vexed and upset that it was impossible for him to sleep.

The afternoon rain fell, making a thunderous clatter against the zinc roof, while he lay in bed and fretted over his ugliness.

Chapter 3

All afternoon he lay in the dark bedroom, listening to the rain pounding against the zinc roof. He heard Carina moving through the kitchen preparing the evening meal. He heard the sons come home from school, and he heard them romping in their bedroom. And when the mail bus thundered through the village, its air horn blasting, he got up and washed his face in the pan of water left by the bed, for it was time to go down to the canoe. But he still had not slept because of all his fretting.

When he got down to the beach, the sun was sinking into the horizon and the shoreline was bathed in the hazy golden colours of the sunset. Stretching all the way out to the breaking reef that was slung across the mouth of the harbour, the ocean was flat and glassy like a syrup. All along the beach, the fishermen were readying their canoes to put out to sea, their woman and wives standing nearby and giving unasked-for advice about the night's fishing.

Mrs. Ferguson was scolding her husband over some little thing, as she usually did before he put out for the night. Her bellowing voice carried down the length of the beach, drawing humorous glances and comments from the fishermen.

Old Mrs. Wilson was helping her husband load a fish trap onto the gunwales of the canoe. The trap was baited with orange peels and was ready to be lowered onto the side of the reef. Mrs. Wilson was complaining about the land breeze and casting anxious glances out to sea. Her husband was old and not as strong as he used to be, and she was constantly fearful that his canoe would be blown away.

Mrs. Hemmings was telling her husband the story of a movie she had seen last week in Port Antonio where she had gone to spend time with her mother. But already she was drunk from too much rum, which made her talk rubbish.

Carina helped Zachariah heave the canoe into the ocean, where it bobbed and rode with a slight list. Wading into the sea, Zachariah arranged the ballast until the craft was trim and even.

"De only time o' de day when negar turn pink," Zachariah muttered, glancing down the beach at the other fisherman whose faces and bodies glowed with the soft pink tones of the sunset.

Carina, however, did not hear this quip, for she had gone down the beach to comfort Mrs. Wilson, who still wrung her hands over her old husband going to sea in a land breeze. By the time Carina returned, Zachariah was hoisting himself over the stern of the canoe and settling into the rear thwart.

Then Carina sensed that something was wrong with him. She did not know how she knew, nor did she know what she knew. But as he shifted in the thwart of the canoe, she knew that something had troubled him and caused him to lose sleep.

"Zach, you sleep today?" she called out to him.

He grunted and picked up the paddle.

"Zach, you don't sleep today!" she cried, wading after him.

"I sleep plenty, woman," he answered.

"But if you don't sleep, Zach," she persisted, the water now coiling above her knees, "you can't stay out dere all night. You goin' fall asleep on de sea!"

"Me all right, woman!" Zachariah replied gruffly.

That was not what he wanted to say, nor had he used the tone of voice he wanted to use. But he did not like to discuss his personal worries in public, for he was shy about being stared at the way people stared at Mrs. Hemmings when she was drunk, or the way they gawked at Mrs. Ferguson when she berated her husband. So he said the gruff thing to quiet Carina's concern. But it was not what he had wanted to say.

The canoe soughed away from the beach and hung off-shore, suspended in the garish, reflected glaze of the ocean.

"Don't fall asleep on de sea, Zach!" Carina cried.

He began to paddle, using short, quick strokes to steer the bow of the canoe towards the opening in the breaking reef.

"You hear me, Zach!" she called out, wading in deeper after him.

"I hear," Zachariah replied, glancing over his shoulder at her. "Look for me a-morning."

These were the customary words that fishermen, as they pull out into the deep night sea, use to comfort their wives.

She watched the canoe pull away from the shore, saw the shining, becalmed water part after it, saw the crooked wake curling off the pointed stern.

"And watch out for de land breeze!" she cried.

But by then, it was doubtful that he could hear her, for he had already reached the opening in the breaking reef. The smell of the exposed reef was sharp and pungent, like mouldy cheese. Sea birds, pelicans, swimming under the lee of the reef, turned and watched the sleek, black painted canoe slip through the mouth of the reef and glide out into the open sea.

Once clear of the breaking reef, Zachariah put away the paddle, crawled into the centre thwart, and ran out the oars. He rowed in long, smooth strokes, driving the painted canoe through the glassy water, aiming her bow towards the fishing shoal where the fishermen took their nightly catch.

Darkness had settled over the shoreline and already lights flickered in the windows of the village shacks. As he rowed, he could dimly make out the low shapes of other

25

canoes pulling away from the shore and slipping through the breaking reef.

The canoe rolled slightly as Zachariah rowed and thought about the bait he would use, and the kind of catch he hoped to have by morning.

He was hoping tonight for a good catch of snappers, which would bring better than fifty cents a pound from the higglers. If he was lucky, he would even land a mackerel or two.

But if he was unlucky, he would catch only goatfish, grunt, and parrot fish, which higglers would pay no more than twenty cents a pound for, and over which they would rage and quarrel if a fisherman demanded a higher price.

When he thought about this, he frowned and looked over his shoulder at the darkening land mass of the promontory that thrust into the sea on the far side of the bay. He did not like to be argued down on his price by higglers. But if he caught only goatfish and grunt he would be in no position to quibble over the merits of his catch and argue for a better price. For the grunt and the goatfish were not desirable for eating. The one is too bony and the other is too bitter. But tonight he would catch only snappers and mackerel. And perhaps he would catch something special and rare — a kingfish — a fish of the deep, deep water whose flesh is succulent and tasty.

An hour later, he was over the fishing shoal. He manoeuvred the canoe until she was lined up with his landmarks, threw down the anchor, and pulled it fast. The canoe swung and held.

He began to fish, casting out first the lines for the snapper, and then the deeper lines for the bottom fish.

The land breeze sprang up; the bow of the canoe swung towards the shoreline, where the lights from the shacks flickered and twinkled like stars.

He took a wrenchman first, a small fish with a sharp, pointed spine that bristled like barbs. Battering the fish

26

against the thwart until it was dead, he worked the hook out of its mouth, and popped out its eyeball for bait.

As he fished, the lights of the other canoes appeared on both sides of him, stretched out against the shoal. The land breeze picked up, scudding the surface of the ocean into sharp spindrift that carried into the canoe and stung his face. The canoe yawed with each gust of the land breeze, but the anchor held her fast against the shoal.

The fishing, however, was bad. Zachariah felt one line and then another, feeling for nibbles of feeding fish. But there were none.

"Rass breeze," he muttered. "Fish don't like de breeze."

Such was the nature of the fish that the slightest thing upset them. Who knew what a fish really felt, anyway, or what a fish thought? For all he knew, perhaps fish could talk to one another. When the alewife was caught, it groaned like a wounded goat. Zachariah always cut off the head of any alewife he landed so he would not have to listen to its groaning. Carina had scolded him often over this, for the higglers did not like to buy decapitated fish. Yet it was better that he cut off the head of the alewife than have to listen to the fish moaning sorrowfully all through the long night.

For the truth was that Zachariah had a soft heart and could not stand to listen to the suffering alewife crying out its longing for the ocean. When he first began to fish, he would often take pity on the alewife and throw it back into the sea. But he hid this action from the other fishermen, because they would think him a lunatic to do such a rash thing. As for Carina, there was no end to how provoked she would become if she knew that he was throwing their livelihood back into the sea. Better instead that he put the groaning fish out of its misery by cutting off its head. But even this he sometimes couldn't bring himself to do.

While the land breeze freshened and the canoe tugged at its anchor, he thought about the alewife, which was a pale, ugly fish with a flat body and bulging eyes, and he tried to imagine why such a creature would want to prolong its dreamless life. But he concluded that the fish did not know that it was merely a fish, and that to all things that live nothing is sweeter than life itself.

He took a swig from the water bottle. As he was replacing the bottle under the thwart, the snapper line gave a sharp tug. He pulled on the line and felt a fish struggling at the end of it.

When the fish was nearly on the surface, he dragged it against the side of the canoe and into the wavering light thrown off by the cresset. He saw that it was a horse-eye jack, and he grunted with pleasure and flipped the fish into the bottom of the canoe, clubbing it until it was still.

He baited the line and threw it back into the sea, hoping for another horse-eye jack, which was a popular fish with the higglers and would bring at least two dollars a pound.

While he continued to fish, he told himself that he had done the right and cautious thing to bring the fish into the light before hauling it into the canoe. This was his way of ensuring that he would do the proper thing — by praising himself when he did right, and by scolding himself harshly when he did wrong. Otherwise he would become careless and leave his woman alone in the world to raise his two sons.

A fish with such a strong pull could have been a barracuda, or an eel, or a mackaback — fish that would sink their teeth into the nearest object and never let go. The barracuda was a dangerous fish to bring into a canoe, especially a big barracuda, for it would leap about until it had flesh between its jaws. This was the way Hopeton, a fisherman from Zachariah's childhood parish of Westmoreland, had met his death. Hopeton had landed a barracuda that siezed his ankle and tore the flesh down to the bone. Before he could row the canoe back to shore, he bled to death. His canoe blew away and was not found for a month. When it finally drifted into Sav-la-Mar, the barracuda was rotting under a thwart, its sharp teeth bared at the man, and Hopeton's corpse was mangled beyond recognition. Sea birds had been feeding on him.

Hopeton should first have looked at the fish when it was still in the water, to see if it was a barracuda. He should have driven the gaff through the brain of the fish and held it wriggling against the gunwales of the canoe, until it was dead. That was what Zachariah did whenever he caught a barracuda. This time, again, he told himself solemnly, he had done the correct thing.

The land breeze gusted; the canoe yawed at her anchorage. Zachariah fished, thinking of one thing and another to wile away the loneliness. He tried not to think about the scene today when the higglers had jeered at his ugliness. But soon he found himself brooding about it.

He told himself that ugliness is the fault of no man, least of all the man who is ugly, and he was preparing to give himself consolation the way his mother had taught him.

First, to give himself consolation, he would try to think of someone worse off than he. Such a man, known by the nickname of Seahorse, used to live in Charity Bay.

Seahorse had been a fisherman whose canoe had blown away and who was lost at sea for fifteen days. Alone on the ocean, he went mad. On land, his girlfriend thought Seahorse was dead and went immediately to a younger man with whom she consorted openly.

On the fifteenth day, Seahorse drifted into Port Antonio. So maddened by loneliness was Seahorse, and so overjoyed by the sight of land, that when his canoe was still more than a mile offshore, he jumped overboard and swam furiously for shore. A shark attacked him no more than two hundred yards away from two other canoes returning from a night of fishing.

On the first pass, the shark tossed Seahorse high above the waves, churning the water red with blood. The canoes

29

raced towards Seahorse who, maddened with hunger for land, ignored the shark and splashed frenziedly for the shore.

On the next pass, the shark tore off Seahorse's right arm below the elbow. The fishermen pulled the mad Seahorse aboard their canoe and drove off the shark with their harpoons. Seahorse was so mad that he did not even know that his right arm was severed. All he could babble about was his loneliness at sea.

Seahorse should have died, but because Port Antonio had a hospital and doctors, he did not. He lived to return to Charity Bay and to find his woman gone away with a younger man. Instead of dying, Seahorse went mad.

His hair growing wild and unkempt, Seahorse gave up fishing and began to wander through Charity Bay singing in reply to all questions. If he went to the shop owned by Mr. Lewis to buy sugar, he would lean the stump of the severed arm on the shop counter and sing about buying sugar. If someone met him on the street and asked him how he was feeling, he would stand right there on the street and sing his symptoms in a loud voice. Moreover, his voice was unpleasant to hear because he could not sing. It would have been better if Seahorse had babbled like an ordinary madman rather than sing in such a voice.

Shunned by everyone, Seahorse went into the bush where he lived among a pack of starving, castoff dogs. For food he scavenged in the village and ate wild fruit. Zachariah began to give him all the goatfish from his catch.

In the mornings when the canoes came in, Seahorse, wild and ragged beyond belief, wandered down to the beach followed by a pack of famished dogs and collected the goatfish from Zachariah. Singing, he then disappeared into the bush.

So Seahorse lived for more years than even a mother would wish. One day he did not come to collect the goatfish. Going into the bush, Zachariah found him dead. The dogs attacked Zachariah when he tried to carry the body back into the village. He killed one dog with his machete and drove off the others. Carrying the body of Seahorse down to the beach, Zachariah buried it under the roots of the sea grape tree.

Giving himself consolation on the dark sea, Zachariah thought about the wickedness that life does to some men and shook his head with pity.

But now, as his mother had taught him, came the second half of the consoling. Now he must number his happiness. He began to do this carefully.

His sons were manly and strong. True, one son had a bad temper while the other was silent and withdrawn.

Carina loved him truly, caring for him and for his sons with gentleness. In fact, she also had a bad temper, and when she became angry she was wild and erratic beyond all reason. Moreover, she was often too mannish in her ways, especially in her desire to always ride on top of him during lovemaking.

His canoe was seaworthy and strong, having neither a blemish nor a weakness. Certainly, he would do better with a motor, but he could not afford one. For the time being, the sail would be enough.

Moreover, he told himself impatiently, in consoling himself a man must look to the good, not to the deficiencies. He frowned at himself because his thoughts were undisciplined. He shifted in the canoe, and the small boat rocked heavily against the chop thrown up by the land breeze.

Now he must think of the worst thing in his life and attempt to make it better by imagining how much worse it could have been. This was not the teaching of his mother, but his own invention.

He closed his eyes and tried to see what was the greatest evil in his life — his ugliness.

At first, he could not see his face clearly because he seldom looked at himself in a mirror. Carina had a small mirror in the house and, if it hadn't been her favourite posses-

31

sion, he would have thrown it away long ago. For he seldom had an urge to see his reflection in it.

With great effort, Zachariah strained to see himself the way he must have appeared today to the higglers in the bus. Only after a few minutes, during which he concentrated so hard that he became dizzy, could he see his face. He saw his jawbone, engorged and thick, insinuating to his features the lascivious looks of a goat. He tried to imagine his face worse than it already was.

After some aimless thinking in which he saw flashes of other faces and had a vivid picture of a crowing rooster, he shrugged and gave up. He had tried to imagine himself with a jawbone twice as big as the one he already had, which would have given him the looks of a donkey, but it was impossible for him to imagine such a face. Moreover, he had no more wish to resemble a donkey than he wished to look the way he now did.

Disgusted with himself but too weary to continue because thinking had made him sleepy, Zachariah told himself that he would not sleep, but he would close his eyes for a few moments and rest. The land breeze was freshening and the canoe was yawing and tugging at its anchor and the incessant bobbing motion added to his sleepiness. And after all, he mumbled to himself, it didn't matter if he closed his eyes for a few minutes. He had four lines running down to the reef, and the first fish to take the bait would jerk him out of his doze.

He was still thinking about this when he fell asleep, his body sliding heavily between the thwarts.

The wind freshened and the canoe tugged at its anchor until the rope frayed loose. Freed from the anchor's grip against the reef, the canoe swirled and lunged to the touch of the land breeze, stepped nimbly over the chop, and swung her bow towards the blackness of the open sea.

Chapter 4

The splash of a jumping fish awoke Zachariah. For a moment, he lay in the bottom of the canoe and could not remember where he was. Holding onto the gunwales, he sat up and peered groggily about him.

All around the canoe, a vast and empty ocean shuddered, sloughing off its night-time coat and sliding into a dizzying blue. Near his feet, the dead horse-eye jack stared glassily at the dawn sky.

He came slowly to his senses and was about to lean over the side and wash his face when he remembered the loud splash. He picked up the harpoon and peered warily into the sea, searching for the shadowless black shark.

He saw nothing. Small waves rose up all around the canoe, swelled, and tore their tops open.

Zachariah cupped two handfuls of water and splashed it over his face.

He was soon wide awake and aware of his predicament. Circled by horizons, the small canoe was drifting alone on the deep. The dread of the ocean came upon him with a quick stab of fear.

Replacing the harpoon, he wriggled forwards, wedged the mast into the hole in the centre thwart, and hoisted the triangular sail.

The small sail unfurled languidly in the morning breeze. Holding onto the end of the rope attached to the corner of the sail, Zachariah crawled back into the stern thwart. He paddled the canoe around so that the sun was astern. The sail flapped in the breeze, stiffened and filled. Bowing gently

33

with the following seas, the canoe ran downwind.

Zachariah was angry with himself for falling asleep, but he did not know where he was, and he could not afford just now to think about his anger. Never before had anything like this ever happened to him. Even though he had slept all night, he was still tired. He told himself that he would not go to sea tonight, but would spend the night resting in his own bed. He tried to think about the bed.

But he could not think about anything else, except what a fool he was for falling asleep, and how much he deserved to be punished for being such a fool. He cast around for a suitable punishment and decided that, much as he wanted to smoke a piece of the donkey-hemp tobacco, he would instead throw it overboard and deprive himself of that pleasure as punishment.

"Damn fool-fool man should be whipped," he told himself sternly, hurling the tobacco overboard in the wake of the sailing canoe.

But even this act of punishment struck him as another piece of folly, proving that he was as ugly a fool as everyone said, for he did not know where he was at sea, or how far he had drifted, or how long it would take him to make a landfall, and in the meantime the tobacco would have given him a little pleasure to take his mind off the sea and its loneliness.

"Damn fool to throw away de tobacco!" he raged at himself, thumping at the air with his free hand.

He turned to see where the tobacco was, but the canoe slid down a swelling wave, and the tobacco disappeared behind its crest.

He could not believe that he had been stupid enough to fall asleep and blow away. Even now, after throwing away the tobacco and raging at himself for doing it, he still could not believe that he was lost and alone on the deep open sea. Such a thing had happened to others. But he did not wish tc think about them, for many had never been found. And some, like Seahorse, had come back as madmen.

Well, he would not think of these unlucky ones. And he would not think of any more punishment for his stupidity. Instead, he would think about where he was and in which direction he should sail to make a landfall. But even as he made this resolve, he began to think about Obediah whose torn body had drifted into Charity Bay, and he had to become severe and scolding with himself lest his thoughts get away from him.

He did not know where he was or how far he had drifted. He knew, however, that in the morning the sun was always at his back when he sailed into Charity Bay. He reasoned that even with the land breeze blowing him out to sea, he could not have drifted far. Jamaica was just under the horizon. If he sailed with the sun astern, he would make a landfall.

Driven by the wind, the painted canoe rose and fell on the following seas. The sun came up and the ocean slipped into its immense blue. The black hulled canoe drove towards the horizon.

Zachariah tried to see Carina in his mind. She would worry about him. When she found out that he had fallen asleep at sea, the worry would turn to anger. He thought about how she looked when she was angry. He saw her face as it had been the time she came after him with a machete. Screaming his name, she had stalked past the hibiscus where he was hiding.

Afterwards, when she was calm and sensible again, she laughed and joked about how, by hiding himself, he had saved her from the gallows. She had laughed longer and louder than he, hanging her head with shame over her foolish temper. It made him uneasy, she had laughed so convincingly. He wondered whether she might really have murdered him with his own machete.

Every woman, whether a lawful wife or a common-law wife, or even a girlfriend, brings down crosses on a man's head. Mrs. Wilson, a lawful wife, nagged her old husband, frequently holding him up to public scorn. At the south end of the village lived Mrs. Ferguson, a common-law wife, who beat her husband once a week. In the centre of the village Mr. Hemmings lived with his drunkard common-law wife. And then there was Mrs. Lewis, a virago if ever there was one, a woman who nagged and bullied every man within her reach. Not to even mention such a one as Seahorse's girlfriend, who drove poor Seahorse mad with her fickleness.

Even when a woman had no vices, she brought trouble to a man. Poor Mr. Roper, who drove the mail bus, suffered with a wife who was a religious lunatic. She went to church as often as she could, sometimes even on Monday, riding the bus all the long way to Port Antonio just so she could attend revival meetings. Frequently she loitered near the bus stop, astonishing passengers by talking in tongues and tearing her dress. When she carried on so, everyone hurried to the bus stop to watch her and marvel at the strange tongue she spoke in. Yet she was not a wicked woman. Many people even said that she had a divine gift of talking in the words of the Holy Ghost.

The canoe yawed to the right, spilling the wind out of the sail. Zachariah paddled, swinging her bow to the left. The sail ballooned out from the mast. The canoe rocked and lunged ahead into the seas.

Carina was by no means the worst woman in Charity Bay. Mr. Wilson's wife was the worst, with her constant nagging and fretting. No, Mr. Ferguson's was the worst. At least Mr. Wilson's wife seldom beat her husband; she merely treated him with scorn. But when Zachariah thought about it further, he realized that he had overlooked Mrs. Lewis, truly the most horrible woman in Charity Bay. Not only did she beat her husband, but she frequently abused any unlucky man within earshot. Once, when she was in a rage, she gave her husband a sound thrashing and, not content with that, leaped over the shop counter and beat an innocent cultivator who just happened·to be passing through the village and had stopped to buy some sugar. Who knows what the cultivator had done to anger Mrs. Lewis? Perhaps he just looked with astonishment while she was pummelling her unfortunate husband. In any event, she jumped over the counter and clouted the cultivator on the head with a large tin scoop used to measure sugar. Without question, she was the worst, vilest, wickedest woman of Charity Bay. Zachariah never allowed her to become familiar with him, never gave her the slighest liberty. Which was why he had made such a fuss when she had warned him against spitting on the floor. For the proverb says, "Play wid puppy, puppy lick you mouth", and such a saying applies especially to viragos. If he did not force her to keep her distance, who knows? Perhaps the next time she was in a rage and he wandered by, she might decide to beat him, too.

"Damn faisty woman," Zachariah scowled, using the patois word for someone who does not know his place in the world.

But then, did not poor Mr. Roper bear a heavy burden, too, having a wife who supposedly talked for the Holy Ghost? What man could live happily with a woman who talked in tongues? Suppose he had something important to say to her and she was seized just then by a wish to reply in tongues, how would it be possible to reason with such a one? Moreover, who could argue with a woman who talked for the Holy Ghost?

No, Carina was immeasurably better. She did not drink much. She talked only Jamaican. She seldom quarrelled with him. True, she had tried to kill him once, but that was only once. True, she liked to be on top during lovemaking and was obstinate about allowing him to be on the top once in a while, but that was not a great fault when it was put up against the faults of some other women.

He steered the canoe and remembered when she had lost her temper and tried to kill him. Afterwards, she

37

promised never to try again. He believed her. She had a cross temper, but she would not try to kill him again.

He sailed the canoe on this vast expanse of landless sea, and tried to occupy his mind with such thoughts. For he could not think of himself riding alone in the bottom of a black-hulled canoe, circled stealthily by empty horizons. And he could not think of the depths that fell away beneath the hull of the canoe, nor of the waiting fish that stared up at the bottom of the passing canoe. For when he thought about such things he became frightened and trembled like a child left alone in the dark.

A man at sea must not think about where he is or what he is up against. He must think about the familiar things in his life. He must fill the emptiness of his mind with his favorite dreams and memories, or he will become bewildered and stricken with a dreadful terror. Above all, he must never consider the immensity of the empty ocean.

It was his heart that guided him in this, and his heart told him that a thing as mighty and vast as the ocean must be gazed upon as if it were a single object, as if a man could reduce its immensities with one quick stare. When a man stared at the empty ocean on which he rode alone and abandoned, he must stare either at one specific, small part of it, or else sweep his eyes over all of it as if the entire vast landless scope of shuddering seas could be comprehended in one darting glance.

He paused in his thinking and the vastness of the ocean unfolded menacingly before his quick glance. He ran his eye over the sail, which billowed out full and brimming with wind. His mind, the canoe, the sky, and the ocean itself were suspended in an enormous silence broken only by the soughing of the waves and the whispers of the prancing canoe.

She was riding as she was supposed to, lifting her hull high and skittishly above the waves, for she was built to dance nimbly on the waves, not to fight and rage against them like a boat with a keel.

He began to think about the canoe, which he had named the Lucky P, after his mother.

She was a seamless and sturdy craft. He himself had cut down the cotton tree from which he had hewed her. He had sawed off the roots and limbs of the tree, leaving the bare trunk. With an adze, he then dug a long, deep furrow into the middle of the trunk. In the furrow he started a coal fire that burned deep into the girth of the trunk, charring an open wound into the wood.

He chopped away the charred wood until the trunk resembled a large gutted fish. Rounding off the ends of the trunk with an adze, he dug deeper into the wood, hollowing out the hull of the canoe.

Zachariah then crawled into the hollowed out space and used a chisel to chip away the scars left by the crude strokes of the adze.

The canoe emerged, curved and bulging in the middle, tapered at both ends, with an underbelly swollen and rounded like a pregnant sow's.

He melted down pitch over a kerosene fire and coated the outside hull with it. Inch by inch he went over the canoe, applying the acrid, viscous pitch. The wood shrivelled and glistened with a waterproof sheen.

He went over the hull once more, rubbing on a second coat of pitch as gently as if he were applying ointment to the belly of a sick child. The wood absorbed the pitch until it could absorb no more. Mixed with sap, the pitch hardened into a lustrous shell.

Five months after he had felled the cotton tree, Zachariah turned the canoe right side up and pushed it into the sea.

For the first week he anchored her offshore and waded out each day to touch her bottom with his fingertips and feel for soft spots in the wood through which the sea could bleed. When he was sure that she was tight and dry inside, he beached her again, installed the three thwarts, and laid down her gunwales of pitchpine. He painted her black and named her after his mother.

Thinking now about this, he stretched his legs out until a toe rested against the one astonished eye of the horse-eye jack. He shifted his foot a little to the right so that his big toe would not block the dead fish's stare at the sky and thought how large the eye of even a small fish was and how distended the pupils of a fish always seemed to be. Then he stopped thinking about the dead jack because there was a limit to which any man could think about a fish, especially one that was dead.

Moreover, he did not like to look too long at any fish that he had killed, for he did not like to kill fish, even though his livelihood required him to do it. He was always roused to pity at the sight of a fish suffocating in the bottom of his canoe, which is why he was known for battering his catch, for bringing in fish that were either decapitated or bludgeoned about the head, or bleeding from numerous wounds. For whenever he caught a fish he tried to kill it as quickly and as mercifully as he could. He killed fish such as the wrenchman, or the grunt, or the snapper, by battering them against the thwart. A big fish, such as a king-fish or a mackerel, he would kill by bludgeoning it on the head with the lingnum vitae club he carried under the thwart. His catch always looked as though it had been violently beaten to death. Higglers who bought from him often complained about the bruises on the fish. Carina scolded him, too, about his habit of battering the fish, telling him that he was taking food out of the mouths of his sons because of his perverse ways with the fish. But it was preferable to kill the fish with a merciful blow to the head than allow it to lie in the bottom of the canoe and suffocate to death, its gills sucking vainly for air. Other fishermen did not care if the fish took an hour to die, during which time the fish shivered and fluttered, slapping their tails against the bottom of the canoe. Some fishermen even said that the sounds of the dying fish kept them awake during the long lonely nights. But Zachariah could not stand to hear such sounds because his heart was too soft.

For that matter, he did not even like to eat fish although he often had to because there was no other food in the house. But he would rather eat goat flesh, or pork, or chicken, or beef, rather that the flesh of the fish. And he especially did not like to eat a fish that he had caught, although he usually had no choice in the matter. Many of his preferences he did not even confide in Carina for fear that she would scoff at him or scold him about having a rich man's palate in a poor man's mouth. So he ate the fish when he had to, although he did not relish it.

He began to think now of the night when he spoke to Carina about his wish to name the painted canoe after his mother. When Zachariah built the canoe, he had not lived with Carina for more than a few months, and they were still childless. He finished the canoe one night and was waiting to discuss naming the boat with Carina, who had gone into the village with Mrs. Hemmings. He sat in the small living room and waited for Carina to return.

But when Carina came home, she was drunk and wanted to wrestle. In those days, when the rum was upon her she loved to wrestle with him. But he was in no mood to wrestle.

In the corner of the living room, Mrs. Hemmings sat beside the kerosene lantern and taunted him for not wanting to wrestle with Carina.

"Man don't wrestle woman," he said with impassive dignity.

"See here, Jesus!" Mrs. Hemmings screeched as only a drunken woman can.

"Me not deaf," he told her crossly, wishing that she would go to her own house and torment her own husband.

"Who man goin' wrestle if not with him own woman?"

41

the drunken Mrs. Hemmings asked, rolling her eyes as if she had seen a duppy.

Carina crouched into a wrestling stance.

"Come, Zach," she growled.

She was so drunk that she could hardly crouch without falling over on her face. Even as she crouched, she weaved, and nearly toppled over.

"Watch out!" Zachariah warned, pushing a chair out of her way.

"Wrestle with you woman, man!" Mrs. Hemmings said with disgust.

"Me don't want to wrestle me woman in me own house!" he said stubbornly.

Carina, still crouching, lunged towards him, her hands outstretched and groping. The kerosene lantern threw a jerky, menacing shadow against the wall. Zachariah stood his ground and refused to wrestle.

"Who woman goin' wrestle with, if no de woman own man?" Mrs. Hemmings argued, spitting out her words. "Dat why man and woman can't live in harmony together as one. De rass man won't wrestle him own natural woman. Is odder woman, is young gal, him want wrestle with! But him own woman? She drop dead 'pon de ground before de rass man give her one rass wrestle. And what de woman ask for? What she want dat so unreasonable? She want no money. She want no big car. She want no luxury or finery or riches. She don't even want a bicycle. All she want is one rass wrestle. And will de rass man wrestle him own natural woman? No, sah! Who? Him? Dis rass man?" She pointed a contemptuous finger at Zachariah who sat calmly watching as Carina stalked him.

Before Zachariah could reply, Carina gave a guttural scream and hurtled headlong towards him. She slammed into his chest and fastened a hammerlock around his neck as the chair fell backwards with a thunderous crash.

"Yes, sah! Yes, sah!" Mrs. Hemmings was on her feet,

dancing and shrieking as Zachariah and Carina grappled on the floor.

"Rass!" Zachariah managed to croak before Carina tightened the hammerlock around his windpipe, cutting off his breath.

"Woman beat de rass outta man!" Mrs. Hemmings exulted.

Zachariah flung Carina off. Still clinging to his neck, she flew through the air, and he thought he heard the sound of his neckbone snap. He grabbed her wrists and pried loose the hammerlock. She twisted her torso and locked his midriff in a scissors-hold with her legs, throwing him bodily against a table, which shattered under the impact.

"Blood!" Zachariah muttered, prying the scissors off his stomach.

"Yes, sah! Yes, sah! Woman beat the rass outta man!" Mrs. Hemmings gloated.

They rolled across the floor, banging into furniture, bouncing off the walls. Zachariah braced himself and threw her off, twisting out of reach of her flailing hands, which groped for his neck. Landing hard on her back, Carina had the wind momentarily knocked out of her. Zachariah pinned her on the floor, spreadeagled and wriggling.

"Damn thief man!" He heard Mrs. Hemmings growl. "Leggo de woman."

Then she leapt on his neck and bit him on the ear.

He wrestled with the two drunken women for at least an hour. Finally, he threw Mrs. Hemmings against a wall and knocked her unconscious. He pinned Carina again and was about to tie her up with a rope when she fell asleep in his arms and began to snore.

Standing up groggily, he was unable to believe his eyes. The small room was in shambles. Chairs were upended and broken. The table was shattered. Slumped against the wall, Mrs. Hemmings lay tangled and unconscious. Carina was sprawled out, snoring among the wreckage.

43

Zachariah revived Mrs. Hemmings and led her through the darkened village street to her house, leaving her on her doorstep where she sang "Rock of Ages" in a loud voice to rouse her husband.

When he got back to his own house, Carina was in bed. That's when he asked her if he could name the canoe after his mother.

She began to cry.

"You such a good son, Zach," she sobbed sentimentally, "If we have any pickney me hope when me dead and gone one o' dem name something after der Mumma."

She sobbed inconsolably over this thought until she finally fell asleep.

That night, as he lay beside Carina and listened to a cricket bleating outside the window, he thought of a name for the canoe. His mother's first name was Pansy and all her life she had been unlucky. He decided to name the boat the "Lucky Pansy".

But when he tried to paint the name on the bow section of the canoe, he made a mistake and left only enough room for the "Lucky P".

By this combination of love and accident the canoe got its name.

Chapter 5

He sailed for several hours, thinking aimlessly about this early period of his life with Carina, expecting landfall at any moment. But the land did not appear.

The sun climbed into the sky and Zachariah could feel the searing heat bleeding the life out of him. But he could do nothing to shield himself. He wanted to reach down into the water with the calabash bowl and splash himself all over, but he did not. The water would only evaporate, leaving salt all over his skin, which would make him itch.

He was weary and thirsty and desperately sleepy. He wondered why he should be tired after he had spent the whole night sleeping. A month ago, he had gone to the mad English doctor at the clinic in Charity Bay, complaining about a strange lump growing at the base of his neck. The doctor had given him an injection and cut the lump out, sending him to the hospital in Port Antonio to have an X-ray taken of his chest. Now he wondered whether this was the cause of his great weariness. But he could not understand how a lump cut out over a month ago should make him feel tired now, especially after he had had a good night's sleep.

He raised his eyes and stared over the bow of the canoe at the horizon, but he saw no sign of land. All he saw was where the ocean and the sky were jointed, and how the sky looked puffed up and white in the searing heat, as though it would blow out at its seam with the ocean.

To fight off the feeling of weariness, he decided to eat the horse-eye jack. Holding the canoe on course with the paddle wedged between the gunwales and his leg, he fumbled under the thwart for the knife, found it, and cut off the head of the jack. Opening the belly of the jack, he gutted the green intestines and placed them in a calabash bowl with the severed head. Then he dipped the jack into the ocean to moisten it, and tried to work some suppleness into the stale flesh before he ate it. But the jack had been dead too long.

Zachariah filleted the jack, exposing the white spine under the jellied flesh. Reaching under the rear thwart, he found the salt and sprinkled it over the strips of meat. Then he chewed on the strips, sucking their juices mixed with the salt.

The meat was bitter and dry. But he chewed on the flesh and swallowed the juices, and his body tingled at the taste of the salt.

After he had eaten the jack, he broke off a bone from its spine and used it to pick his teeth. Then he threw the spine overboard, washed his hands in the sea, and took a drink from the water bottle.

The canoe, meanwhile, had yawed off course. The sail had spilled its wind, and the small craft was now drifting with the following seas. Zachariah looked around the boat and saw that she was surrounded by rising groundswells. The waves began deep and flat, swelled ponderously, and ruptured into white crests with a ripping sound. He was fortunate that the wind was not blowing. For with a strong wind in such seas, it would be almost impossible to steer the canoe.

He swallowed two more mouthfuls of water and swirled the cool liquid inside his mouth and trickled it gently down his throat. His windpipe seemed to quiver with excitement. Then he put the water bottle under the thwart and tried to concentrate on land.

Land had to be just under the horizon. He had been sailing now for at least seven hours. The sun was already falling towards the sea. If he did not make a landfall soon, he would

46

have to spend the night alone on the open sea. He looked around the canoe at the rolling groundswells and was overcome by a feeling of stark terror. It did not last long, but suddenly he knew how alone and weak he was, and how small and frail the painted canoe was against the might of the ocean, and his heart was filled with dread.

But the dread quickly passed because he became angry at himself for feeling the fear of children and he refused to think about it.

So he thought just now, when the fear was upon him, that he would sing it away, because his mother had taught him that song was the enemy of fear. Moreover, the sound of his own voice would give him comfort. He was afraid to talk aloud to himself, for he believed that this was the first sign of madness. But he was not afraid to sing to himself. The words of the song would console him. He cleared his throat and steered the canoe so that the sail filled with wind. The· small canoe lunged over a groundswell and slid into its trough with a hiss, while Zachariah tried to think of a song to sing.

He wanted to sing a church hymn, but he refused to do it because of his belief of not calling out to God unless the need was desperate. Being temporarily out of sight of land was not reason enough to go bawling to God.

"Negar bodder him so much him don't know what to think," Zachariah muttered, referring to God.

Now there he did it – he was already talking out loud to himself. Better to think and conserve his voice so he could hail any passing ship. Later, if he was still at sea when night fell, he would need the sound of his voice.

So he began to sing a song he had learned in his childhood, a song about the cricket victory the West Indians had scored over the English. And though he did not remember all the words, nevertheless he sang this song, which had the refrain, "Ramadin and Valentine and Gomez too indeed, West Indies take the lead."

Ramadin and Valentine were spin bowlers. The second of the two, Valentine, had an ugly mouth because of terrible buck teeth. But he was a skilful bowler who could make the ball take to the air as lightly as a hummingbird, who could put such a soft flight on the ball that the batsmen would become confused and swing long before it got within reach of their bats. Moreover, Valentine — who bowled a leg-break — would put such a spin on the ball that it would break sharply for the wicket after it hit the pitch. When Zachariah was a young boy, he used to go down to the village shop to listen to the cricket game over the radio, and to hear the stories the men told about Valentine's prowess as a spin bowler.

So Zachariah sang the song about Valentine and the West Indian victory over the English. But after he had sung only two verses, which he garbled because he did not really remember all the words, he felt foolish singing with rolling green seas piling up around the canoe. He stopped singing and was suddenly aware of the endless, vast, empty ocean.

His heart jumped with fear. The waves were everywhere around the canoe. Stretching as far as the eye could see, nothing moved but the endlessly roiling seas. And the canoe was so small and frail in comparison that any man would have cried out just then for his mother, so vast and surging was the sea, so stark and empty was the horizon, so lonely and friendless was the man in the small painted canoe.

But Zachariah fought against the fear that welled up in him. He refused to listen to its voice. He calmed himself and became stern and scolded himself for having the timidity of a child. Yet he was not ashamed of the fear. More than once the fear had saved his life. Fear made him cautious and prudent. It was fear that had prevented him from going to sea on the very night that Obediah was lost. Zachariah had stayed home because he had been fearful of the norther that his nose told him was in the air. And there was another time when fear had saved him from a shark. He had lost a fish trap on the shallow side of the fishing shoal and was thinking about diving to the bottom and retrieving it. But he was fearful of the hammerhead shark he had seen in these waters. As he was staring over the side of the canoe at the trap, the hammerhead had glided past, its ugly head moving from side to side in search of prey.

"Is all right. Let de heart beat fast. It don't trouble nobody. Go on, heart. Beat fast all you want." He muttered this to himself as he thought about this fear.

But he must not talk to himself. A man could go mad talking to himself at sea. He must think; he must think quickly, and he must always have something to think about. He would think first about Carina. After that, he would think about his first son, George. Later, he would think about his other son, and about his own mother.

"Never make de ocean find you without a thought in you brain," he warned himself.

The canoe rose with a swelling wave. The sail began to luff. Zachariah steered to the right until the sail had filled with wind. He was now sailing at an angle to the horizon, because the wind had shifted. But that was all right. He would have landfall west of Charity Bay. But he would still make land today. He began to think about Carina.

First, he thought about her own singing habits. Always she sang when she was in the pit toilet. She had a terrible voice, flat and reedy like the voice of a goat. Fortunately, she sang only on the toilet. It did not matter when she was on the toilet, whether in the morning or late at night, if she was there she was singing.

Zachariah did not understand how anyone could sing on a toilet. Moreover, he did not understand why she sang certain songs and not others. Sometimes she sang some of the old tunes of their childhood days, "Linstead Market", "Night Food", "Old Lady You Mashing Me Toe", light mischievous songs. Sometimes she sang the Jamaican

49

National Anthem, not the one they were taught as children, but the one the children now had to learn because of Independence. He himself did not know the exact words of the new song, but he recognized the tune when he heard her singing it.

He did not understand why a woman would lock herself up in a pit toilet and sing the Jamaican National Anthem. Moreover, he was certain that the Prime Minister would not approve of such a thing. The Prime Minister frequently railed at Jamaicans for being undisciplined. Sometimes, when the Prime Minister was vexed about something, he would talk to the people on the radio about it. Sometimes he talked for eight hours, scolding them over something he did not like. Nobody else on the island could talk as long, or as loud, as the Prime Minister.

Zachariah shook his head and marvelled about how the Prime Minister could chat, and how Carina could sing to herself when she sat on the pit toilet, and he reached over the sides of the heaving canoe and scooped up some water to wash his face with, for his thoughts were becoming jumbled and confused. One minute he would be thinking about Carina and the next minute his thoughts would be mixed up and he would be thinking about the Prime Minister. And even as he washed his face, he found himself thinking about the hammerhead shark he had seen several times on the edge of the reef where he fished.

"Which man understand woman?" he asked himself out loud, trying to bring discipline to his thinking.

He did not. Only two women had he ever lived with, his mother and Carina, and he understood neither one. Once he thought he understood his mother and why she so often told him that he was ugly. But later he decided that he did not understand her after all.

All his life his mother had been religious and unlucky. She went to church, prayed, sang, and spoke in tongues more

50

often than Mrs. Lewis. Her life was filled with hardship and misfortune. Zachariah was her only child and he was — as she often reminded him — unspeakably ugly.

During revival meetings, his mother sometimes made him stand up in church and, as he stood in the pews feeling like a fool, she would carry on about his ugliness, telling everyone that he was ugly because she had committed dreadful sins.

"Look upon me pickney," she would bawl in a horrible voice, and everyone in the small stone church, though they had heard it all before, would turn and look at Zachariah.

"Look upon dat jawbone! Is normal jawbone, dat? Which jawbone man or woman ever look upon dat ugly so? Which jawbone? Only on goat you find jawbone like dat one! What cause dat jawbone to look so ugly? Sin! SIN! SIN! ME SIN!" And, as she screeched this out, she would point a trembling finger at Zachariah, who would shift clumsily from one foot to another and pretend that he was dead.

After this outburst, his mother would tell the story of her sin, or talk in tongues, or sing in a cracked, treble voice about Jesus.

All this took place when Zachariah was a boy and when he suffered from his disease, which no doctor could treat or understand. He suffered painful headaches, as though his skull were being forced against its will to expand. Sometimes, he would be in such agony that, though he was supposed to be tending to the goats, he would crawl under the cool shade of a bush and sleep through the day. It was also during this terrible time that his jawbone grew ugly and monstrous, and his hands swelled and became like the dangling paws of a beast. He only dimly remembered what he used to look like before this dreadful sickness came upon him. His mother did not even have a picture of him as he appeared in those days.

She took him to the only doctor nearby, a foreigner who practiced at the Frome Sugar Estate. There, before this strange brown man, she wailed and carried on about

51

how her son was turning ugly before her very eyes. The doctor examined Zachariah but could find nothing wrong with him.

"Him jawbone get bigger and uglier every day," his mother wept, wiping her eyes with a dirty handkerchief.

"There may be something glandular that's wrong," the doctor said in a funny accent. "You'll have to take him to a specialist at the University."

So they took the bus through the Junction Road and into Kingston, spending the night on the bare benches in the outpatient room while they waited for a doctor to examine Zachariah. All around them were weeping, moaning people, some with horrible wounds that bled on the benches, others with scabrous sores that covered their faces and limbs. Children wailed incessantly under the battery of fluorescent lights. Grown men held their bellies and doubled over on the floor. The nurses were sullen and angry, calling out the names of the sick to be attended to in loud, bellowing voices.

When it was his turn, Zachariah was taken into a small room and examined by a white man and peered at by respectful students dressed in white coats.

"Is obeah him obeah dat him jawbone turn ugly so," his mother whimpered, blowing her nose.

"No blow you nose in here!" the brown-skinned nurse snapped, glaring at her.

When the examination was finished, the doctor said something to the students who laughed as though he had told them a joke.

The nurse led them out of the examination room and down a narrow, dirty hallway, at the end of which she went behind a counter and came out with a bottle of medicine.

"No medicine on earth can help ugly pickney turn pretty, you hear, me love," the nurse said tartly, as she showed them the way out of the hospital.

His mother grew vexed and exchanged harsh words with the nurse, who shrieked that it was no wonder that

52

the island was in such a dreadful way, with all the ungrateful, dirty country people who were always coming to town begging for help over foolishness. The row was carried on in such loud voices that a constable came and ushered Zachariah and his mother out of the hospital and showed them to the gate.

So the conclusion of all this examining by doctors was that no one could find anything wrong with him. But his mother knew better, for she could see how ugly he was becoming. She therefore assumed the next reasonable thing, that he was either obeahed by an enemy, or that he had become possessed of the devil who was out to warp and deform him until he looked like a demon. From that day on, she carried Zachariah every Sunday to church with her and screeched about her sinfulness. The congregation would sing and dance around Zachariah. Once in a while, the Minister would fall into a trance and flog Zachariah with a strip of cowhide. For his mother was a member of the Pocomania Sect, and they believed in whipping sinners to rid them of the devil. But no matter how he was whipped or prayed over or danced around, Zachariah continued to grow misshapen and grotesque looking. By the time he was an adolescent, his face had become monstrously deformed and ugly. Eventually, the sickness passed, but not before it had wreaked a dreadful ruin on his face and body.

Zachariah scowled as he remembered how the parson used to beat him with cowhide, and how his mother used to wail about her sinfulness. What if he had been handsome and intelligent? What would she have had to moan and weep about then?

Sometimes, for spite, he wished that he had been born good-looking. Just to spite his mother and show her how ignorant she was. Often, when she would moan about his ugliness, he would scowl and think her a fool-fool woman. Even now, he did not understand how she and the Pocomania people could believe such wickedness.

"Fool-fool woman," he muttered.

But he quickly regretted his words. She was dead and gone now. In spite of his ugliness, she had loved him.

"It over and done with," he said aloud.

If he was not in the right frame of mind when he thought about his mother, he became bitter. Usually, to be in the right frame of mind, he only thought about her when it was shady and cool. He should never think about his mother during the fiery heat of the sun. He should wait for night. Meanwhile, he would think about Carina.

Even Carina he barely understood. He understood fish better than he understood any woman. He understood the slyness of the wrenchman, the stupidity of the goatfish, the bad temper of the barracuda, the brutishness of the shark. There was little about fish that he did not understand. But he did not understand women.

When he first met Carina in the bush, for instance, it never occurred to him that she might have a bad temper. Only after months of living with her did he discover this trait. Even then, he did not believe.

He began to remember the day when he found out about her bad temper. They had been to the standpipe together and were returning to their shack. She was carrying a large can of water on her head and grumbling at him for not helping. He walked beside her, slapping her fondly on her bottom.

"Don't do dat!" she snapped.

But she said it in a voice too much like a command. He hit her again, this time hard, a stinging blow on the bottom with his open palm. That was when he found out about her terrible temper.

First, she threw the can of water at him. Then she tried to bash his skull with a rock. He ducked just as the rock sailed pass his head. She ran down the road, scurrying into the bushes, looking for more rocks.

He was so astonished he did not know what to do. He thought she was joking. A fusillade of rocks spun towards

54

him and he saw that she was not joking. He ducked, pointing a threatening finger as he dodged the rocks.

"Stop dat!" he yelled.

She ran behind a bush and he could hear her scratching the ground for rocks and muttering obscenities under her breath.

"Behave yourself!" he warned. "Come outta dere!"

The bush exploded with a flurry and she was standing before him with a mad glint in her eye, panting and blowing with rage. Taking deliberate aim, she hurled a rock at his head.

"Rass!" he yelped, ducking.

With a yell of frustration, she hurtled at him, wielding the rock in her hand like a club. He dodged the first swing and ran wildly down the road, clutching the back of his head for protection.

Rocks sailed past him as he ran. A half mile down the road, gasping for breath, he paused under a tree. He turned just in time to see Carina tiptoeing towards him, clutching a rock in each hand.

"Blood!" he managed to exclaim before she was upon him.

He ran down the road as fast as he could with Carina chasing after him, hurling rocks and obscenities.

He hid for three hours in the bush. The sun had begun to set when he finally thought it safe to come out.

That was how he found out about Carina's temper. Something so obvious in her character had escaped him, a thing well known to all the other village men, which explained why she had been living alone when he first met her. Clearly, he did not understand women.

Even mad Seahorse had known about Carina's temper though he had never said a word to her in his life. When Seahorse was sane and had a girlfriend, he had lived at one end of the village while Carina lived at the other. They knew each other only by sight.

But once, during his madness, Seahorse came down to the beach to collect goatfish from Zachariah. The dogs, lean and starving and mottled with mange, sat on the side of the road and waited for Seahorse. Zachariah was unloading his catch, separating the goatfish from the other fish. Carina stood nearby, waiting with a basket to collect the fish she would sell to the approaching higglers. Seahorse put his mouth close to Zachariah's ear and sang in a whisper.

"Zachie, you woman have one rass of a temper."

It took Seahorse awhile to get the sentence out because he sang its words to the tune of "Silent Night".

Zachariah stared at the unkempt Seahorse with astonishment and respect. Confused by Seahorse's singing, he almost began to sing his reply, but he caught himself in time and asked Seahorse in a gruff tone, "How you know dat?"

Seahorse looked around him like a thief and rolled the whites of his eyes.

"Me can tell by her nose," he said, pointing significantly to his own nose.

Zachariah grunted and unloaded the fish, ashamed to admit that even mad Seahorse, who lived among wild dogs, knew more than he about women.

But that was how Zachariah was. He did not understand women; he understood fish.

Chapter 6

Zachariah had almost dozed off, his head slumping against his chest, when out of the corner of his eye he saw the soaring gull.

"Bird!" he exclaimed joyfully, leaping to his feet in his excitement.

The canoe collapsed on its side, skidded out underfoot and hurled him headlong into a swelling wave. The water closed over his head. Then he was blindly scratching and clawing for the surface.

He broke the surface on the crest of a wave, gasping for breath and looking around for the canoe.

"Shark!" he thought, with terror. "Shark!"

He spotted the canoe rising on a swell some thirty feet to his right.

He began to swim for it. Another wave rose up before him and the canoe vanished behind its swelling crest.

He splashed frantically at first; then he told himself to relax or he would tire before he could reach the canoe. He forced himself to swim slowly, making no splash that would draw a shark.

Her sail luffing, the canoe wallowed clumsily in the groundswells while Zachariah swam towards her, using a breaststroke.

Finally, he grabbed the gunwales and tried to pull himself aboard. But he mistimed a swell and the canoe nearly overturned on top of him. So he waited while the canoe sank into the trough of a groundswell, and he carefully steadied himself against the gunwales and pulled himself aboard, hanging on to a thwart and taking care not to capsize the small canoe.

When his legs were finally out of the bottomless blue water he gave a spasm of relief.

Exhausted, he lay in the bottom of the canoe and scolded himself.

"What a rass man is dis, eh sah?" he muttered between gasps of breath. "Fourteen years at sea and him jump up in a canoe."

He scolded himself fiercely as he lay exhausted in the bottom of the canoe, which wallowed helplessly between the groundswells.

"Worthless man," he was muttering over and over. "Worthless man."

What punishment could fit such an obvious and foolish blunder? If a shark had come along just then and taken him, he would have had only himself to blame. For how could a man with so many years at sea, a man who made his livelihood at fishing, a man who had sailed in rough seas, calm seas, night seas, day seas, how could such a man jump up in a small canoe over the sight of a bird? It must have been a duppy that had made him do it. Fishermen spoke of such things, saying that sometimes the fish will send a guileful duppy to trap a fisherman, to get him to do a foolish and deadly thing. For as everyone knows who has been at sea for a long time, there is no end to the trickery that the fish will resort to in their effort to escape the hook and the net. Perhaps it was therefore not a gull he had seen but a duppy sent by the fish to snare him. He lay in the bottom of the canoe, dripping wet, his heart still pounding from shock, and thought about what he had seen.

Looking around the canoe and into the skies, he saw no trace of the gull. He could not tell in which direction it had flown. All he saw gathering mountainously about the canoe were green groundswells.

"Worthless man!" he was muttering, when he suddenly

realized that the paddle was missing. Without a paddle, he could not steer the canoe under sail.

He looked frantically around at the roiling waves and caught a glimpse of the paddle.

Clambering into the centre of the canoe, balancing himself carefully in the rising seas, he took down the whipping sail and ran out the oars. Working the oars, he held the canoe stiff and steady so that her stern pointed at the incoming seas.

"Watch yourself, now! Watch yourself!" he warned as he prepared to turn the canoe.

If the canoe were hit broadside by a groundswell, she could capsize. He would have to time the oncoming seas just right.

He waited until the canoe began to rise on a groundswell, then he pulled hard on one oar and backed the other.

Climbing with the wave, the canoe began to turn. She spun sluggishly and came about as the wave fell and the seas shuddered all around her, blocking the horizon from Zachariah's eyes. A giant wave hit her obliquely, pushing her high and tilting her down to her gunwales. But she quickly righted herself and began to ride high and light with her bow pointed into the seas.

Zachariah rowed towards the paddle. The waves were heavy and the current was against him, but he was used to rowing the canoe in heavy seas. His muscles, strengthened by fourteen years of rowing a canoe, pulled hard on the oars, skimming the canoe into the troughs, propelling her up the sides of the swells and towards the paddle. The canoe took the seas as she should, light and dry as a cork, and Zachariah exulted with love and pride over the way she rode.

He retrieved the paddle and repeated the manoeuvre to turn the canoe back on course in the direction in which he expected to make a landfall. Soon she was sailing once again with the wind at her stern.

The canoe had taken on a little water. He bailed with the calabash bowl until she was dry. Then he checked to be sure that nothing had been washed overboard, taking inventory of the water bottle, the gaff, the harpoon, the knife, the bag of salt, and the cresset. Everything was where it should be. He was especially relieved to find that the water bottle was intact under the thwart.

But now that he was safely aboard the canoe again, and she was lunging over the groundswells with the wind at her back, he became severe and furious with himself for standing up to observe the path of the gull's flight.

"Worthless man," he muttered under his breath, telling himself that his mother had been right, that he had been conceived in sin, and that because of this he had therefore turned ugly and stupid. But after he had said this a number of times, he became angry at himself for saying so. He did not believe that his mother was right. Moreover, though he had been foolish to stand up and look for the gull, that did not necessarily mean that he was stupid. This was carrying chastising too far. If he believed such a thing about himself he would become downhearted and discouraged. Therefore, while he admitted that he was foolish to stand up in the canoe, yet he refused to admit that he was stupid, or that he had become ugly because of his mother's sin.

"Brainier man dan me do worse thing while dem alone on sea," he muttered.

And this, indeed, was a truth that was easily proved. Hopeton, who had been a good domino player, had brought a live barracuda into the canoe with him and paid for that mistake with his life. And Obediah, too, had put out to sea in the norther and been blown away. Then there was even a further case, of a man named Stegbert who used to fish in Sav-la-Mar, the town in Westmoreland where Zachariäh came from. Stegbert had a hunchback but was said to have been among the most cunning of men in Westmoreland to ever go to sea Yet Stegbert lost his life while fishing among

60

the mangrove swamps — an area he knew well. He came out of the canoe and waded into the swamps in search of eggs from the booby birds nesting in the mangrove crowns. But he took a wrong step and ended up, instead, in the quicksand, which quickly sucked him under. No one knew for sure what had happened, for Stegbert's body was never found. But his canoe was found, nestled in the mangrove bushes among the swamps. And his hat was seen floating in an area of the swamps known for quicksand.

So Zachariah refused to admit that he was born stupid, though he readily confessed to having done a foolish thing by standing up in the small canoe to look at the gull.

After he had chastised himself and was sure that he would never again stand up in the canoe — "not even," he swore, "if a rass mermaid fly overhead!" — he began to think of the good side of what had happened.

The good side was that he had seen a gull, which meant that land was nearby. He would have a landfall before dusk. It was just as he had reasoned. Jamaica was just under the horizon.

The sun was falling towards the ocean. Already it was about four o'clock. Nevertheless, he hoped to see land before the sunset. But even if he did not reach land before the darkness came, he would see the Port Antonio beacon and be able to make a landfall by it.

In the meantime, he must guard against falling asleep by thinking. He must be constantly thinking. He must think about Carina, about his sons, about his mother. He must not stop thinking.

"And watch out for too much talking, too," he reminded himself.

True. A man who talked to himself at sea could go mad. He must not talk; he must think and stay awake and watch for the Blue Mountain Peak, the highest point of land on Jamaica, or watch for the beacon from Port Antonio, which came on at dusk.

61

The ocean gathered and stretched, puffing itself out on the horizon. The sun stalked the canoe like a predator. The wind moved across the ocean driving the painted canoe towards the horizon.

Zachariah began to think about George, his first son.

George had the temper of his mother. He was only a small boy, but even now he sometimes defied Carina. One day there would be a bitter row between them and George would leave and never return.

When George was mad, he looked just like his mother. A dangerous gleam came into his eyes; his lower lip curled; two sinister lines stiffened on his chin. And he was just as stubborn as his mother could be. Sometimes, Carina would fly into a towering rage and beat him, and George would confront her defiantly, his face twisted into a helpless fury which no blow could erase. He had a small body; his limbs were delicate and weak. But the mad stubborn temper of the mother had been passed on to the son.

On the open sea in the painted canoe, Zachariah was filled with sorrow as he thought about his wife and his first son, how the two walked side by side warily together, but how, later, when the boy became a man and no longer in need of a mother, they would row and part forever. The indomitable temper of the mother, passed on to the child, would one day turn against her.

Zachariah could see the rashness of Carina festering in the heart of George, but he was still proud of his first son, of the way he carried himself in his young years — even though his body was underfed and weak — of the way he was filled with fearlessness.

When George was in a rage, he was courageous and stubborn. Frequently, he came home bloodied and beaten from fighting with boys much bigger than himself. Once he was even sent home from school for defying the Principal.

Zachariah recalled the incident, which had taken place

62

last year. On the playfield, the school children were playing "Farmer in the Dell," a game even Zachariah had played during his brief schooldays.

Zachariah remembered how the game was played when he was a boy. He remembered how the children would form a circle, singing the innocent song,

> The farmer in the dell
> The farmer in the dell
> Hi-ho the dairy-o
> The farmer in the dell

One of the children would skip inside the circle while the others sang,

> The farmer takes a wife
> The farmer takes a wife
> Hi-ho the dairy-o
> The farmer takes a wife

The child skipping in the circle and playing the farmer would then choose a wife from the children who formed the circle, and the two children would skip within the circle while the others sang. Then the wife would choose a child, the child a nurse, the nurse a dog, the dog a cat, the cat a rat and, finally, the rat a cheese. The children would all hold hands and laugh and dance and skip inside the circle and sing the song. Then all the children would rejoin the circle and hold hands, leaving the child playing the cheese to stand alone in the middle of the circle while the other children laughed and sang:

> The cheese stands alone
> The cheese stands alone
> Hi-ho the dairy-o
> The cheese stands alone.

The trouble began when George was chosen to become the cheese but refused to play the game. He complained that he had been the cheese three times last week. He scowled that if he became the cheese once more, he would be nicknamed "Cheese" by his classmates. The teacher got vexed and ordered George to become the cheese. George refused.

The Principal was summoned. While all the children stood holding hands in a circle and looking bewildered, the Principal ordered George to become the cheese. George said that he would not.

Going back to his office, the Principal returned to the playfield carrying his leather strap. He hit George three times with the strap, bringing the strap down hard across the boy's back. Then he commanded George to take his place within the circle as the cheese. Sullenly, in a whisper, George refused.

Furious, the Principal beat him some more with the strap, slashing it across the boy's back with six hard strokes. George began to cry with pain. The other children became frightened. They shuffled their feet and wet their lips nervously.

Believing that George had now relented, the Principal ordered the game resumed with George in the part of the cheese. George was in tears. But his lower lip was curled, and his eyes were defiant. Between sobs of pain, he gasped to the Principal, "You better kill me now. For me not being no cheese!"

The Principal, taken aback and not knowing what to do next, flew into a rage and gave the children a stern lecture on what it meant to be living in an Independent Jamaica, and how British Colonialism had ruined the national character as exemplified by George's refusal to become the cheese. This was the very sort of thing the Prime Minister was always complaining about, the Principal raged, the pettifogging selfishness of the average Jamaican. The children blinked and stared at the Principal. For, the Principal demanded, pacing up and down around the cowering but defiant George, how could Jamaica become a just socialist society when everyone was determined to have his own selfish way? When everyone was determined to become a farmer and no one was willing to be the cheese? And everyone knew, the Principal said, speaking so furiously that he sprayed spittle on the heads of the mute children, that a society not only needed farmers and wives and cats and dogs; but cheese, too, was necessary in any society. He was, of course, the Principal glowered, speaking metaphorically. George sniffled and refused to budge. The children looked very solemn. A few were on the verge of tears.

In the middle of this metaphorical speech, the Inspector from the Ministry of Education drove up in his black Mercedes Benz.

Still standing in a subdued circle, the children limply held hands and began to whimper while the outraged Principal explained the incident to the Inspector.

Nodding briskly, the Inspector took charge. First, he demanded an explanation from George about his refusal to become the cheese. In a small, faltering voice, George explained. He had been the cheese three times in one week. If he became the cheese one more time, his classmates would nickname him "Cheese."

The Inspector then turned to the other children. Glowering officially at them, he demanded to know whether or not they intended to nickname George "the Cheese". With wide-eyed innocence, the children assured the Inspector that they did not.

Facing the obstinate George, the Inspector then gave him the assurance of the Jamaican Government that if he consented to become the cheese just once more, he would not be nicknamed "Cheese" because of it.

Unconvinced, George refused. In compromise, he volunteered to become the rat; but he refused to become the cheese.

Both the Inspector and the Principal flew into a rage and took turns browbeating George and flogging him with the leather strap. But still, although he cowered on the ground with pain, George held his ground. The other children became hysterical. Girls moaned and cried for their fathers;

boys urged George with sly movements of their eyes to become the cheese. Finally, his body covered with welts from the strapping, George was sent home.

The incident caused a terrible row between Zachariah and Carina. Carina sided with the government, raised her voice angrily against her defiant son and swore that he would grow up to become a gunman. Zachariah got angry too, and vowed that he would chop the Principal with a machete for strapping George so brutally. Carina accused George of being an undisciplined "negar". Zachariah retorted that if the boy was a "negar" he was so because that was also what his mother was. Then they had a loud row about which of them was more of a "negar". Carina brought out the small mirror and held it in front of Zachariah so he could see his nose, swollen with blackness, and his thick negro lips. Zachariah pointed to his skin, which was lighter than Carina's, as proof that he was less "negar" than she. All afternoon and into the early evening, the argument raged.

But the next day, after Zachariah had come in from the night of fishing, they made up and lay in bed together. Carina admitted that Zachariah was less negro because his skin was lighter. Zachariah confessed that his nose was more swollen and his lips thicker than hers. In compromise they decided that she had less negar in her face but more in her skin; he had the negar in his face, but less so in his complexion. Then they made love.

"So naturally, she ride on top o' me like me is a damn donkey," Zachariah muttered, as he remembered. And even as he said this, there was the grievance at her unreasonableness to not allow him to be the rider for just twenty times.

Nevertheless, he was alone at sea and his heart was longing for his woman and his sons. And he was surrounded by nothing more than empty horizons and surging groundswells with only the painted canoe between him and the ravenous fish below. Yet he still felt the grievance over the business of who should ride who. But that was not

66

necessarily a wrong or a bad thing, for a man who feels a grievance over such a thing still has a lot of fight left in his heart, no matter how alone he is, or how surrounded by emptiness.

"Dat's why a man alone at sea must think," Zachariah told himself with a smile. His lips, however, dried from the hot sun, cracked when he tried to smile. So he reached under the thwart and moistened his lips with a mouthful of water.

He sailed all afternoon and into the evening, expecting Jamaica to rise out of the ocean across the bow of the canoe. The sun fell into the horizon. The heat cooled and the sky, oozing with gaudy colours and hues, seemed to become limp and wrinkled at its edges.

All over the ocean, and all over the sky, and everywhere that the two came together, there was a jubilant loosening. The heat dissipated and was borne off by a cool breeze. Blackness blew across the water, and the night glided in over the ocean.

Into the direction of the setting sun Zachariah sailed, believing that Jamaica was just ahead on the horizon.

But Zachariah was wrong. When he was only six, his mother took him out of school and put him in charge of a herd of goats. He had barely learned to sign his name, could read only a few words, and had not yet learned geography. He did not even know the shape of Jamaica, nor the exact location of Charity Bay on the map.

And this was the reason for his error. When he fished, he sailed only by dead reckoning, always within sight of land. He knew nothing about navigation, nor could he plot a course from the stars. He knew only that the sun was always at his back when he sailed into Charity Bay after a night's fishing. And so he reasoned that if he sailed with the sun at his stern, he would have a landfall.

67

But if he had considered the location of Charity Bay on the Jamaican map, he would have seen his mistake. For the village sits close to the eastern tip of the island. And when the land breeze had blown him away, it carried him to the north and then to the east. Jamaica was not in front of the sailing canoe. The eastern tip of Jamaica lay to the starboard, lurking just under the horizon on Zachariah's right.

Ahead of the painted canoe, across a thousand miles of merciless ocean, lay the Isthmus of Panama.

Chapter 7

Consternation was in the hearts of the villagers of Charity Bay, when they learned that Zachariah was missing. Wives, sweethearts, old men, even children and dogs, wandered down to the shore where the canoes were beached and stared out into the green sea. Arguments and petty quarrels were set aside; antagonists who had not spoken to each other for weeks over some foolishness, now stood side by side on the beach, straining their eyes over the ocean in search of the painted canoe. Women who had yesterday bickered with their men, were now so joyful over their safe return that they could not touch them gently enough.

The villagers gathered in small groups, speculating on what could have happened to Zachariah, talking in subdued tones about whether the land breeze had carried him off, or whether a shark had taken him, or whether he had become sick last night and died at sea and was now drifting aimlessly on the ocean. The fishermen huddled under the spiny shadow of a coconut tree and discussed the strength of the land breeze and talked about who last night had last seen the light from Zachariah's canoe before it blew away.

Even the higglers, who came down daily to the beach to buy fish from the incoming canoes, laid their wicker baskets down on the sand and sat in a group and talked morosely about what dreadful fate could have befallen Zachariah, the ugly fisherman whose catch was always battered and bruised. Anecdotes about him were exchanged. Stories were told about his prodigious stubbornness, about how obdurate he had been over the price of his fish. Fingers pointed furtively to where his grieving woman stood, peering intently out to sea.

"Man eat fish," one dour, obese higgler declared, flashing her eyes darkly over the harbour, "and fish eat man. So it go."

There was so much chattering and visiting on the beach that it was like Christmas, or Festival, or a holiday, except that the groups of people were sombre in their talk, and there was no carousing, no music, no wild laughter. But there were plenty of omens. For everyone now recalled a sign of yesterday, or of last week, which had pointed to this loss.

Mrs. Hemmings reported on the galliwasp lizard she had dreamed of, how she saw the lizard come out of a crack in the wall, creep up to a fisherman mending a net on the beach, leap up and bite him fatally on his neck. And as everyone there knew, she pointed out, Zachariah was weaving a new net, so who else could her dream have been about, except to foretell that some calamity awaited him?

Mrs. Roper became excited and clamoured scripture to anyone who would listen. She wandered from group to group, reading from Deuteromony, and from the Prophets, finding signs that foretold not only the end of Zachariah, but the end of Charity Bay, and Port Antonio, and of Jamaica itself, or even of the world. Earthquake, hurricane, pestilence, ravenous beasts, plagues of mongoose, all these things she foretold by reading from the Bible. From group to group she wandered, spreading the dreadful news. One or two of the fishermen shooed her impatiently away. The women all listened respectfully, for they knew that Mrs. Roper talked in tongues with the spirit of the Holy Ghost.

Mrs. Lewis told herself that she was glad that she had not lost her temper with the ugly brute and hit him on the head with a broom as she had been tempted to when he had quarrelled with her in her shop. For if she had brained him, the blow would now be on her conscience. But in another breath, while she wandered from group to group exchanging hopes and fears with the villagers, she could not help but think that if she had brained him he would not have gone out to sea, which would have spared his life. And she took this as another sign of what her Maroon mother had taught her — that women were put on this earth to master and discipline men, and that where an unruly man was concerned, a woman should never spare the switch. So when Mr. Lewis wandered onto the beach and took liberties with his wife, thinking that the tragedy of the moment would incline her towards leniency, he was repelled by such a severe clout on the head from her that he fell face-forwards into the sand.

"Go mind de store, you worthless brute!" his wife stood over him and commanded.

"You don't have no respect for de dead, woman," Mr. Lewis began, staggering to his feet.

"Go mind de store before I dead you," she glowered.

"Rass woman," Mr. Lewis muttered in an undertone, scrambling away from the beach, followed by the village dogs who thought that his fall on the beach meant that he was out for a romp.

Carina, too, had had an omen — a bad dream about a green alligator who had crawled into bed with her and rubbed his scaly belly up against hers. And she woke up and knew that a duppy was in the dark room peering at her from a far corner, knew that something had befallen Zachariah at sea. She wandered most of the night from room to room, protecting her sons against the presence of the duppy, pausing to look out the windows of the shack at the lights of the fishing canoes that rose and fell with the undulations of the ocean. Even then she knew in her heart that misery had befallen her man, knew as only a woman can know such a thing.

"So God give woman heart to suffer," Mrs. Wilson

71

said in a gloomy voice as she heard this story.

"Is so God make woman," Mrs. Ferguson agreed.

"Women heart make to broke," Mrs. Hemmings added, sober for the first time in a week.

"Woman must suffer, whether or not she do no wrong," Mrs. Lewis agreed, rubbing in the cool sand the sore fist with which she had just clouted her useless husband.

Sitting among the grieving women, her hair undone, her small, intense eyes darting over the harbour reef and out to deep sea, so Carina told the story of the night when Zachariah was lost at sea.

The duppy had come to take her too, having taken Zachariah, but she drove him off with an ointment purchased from Lubeck, the obeah man. Some do not believe in the obeah man. And others deny the existence of duppies. But men and women everywhere who have sense and who do not wish to be devoured by darkness, know better and take precautions.

"Know better for true!" Mrs. Lewis grunted.

All through the long hot day, the villagers wandered along the stretch of beach, staring out into the ocean for signs of the painted canoe. The higglers stayed for an hour or so, lamenting the general sorrow, but then they bought the fish they had come to buy and rode off carrying the fish in boxes strapped to the pillions of their motorcycles. The fishermen, their catch sold, beached their canoes and scrubbed the smell of dead fish from the boats. But there was a strange, unhurried air to their movements. For no one would go to sea tonight, not so soon after the sea had killed. They would wait at least a day. Some, nagged by their women, would wait even longer. A few would even give up fishing altogether and go into the bush to plant yam, corn, cassava, and try to scratch their livelihood from the earth.

The crowd on the beach soon attracted a passing country bus, for in the islands nothing draws people more quickly than a cricket match or a drowning. The strangers

72

from the bus wandered down to the beach to enquire of the reason for the crowd, and when they were told that a fisherman was lost at sea, they asked questions about him, and speculated on what fate he could have met. A few of the strangers even became loud and excitable in their mourning though they did not know the missing fisherman. Some of the strangers, however, had themselves met sorrow from the sea, and now mourned as though Zachariah was one of their family. A toothless old woman raised her voice and lifted her arms to the sky and wept real tears, remembering the son she had lost years ago to the sea. A burly man, who said he was a constable from Port Antonio, went around from group to group asking officious questions about the disappearance, and writing down the answers in a small note book. A man who had only an ugly stump where his right arm should have been, told everyone that he had once been a fisherman, and that a shark had taken off his arm one night as he leaned over the side of the canoe to free a line. Everyone peered closely at the stump, while the stranger pointed out the teeth marks of the shark in his flesh and swore that he would never again even wade into the ocean. Eventually, however, their curiosity sated, the strangers boarded the bus and it rattled off down the country road.

The sun climbed and the heat came down like a patterless dew. Gradually, the crowd thinned. Weary and hungry, the fishermen drifted off the beach and crossed the road to where their shacks stood under the shadows of coconut trees.

Carina stayed on the beach, watching all through the long, hot day for the yellow sail. Women came and sat with her on the sand and tried to give her hope and consolation. The two sons came from school and cuddled beside her. Wilfred, the silent one, stared out to sea with tears in his eyes. George scraped up fistfuls of the sand and threw them against the hull of a nearby canoe. Seeing the tears in his brother's eyes, George scolded, "Stop you crying! De sea can't kill me Papa!"

Old Mrs. Wilson led the sons away, leaving Carina alone on the beach, sitting under the shadow of a sea grape tree, and peering out into the harsh glitter of the daytime sea.

The sky sifted white, yellow then red. The sun fell into the horizon and the line between the sky and the sea wavered and disappeared in the gathering darkness. Undulating like fish, flocks of bone-white birds floated overhead towards their roosts.

When Carina saw the birds, she stood and dragged herself across the asphalt road towards her house, where the fishermen and their women would be gathering to comfort her, and to shield her from the wiles of duppies.

Turning, Carina threw one last hungry look across the bay. She saw how the night fell over the ocean and she thought about how the darkness smothered Zachariah, alone and adrift in the painted canoe, and she felt so much rage at the darkness that she trembled beside the trunk of a coconut tree.

But as quickly as it had come, the anger disappeared when she considered how cold and frightened Zachariah would be tonight. There was no moon. He would have only the light from the kerosene cresset. The glow from the stars would not be bright enough to show him the way home. And he would be so lonely out there, alone and friendless on the guileful ocean.

She began to cry her grief and helplessness. She cried long and loud, choking the sobs in the palms of her hands.

Straightening her back, she stopped crying. Her eyes glinted as the rage came back.

"Fight him, Zach," she hissed under the coconut tree.

She was facing the ocean when she said it. Her voice carried into the shadows and floated away on a breeze towards the ocean.

"Fight him, Zach!" she hissed again, this time louder and with murder in her voice.

74

"Fight him, Zach!" And this time she screamed it, her body fluttering with a spasm as if to spit out rage and love to be borne off by the wind to Zachariah, lost and drifting alone on the ocean.

Women hurried from the small shack and gathered protectively around the sobbing Carina and led her inside.

Under the starlit night, the ocean heard. Furled up against the shoreline, the green ocean heard, peeled off three small waves and hurled them against the shore. The water purled over the sand, turned white and flat like a flounder, reached out and gathered pebbles on the beach. The water withdrew, pulling the pebbles after it, giving off, in reply, a faint, malicious cackling.

Chapter 8

He panicked, that first night at sea. He was unnerved by the terrible darkness of the deep, by the sighs of the slumbering ocean. He yearned to see even the flicker of light from a peeny-wally — for so Jamaicans call the firefly — and he looked everywhere around him, hoping to glimpse even the running lights of a distant freighter. He was adrift in the sea lanes of the big freighters. Surely if he looked hard enough, he would spot a light on the horizon. But no matter how hard he looked, he saw nothing but the enormous blackness. He heard none of the sounds the fishermen usually made at sea. No voices called to one another out of loneliness. There was no crack of surf against a distant promontory. Even the rustle of the ocean was different this far out. It was so dark and lonely that he began to shiver.

The wind had died and the sail drooped on the mast. He took down the sail and thought about lighting the cresset but refrained from doing so because he wanted to keep his eyes sharp and clear to see the Port Antonio beacon.

The ocean rolled into fat swollen waves that did not break. Wallowing up and down, the painted canoe drifted aimlessly. Now that the sun had gone down, he was in danger of forgetting the direction in which he should sail for a landfall.

He decided, therefore, to row the canoe. Rowing would keep his mind occupied. Moreover, if he rowed now he would hold the canoe on the proper course for a landfall. So he crawled into the middle of the canoe, took down the small sail, ran out the oars, and began to row.

The canoe lurched through the waves, and the rope oar-locks groaned with each pull on the oars. He rowed and every now and again he turned and looked over his shoulder for the beacon. It was a five second light, a powerful yellow flash into the dark night. But though he looked until his eyes watered, he saw nothing other than the immense darkness.

He rowed. The oarlocks groaned. The stars stayed stubbornly where they were; the beacon did not flash. He was breathing hard as the dew fell on the painted canoe.

He rowed some more, pulling on the oars until his shoulders ached. His arms became numb. His body begged him to stop. But he would not stop. He was afraid of the deep. The darkness terrified him and made his heart beat fast. He would not look at the stars that glittered on the becalmed water like the eyes of inquisitive fish.

Over the dark ocean, the painted canoe moved, but the beacon did not appear. Like a sly spider, the ocean un-ravelled a vast, unmeasurable web before the painted canoe.

Zachariah rowed and rowed and the oarlocks groaned and the canoe wallowed and rocked because he was too weary to dip the oars evenly into the water. And he was so exhausted that, without his knowledge, the canoe had turned in a slow, lumbering arc and was now moving in the opposite direction.

But he would not stop rowing, for he was driven by fear and loneliness. His heart curdled into a painful knot. His lungs burned. His throat was raw from sucking for air. His hands began to swell. Reeling with exhaustion, Zachariah collapsed in the bottom of the painted canoe.

He was dizzy and the canoe seemed to spin under him. The fear came and spread through his limbs like a chill. Suddenly, he was cold and shivering. He hugged himself and clenched his teeth to prevent them from clattering.

All around the canoe the sea was dark and friendless. Above, the sky glittered its frightening immensities. He

77

was afraid to raise his head and look around into the darkness. He did not know what he would see, but he was afraid to look. He began to sob.

He sobbed and shook with fear and the canoe quivered under him. He knew now that he was lost. He would not see the Port Antonio beacon. He did not know where he was. Raising himself painfully in the bottom of the canoe, he looked around him and saw the darkness, the stars, the brooding, luminous sea. He could stand no more. He closed his eyes and cried out the name of the woman he loved.

"Carina!" he called, his voice hoarse and tired. Then he called her name again, and again, and again.

His words drifted out of the bottom of the painted canoe and blew vainly across the empty sea.

He tried to beat down the fear. Rubbing his face and his hands to drive away the chill, he tried to think about wives and the crosses they bring a man. And when he could not concentrate on that, he tried to think about his second son, Wilfred, who was silent and stealthy as a fish.

Wiping his eyes, he told himself that it was shameful for a grown man to carry on so like a frightened child. Then he told himself that he would call out to God, and ask God to help him find the way home. But in the very next breath he dismissed this idea because of his belief that a man should not run to God over every little thing, but should wait until his trouble was dire and beyond all hope. And he was not yet beyond hope. The canoe was not foundering. He was not on his death bed with sickness. His heart was still strong. What, really, were his present troubles?

Well, he was hungry. And this thought brought a chuckle out of him, for he was afloat on God's deep sea where the fish were plentiful and nourishing. Moreover, he had fishing lines and hooks and skill to land the deep water fish. He also had the wrenchman for bait. So though he was hungry he was in no danger of starving. And there was no reason to call out to God simply because of a temporary hunger.

Well, then, he was thirsty. And as he thought this he reached under the thwart and took out the water bottle and put it to his lips and drank. The water tasted sweet and satisfying and in no time his thirst was slaked. So he held the water up to the light from the stars and saw that the bottle was half full. He had enough water for the time being. This was the rainy season. Tomorrow or the next day would come a squall that would fill the bottle with water, giving him more than enough to satisfy his needs. So there was no reason to call out to God because of the lack of water.

Then he told himself that he was frightened by the loneliness of the deep, and by the darkness of the night. And this brought a scowl to his face.

"Pickney and woman afraid o' dese thing, not big man," he muttered.

And certainly, there was no reason for a lonely man to call out to God when he had memories of his woman and his children to comfort him.

"So what you bawling out to God for, you ugly rass, you?" he concluded by scolding himself.

And he could give no answer, for he could find no reason to go running to God just because he was temporarily lost at sea.

"Damn ugly man behave just like a pickney at sea," he muttered to himself as he pulled in the oars and tried to decide what he would do next.

The canoe drifted on the dark sea, rising and falling with the gentle movement that mothers use to rock a cradle, and Zachariah scolded himself and muttered several times that he was stupid and ugly and tried to think of what he should do now.

He was thinking when the ocean behind him exploded with the splash of a jumping fish.

He looked quickly around the canoe, expecting to see a shark. Reaching under the thwart, he raised the harpoon.

79

Another splash, louder than before, exploded off his right. He swung around and peered into the darkness. By starlight he saw where the ocean had been punctured by a leaping fish and where the ripples now coiled off and ran soothingly over the wound.

He told himself to be careful, for this would be a deep water shark and a dangerous fish. He twisted and looked all around the canoe. Seeing nothing, he spun quickly and looked around the side and flashed a glance across her stubby bow. And when he still could not see a sign of the shark, he laid down the harpoon and lit the cresset and held it up over his head so that it threw a wavering glow into the dark ocean.

The dark surface of the water trembled under the stab of light. A fish leaped out of the water, arced towards the wavering light, and landed on its side with a loud splash.

"Bonito," Zachariah said, with exultation.

He had drifted into a school of feeding bonito.

Quickly, he hoisted the cresset over the bow of the canoe, threw the green bowels of the jack overboard, and baited a hook with an eye that he popped out of the jack's head. He threw the line overboard, got an immediate strike, and yanked a bluefin bonito into the canoe. With a quick blow from the club, he shattered the head of the bonito, popped out its eyeball with the tip of the hook, and threw the baited hook overboard. Within seconds, he had another strike, and pulled another bluefin into the canoe.

He had landed four of the big, deepwater fish within minutes — enough meat to last him a week — when the ocean was torn by a sudden, violent flurry and the bonito leaped into the air, splashing frantically around the canoe. It was then Zachariah saw the black fin rise out of the deep and slash through the feeding bonito.

The ocean was torn by the sounds of the bonito trying to escape. Zachariah watched the fin slice through the water and slink into the darkness. He moved forward slowly, carefully, and blew out the lantern. Then he sat in the bow of the canoe, waiting for the shark to move on, listening to the sounds made by the bonito as they hurled into the air and slapped against the waves.

His eyes gradually adjusting to the darkness of the night, he sat and listened. The bonito had moved away, swimming to escape the shark. He fumbled for the match and was trying to light the lantern when he heard a thud against the side of the canoe, as though the boat had drifted into an obstacle, and felt the canoe lunge sideways.

He sat deathly still, without moving a muscle. The ocean rustled and sighed as though a big fish had glided past. Zachariah reached down and took up the harpoon. His heart was racing and his mouth was dry. With his other hand, he moved the lignum vitae club near his feet, where he could reach down and get it in a hurry. Then he fumbled under the thwart for a match, and lit the lantern. But his hand was shaking so badly that it required two matches to light the kerosene wick. Holding the lantern above his head, he searched the water for signs of the shark.

The flickering lantern threw out a feeble glow over the still water. Zachariah looked all around him, searching for the shark. But he saw no sign of any fish. The ocean trembled under the wavering light.

"A-hoa," Zachariah grunted, almost frightening himself with his own voice.

But even as he said this, the black fin slunk out of the deep, no more than four feet away from the canoe, and the ocean sighed as the shark drove past the canoe and into the wavering light. The shark rustled out of the flickering glow of the cresset and disappeared into the darkness, sliding past with the stealth of a thief.

"Hammerhead," Zachariah whispered, his heart racing. He had glimpsed the fish as it slithered out of the glow of the cresset.

"You don't 'fraid me with dat fish," Zachariah said out loud. But even as he said this, he knew the terror that children feel. And he quickly doused the light from the kerosene lantern so the shark would not have anything to draw it to the canoe. Then he sat in the darkness and waited, and listened to the throbbing of his frightened heart.

It was a malign and humourless beast that the sea had sent up to greet him. A hammerhead shark, the ugliest of all fishes, a fish the fishermen said was brother to the devil, a fish so ugly and deformed that even a glimpse of it could make a man sleepless.

"You don't 'fraid me with dat fish," Zachariah repeated out loud, moving back to the centre of the canoe, feeling his way over the thwarts.

But he knew that his heart was afraid, for he could feel it racing in his chest. And he knew that his limbs were afraid, for he could feel his hands trembling and unsteady as he made his way across the thwarts. And he knew that even the painted canoe was afraid, for he could feel its skittishness on the becalmed sea.

He took a drink from the water bottle and he gripped the harpoon and waited, listening to the soft whispers of the water against the side of the canoe, hearing the frenzied beating of his own heart. But he heard no sounds of a shark stalking around the canoe.

"Don't throw no fish parts overboard," he warned himself. "You just goin' draw him back."

Now he was talking to himself, which was another bad sign. But it was the fear that caused him to do so. For the hammerhead was a merciless and persistent fish. And sometimes, once a hammerhead spotted a canoe, it would follow the boat for hours. And sometimes it would swim close to the canoe and touch the cottonwood with its ugly snout, sniffing after flesh. The fishermen said that once the hammerhead had tasted the flesh of a man, it wanted no other kind of meat. Fish was no longer satisfying to it. Perhaps this hammerhead had eaten a man or a woman or a child once before and liked the flesh, and was now hungry for more.

"Foolishness," Zachariah said out loud.

There was no end to the number of ways a man could torment himself when he was lonely. There was no counting the number of fears a man could hide in his heart. But he would pay no heed to the fears inside him. He had other things inside him too, things that would counteract his fears.

"Remembrances," Zachariah muttered, "happy remembrances."

Now he had said that word, "happy", something his mother had taught him a poor man should never say. For when the poor man confesses to happiness, it meant one of several bad things. First, it meant that he was content with his poverty, which also meant that he would be poor all his life, that his children and his woman would be poor all their lives, too, and that he would die a pauper and be buried in potter's field, with not even a stone to mark where he lay. So, according to the teaching of his mother, a poor man should never say he was "happy". He should always call himself miserable. And if he persuaded himself that he were indeed miserable, he would work hard to rid himself of his poverty.

The second reason that a poor man should never confess to happiness, was the envy of the duppies around him. The duppy ate out its heart when it witnessed a poor but contented man. For the duppy was doomed to wander, searching for peace which it could never find, wailing and gnashing its teeth with rage at the tranquillity of mortal men, looking to make mischief whenever it could. And if a duppy heard a poor man confess to being happy, it could quickly try to bring evils and wickedness upon his head.

The ocean shook with a strange restlessness and Zachariah immediately put away his thoughts and turned his head to listen to the sounds the dark water made around the painted canoe. He heard a loud rustling through the water that told him the shark was still treading around the canoe, its fin slicing through the surface. His heart skipping with fear, he heard the rustling of the shark grow louder, and he felt and heard a dull thud against the hull of the boat. The canoe shivered and rocked as though it were being shoved from underneath.

"You rass, you!" Zachariah shouted, his heart mad with fear. "You rass shark!"

Quickly, he lighted the cresset, though his mind told him that he was making a mistake, that he should instead sit quietly in the darkness and do nothing that would arouse the beast. But he could not bear to sit and wait any more, while the hammerhead swam around the canoe and rammed its hull testingly. So he lit the cresset and he raised the harpoon and craned carefully over the side, looking to drive the spear into the heart of the malign fish.

And though Zachariah was not a profane man, yet he was so frightened that he was cursing the black fish of the deep that slunk like a murderer around the canoe. When he cursed, he heard the sound of his own voice, and he felt the defiance of his own heart, and he forgot about his fear. So he raised the harpoon, its filed down machete blade glinting in the flickering light, and he searched the waters for the shark.

"Come, you rass, you," he told the hammerhead. "Don't hide in de dark. Come. Me have somethin' for you. Come, you blood."

But after he had looked around the canoe and listened to the ocean, he neither saw nor heard the shark. It was folly to stay awake with the cresset lighted and the harpoon ready, watching all night for a prowling, sleepless fish. Soon Zachariah would become tired. Then he would get careless. Moreover, he needed to keep his strength for rowing the canoe in the daylight hours.

He laid the harpoon across the thwarts, where he could reach it in a hurry, and under the yellow glow of the lantern, he worked on preserving the bonito.

First, he cut off the head of a bonito, sawing through the spine bone with the knife. Then he inserted the point of the knife into the throat of the fish, and opened up its stomach, so that the green bowels and water spilled out onto the thwart. Then he scraped the insides of the bonito clean, gathering the bowels onto the thwart. Because the shark was lurking nearby, he dared not throw the bowels overboard. So he laid the bowels, coiled and green like a slippery worm, on top of the head in the calabash bowl, and stored the bowl under the thwart.

Next, he skinned the fish, exposing the firm flesh. With the knife, whose blade was razor sharp, he filleted the bonito and rubbed salt into the thin strips of meat.

Tomorrow, he would lay the salted strips on the forward thwart of the canoe, where they would dry and stay fresh for the days ahead.

When he was done, he blew out the lantern, ate some of the salted fillet, and drank from the water bottle. By his side, as he rested against the thwart, was the harpoon. Nearby, were the club and the knife.

He ate the fillet and listened to the sounds of the canoe soughing through the still seas. He listened also for the sounds that would tell him of the return of the shark. And as he ate and listened, he thought about the hammerhead and hoped that the shark would eventually wander off.

Such an ugly fish had killed Sedak, known as Seddie, a calypso singer and sometime fisherman in Westmoreland, where Zachariah had come from.

Seddie used to wear a yellow towel tied around his head whenever he sang. He played the guitar and the banjo and sang the old-time songs from his childhood. The guitar he

85

had made himself. Some people said that Seddie had been a thief in Montego Bay, and that he had stolen the banjo from a white man. But Zachariah did not believe these stories, because he knew Westmoreland and the hearts of the people there, and he knew that even a saint would get a bad name from them.

When he was not fishing, Seddie used to wander through the bars, singing calypsos and dancing to his own music, trying to beg a little rum with his music. And there was always a fisherman or two present who would buy Seddie a jigger of white rum, which would fire him up and cause him to sing and dance all night. Seddie loved nothing more than white rum, loved it even more than he loved his woman, who was a higgler, or than he loved his one child, a boy who had gone deaf from disease.

When Seddie was drunk, he sang the old calypso songs such as "Give Me Back Me Shilling Wid De Lion 'Pon it", or "Old Lady, You Mashing Me Toe". But his favourite song was a rude calypso, "Night Food", which was about a precocious schoolboy trying to seduce his female teacher. And sometimes, when he was singing this lewd song, which was done in the quick, jerky rhythms of the calypso, Seddie would weep. Yet it was a mystery to everyone that Seddie should weep over such an unsentimental song. People whispered that perhaps, when Seddie was a boy, he had once loved his teacher.

Seddie's life was ended by a hammerhead shark. Zachariah was then a young man who had no canoe and therefore fished only from the shore. Once in a while, one of the older fishermen would carry him out to sea to help run out a net. But the morning that Seddie was killed by the hammerhead, Zachariah was in the bush, tending to his mother's goats. Later, after Seddie was already dead, Zachariah heard the story about how the shark had killed him.

Some said that Seddie had caught a snapper and was

pulling the fish to the surface, when the hammerhead lunged out of the ocean and cut the snapper in two. So astonished was Seddie by the sight of the ugly, striking shark, that he jumped backwards with fear and fell out of the canoe. Before he could clamber back in, the hammerhead cut off both his legs. Seddie thrashed around, vainly reaching for the gunwales of the canoe, while the shark devoured him.

Others said that they saw the hammerhead ram the canoe and tip it over, spilling Seddie and his catch into the sea, where the shark devoured him. One older fisherman swore that this was what had happened. For months afterwards he told and retold the story of seeing the shark's fin suddenly appear off the side of the canoe, and seeing the shark swim into the canoe, capsizing it. But few of the fishermen believed his story. It was not that they doubted the malignity and cunning of the hammerhead, for they too had had sharks come up against the hulls of their canoes and touch them with their snouts. But the man was known as a great liar, who always told lies about his fish.

What was left of Seddie, after the shark had devoured most of him, was recovered by the fishermen and buried under the front doorstep of the house in which he had lived with his woman. His guitar and banjo, the woman sold to a breadfruit vendor, whose son had ambitions to become a calypso singer as popular as the great Sparrow from Trinidad.

But even now, as he drifted alone on the deep and thought about Seddie who had been killed by a hammerhead, there was sadness in Zachariah's heart about how a poor man could so easily and completely vanish from the earth, and never be remembered. Every man would meet his death someday, although all sane men wished that that day be far distant in the future. And it was a great pity that Seddie, a man who loved song and who wept sentimentally over the words of a rude calypso, should have been killed and eaten by such a brute fish as the hammerhead. But it was an

87

even greater pity that his bones should have been buried under the doorstep of a shack, with neither marker nor headstone nor words to commemorate his resting place. Even now, probably no more than a dozen people knew where Seddie's bones lay. Just before Zachariah left Westmoreland, the government tore down the shack where Seddie had lived. The bulldozer drove its blade through the wattle-and-daub walls, and scraped the stone foundation clean from the ground. When the old foundation had disappeared, the workers came and built new houses, houses bigger than the ones the bulldozer had torn down, houses with inside toilets and running water. The Minister came to the dedication of these houses, which were turned over to the poor people who had formerly lived on the property, and he said it was a wonderful thing that the government had done. But all Zachariah could think of when he heard the Minister speak, was that Seddie's bones were now scattered forever in the dust. Some of his bones rode inside the belly of a great hammerhead. Others were sunk deep and unnoticed into the earth.

Zachariah remembered when the bulldozer first came. He had seen Seddie's woman at the market and offered to help dig up Seddie's bones and move them to a place where later, when she was more prosperous, she could mark them with a headstone. He remembered how the woman had looked at him out of the corners of her eyes, looked at him as though he were drunk or mad or worse.

"De man dead and gone," she said finally, with a contemptuous shrug of her head. "Him in heaven. It don't matter what dem do wid him bone."

"But when him pickney grow up and want know where him father bone lie," Zachariah argued, sitting down on the dirt beside her.

The woman became cross and growled at him to not sit with her as though he was her "friend", meaning that she did not wish people to think that such an ugly man was her lover.

"When him ask," she replied, after Zachariah had stood and moved away to a respectful distance, "I goin' tell him him father in heaven. Man not make of bone, Missah Zachariah. De shark don't eat Seddie. Him eat only a dry bone. But Seddie live now and walk 'pon de ground of heaven just like you see me here sit in a de dutty selling fish. For me know dat me see Seddie one night wid me two eye, me see him plain as day rowing one canoe 'pon de waters of de heavenly kingdom. God bless de day de shark take him dry bone and free him spirit to fish de waters o' heaven. And me wish is me de shark did eat instead o' him, den me would be fishing in heaven and him would be selling fish in Westmoreland."

Zachariah knew that she did not wish to talk with him about Seddie any more. Whenever a woman called him "Missah Zachariah", it meant that she was trying to discourage familiarity, trying to teach him his place. So he told her "Good evening" and went about his business. But in his heart he knew that the woman was wrong, and that some marker should have been made to show the spot where Seddie's bones rested.

Only the poor man's bones were hidden unmarked in the ground. This was not the way of the rich man. Zachariah knew this because he had once worked for a rich "backra" in Westmoreland, a white man who owned more land than anyone else in the parish. His land rolled over pasture and gully and bushy hill. This rich man, whose name was Backra McPherson — the "backra" being the traditional term of respect given to rich white men — had taken a liking to Zachariah for a foolish reason. Backra McPherson said that he had never met an ugly man who was a thief. He also said that Zachariah was the most honest man in Westmoreland, because he was the ugliest. Zachariah did not like to hear this kind of comment from the backra, and if the backra had said these things repeatedly, Zachariah would not have worked for him. But he said these things only in the beginning, when he first hired Zachariah to work as a day labourer in the fields. And after that, he would only mumble these comments if Zachariah happened to be nearby when the backra was drunk.

The backra lived in a big house on top of a green hill that was always cooled by a refreshing breeze. The veranda of the house overlooked grazing pastures and fruit orchards. Next to the veranda were gardens of wild orchids and English roses. Flowering vines mounted the trunks of bountiful mango trees. Hibiscus and bougainvillea bloomed on the backra's doorstep. And in this garden, Zachariah sometimes worked, weeding the flower beds and cutting the grass with his machete.

And so he got a good chance to see how the backra lived and what the backra's hopes and dreams were. He sometimes overheard the backra talking to his woman; he often overheard the backra giving instructions to his children. Moreover, Zachariah saw the things that worried the backra, and the things that made him content with his life.

So Zachariah knew that it was not the way of rich white men to plant the bones of their family in unmarked graves. Indeed, three times the backra had taken Zachariah to work in the family graveyard. Here the backra's family, his fathers and his grandfathers, lay under imposing marble tombstones. Here, to mark the resting place of the backra's mother, was a marble angel blowing a horn at the sky. And where the backra's grandfather lay, was marked by a squat marble house. The names of the dead were written in the marble with a chisel, along with a prayer and the times in which they had lived. Neither rain nor sun nor wind could erase the names from the stone. And every week, the backra took a worker into the graveyard, and saw that the grass was trimmed, and the weeds were removed, and the vines were lopped back and prevented from twining over the mounds of the graves.

It was only the poor man whose bones were laid unmarked in the earth. The rich white man marked the burial sites of his dead, and wrote their names and years of life in the most durable of stone.

"Everywhere you turn in dat place, you see another McPherson," Zachariah muttered, remembering the grave-yard.

He ran his hand over his chin as he said this, and he could feel the stubble of a day-old beard. He traced the growth of the beard down the side of his neck until he came to the scar beside his collarbone where the mad English doctor had cut him.

Now here, Zachariah thought, was a white man unlike any other on the island, a foreigner with such strange, perverse ways that, by common consent, everyone in Charity Bay called him "mad". Zachariah tried to visualize the face of the Englishman but could not, for he did not have much practice with either seeing or recalling white faces. One white man looked very much like another to him. The Englishman was the only white man who came regularly to Charity Bay. He came to the clinic there every Thursday, and treated patients.

Then Zachariah began to think about why everyone said that the Englishman was mad. He had a violent temper. In his bag with his medicines and instruments, he carried a large gun and had more than once threatened to shoot a patient who provoked him. Only last week the Englishman had sent a message to Lubeck, saying that he intended to shoot him "as soon as possible". The wording of the message was a symptom of his madness, for no one who intends to shoot another threatens to do it "as soon as possible". Only a lunatic would send such a message.

But that was exactly what the English doctor told Karlene, Obediah's widow, to tell Lubeck — that he intended to shoot Lubeck "as soon as possible" — forcing the poor woman to sit on the examination bench in the clinic's treatment room and repeat the message several times in exactly those words so she would not forget. After the doctor was sure that Karlene knew the message by heart, he allowed her to leave.

She delivered the message to Lubeck — and to everyone else in the village. People heard and shook their heads with horror. But what could anyone do? The Englishman was the only doctor in the vicinity. Yet he was a madman.

Zachariah's own opinion was that anyone who wished to shoot Lubeck was quite sensible and not at all mad. Several times Zachariah had privately wished to chop the obeah man. Lubeck was a scoundrel and a thief. He sold useless herbs and weeds and chicken blood to anyone, especially women, who believed in him. He boasted that he could cure sickness and disease with his herbs; he claimed that he was able to cast spells on enemies, cause bellyaches, blindness, deafness, even death; and to do all these dreadful things, he used herbs and weeds, killed chickens, and wrote unreadable words with chicken blood.

"Foolishness!" Zachariah said aloud, the sound of his own voice startling him.

When he was a boy suffering from terrible headaches, his mother carried him into the bush to be treated by such men. They daubed him with chicken blood, bathed him in juices of weeds, and performed all kinds of magic over him. One of these same obeah men, a muscular Indian with not even a single tooth left in his mouth, nearly drowned Zachariah in a slimy pond, holding him under the green, brackish water and muttering spells over his head while he drowned. From the banks of the pond, Zachariah's mother looked on, beaming at the antics of the obeah man. Only by biting the Indian severely on his calf did Zachariah escape being drowned. Afterwards, there was a terrible row. The Indian screamed and hobbled out of the pond, bleeding from where Zachariah had bitten him, breaking loud oaths and swearing that he would revenge the bite by inflicting dreadful sickness on both mother and son. While the Indian was howling for vengeance and hopping on one foot to ease the pain of the bite, and his mother was shrieking that she had done nothing, Zachariah crawled out of the pond, so weak he could hardly breathe. Then the two of them took turns flogging him with a green switch. For what? Because he was not content to be drowned by a toothless Indian who claimed he could cure headaches with obeah magic.

So if the Englishman wanted to shoot Lubeck, or for that matter, any other obeah man, it was perfectly understandable to Zachariah. There was no madness in this desire that he could see.

Carina, however, believed in Lubeck. Several times Zachariah had argued with her about Lubeck, without changing her mind. She would get mad and rage, and Zachariah would prudently withdraw, ending the argument.

But when he first came to Charity Bay, the Englishman also swore that one day he would shoot the Parson. What could this be but madness? Even this, however, was understandable to Zachariah, who had often felt like chopping the Parson with a machete. For in addition to always ranting foolishness in the pulpit, the Parson also had another bad habit which was very provoking.

His habit was this: when he was through with service, the Parson would run quickly to the front door to waylay worshippers and, with little barbed comments, apply his sermon individually to each of them.

Zachariah scowled as he thought about this bad habit. After sitting in a church for over an hour listening to the Parson preach, no one liked to be accosted at the church door with more preaching.

The last time Zachariah had sat through an entire sermon, the Parson — sweat dripping off the creases of

93

his neck — had ranted and raved about hell; then he ran to block the doorway where he met Zachariah, who was, as usual, trying to sneak out the church before the Parson could waylay him.

"Brother Zachie," the Parson said loudly, puffing breathlessly, "you think you jawbone is big now, eh? You think it big? Wait'll you see de jawbone dat devil have! Now dat's jawbone! 'Cause hell have jawbone dat make your little thing dere look like bird jawbone!"

Zachariah frowned angrily and tried to shove his way past the parson.

"Aim for heaven, brother Zach!" the Parson exhorted, refusing to budge out of the doorway. " 'Cause when you reach heaven, brodder Zach, all de jawbone trouble you got is over! Over and done with! Suddenly, you handsome and pretty again like me, and everybody goin' love you!"

Furious, Zachariah glowered at the Parson and was about to curse a bad word when Carina nudged him in warning. He pushed past the Parson and stepped into the morning sunshine.

"You never see nothing prettier dan angel jawbone, brodder Zachie!" the Parson flung over his shoulder with a boisterous laugh.

Zachariah was so enraged that Carina had to grab him by the elbow and lead him away.

"No wonder de white man want to shoot him," Zachariah growled as he thought about the Parson's rudeness.

But this habit which the Parson had was not the cause of contention between him and the Englishman. The trouble between them arose because of Seahorse.

After Seahorse lost his arm and went mad, the doctor tried several times to see him. But in those days Seahorse was elusive and difficult to find. The doctor was in Charity Bay only on Thursdays, and he was always busy with sickness and injuries that had accumulated during the week. He gave messages to the patients he saw, asking them to locate Seahorse and bring him into the clinic for treatment. Several people told the doctor that they would.

Then, one Sunday, the Parson gave a silly sermon about God and suffering in which he used Seahorse as an example. He told the congregation that God intended everything to be the way it was — that God even intended Seahorse to lose his arm to a shark and go mad. Seahorse, the Parson said, was carrying on God's work by consenting to go mad and suffer. The Parson went on and on in this vein, even going so far as to imply that God's teeth, and not the shark's, had severed Seahorse's arm.

Zachariah, when he heard this rubbish, immediately got up and stalked out of the church. For he thought the sermon rude and indecent.

The following Thursday, however, a woman who had gone to see the doctor told him about the Parson's sermon. The doctor flew into a wild rage, throwing his bag against the wall and cursing in a loud voice. Some said that he was drunk. Others swore that they heard the doctor take violent oaths, daring God to strike him dead on the spot. When God did not strike, witnesses said, the doctor laughed and his eyes flashed like a lunatic's.

Zachariah did not know what to believe because others who were supposed to be at the clinic during this demonstration denied that anything of the sort had happened.

One thing all agreed on, however, for everyone heard it: the doctor swore that if he had been in the church during the sermon he would have shot the Parson dead in the pulpit. Several people related this message to the Parson who became mysteriously ill and did not show up in Charity Bay for a month afterwards.

By common consent, the doctor was thereafter nicknamed "the madman."

When Carina found out that Zachariah had gone to the madman for treatment, she became vexed at him. She told him that he should have gone to Lubeck instead, who would have treated the lump with herb tea. They had an argument over whether an obeah man was better for sickness than a doctor. Zachariah told her that even a mad doctor was better than a sane obeah man. She scowled and muttered at him. He asked her to tell him which university an obeah man had gone to. She kissed her teeth with contempt, making the scornful sound that higglers make by sucking air against their teeth, and retorted that doctors killed more people than sickness.

But afterwards, they made up, and she looked at where the doctor had cut him. The juices and sweat from his muscles, she said, had gathered into his neck and caused the lump. She boiled some green bush tea which she forced him to drink. That night she was tender with him the way they used to be long before the daughter died.

Rubbing his finger onto his neck, Zachariah could feel the scar. Moreover, he could also feel another harder lump swelling at the site of the scar. He had not told Carina about this one, for fear of causing her worry. Nor had he shown it to the Englishman for fear of more cutting. When Zachariah touched the new lump, it stayed stubbornly in place, as though it had a root.

His thoughts left him and he came back to himself in the bottom of the painted canoe. He cocked one ear and listened to the sounds of the sea for the shark, hearing only the whispering of the water against the hull. Then he glanced at the stars and saw that it was late, and remarked to himself how when a man's mind is full of thoughts, time passes quickly.

But now he was weary and needed sleep, so he reclined between the thwarts, his head resting lightly on the shaft of the harpoon, and prepared to rest.

A new moon rose, sharp and pointed at both ends, its pinchers fastened stiff and hard around the dull body of the old moon.

He would be damp and cold sleeping in the bottom of

the canoe, but if he did not sleep tonight he would fall asleep during the blazing sun tomorrow. He looked around the canoe. The ocean was calm and shiny in the moonlight. Dew flecked out of the dark sky. Weighted with prey, the new moon blew sluggishly over the horizon.

Lying in the bottom of the canoe, Zachariah covered his eyes with his hand so he would not have to stare into the darkness of the heavens. Almost immediately, he fell asleep.

Stars dipped and fell into the ocean and were replaced by great multitudes of stars lifting out of the sea. The moon climbed into mid-heaven, and the dark, languorous ocean swayed under the pinprick of starlight and the luminous pith of the moon.

Flying fish leaped into the air and skimmed the waves, flashing silver in the moonlight. Out of the east, a small breeze lifted, and the painted canoe was carried off by this night wind.

While Zachariah slept and the canoe drifted, a mountain rose off her starboard, and the beacon from the Morant Point lighthouse stabbed furtively through the darkness. Then the horizon curled over the mountain and the light disappeared.

The hammerhead, however, did not sleep. The black fin slunk out of the deep and circled the canoe. The shark drove past the gunwales of the canoe, and the ocean rattled like a snake in the wake of the slicing fin. Then the fin sank back into the deep, leaving a meticulous ripple shivering in the moonlight.

Chapter 9

The Island Queen, a sternhouse freighter of 4,000 tons whose holds were half-filled with copra, was pounding her way through the morning seas on her regular run to Belize. Though the sea was flat and glassy, the freighter still rattled and shook and made a terrible din. Her twin screws were partly out of the water and she was churning off a splattering wake behind her.

The first mate, a chain-smoking Honduran, was playing two-handed poker with the Trinidadian helmsman. Occasionally, the mate would glance into the dirty radar scope for a single sweep, peer out of the wheelhouse over the tangle of cranes on the deck, and return quickly to the game. With the Pedro Banks well astern, the mate assumed that the freighter had nothing ahead of her but deep, empty seas. She was therefore sniffing her way through the dawn skies under automatic steerage while her crew played cards on the bridge.

Yawning, the mate stood up from the chart table, stretched, and glanced into the radar scope. Resuming his seat, he picked up the hand the helmsman had just dealt and found himself looking at a natural full house. He hid his delight by coughing into the cupped palm of his hand.

Just. then, the Island Queen was crashing through the glimmering dawn light and bearing down noisily on the painted canoe.

Zachariah was dreaming of Carina. He was dreaming of his homecoming and about how she would greet him. He heard her scream his name and he saw her plunge recklessly into the surf and swim towards him. His heart bursting with love and joy, he rowed the canoe in his dream and screamed out the name of the woman he loved. In the dream, he was weeping like a child.

And he would have heard the freighter, except that he was upwind from the vessel and the dream was so pleasant that he did not wish to wake up. But finally, he heard a terrible pounding, which started from a distance and grew louder and louder until he could bear it no longer. He jumped awake just as the freighter was crashing past the canoe.

The stern of the freighter slid within feet of the canoe, tossing the small craft high into the air, spilling Zachariah out into the sea. The canoe banged headlong into the wake and swirled after the freighter, caught in the drag of her exposed screws.

Zachariah sank into the dawn sea. Flailing and twisting, he fought and clawed his way to the surface, the underwater sea dim and gauzelike before his startled eyes. He did not know where he was, or what had happened.

He broke the surface, sucked deeply on the morning air, and looked wildly around him. The freighter was thrashing two hundred yards away, steam puffing out of her stern stack. Zachariah waved and screamed to attract attention.

Half a mile away, the canoe bobbed free of the freighter's wake and swirled on the open sea. The freighter pounded into the distance, trailing a long, shivering wake after her.

He began to swim for the canoe, his mind crowded with thoughts of terror. He remembered the hammerhead and hoped that the fish had moved away. Swimming cautiously towards the canoe, he looked around for the black fin. He felt as though his legs were dangling deep into the bottom of the sea, enticing the shark.

He was swimming into the rising sun. Yellow, red splotches fell across the flat surface of the ocean, and shimmered there like a glaze. In the distance, the freighter had shrunk to the size of a small motor boat. Steam rose in a curly wisp after her.

Paddling like a dog, taking care not to make a splash, Zachariah swam for the canoe, counting off to himself the remaining yards. He swam and fought to control the frenzied beating of his heart, and paused every now and again to scan the glazed surface for the shark.

The water was blue and bottomless beneath him. When he put his head under and opened his eyes to search for the stalking shark, he saw only the impenetrable smokiness of the deep.

"Soon reach, now," he told himself, drawing slow, careful breaths.

He was within two body lengths of the canoe when the shark came.

First, he saw the shadow slink underneath him, and his heart nearly stopped when he saw the enormous size of the fish. Then he saw the fish curl into a slow turn, and he made out the ugly, disjointed head as the beast rose up out of the depths to attack him.

Zachariah screamed. He put his head under just as the shark hurtled out of the deep and fastened its jaws around his left leg, and he screamed his terror and flailed at the shark's eye with his hand, trying to gouge it out with his thumb. Blood billowed off his leg in an enormous, coiling plume that blinded him. He thought he heard the snap of bone. Then as suddenly as it had come, the shark curled away and disappeared into a hole in the ocean. Zachariah lunged for the canoe, grabbed onto the gunwales, and hoisted himself aboard.

But he would not look at the leg. He clenched his teeth and stared at the sky and screamed his horror and agony, but he would not look at the leg. For when he had climbed into the canoe, he felt only one leg come out of the ocean, so he knew that the shark had taken the leg and even now was slinking into the deep chewing on his flesh.

"Rass!" he sobbed, rolling his eyes at the dawn sky. "He got de foot. He rip de foot clean off!"

And even then he would not look, for he could not stand to look at his own blood spurting into the canoe. So he lay against the thwart and screamed at the sky, but he would not look at the leg.

Out of the corner of his eye, Zachariah saw the fin surface and slice towards the painted canoe. A rage took hold of him, a rage that defied his fear and instilled him with such a madness that he nearly leapt into the ocean to fight the shark with his bare hands. But he restrained himself and fumbled for the harpoon. And when he couldn't find the harpoon, he searched under the thwart and found the stout lignum vitae club, and he stationed himself on the centre thwart and raised the club and watched as the stumpy, black fin slid up against the side of the canoe. Just as the fin drove past, Zachariah slashed at it with the club and felt the wood crunch against the black body of the shark, and saw the fish sound quickly into the depths. But still, he refused to look at his leg. He craned over the side of the canoe watching for the return of the hammerhead, and felt the weakness of death upon him, causing his limbs to shiver, his mouth to become dry, his heart to pound as though it would shatter in his chest.

He was sure that if he lay back against the thwart and closed his eyes, he would die. He would die as easily as a weary man slips into a sleep. He was certain of it. All he had to do was lie back against the thwart and allow death to take him.

But he would not do it. He put the club down against the bottom of the canoe, averting his eyes so he would not have to look at the severed leg, and he covered his face with his hands like a frightened child and forced himself to fight against the weakness of death.

He would look at the leg. He trembled as he thought about doing this, but he would force himself to do it. If the leg was severed, as he expected it would be, he would pack the stump with salt and wrap it up tight in the sailcloth. Closing his eyes, he fumbled in the bottom of the canoe and found the brown bag of salt. Pouring a handful of salt into his cupped hand, he opened his eyes and looked furtively at the leg.

The bone was not torn off. Instead, the leg was covered with blood so that not even an inch of black flesh showed. Through the coating of blood, he glimpsed the outline of the leg and saw that the limb was still attached. But the flesh was hideously mangled and shredded.

Watching for the lurking shark, Zachariah found the calabash bowl and drew water from the sea which he poured over his leg, washing away the blood. He cleaned the leg until he could see the teeth marks that punctured his flesh, running from above his knee almost down to his ankle bone. Some of the wounds were so deep that the bone showed through.

Sobbing and muttering over his injury, he packed salt into the bleeding punctures. When the blood continued to gush, he crawled to the bow of the canoe, found the fillets of bonito, cut them up and pressed the pieces into the wounds, pushing the salt deep into his flesh, causing the leg to burn as though it were on fire. Then he took his shirt and tore it into strips, which he used to bind the leg.

The hammerhead glided under the canoe, slinking past like a shadow. Zachariah held the club and watched to see what the shark would do next.

A terrible, weakening fear took hold of him and made him feel giddy. His heart was racing and his limbs were weak and trembling. He felt a strong desire to urinate. Though the morning sun was beating down on him, he felt so cold that he began to shiver.

But he fought against this weakness. He took a drink from the bottle of water, which he found wedged under the thwart, and he turned his mind to what he had to do. His body was swept with spasms of trembling, but he fought mightily against them.

"You get worse wound dan dis before," he told himself, looking around at the becalmed sea for the harpoon. And when his limbs still continue to tremble, he became stern with himself, scolding the weakness and fear that had come upon him.

"Man give you worse injury dan dis already," he told himself in a firm voice.

Holding on to the gunwales, he raised himself cautiously in the canoe, and searched the glassy water for the harpoon. Seeing an object floating some distance away, he crawled into the centre thwart, took out the oars and rowed towards it.

But even as he rowed, he was still trembling. His leg burned and his heart raced and he was lightheaded and faint. But still he rowed towards the object he had seen floating. And by craning in the thwart and looking, he eventually found the harpoon and the cork-handled knife and retrieved them from the sea.

Searching the canoe, he also found that the gaff was not lost, nor the cresset, although the wick was wet. So he placed the cresset on the thwart to dry out the wick, and he dipped a piece of his shirt into the sea, making sure that the shark was nowhere nearby, and cleaned the blood off the bottom of the canoe. When he was finished, he was exhausted. His mind was racing with thoughts about the shark. Moreover, he kept seeing the ugly hammerhead gliding out of the depths to greet him. And he kept thinking of the way the beast had seized his leg between his jaws. But he had to fight against these thoughts. He could not think about how he had nearly been devoured by the hammerhead. If he thought about such a thing, his heart would pound in his ears and he would pass out.

He told himself that he knew what was happening. His leg, which bore the marks of the beast in its flesh, wanted

103

him to feel pity over it, wanted him to console it over the injury. That was how an injured limb was — needing sorrow and pity. When Zachariah had once nearly cut off his finger, for days all his mind could think about was what might have happened to the finger. He would close his eyes and try to sleep, and think of the finger. He would be smoking a donkey-hemp cigar, when thoughts about the wounded finger would come to his mind. No matter what he was doing or where he was, he was compelled to think about the injured finger.

And now that was what his leg was doing — expecting remorse and worry and sympathy. But Zachariah would not give in to such thinking. His heart was already skipping and his head was light and giddy. He could not afford to harbour any thoughts of what might have happened.

He looked around the canoe at the flat, empty expanses of becalmed sea. Even the freighter had disappeared on the horizon. The sun hung low over the bow of the canoe. Hoisting the sail, he returned to the rear thwart, paddled the canoe so that the sun was at its stern, and waited for the wind to come up.

While he waited, he started to pray and ask for God's help, but stopped himself before he had said more than a word or two. If he had lost the leg, perhaps then he might have called to God, because his plight would have been terrible. But he was in no immediate danger at the moment, and there was no reason to call to God over every little foolishness.

His leg would not agree that the bite of a shark was a little foolishness, but nevertheless it was his mouth that said the prayers, not his leg.

"In fact, when you think 'bout it," he mumbled, "de leg is no rass good to a man in a canoe. Where him goin' jump and run? Where he goin' walk to? Better the shark bite off a man leg dan him hand."

104

Laying his head against the stern of the canoe, he waited for the wind to spring up, while he tried to fight off the horror of the shark and the compulsive thoughts about the wounds in his leg.

He thought, instead, about lovemaking with Carina. He was trembling and his heart was racing, but he forced himself to think about lovemaking. His leg began to throb and he noted the throbbing with satisfaction, because it meant that healing had already started. Yet he did not pause to reflect on this, but continued to think about lovemaking.

First, he thought about the first time they had made love. He had been staying under her roof for three days when she approached him. He remembered the night well. A patou was bawling in a tree. The moon was full. A warm night breeze wafted off the sea and blew into the room. He was by the window, watching the light of the moon sparkle on the ocean, when she approached him. She sat down beside him on the floor and said, "Make me see what you have in your pants, man." And even as she said this, she dipped her hands into his pants and took him between her fingers, causing him to swell up and burn with a passion. And this was the first time in his life that a woman had ever touched his private parts.

Country women were this way — very forward in their lovemaking. Indeed, his mother had repeatedly warned him against them, claiming that country women brought sickness and disease on a man, for they were loose like goats and quick to dip their fingers into a man's breeches.

Nevertheless, there was no refusing Carina that night. Even if his own mother had been standing before him with a switch ready to beat him, he could not have refused Carina. For when she took him between her fingers and stroked him, his heart exploded with loud thumps and his organ began to throb.

She laughed at this, and stroked him until he felt as though he would burst.

Then she took him into the bed and laid down with her clothes off, while he fumbled his pants to the floor and lay down beside her.

What else could he do? He had no idea what was to happen next, or what he was expected to do.

She clambered on top of him and opened her legs and took his organ again between her fingers.

"You big like a donkey," she grunted, putting him deep inside her.

And what a feeling it was, that first time, to feel his body sliding deep into hers, to feel her wet and warm private parts enclose his organ!

"Hmm, hmm," she groaned, licking his ear, "you bigger, dan bulldog." But from the low, contented moan in her voice, he knew that she was pleased with the size of him.

But he did not understand what he was expected to do next, so he lay there on his back, thinking that what would follow next would happen automatically. She began to pump him, slowly at first, moving up and down on top of him, sliding him deeper and deeper inside her, until he felt himself down to the shaft and could go no further.

"Lawd, man," she whispered, riding him gently, "how you so big and sweet?"

He almost laughed when she said this, it was so strange to hear a woman call him sweet as though he were something delicious she was eating. No woman had ever used such a word with him before. He laid his hand across her naked, pumping bottom, and pressed her firmly down on top of him, sinking into her body until he could go no deeper.

"Hoa, hoa," she whispered. "One donkey hood inside me poor pum-pum."

He thought she meant that he was hurting her so he started to withdraw, but she shoved herself down on top of him and rubbed it in even deeper, growling, "Leave it dere, man. Leave it dere."

But the first time he was not very satisfying to her,

because he could not control himself and in no time at all was through, bringing a scowl to her face.

"You done already?" she asked, staring down at him with peevishness in her eyes.

She would have reason to ask him this question many times afterwards. Because he did not know what he was expected to do, nor how long he was expected to wait. Moreover, he did not know whether it was possible for a man to wait under such circumstances.

Even this she had to teach him, explaining to him what was expected of a man, and how he was to try and control himself so she could have her pleasure.

The only way he could control himself was to close his eyes and think about fish while she rode on top of him and took her pleasure. Underneath her, his eyes tightly closed, he would think about the reef, about the painted canoe, about the character and disposition of fish. He would imagine what it was like to be an alewife, to swim on the bottom of the reef, eating weeds and pebbles. He would take on to himself the character of the parrot fish, whose sharp beak was useful for breaking off coral for food, and while Carina rode on top of him, grunting and whispering with pleasure, he would grind his teeth as though he were a feeding parrot fish.

"What you doin' wid you teeth?" she asked him crossly one night.

"Piece o' breadfruit stick in it," he said.

How could he explain to her that he had just now been at the bottom of the sea, in the character of a parrot fish, eating a piece of reef?

Sometimes, he pretended to be a puffer fish blown up with air and gliding above a reef. When he took on the nature of this fish, he filled his cheeks with air and imagined what such a fish felt like.

Using these tricks, he was able to control himself long enough to satisfy her regularly, although he would sometimes

107

be unable to bear the sheer pleasure of it, and would quickly shed the character of a fish, come back to the lovemaking bed, and be done in a hurry. Fortunately, he did not have such relapses often, because as everyone knows, country women love their hoods and are unwilling to endure a man who cannot give them satisfaction. This impatience of women has been the theme of many calypsos by Sparrow. In one such song, Sparrow told the story of lovemaking with a Trinidadian woman — "grinding" as the words of the song call it — and of coming too soon to please her. Whereupon, the woman jumped off the ground, grabbed a stick, and began to beat him. The song was humorous, but such an incident would not be humorous if it really happened.

For after all, how long could any man, whose woman was whispering in his ear and riding gently on top of him, be expected to think of himself as a parrot fish, or a puffer fish, or an alewife, all the time waiting for the woman to achieve satisfaction? What woman could understand how difficult such a thing was to accomplish?

"Damn women have no appreciation," he mumbled, coming back to himself in the canoe.

He had been so engrossed in his thoughts about love-making that he had forgotten about his throbbing leg. But now that he thought about it, he could see that the leg was still bleeding, and that fresh blood had dripped into the bottom of the canoe. He wiped up the blood and he poured some sea water through the bandages onto the wounds in his leg. Then he crawled forward and ate a fillet of the bonito and drank a mouthful of water.

A breeze began to blow. The sail waved and filled and the canoe surged through the water.

But now the tripping of his heart was under control and the weakness had left his limbs and he was conscious again of the heat of the sun. The chill was gone from his body. Only the throbbing pain in his leg was left. He was no worse off than before, he told himself. He could have a landfall today.

He could go to Port Antonio and be attended by a doctor. His leg would heal quickly. He had the body of a poor man. Everyone knew that the poor man who was not tough, was buried. So he was no worse off today than he was yesterday.

He was thinking this, trying to console himself over his latest misfortune, when the hammerhead surfaced behind the canoe, drove at its stern, and then sank quickly, vanishing into the duskiness of the deep sea. Zachariah heard the faint rattling of the waves. But when he turned and looked, he saw only the curling wake of the sailing canoe.

Chapter 10

But then the fever came, bringing bad dreams. He sailed aimlessly all day. The sun sucked the life out of him. Blood seeped from his leg, dripped onto the bottom of the painted canoe and dried. Yet he consoled himself that because of his black skin, the sun would have a hard time killing him. But if he were a white man, his skin would turn red and blister. The heat would dry up his vital juices. In a matter of days, he would be near death. Only the black man could endure the scorching sun on the open sea. His body would burn, his tongue would swell, his eyes would sting from the glare, but he would live to sail the painted canoe. So even such a thing as a black skin, which no sensible man would wish these days on his children, would help to save his life.

The day dragged slowly over the glittering ocean. He was cramped and stiff. His wounded leg had no feeling in it. The sun sank into the sea and the soft colours of another sunset drifted into the sky. With night came the fever.

He expected the fever, but he did not expect it so soon. By nightfall he was burning up. Sweat poured off his body. He poured sea water over his body to cool it and fell asleep without eating any of the bonito. By morning, he was in a delirium.

He saw duppies and dead people from his childhood. His mother came and sat facing him in the canoe, carrying the switch she had often used to beat him with. Seddie sat on the thwart beside him, played the guitar and sang. But the delirium was nothing worse than a lifelike daydream. And at first none of the visions were malign. He would fall into a fretful sleep and groggily awaken to find the dreams sitting on

110

the thwarts of the canoe, peering inquisitively at him. But if he made an attempt to fully wake up, they would disappear.

This was the fever, not madness, so he did not fight too hard to be rid of these dreams. It was good to see his mother again, though she was long buried under a star-apple tree in Westmoreland. It was good even to see the face of Seddie again, and to remember how he once used to sing.

But when the heat of the sun was most powerful on him, scorching him to an unbearable degree so that he could not even focus his eyes on the sea, then the dreams became malign. And he took this as the first sign of madness.

He saw a dog sitting on the forward thwart and baring its teeth. He blinked and looked into the eyes of the dog and saw flames flickering in its pupils. So he knew it was a duppy come to goad him.

Gathering the harpoon at his side, and the club, and the knife, Zachariah sipped from the water bottle and tried to stay alert so he could watch the movements of the duppy dog. But the dog did nothing more than bare its fangs when he looked into its eyes. And even in his madness, though he knew the dog was a duppy, even then Zachariah did not call out to God. The duppy could instil fear into the heart of a man, could make a man's heart beat as though it would burst. But the duppy could not do him physical harm. So he looked into the eyes of the duppy dog, and he felt his heart beat fast, but he did not call out to God.

"If I was on land, I'd give you a chicken bone to chew," he told the duppy dog as a joke, which enraged the creature so much that it snarled and barked soundlessly. Zachariah fell into another fitful sleep while the duppy dog was baring its teeth. When he awoke, the dog was gone.

But in its place sat a huge, groaning alewife. This was the most monstrous alewife Zachariah had ever seen. As he peered suspiciously at it, through the dimness of delirium, the fish gasped and choked for air. It did not lie on the

111

thwart, like a fish, but sat on the end of its tail and peered sullenly at him.

"If I had de strength, I'd cut off you head and put you out of you misery," he muttered to the alewife. The fish flew off the thwart and hurtled headlong at him. But when Zachariah waved the knife at the hurtling fish, the duppy vanished.

"More duppy on de sea dan fish," he muttered, trying to make himself comfortable between the thwarts. Within minutes, he had dozed off again.

He awoke in the afternoon just as the long wavering shadow of the canoe shivered on the sea. The sail drooped listlessly from the mast. The sea was glassy and calm. He sat up in the bottom of the canoe, groaning with stiffness, and looked around him. And then he saw the hammerhead. When their eyes met, the shark seemed to grin malignly at him, showing curved rows of sharp teeth.

Zachariah screamed and clutched for the harpoon. The shark was sitting in the bow thwart of the canoe, its ugly disjointed head waving in the shining heat. He saw that it was another duppy come to torment him.

He sagged against the thwart and gazed fearlessly at the duppy.

"You like de taste o' poor man flesh, eh?" he asked the shark. "Poor man tough like ole chicken. Black man taste like shoe leather."

Before Zachariah's eyes, the hammerhead began to chew on the leg bone of a black man. He saw the fish crack the bone below the knee, and suck at the marrow. And though his heart was leaping with fear, Zachariah still gazed fearlessly at the hammerhead and refused to cower before the fish. The shark was devouring the knee bone, when Zachariah fell into another delirious sleep.

He awoke to hear Seddie singing the rude song, "Night Food." Seddie's voice came from a far way off, as though he were locked in a room and singing through the closed door.

112

And when Zachariah rose out of his dream, he saw in the glittering, blood-red light of the sunset, that the hammerhead was hovering over the bow of the canoe, weeping over the words of this song.

Zachariah could not endure this mockery. He willed himself to get out of the bottom of the canoe, and he dragged himself up until he was sitting on the thwart. The hammerhead hung over the bow of the canoe, weeping like a child. From every corner of the sea, came the sound of Seddie's song. Zachariah gripped the shaft of the harpoon and hoisted the weapon over his shoulder. He took aim at the open maw of the hammerhead, intending to drive the harpoon into its heart. But even as he aimed and drew back his arm to hurl the harpoon, he saw the hammerhead bite down and chew, and saw that the head of dead Seddie, still singing, was fastened between its jaws. The fish bit down, cracking the skull, and chewed on the head. Zachariah screamed and threw the harpoon into the mouth of the shark. The madness suddenly left him and he became aware of the canoe, of the light of the stars, of the surrounding vast and empty seas.

He took a drink from the water bottle, to clear his head. Then he fumbled forward and lit the cresset, and held it above his head and searched the dark seas for the harpoon.

"You throw 'way de harpoon, you foolish rass, you," he told himself. Scanning the sea for the harpoon, he forgot about his injury, tried to stand, and nearly fell headlong overboard. His head was spinning. The canoe seemed to be whirling in circles on the dark sea.

"Behave youself," he warned, sitting cautiously again in the bottom of the canoe. "Steady you head. Look for de harpoon."

When he was no longer dizzy, he sat on the thwart, and looked around for the harpoon. A fish jumped beside the canoe, making a loud splash. Zachariah raised the cresset, and its light fell waveringly on the sea. Staring into the dim.

flickering light on the sea, he saw the black fin rustle out of the darkness and glide past the canoe. The shark passed so close that the canoe rose and fell as the fish swam by.

"Duppy," Zachariah whispered, sitting down in the canoe. His heart was tripping with terror.

"Duppy," he told himself. "It not real."

But he blew out the light and sat in the bottom of the canoe and held on to the thwarts in case the shark should bump the hull of the canoe. He sat in the bottom of the canoe and listened. Soon he was in another delirious sleep.

When he woke, it was raining. Bolts of lightning stabbed the inky blackness; peals of thunder rolled over the ocean. Crawling through the canoe, he gathered the calabash bowls and laid them out to catch the rainwater.

It was nearly dawn. The morning light, pale and cool as a mountain mist, glowed on the horizon. Raindrops pelted his body and dripped over his limbs and face. He was ravenously hungry. But the fever was broken.

By the time the rain stopped, he had more than half filled the bottle with fresh water.

He unwrapped the bandage and saw that the teeth marks of the shark had filled with pus. But the salt had stopped the bleeding and the flesh of the bonito pressed against his wounds had started the healing. He carefully stripped the fillets off his leg, exposing his wounds to the morning air. Then he washed the dried blood off the fillets and ate two of them. The others he cut into small pieces and used to bait two hooks with which he began to fish.

The sun rose out of the ocean and still he had not caught a fish. Finally, after fishing for nearly two hours, he landed a small kingfish, battered its head against the thwart, popped out its eyeballs on the barb of the hook, and threw the line into the sea. Twenty minutes later he had a strike. He was pulling the struggling fish to the surface when the line stiffened and went slack. He pulled in the line and the head of a bonito came spinning out of the ocean, two incredulous eyes staring with distended pupils at Zachariah. So he knew that the hammerhead had ripped off the body of the fish, then slithered into the shadows beneath the canoe. He peered into the depths of the dawn sea, trying to spot the black shark.

"And you lose de harpoon to a rass dream," he rebuked himself.

He cut up the kingfish and salted the pieces, which he laid out on a thwart to dry. Then he wetted the rag that he had torn from his shirt, and he cleaned out the bottom of the canoe, swabbing away all traces of his blood, scrubbing the smell of his wounds and the stale smell of fish off the cotton-wood.

Kneeling unsteadily on the centre thwart, he scanned the glassy surface of the sea for signs of the harpoon.

But the weapon was lost. By now, he told himself, it would have drifted miles away. He sat down and thought about his predicament, and about what he should do.

There was no wind. Left alone, the canoe would simply drift. He took in the listless sail and furled it under a thwart. Then he ran out the oars and began to row.

Once he had settled into a rhythm for rowing, he sang a song to help him forget about the vastness of the sea, about the lurking shark, about the injury to his leg, about his terrible loneliness. He sang a quiet song that mothers on the island sing to their frightened children. The words of the song told about a child who stayed awake at nights, fearing the duppy. Then the mother comes into the room, takes the child into her arms, and comforts him. She tells him that tomorrow the "Doctor breeze" will blow, shaking fruit off the trees for the child to eat. She tells him that tomorrow the sun will shine, and the cane stalks will grow tall and sweet. She comforts him that nothing can harm the heart of an innocent child, for God is in the moonlight, and the duppy is helpless. Holding the child against her bosom, she sings him so to sleep.

115

Zachariah sang this song in a loud, robust voice as though he were a boastful schoolboy in a church choir showing off his fine voice. The canoe soughed through the becalmed sea while he sang.

Circling warily at a great distance, the hammerhead came out of the deep. Zachariah saw the black fin break the surface, and he saw the way the fish rustled through the water as though to listen to his song. His heart began to pound with terror. But he would not stop singing. He sang even louder, sang until his throat was hoarse. And while he sang he watched the malign fish circle the painted canoe and slash across its bow.

His heart filled with hatred and rage against the evil fish. One more thing in the world trying to kill a poor man, he told himself. Another thing that did not care what a man had in his heart, or what his dreams were. All it cared about was its hunger for flesh. He looked at the fish out of the corner of his eyes, and he determined that he would find a way to kill it.

He rowed and sang and plotted in his heart how to kill the black shark. If he had the harpoon, he would try to lure the fish close to the canoe and drive the machete blade into its brain. But the harpoon was lost. Moreover, the hammerhead is a wily and cautious fish. He would get a chance for one blow. And it would have to be a lethal blow. Enraged, the shark could hurtle into the canoe, capsizing it. Sharks had done this before. So he would have perhaps one chance to kill the hammerhead, while the fish would have many chances to kill him.

This was the wicked and guileful way of the sea, to plot mischief against the life of a poor negar. The rich man went to sea in a tall ship, immune from most of the sea's trickery. But the poor negar went to sea in a hollowed out tree, with nothing between his body and the perils of the ocean but a thin layer of cottonwood.

He remembered the backra McPherson, whose boat had

116

two mighty motors that roared like lions. The backra's boat had beds and tables and toilets. It had a shower and a radio and a gramophone. It had things in it that a poor negar such as himself could not afford to put even in his home.

Zachariah had gone to sea with the backra a half-dozen times in this wonderful vessel. In almost the wink of an eye, the boat sped through the harbour, cleared the breakwater reef, and was rearing on the waves of the open sea. The backra ran out steel lines from outriggers, and fished with strong steel lures. And once, when they saw the fin of a shark nearby, the backra went down into the cabin and brought out a rifle, which he used to shoot at the fin.

Against such a boat, against such a man as the backra, the sea was docile and obedient. But let a poor negar put out to sea in a small canoe, and every kind of evil that the sea could dream of, it hurled at him. It sent sharks to devour him, jellyfish to sting him, eels and barracudas to bite off his feet, storms to founder him, rain to drench him, sun-hot to scorch him, lightning and thunder to terrify him, hail to beat him on the head, and duppies to beguile him. In the face of such evils, the poor man had nothing to aid him but the strength of his body, the hope in his heart, and the memories in his brain. He could sing a song, he could dream of things to come, he could comfort himself with wishes. But there was nothing else on his side.

Some, however, such as the fat Parson of Charity Bay, said that a poor man should turn to God for help. Because of this teaching, every time a poor negar bucked his toe against a rockstone, or jooked his finger on the thorn of a makka bush, or felt a pain in his belly, he bawled out to God to help him, Jesus to heal him, Holy Ghost to whisper to him, Virgin Mary to plead for him. And let a poor negar die and listen to what everyone said about him! He was in heaven. He was at peace. He was sleeping the great, timeless sleep. No one should weep over the grave of a poor negar.

When Obediah's body had washed up onto the beach,

117

the Parson declared in a funeral sermon that Obediah was in heaven. Zachariah sat in the pew and heard the Parson preach this. Obediah was in heaven, puffed the Parson from the pulpit, because Obediah did not drink; Obediah did not carouse; Obediah did not smoke the ganja weed; Obediah did not keep women on the side; Obediah had worked and slaved all his life to put food into the mouths of his children. All these things the Parson declared in an impertinent, foolish sermon. Zachariah did not walk out, however, because he did not wish to hurt the feelings of Karlene, Obediah's frail woman. So he sat through this long-winded sermon while the Parson talked foolishness he had picked up in America.

And the conclusion of the Parson? That Obediah had gone to heaven. That it was selfishness to weep over a man whose soul was in heaven. That whoever wished to see Obediah again should follow his way of life and get to heaven, too. Then, there would be an eternity of companionship with Obediah. No more pain or suffering. No more fishing on the lonely sea at nights. No more worry about drowning or starving, or clothing the children. (All this talk, mused Zachariah, from a big-bellied Parson who had never been to sea in his life, who had no children to feed, who kept a fat-bottom woman in Port Antonio, who drove an American car and lived in a concrete house, all this talk about starving and fishing and drowning from one such as this. The proverb says, "Rockstone on river bottom never feel de sun hot." This was the case of the Parson. What did he know about lonely nights at sea, or hungry children, or drowning? Which American university taught him about such things?)

If it weren't for the presence of Karlene, Zachariah would have stomped out of the church. For he was in a mood to wail and weep when he saw the torn body of Obediah washed up on the beach. Zachariah had gone and looked closely at the body. He saw that one leg was missing,

118

and that the loose flesh hung off the severed end of the limb which a shark had taken off with one careless bite. He saw how the sea had flayed the flesh off Obediah's back, peeling off the black skin and showing the naked raw meat to the sun. All these things Zachariah saw when he looked at the battered body of poor Obediah.

True, Obediah had gone to heaven. But he had gone to heaven because God was not so wicked as to heap any further miseries upon the soul of a poor negar. Parsons could preach what they wanted to preach; but Zachariah could never be made to believe that a poor man's soul would suffer after he was dead.

But the Parson was especially wrong in encouraging the congregation not to weep over dead Obediah. They should have wailed over what life had done to his body. They should have carried on about how the fish had opened his eyes, and how the sea had flayed the skin off his back, and how the shark had severed his leg. But at the graveside, except for the silent weeping of Karlene, everyone did as the Parson urged and stood respectfully around the grave, and did not lament the passing of a poor man.

Yet let a backra die, a man who had lived a long, full life, a man who had caroused and kept women and beaten his children and drunk rum every night of his existence, let such a one die and listen to the howls of sorrow the backras make over his grave. When the backra who used to be Superintendent of Police for Westmoreland died in his sleep, an old and feeble man, the other backras raised a terrible outcry over his grave.

Zachariah was then digging graves for the Catholic church once a week. He happened to be working on a grave when the funeral procession filed into the cemetery to bury the old Superintendent. There was so much wailing and weeping from the other backras that Zachariah could not concentrate on grave-digging. Yet here was a white man

119

who lived a wicked life, a man who boasted even in his old
age about his bastard children, and here stood all the rich
backras in Westmoreland, weeping and wailing over him. And
he had died an old man, with a big belly from eating more
food than he ever needed. His hands and limbs had gone
soft and puffy in his old age, from lack of labour. All his
life he had slept in a warm bed with a blanket. Rain never
fell on his head at sea. Hunger never gnawed at his belly.
Yet the wailing and weeping over such a man by the backras!

Once, Zachariah had gone out with the backra
McPherson in the backra's motor boat, and the Superintendent, by then an old man who should have been begging
forgiveness for his sins, was boasting about the women he
had had.

"Nobody in this world give a grind like a black woman,"
the Superintendent told Backra McPherson. "Ask me, I'll
tell you. For I grind white and I grind Coolie and I grind
yellow and I grind Chiny. And I grind every colour of brown
skin gal dat eye can see in the mud or the ground. No brown
skin colour live on this earth that I don't grind. And lemme
tell you something, man. No woman alive, grind sweet like
a black woman. She grind like sugar. She grind like a mule.
When you give the hood to a black woman, she jump up and
push her bottom in the air like she take a sugar stick. She
wriggle and she holler bloody murder and she give you a
ride like a donkey with makka stick jook up its ass. And
Lord himself save you soul if you stick you hood up a virgin
negar. Is like hurricane and storm and lightning lick you on
you head, all at once. She bawl like goat and she kick like
mule and she bite like a green lizard. And lemme tell you
something, Mackie. If you find pussy in heaven, it goin'
be black pussy."

The backra McPherson, who was liquored up, laughed
loudly over the Superintendent's humour. The two of them
spent most of the fishing trip drinking and telling slack
jokes while Zachariah tended to the boat and the fish.

This was the way of backra — to talk scornfully about negar even though a negar sat right under his nose listening. It was as though the backras believed that negar had no ears for such things as they said about him.

Later, during the day, when the boat was rolling through the groundswells, the Superintendent boasted about his pickney. He claimed that he had more pickney than any other man in Jamaica, that he had mulatto pickney, and half-Chiny, and half-Coolie — more pickney, he chuckled, than mango tree have mango.

"You and me know, Mackie," the Superintendent said, "dat only goat and rabbit breed more plentiful dan negar woman. And she especially love to breed for a white man, for she don't love pickney dat have skin black like her own. And lemme tell you something, Mackie, I breed pickney, you see, sah! Lawd God Almighty, I breed black woman wid pickney! Pickney like fish in de sea or flea on a goat! I just push in de hood one time so and bam! — another pickney drop on de ground nine months later. Pshaw! I have more pickney dan Sav-la-Mar have thief, dan Kingston have criminal! Some o' dem I don't even know. One woman come to me house de odder day and bring a brown boy with her, and I look into the boy eye and I say to meself — 'Kiss me Granny, is not me father dat looking in me eye?' Mackie, I couldn't lie to you. De boy was de spitting image o' me Daddy, down to the very buck teeth! 'Oyea, Woman,' I say to her ('cause I don't remember her), 'where you get dat boy from?' She laugh and she say, 'Backra, is you give him to me, sah.' And Mackie, when I look, and I look, and I look, and I look 'pon her till me eye water in me head, I don't remember grinding de woman. Then it come back to me. One night, in Clark's Town, in the rass cane field. One grind — it don't even last three minute — and it's like me own Daddy come back in brown skin!"

The backra McPherson thought this was a very funny incident and laughed so hard that he cried.

121

When they were returning to port, the Superintendent, who was then feeling the rum, pointed to Zachariah and said, "Now, take dis one here. I could be his Puppa except that him so damn ugly. Hey man, where you get dat dere jawbone from? Kiss me Granny backside, I never see a uglier man in all me rass life."

Zachariah gave him no answer and eventually the Superintendent stopped goading him. Only once, as they were pulling into the breakwater did the Superintendent make another remark about Zachariah's ugliness. He looked into Zachariah's face and muttered an oath to himself.

"Backfoot and crosses!" the Superintendent said.

What was the cause of the great differences between the lives of men? Why were some men so prosperous and lucky, while others were so poor and wretched? Why did some men live long, comfortable lives to die peacefully in their beds, while others suffered and toiled every day to die suddenly in their prime? These were puzzles that Zachariah's brain could not understand. There was no sensible explanation for the unfairness of life.

He began to think about his mother and what she had taught him about life. She had been among the unlucky ones — born poor and died poor. All her life she had toiled at menial labour, working for heartless, stingy backras. She had received no schooling, yet she had memorized hundreds of prayers and hymns and passages from the Bible taught her by her own mother. She used to recite these constantly to Zachariah when he was a little boy. Even now, if he sat down and tried, he could remember some of the things she used to recite. But he had no wish to remember her sayings, for they only made him downhearted.

Negar, she said, was put on the earth to suffer. Negar had done some terrible thing many generations ago, which all generations of negar since then had suffered from. This was the lesson she had drummed into him. Negar must suffer because he was negar.

122

She used to take him down to the river once a week, and give him a bath. The river tumbled green through a gorge in the mountains. In some spots it ran flat and smooth over thick, silt-filled banks. In other places it bubbled and sparkled, making a noise like playing children.

One morning she handed him a bar of hard brown soap and sat on the bank of the river under a bamboo bush while he waded in naked and washed himself. When he had soaped down, he braced himself between two huge stones and lay on the bottom of the river bed so that the cold sparkling water could pour over his body and rinse off the soap. But when he came out to dry off in the sun, she told him that he still looked dirty and that he should go in and wash himself again. It was chilly in the river. A breeze moved through the gorge, rattling the limbs of the bamboo. He waded back into the water and soaped down once more.

She was in a bad mood, and she had a wicked look in her eye. Moreover, she was muttering under her breath, a sign that she was especially cross.

He rinsed off and came out of the water.

"You still dirty, boy," she scolded. "Go back in the water and wash youself proper."

"But Mama," he protested, "I done wash twice already."

"Wash till de dirt come off!" she said crossly.

He waded back into the rippling water, soaped down, and splashed into a deep part of the river. Dripping and shivering, he came onto the bank.

"I done now, Mama," he said.

"You still dirty. Wash one more time."

"But Mama! De water cold."

She stood suddenly, grabbed his ear, and dragged him into the river. Standing over him, she soaped his face, his neck, his body, rubbing her calloused hands hard over his skin. When he was covered with soap, she pushed him into the water and rinsed off the soap.

"Is a lesson I bring you down here to teach you," she

123

said, holding onto his neck while he shivered from the cold breeze. "Look 'pon you skin! What you see dere? It look clean to you?"

"Yes, Mama. It clean!"

"It no look black like mud to you?"

"But me have black skin, Mama!"

"Now you learning de lesson. You have black skin. You could wash till judgement day, you skin still going black like mud. 'Cause soap can't wash negar skin clean. You born negar and you goin' dead negar. What you learn from dis?"

"I don't know, Mama."

"You don't know? Well, is teach I goin' teach you. You learn dat dis world don't love negar! And negar don't make for dis world! And you could rub rub and scrub scrub till de river run dry, you is still negar and de world don't love you! What me say?"

"You say de world don't love negar, Mama."

"Me can't hear you."

"Mama, you say de world don't love negar."

"So negar wid sense don't worry himself 'bout dis world. Him don't worry 'bout name and riches. Him don't bother 'bout big car and big house. 'Cause him know dat him don't make for dis world. Negar wid sense put him mind 'pon heaven! What negar wid sense do?"

"Him put him mind on heaven. Mama, de breeze cold."

"Cold don't trouble negar. And heat don't mind negar no business. For negar wid sense thinking all de time 'bout heaven. You hear me, boy? You hear what you Mama tell you?"

"Yes, Mama, I hear."

"A-hoa," she grunted, letting go of his neck. "Is a lesson you learn today. Wipe off and come, make we go home."

She prayed constantly, especially on dark nights. Their shack against the mountain side stood under a dark cotton tree. Croaking lizards grunted throughout the nights, and

124

whistling frogs howled in shrill, piercing tones. If she woke up, she would raise her voice in loud prayer. Sometimes she would even lie on her pallet and sing a hymn in the dark.

When he was a little boy, he would be awakened by her praying and singing, and she would force him to join in. But by the time he was a young man in his teens, he had become such a sound sleeper that no matter how loudly she prayed and sang, he would sleep undisturbed. She used to be provoked by his sleeping through the night. But she never dared creep across the shack to shake him, for she was deathly afraid of stepping on a scorpion.

Now she was gone. She took sick one Christmas. Her belly swelled up. She lay in bed praying and mumbling verses from the Bible. He stayed up with her, wiping her face with a moist cloth and listening to her prophecies.

"Zachie," she told him, "is dead I goin' dead tonight. I feel it in me bone, Zachie. But is all right. Dis is one negar not afraid to dead."

She began to cough. The weather was bad for one suffering from a coughing sickness. The rain was falling so hard that the damp air seeped through the walls of shack and into its small rooms. She complained that her belly was full of air and that she could feel water pressing against her brain. He brought his pallet beside hers and sat up half the night wiping her forehead. But he did not really think that she would die. For she was always groaning and fretting about death.

"Zachie," she whispered, "bad times ahead o' you. Wha' you goin' do without you Mumma? You don't learn a trade. You can't read and you can't write. You don't have a woman to look after you. Wha' you goin' do? You negar Mumma do her best for you, Zachie. She don't give you much, but she try her best."

He wiped her forehead and told her that she had done plenty.

"I teach you right from wrong," she sighed. "I teach

you dat you is a negar and de world don't love you. I teach you to love God and respect youself and not to trust young gal. I feed you what little food I had and I put clothes on you back so de sun don't burn you. Body can't do no more."

"You do plenty, Mama," he grunted.

He had wanted to say other, more cruel things. He had wanted to gripe about her foolish ways and her constant praying at nights. He had wanted to bring up many things she had done to him which he did not like. But he restrained himself because he saw that she had a fever. Moreover, he had learned from bitter experience that it did no good to complain about her to her face. She would only wail about how he had grown into an ungrateful son.

He did not really believe that she would die that night. But she did die. When he awoke the next morning, she was lying rigid and cold against the wall. Her mouth hung open, showing her toothless gums. The whites of her eyes shone like pebbles on the shallow bottom of a river. For the first time, he noticed how bony and thin she was.

He buried her in the graveyard beside the stone church. He himself spent two days digging the grave. The church was on the sloping side of a hill, and the ground was rocky and tough to dig. He borrowed a pickaxe and shovel from a man who worked for the Public Works Department, and he dug the grave under the blossoming limbs of a star-apple tree. At first, the preacher did not want Zachariah's mother buried on the church grounds. The cemetery, he claimed, was old and not used any more. People, he told Zachariah, should bury relatives in the yard where they had lived. That was the custom among country people. But Zachariah had already made up his mind to move away from Westmoreland, and he knew that once he was gone, someone else would occupy the shack. He could not bury his mother in a yard that would be occupied by strangers. So he begged the preacher to allow him to bury her on the church grounds, making up all sorts of stories to sway him.

The church members came to the funeral and the preacher said a few prayers and gave a talk. But during the sermon, it began to drizzle, and then to rain very hard, causing the preacher to say less than he had intended.

When the sermon was done, Zachariah clambered down into the muddy bottom of the grave, reached up to its lip, took his mother into his arms, and lowered her onto his feet. Then he pulled his feet slowly from out under her and climbed out of the slippery grave. Mud and rain were already pouring down on the body, soiling the death sheet. He had barely shovelled dirt over the body when the mourners, drenched and peevish, began to drift off, trying to appear as though they weren't hurrying to get some shelter. Soon he was alone in the downpour. He filled the grave, tamped down the dirt with the blade of the shovel, and stood there with his head bowed, weeping over the grave of his dead mother.

But it did not seem right that she should lie in an unmarked grave. The other graves in the cemetery were marked only by a circle of whitewashed stones. One or two of the earlier graves had wooden markers, but rain and heat had weathered them to rotted stumps. Zachariah approached the preacher and asked permission to put a stone marker over the grave of his mother. The preacher lectured him about worldly vanity before finally consenting.

First, he went into Sav-la-Mar and visited the stone cutters. One said that a stone marker would cost at least a hundred pounds; another said that for one hundred and fifty pounds he would provide a marker that not even a hurricane could blow away. The third, a member of the Rastafarian cult, a worshipper of Haile Selassie, said that he would supply a black stone marker with an engraving for seventy pounds. He took Zachariah into the yard of his shack and showed him a similar stone he was preparing for the mother of a powerful backra. The stone was so smoothly polished that it felt almost warm under Zachariah's finger-

127

tips. Moreover, the writing on the stone was neat and impressive. Zachariah went away, determined to purchase such a marker for his mother's grave.

He therefore went to work to earn the money. He worked as a gravedigger for the Catholic church, and as a day labourer for Backra MacPherson. In the evenings, after his day labour was done, he worked as a garden boy in the backra's garden, weeding and hoeing until dark. For all his long labour, he earned little more than three pounds a week. He buried his weekly wages at the roots of a guinep tree so he would not be tempted to spend them.

At the end of four months, he returned to the stone cutter and ordered the marker, paying down half the money. The stone cutter wanted to begin work on the engraving as soon as he had dug up the stone. He asked Zachariah for the name of his mother and the dates of her birth and death. Zachariah, however, did not know her birth date. Country people seldom kept such records. So the stone cutter said he would write on the stone any date Zachariah wished to have there. Zachariah could not make up his mind. He went away to think about it.

To begin with, he knew that his mother had been in her seventies when she died, but he did not know her exact age. Neither, for that matter, had she. Moreover, he could not do the subtraction required to find an approximate date because the numbers were too complex for his brain. He therefore went to the preacher who worked out the subtraction for him and who advised Zachariah to use December 25th as the birth date if he could not find the real date.

"That's when Christ was born," the preacher said, looking very solemn. "What better date to use?"

But Zachariah did not agree. It did not seem proper that his mother should have been born on Christmas Day.

"Why you don't use September 29th, then?" the preacher suggested, scanning a calendar. "Michaelmas day.

128

The feast of Michael the Archangel."

Zachariah nodded. September 29th seemed like an appropriate day. He went back to the stone cutter and told him to engrave September 29, 1879 as the birth date.

Five months later, the stone was engraved and ready to be laid. Zachariah had earned the second instalment of the payment, which he gave to the stone cutter.

One morning, the stone cutter, accompanied by Zachariah, set out towards the church in a dray cart drawn by a mangy donkey. The stone cutter grumbled and complained the whole way up the hill that he didn't know he would be required to travel so far or he would have charged more. And when he saw the broken down old cemetery in which the stone would be laid, he became vexed with Zachariah.

"You know how hard me work on dis stone, sah?" he asked peevishly, "And it not even goin' lay in proper graveyard. Why you use me so? You make me think de stone goin' sit in proper graveyard where man come by and look on me workmanship and say, 'Ah, yes boy, dis is a stone! Is so stone to cut! Which hand cut dis stone?' Not even cow or goat come in dis yard. Only mongoose and rat goin' see me hard labour. Why you use me so, Missah Zachariah?"

But eventually, the stone cutter set to work, laying the slab. First, he felt the soil to be sure the earth had settled firmly enough to bear the weight of the stone. Then he laid a bed of wet cement over the grave, and imbedded the slab in it. After that, he set up the polished black headstone, cementing it on to the slab.

The man worked cheerfully, whistling to himself, sometimes talking to Zachariah's mother as though she were peering over his shoulder supervising his labour.

"See dis, Mumma," he told her, after he had smoothed over the layer of cement, "is a nice, proper bed I make for you here. See how smooth and even I make de strokes. You resting place goin' look nicer dan a backra house when me done."

And when he had laid the slab, he said, "I hope de weight not too heavy on you, eh Mumma? You is a woman, and woman when dem live learn to take de weight of man. Is all right, though, Mumma. You not goin' feel dis weight."

Finally, with Zachariah's help, the stone cutter laid the headstone, attaching it to the slab with smooth, creamy strokes of cement.

"Watch dis final stroke, Mumma," he said, brushing the cement with a trowel. "Watch how me work de cement so it look smooth like stone 'pon a river bottom. See how man supposed to work stone, Mumma?"

When he was done with the labour, the stone cutter sat against the trunk of the star-apple tree, and smoked a joint of the ganja weed, because that was part of the Rastafarian belief. Zachariah would have none of the weed. His mother had warned him repeatedly against it. Moreover, he was not a Rastafarian and had no religious reason for using it.

"Dem bring de poor woman here, to Jamaica, from the modderland of Africa, and dem work her to the bone. And when she dead, dem hide her inna de earth like dead fowl. What a wickedness dem people have in dem heart 'gainst negar, eh, Missah Zachariah?"

"You sure rain can't wash 'way de words you put in de stone?" Zachariah asked, staring at the polished grave marker.

"What do you, man?" the stone cutter asked crossly. "When me chisel word inna stone, Haile Selassie himself can't rub it out. Rain could fall and breeze could blow and sun could hot 'til doomsday, me tell you nothin' can trouble de word in de stone."

When he had smoked the weed, the stone cutter stood beside his handiwork and ran his fingers lightly over the polished stone.

"Me not goin' dead in dis country," he said. "Me goin' back to Africa where me Puppa come from, and dere me goin' dead. Dem goin' put me bone in me homeland soil,

130

where all me people bury."

All over the graveyard, like a crowd of respectful mourners, the evening shadows quietly assembled. The star-apple tree threw off an impenetrable shadow that hung mosslike onto the walls of the church. High in the dim sky, flocks of mosquito eaters darted and lunged in a feeding frenzy. Peeny-wallies flickered against the backdrop of darkening bush.

On the way down the mountain, the stone cutter talked about his God, Haile Selassie, and about how the Rastafarians would one day be repatriated to Africa.

"We send a delegation to Haile Selassie," the stone cutter said, "Telling him of de wickedness Jamaica doin' to him chosen people. Him soon send one rass army to liberate us. We goin' load up every black man, woman, and child in a ship and we all goin' home. We even goin' carry de bones of de dead back wid us to bury in Africa soil. Dem goin' have one rass war 'pon dis here island. De ground goin' run red wid blood."

Zachariah listened politely and encouraged the man to talk because the road was dark and the silence broken only by the sound of the stone cutter's voice and the clop of the donkey's hooves.

The headstone, however, caused a row among the villagers who attended the hillside church. Some of them ridiculed Zachariah as a "forward negar", meaning a negar who didn't know his place, to put such a stone in the grave-yard. Others who had family buried under worn and shabby wooden markers were vexed because the headstone put them to shame. The preacher complained that if he had known the headstone would have caused such a fuss, he would never have allowed Zachariah to lay it. Nevertheless, there was no removing a gravestone once it had been laid. So although the stone marker caused much grumbling and backbiting, it was not removed. Shortly afterwards, Zachariah moved from the village and went into the town of Sav-la-Mar to

131

live.

He recalled all these memories as he sailed the canoe over the empty seas, the hot sun burning fiercely on his head. The surface of the ocean glittered so brightly in the sunlight that he could not even glance at it without being temporarily blinded. His injured leg had no life in it. Overhead were no birds of any kind, only a line of small white clouds with firm, rounded edges. The horizon tightened like a noose around the solitary painted canoe.

The hammerhead appeared off the port. The fin rose out of the deep and the ocean rippled as the fish circled the canoe.

"One more thing dat hate negar," Zachariah muttered, watching the black fish that slithered past the canoe.

He studied the fish that swam past. He saw it sink into the deep and vanish. He looked over the sides of the canoe, trying to spot the black shadow below the canoe. Straining, he saw the fish swim under the canoe, passing like a shadow through the vast green pupils of the ocean.

Then he leaned back against the gunwales, his skin crawling with fear over the persistence of the hammerhead, and he tried once more to think of a way to kill it.

He thought about how the fish had seized his limbs in its jaws and he thought about how it had nearly devoured him. Delirious fears about the shark passed through his mind. It was the sea that was determined to break his bones between the jaws of a fish, and grind up his flesh in its dark bowels. It was the sea that was out to kill him.

He leaned over the canoe and stared down into the fathomless depths of the ocean, and it was like staring into the eye of the enemy. Then he scornfully dipped his hands into the water and washed his face.

"Negar not easy to kill," he whispered to the sea, and returned to sailing the canoe.

Chapter 11

The English doctor drove his new green Volkswagen motor car from Kingston to Port Maria. Whenever he came to a pothole in the road, he hurled curses at the government and slowed down to avoid damaging the front end of his new car.

Just as the English doctor set out on his rural rounds, the Prime Minister began to speak to Parliament. Neither of the two radio stations on the island wished to hurt the Prime Minister's feelings, so both were broadcasting the speech, leaving the doctor with nothing else to listen to on the radio. But, promised the Prime Minister as he began, the speech would take only seven hours, at the most, providing the Opposition did not interrupt too often with scurrilous irrelevancies. The Leader of the Opposition leaped to his feet and protested "scurrilous irrelevancies," and the Prime Minister sighed and wondered out loud when this insane colonial sensitivity to harmless adjectivals would pass from Jamaica, allowing free discourse to take place again.

At the Port Maria clinic, the English doctor found one case of leprosy, a case of yellow fever, delivered one baby, signed four death certificates, and discovered one case of lockjaw. He stitched up a machete wound and sewed back on the scalp of a man whose common-law wife had removed it with a rock. He dressed a festering wound on the foot of a child and instructed the nurse to administer her a shot of penicillin. The nurse shrugged.

"We don't have any, sah," she explained.

"Where is this week's supply?" the doctor demanded.

The nurse took the doctor aside, out of earshot of the patients.

"De driver don't pick up no supplies dis week, sah," she whispered.

"Why not?" the doctor asked wrathfully.

"Him say him have grievance with the government, sah. Dem short him pay."

"Why didn't someone else use the van and fetch the supplies?"

"But him have de only key to de van, sah," the nurse explained patiently to the mad foreigner, "and him hide it."

The doctor nodded, took up his black bag, walked around to the rear of the clinic, and pounded on the door of the driver's living quarters.

The door creaked open; the smell of stale sweat and old beer wafted into the outdoors. Blinking furiously, the driver stared into the sunlight, recognized the doctor, reluctantly pulled his pants on, and stepped out into the yard.

The doctor walked away from the clinic building and stood under the boughs of a guinep tree where he could not be seen from the clinic windows. Scratching and blinking, the driver shambled over and stood by his side.

"Dem short me pay, sah," the driver moaned. "Man can't treat man so wicked."

"I need those drugs from Kingston," the doctor said brusquely. "Go and get them or give me the van key."

"Den what about me pay, sah?" the driver grumbled, his mouth hardening. "How man can work wid short pay? Three months now and me tell dem me pay short, dem don't do nothing yet. How man can live on short pay?"

The driver reached into his pocket and pulled out a scruffy scrap of yellowing paper on which his pay shortages were listed in neat columns. The doctor opened his black bag, took out an automatic pistol, cocked it to inject a bullet into the firing chamber, and pointed the muzzle a foot away from the driver's nose.

"Give me the key to the van, or I'll blow your head off," the doctor commanded in a steady voice.

"Me no dog, sah," the driver whined sullenly. "You can't shoot me down like dog."

As the doctor's finger tightened on the trigger, the driver recalled that the Englishman was mad and quickly surrendered the key, whining, "Only in Jamaica white man shoot down black man like dog in him own country."

Nodding brusquely, the doctor uncocked the pistol, put it back into his bag, and hurried to the clinic. He turned the keys over to the nurse who gave them to her sister who drove off in the van.

Meanwhile, the driver began to howl and curse outside the clinic, flailing a machete into the air and vowing that he would chop off the doctor's head. The nurse heard and hurried to the doctor's side.

"Dr. Richardson," she asked, looking at him with astonishment, "you pull a gun on Newton?"

"Of course not," the doctor reassured her, cutting away dead flesh from the foot of a cultivator who had been bitten last week by a wild dog.

Soon, the mad doctor was driving again along the tortuous road. The sea flashed green and blue on his left. Sometimes his car was straddled on either side by lush vegetation; sometimes fruit trees that hung over the road scratched at the roof of his new car, and the lilting green of a cane field ran skittishly past his right fender as barbed wire threaded out along the roadside and undulated crookedly from post to post. And sometimes in the middle of the road the potholes gaped full of mud and water from a morning rain, and the doctor would swerve violently and curse the government.

"Take a kotch! Take a kotch!" the Prime Minister was saying in Parliament, which meant that the speech had lumbered along to the stage where patois expressions would be liberally sprinkled into the text, demonstrating to the country that the Prime Minister's party was no dupe of colonialism and its wicked tongue — standard English.

135

The doctor turned off the radio before understanding what or whom should take a kotch, focusing, instead, on the malevolent asphalt roadway that was determined to ruin his new car. He swerved to avoid a monstrous pothole and cursed the government some more.

As he drove, the doctor planned a story to tell the constable who would come next week to investigate the alleged gun threat against the driver. He tried to remember if there were any uninvestigated complaints pending against him but couldn't, so he turned his attention to how he would answer the driver's complaint.

Last time when the constable came, the doctor flatly denied that he had threatened to shoot the electrician who refused to repair the fuse box in the clinic because the requisition for the work had not come from the Ministry of Health in triplicate. According to the electrician's sworn statement, the constable had explained carefully, the doctor allegedly required the use of the X-ray machine and had stood guard with a loaded gun over the electrician and forced him to fix the fuse box on overtime.

"Nonsense!" the doctor said smartly.

Looking discomfited, the constable wrote "nonsense" in his report pad.

"How come so much people claiming dat you want to shoot dem, sah?" he asked the doctor painfully.

"Hatred of the English," the doctor explained. "Xenophobia. Prejudice against foreigners."

"How you spell dat word, sah?" the constable asked. The doctor spelled the word for him; the constable wrote it down in his report; the doctor signed his name to the statement.

Afterwards, the constable apologized officially to the doctor for the bad manners of the Jamaican people. The two of them went off to a bar and drank rum. After the constable was thoroughly drunk, he took the doctor aside and confided in him that he wished someone would really shoot that

136

"thiefing electrician."

"Perhaps someone will," the doctor murmured hopefully. The constable broke into a sly and knowing grin, and the two of them drank a rum to their mutual hope.

The constable showed the doctor his revolver, and the doctor showed the constable his automatic that he kept in the black bag.

They drank more rum and took turns spinning the cylinder of the constable's revolver. The doctor confessed to the constable that he never kept his automatic loaded and, to prove it, he fired a shot into the ceiling of the bar.

"Oh, I'm terribly sorry," the doctor said, looking puzzled.

"It's nothing, sah," the constable waved airily.

They had another drink and discussed the hole the bullet had made in the ceiling. Then, to reassure the doctor, the constable took aim with his own gun and fired into the ceiling too, and they had another rum and argued genially over which gun had made the larger bullet hole.

A small crowd gathered and examined the holes, and two factions quickly formed. A noisy squabble followed; bad words were heatedly exchanged over the holes in the ceiling. Finally, as everyone got drunker and the tension mounted, the proprietor got a ladder and went up to the ceiling with a ruler, measured the diameter of both holes and announced a draw. Dissidents from either faction challenged the judgement but by then the principals, the doctor and the constable, were too drunk to care, so everybody had another rum and the talk drifted around to Manning Cup Football.

At Annotto Bay the doctor treated a case of yaws and sewed on a finger to the hand of a labourer whose wife had chopped it off because of a boast she overheard another woman making about it.

"Is a lie, sah! Is a dutty lie!" the man blubbered, turning his face away because the sight of his own blood made him nauseous.

"Shut up and be still!" the doctor growled, trying to clamp the finger into position to be sewed.

After the finger was sewed, and as the Pentecostal nurse scowled her disapproval, the doctor jocularly explained to the labourer that, because its muscles had been severed, the finger would from now on be permanently stiff and even more to the girlfriend's delight. Inconsolable, the man cradled his finger and hurled curses at his wife, moaning in the clinic, "She stiffen me finger for life! Sweet Jesus, she stiffen me finger for life!"

Finally, the doctor got mad and ordered the squealing labourer to get out of the clinic.

The doctor drove to Buff Bay. There he treated a case of typhoid, a case of dysentery, and gave inoculations against polio.

He worked without a nurse. The village nurse had left a message with the gardener asking the doctor to come and fetch her at her mother's house before seeing the patients. But the doctor had been in Jamaica too long to be so easily taken in. He knew that it was unlikely that the nurse would be still at her mother's house when he got there; that he would be sent chasing to the house of one relative or friend after another; and that, if he was lucky, he would end up having to drive only to the next parish to retrieve his nurse. So the doctor ignored the nurse's message and attended to the patients by himself. Before he drove off, he tacked a note to the nurse's desk in the clinic:

"Be here next time I'm due or resign."

"Is not one time monkey want wife!" the Prime Minister was shrieking over the radio as the doctor drove out of Buff Bay.

Switching off the radio, the doctor drove towards Charity Bay. He came to an overhanging tree, pulled off the road and into the tree's shade, and ate an avocado sandwich for lunch. While he ate, he read a portion of his wife's last letter:

The shortest distance between two points in Jamaica, you say, is a maze, and yet you want me to bring our children back into the dreadful country. I will never, never come back there to live. If you love me and your children, you'll return to England. Doctors are as desperately needed here as they are in Jamaica. Everything needn't be quixotic and faraway. There are many plain, ordinary needs in the world, and most of them are to be found right here in England.

Yesterday Michael came home complaining that the other boys had laughed at him for saying, "Me naw come," the first completely civilized reaction he has had to the Jamaican dialect. I expect that other such civilized reactions will soon cure him of the disgusting language and force him to speak normal English. Grandmother Grandfather and I eagerly look forward to that day.

Father advises you to stop threatening to shoot people because they won't do as you wish. He recalls a missionary to the Belgian Congo with a very similar tendency who was terribly resented and eventually eaten by the natives. I had tried to convince him that Jamaicans do not eat people, but he is firmly of the opinion that if they don't, they used to, and could have a relapse. I can't imagine, however, that you would be very tasty, even to a hungry cannibal. More than likely you'd be stringy and tough like an old field rabbit.

No, I won't give you a divorce; yes, I mean to contest any action you choose to file against our marriage. I love you; we have children. I have nothing more to say on that painful subject.

Inflation is terrible here, and the government is dreadfully revolutionary, but still, home is home, and there's nowhere else on earth like England.

No doubt you are doing much good in Jamaica by helping those poor and wretched people there, but

*please try to remember that we are your family and that
we all, Jenny, Michael and I, miss you very, very much,
and long for the day when you will return to where
you belong.*

The doctor sighed, crumpled the letter and threw it
out the window. He opened his black bag, took out a pad and
pen, and started to write a reply, which began, "Dear Janet."

After he had stared at the page for ten minutes, he
scribbled: 'The latest chapter from Fox's Book of Martyrs
arrived here yesterday. I refer, of course, to your letter."

He tore up the page and began again.

*I have found a girlfriend and am living with her. She
is quite black and very vulgar and holds unspeakable
opinions about white people. You might be interested
in some of her carnal opinions – I find them very
amusing myself.*

But he tore up that page, too, and tried to write the letter a
third time.

*Blast it, I will have my divorce whether or not you'll
give it to me. I'm sick and tired of your simpering
letters. Don't bring the children into this – it's entirely
between you and me.*

He had worked himself up into such a temper that he bit his
knuckles and pounded on the steering wheel of his new car.

Turning to a fresh page on the pad, he tried to write a
poem. He wrote the first four lines and stopped, searching
for an appropriate image. Scribbling furiously, he covered
the page of the notepad with lines of free verse. When he
was finished, he read the poem aloud.

It struck him as laboured and artificial. He went over
the lines with the pen, striking out words and images, splicing
in passages here and there. But the more he read and
reworked the poem, the more rage welled up inside him,

until finally he crumpled the page and threw it out of the window, startling a kling-kling bird that had been peering at him from a dense thicket.

The doctor reached stealthily into the back seat of the car, took out his automatic, rested the butt against the window, and took aim at the bird. The kling-kling gave an alarmed cry and flew high up into a tree, where it perched on a limb, tilted its head to peer down at the doctor, and made a frightened, squealing noise.

The doctor laughed. Impulsively, he pressed the muzzle of the automatic against his temple. He could feel a vein pounding under the bore of the gun. He touched the trigger playfully while moving the muzzle caressingly against his greying temple. With a sigh, he lowered the gun and put it back into the black bag. Then he got out of the car and retrieved the crumpled poem from a tussock of guinea grass. Sitting on the fender of the car, he read the poem again, his eyes moving slowly over the scrawls and scribbles on the page. When he was done, he crumpled it up and threw it back onto the grass. Then he urinated on it, returned to the car, and fell asleep in the front seat.

Half an hour later he woke up. The kling-kling bird was still staring down at him from high in the tree. He drank a cup of tea from a thermos bottle, threw out the crumbs from his sandwich, tucked his shirt into his pants, got into the car and drove on to Charity Bay.

"Dem say is so it go, so dem say!" the Prime Minister was raging, "but me know is not so it go! 'Cause me know de old saying, 'Everytime fowl lay egg him try to tell de whole world.' "

The doctor switched to the other radio station, but the Prime Minister was there, too, and this time he was cackling loudly as party members celebrated his wit by pounding boisterously on the parliamentary benches.

At the Charity Bay clinic, the doctor found the dead chicken — its throat gorily cut — nailed to the transom of

141

the front door. Over the door the wrathful symbols of an obeah curse were luridly scribbled in chicken blood.

Inside the small clinic the frightened and apologetic nurse waited.

"Him put it dere before me come, sah," she said diffidently.

"No patients today, Nurse?"

"Dem fearful of de obeah, sah."

The doctor nodded, put his black bag down on the make-shift bench that served as an operating table and a utility desk, went over to his car and took a pair of pliers out of its trunk.

Climbing onto a chair, he took down the dead chicken. A few fishermen loitered nearby, watching the doctor out of the corners of their eyes.

A group of higgler women walked past and eyed the doctor with suspicion. The doctor went into the clinic, jauntily swinging the dead chicken by its feet.

"Me tell you, doctor," the nurse said ominously, "you can't threaten to shoot obeah man. It don't work so in Jamaica."

"Cook the blasted thing," the doctor snapped, handing the chicken to the nurse.

"Me, sah?" the nurse asked with a show of extravagant horror.

"Yes, you. Cook the bloody thing."

"Me, sah?"

"Yes, you! You! You blithering fool! Cook it!"

"Where me must cook it, sah?"

"Use the portable stove. Go to your house. Get a pot. Get some salt. Just cook it."

"Me naw cook no obeah fowl, sah!" the nurse recoiled with horror, flailing the extended chicken away with her hands.

"Then fetch me a frying pan and some salt, and I'll cook it myself."

142

"Yes, sah," the nurse muttered wild-eyed, then hurried out of the clinic towards her house, spreading the word breathlessly that the mad Englishman intended to cook and eat an obeah chicken.

By the time she returned with the frying pan and the salt, the doctor had plucked and gutted the chicken and was cutting it into frying pieces with a scalpel.

Word spread through the streets that the insane doctor intended to eat an obeah chicken, and a crowd gathered silently outside the front door of the clinic.

"Nurse, where's the thyme?" the doctor asked peevishly, as he salted the chicken.

"Thyme, sah?"

"Yes, damn it! Thyme! Who in Jamaica can eat a chicken without thyme?"

"Who can eat obeah chicken?" the nurse retorted fatalistically, then set off to fetch the thyme.

"Thyme! Him want thyme to season the obeah chicken!"

The word spread into the streets; the crowd shifted restlessly, sensing incongruity and impending doom.

"Mad to rass!" a voice swore, and a chorus of other voices picked it up and chanted liturgically, "Mad to rass!"

The nurse hurried back with the thyme. The doctor seasoned the chicken and complained about having no onions, so the nurse scurried again to her house in search of an onion. The cry for onions was taken up in the street and derisive voices chorused, "Mad to rass!" and "Onion to rass," as the nurse hurried back, holding the onion disdainfully over her head so that all could see that she did not wish to participate in the cooking of an obeah chicken but was forced by the lunatic doctor to fetch these blasphemous seasonings. And, to be sure that there was no misunderstanding and that word would reach the obeah man of her non-complicity, she shouted to a familiar face in the crowd, "No me doing! No me doing!"

The face picked up the cry and it swept from mouth to mouth in a choir of firm disclamation: "No me doing! No me doing!"

The crowd was thickest, and the nurse was sick in the waiting room, and the mad doctor was frying the seasoned chicken on the portable stove when the constable arrived on his Honda.

On learning what the mad doctor was about to do, the constable tried to leave discreetly but was pressed against the door of the clinic by the milling crowd. The door burst open and the constable flew inside just as the nurse — not wishing to witness the eating of an obeah chicken — ran hysterically out. Suddenly, the constable found himself facing the mad doctor who had raised the drumstick to his mouth preparatory to taking a bite but who, out of politeness, now transferred the chicken to the other hand, shook hands with the constable, and offered him a wing. The constable firmly declined; the mad doctor shrugged, strolled to the open window and, standing in full view of the teeming crowd, bit into the leg of the obeah chicken, tearing off a mouthful of flesh and swallowing it with demonstratory relish.

A cry of terror rose from the crowd. The people recoiled from the window, grimacing and wiping their mouths with revulsion.

"Sah!" the constable began lamely, impassively watching the madman chewing on the chicken flesh. "We have another complaint from somebody about you, sah."

"Oh yes?" the doctor registered mild surprise and licked his fingers. "A complaint? Lodged by whom?"

"A man call Lubeck, sah. He live in de bush."

"Never heard of him."

"People say he is a obeah man."

"Doesn't mean a thing to me, sorry," the doctor said cheerfully, smacking his lips.

"He say you send a message threatening to shoot him with your gun," and here the constable referred to his com-

144

plaint pad and read with a stoical expression on his face,
" 'as soon as possible.' "

"Obvious rubbish! What rational man would word a
death threat like that ?"

The constable blinked, looking confused and dubious.

"Him say," he continued doggedly, "you and he have
differences about some married woman that come to you
for doctoring and then come to him for obeahing, and that
you say he nearly killed the woman with a herb and threatened to shoot him because of dat."

"Have some chicken, Constable," the doctor invited,
extending a chicken leg to the constable.

The constable stood his ground cautiously.

"Sorry, sah. Can't eat on duty."

"Too bad. Too bad." The doctor declared, biting into
the chicken leg and chewing noisily on the meat.

"So what you have to say about dis one, sah?" the
constable asked officiously as the doctor ate.

"Xenophobia!" the doctor replied, wiping his mouth.

Beckoning the constable to follow, the doctor went
to the front door, opened it, and stood in full view of the
watching crowd. He chewed on the chicken leg and pointed
casually to the bloody symbols written above the doorway.

"Funny country, isn't it, constable?" the doctor said
loudly enough for all to hear. "I found this delicious chicken
nailed to the doorway, with this rubbish written above it."

The constable assumed an official countenance.

"You making a complaint, sah?"

"Who, me?" the doctor guffawed, turning to face the
crowd and simultaneously tearing off a chunk of chicken
flesh with his teeth. "Complain about this chicken? Never!"
Then, with a dramatic and resounding flourish, he cried
again, "Never!"

The crowd peered expectantly at the doctor; the doctor
chewed on the chicken leg; the constable cleared his throat
and was about to speak when the doctor suddenly clutched

145

his Adam's apple with both hands and spat out the chewed chicken meat. A cry of horror arose from the crowd. Triumphant and vindictive shouts came from the obeah man's followers. The doctor staggered, bellowed an oath, and shrieked for his nurse.

Flustered and hysterical, the nurse ran through the crowd, screaming, "Yes, Dr. Richardson! Yes, Dr. Richardson!" – fully expecting to find the doctor dead or in the fatal grip of an obeah paroxysm.

"No pepper!" the doctor roared wrathfully. "How can I eat chicken without pepper?"

The crowd fell into a stupefied silence. The doctor glared dramatically, enjoying himself immensely. Overwhelmed by anti-climax, stricken with confusion and fear, buffeted by the afternoon sun, the nurse keeled over in a faint.

The constable and the doctor carried the unconscious nurse into the clinic and laid her on the wooden bench. The doctor fumbled in his bag for smelling salts, and the constable glimpsed the butt of the black automatic nestled among medicines and instruments.

On the yellow report pad, the constable wrote out a brief statement beginning with the sentence, "According to Dr. Archibald Richardson, xenophobia caused the complaint of one Lubeck."

The nurse revived, shaking her head with the recollection of recent horror. The constable presented the statement to the doctor, who signed it.

"A local problem, sah," the constable murmured knowingly, "a local problem."

"Quite so," the doctor agreed.

They shook hands. The constable mounted his Honda and puttered off. The doctor went out the back door of the clinic and fed the rest of the chicken to the village dogs. The crowd flowed around to the back of the clinic and sat watching the dogs devour the chicken. Returning inside the

146

clinic, the doctor firmly closed the door. The dogs devoured the chicken, bones and all, and trotted off to take a nap, followed by the crowd that was now arguing noisily about the English doctor.

"Nurse!" the doctor roared inside the clinic. "To business!"

Twenty minutes later, a man walked in complaining of food poisoning. A case of malnutrition came in, followed by a suspected case of tertiary stage syphilis. Then the assorted cases of violence gathered in the waiting room as a pathetic and raggle-taggle assembly of knife, machete, brick, and cudgel wounds bled copiously, were stitched, mended, and gauzed over, the victims tacked up and sent back out into the world of love and jealousy. Scheming to induce a case of hysterical blindness in his enemy Lubeck, the doctor whispered to each of these patients a message that Lubeck would be stone-blind by the end of the month.

The blood flowed then dried up. The wounds thinned out. The sickness disappeared as the sun began to hover above the mountain range.

Exhausted, the doctor sat in his office, drinking tea and reading the clinic mail. He threw out the drug ads, the administrative notices in triplicate from the Ministry of Health, the officially entered copy of an earlier statement to the constable; he read a short note from an English girlfriend inviting him to a polo game in St. Ann's Bay; and a letter from a mother in Hector's River advising him that she intended to name the daughter he delivered two months before after him. The doctor sighed and drank tea and thought about a daughter named Archibald, shrugged, and resumed reading the mail.

On the makeshift desk a small lizard stirred, surveying the vast wooden plateau with a critical eye and flickering its tail in insouciant, serpentine sweeps. Angered by its presence, the doctor took out the scalpel he had used to carve the chicken, seized the lizard and sliced off its head.

147

He swept the twitching, convulsing body into a trash can, absent-mindedly leaving the head on the table.

Under the pile of mail he found the brown envelope from the pathologist, opened it, spilling out the results of blood tests, pregnancy tests, urine tests, stool tests. He pored over them: confirmed case of diabetes; pregnancy negetive; syphilis negetive; gonorrhea positive; syphilis positive; and almost slammed his fist down on the table in an outburst of anger.

"N-e-g-a-t-i-v-e, damn it!" The doctor spelled out the word for the anonymous typist. "N-e-g-a-t-i-v-e!"

Finally, he came to a long, cumbrous sheet, signed by the Kingston pathologist, and swept his eyes over it, picking out an odd word here and there — "carcinoma confirmed," and "prognosis termenel" — and shouted furiously, "T-e-r-m-i-n-a-l, you bitch! Terminal!"

Weary, exhausted, frustrated, the doctor looked at the patient's name, Zachariah Pelsie, and tried to remember his face, to pick it out from among the hundreds of anonymous black faces crowding in on his fatigued memory. Putting his hand to his brow, the doctor focussed intently until among the swirl of hazy black faces a face of incredible ugliness rose up, crystallized, and stayed firmly in his mind. He remembered the brutally ugly fisherman with the monstrously deformed jawbone who had come in a month ago with a big tumour on his neck, recalled how he had biopsied the tumour and sent the fisherman to Port Antonio to have a chest X-ray taken. Now, a month later, the report drifted back to the clinic with "prognosis termenel" typewritten on it.

"Cancer," the doctor said aloud. He began to laugh as he looked around him at the plain concrete block walls, the curtainless, crude louvred windows, the makeshift wooden bench that served as an operating table and a desk, and he was laughing louder when he suddenly noticed the head of the lizard, the big green artery bleeding through the neck stump, the faintly white bone caressed by delicate grey tissue sticking out of the neck, the eyelids thick and drooping over the protruding eyeballs; and the doctor flew into a rage because the mouth still gaped and gasped with shock in autonomic defiance, and he slammed his fist down on the head, shattering the skull and spilling a rich, greenish-red paste over the brown envelope.

"Die, damn you, die!" the doctor shouted.

Then he laughed again, this time at a maniacal pitch, shrill and humourless. In the next room, the nurse heard, shook her head, and made up her mind to resign.

She knocked decisively on the door and entered. The doctor looked up at her with weariness in his eyes. In spite of his madness, she felt pity for him. But she quickly suppressed the sympathy because she could no longer work for an English lunatic.

"Do you know Zachariah Pelsie?" the doctor asked abruptly before she could resign.

"Yes, sah. Him blow away de odder day."

"What do you mean?"

"Him is a fisherman, sah. Him canoe blow way with him in it."

"You mean, he's lost at sea?"

"Yes, sah. Him lost at sea."

The doctor cradled his head between his hands and gave off a low, cynical chuckle.

"Sah," the nurse began truculently, "me is a Christian woman, you know say."

"Resign if you want to. I don't give a damn," the doctor said, standing up and stretching. He had heard it all before and bloody well wasn't going to listen to it now.

The nurse was so taken aback that she quickly changed her mind about resigning and hurriedly lied, "Me just telling you, sah, dat me is a Christian woman."

"So what?" the doctor challenged, looking at her irritably as he packed his medical bag.

149

"Me going pray for you, sah," the nurse said, hanging her head with shame over her cowardice.

"Pray for Pelsie, Nurse. He's lost. I'm not."

"All of us is lambs of God dat is lost," the nurse said smartly, getting in a good doctrinal knock. Then she hurried out of the room before the doctor could reply.

The doctor packed his blood samples, urine samples, stool samples in a cardboard box and loaded it into the trunk of his new Volkswagen.

The sun had fallen behind the mountains and an orange glow spilled into the twilight skies. In the small clustering shacks, the kerosene lanterns flickered on. Overhead, foraging bats swirled, dipped, and spun erratic somersaults.

The doctor drove along the road bordering on the green sea.

"Barking saves biting," the Prime Minister was snarling over both radio stations.

When the doctor came to the beach on which the small black canoes were drawn up, he pulled the car over, got out, sat on its fender and thought about cancer.

It did not belong here, he thought angrily. It belonged in the fashionable districts of sickness. It belong on Harley Street in London. But not here, not in impoverished Charity Bay.

Here leprosy belonged, and yaws, and dysentery, and syphilis, and lockjaw, and all the old ravagers of human life that destroyed the body crudely, all the diseases that suppurated and scabbed — they belonged here. But not cancer. Cancer was too subtle, too mysterious, too Oriental. Cancer brought studies, placebos, viral theory, natural selection, psychoanalysis, metaphysics, with it. And none of these belonged here.

A cooling breeze sprang up and the green ocean shivered. Against the bay the sea clung, obedient to the contour of the land, lapping the shoreline with unaccustomed docility. Over the brown reef small waves shattered, as fat groundswells

150

broke and planed off in sleek, silvery sheets towards the shore.

It was all so lovely and tranquil, and it all seemed so idyllic and wistful that the doctor could not bear to think of so reptilian a sickness as cancer that curdled flesh, gnawed bone, and rotted tissue.

He looked out to sea. The sea stretched out beyond the clutch of Charity Bay and unwound to the horizon, crinkling domestically.

Sitting on the fender of his new green motor car, the doctor thought about the fisherman with the cancer inside him who was now lost at sea, and the doctor whispered to the green sea, "Eat him!"

And the more he thought about it, the more intensely the doctor whispered, "Eat him, sea! Eat him!" Until he was sitting on the car fender and hissing malevolently the same words in Jamaican patois, "Nyam him, sea! Nyam him, sea!"

The doctor suddenly became aware that he was being watched by a lonely fisherman who knelt on the sand repairing the hull of his canoe. Their eyes locked in the twilight.

"Good evening, sah," the fisherman said, because the doctor was mad and should be cared for gently.

"Good evening," the doctor replied, jumping into his car and roaring off.

He drove west through Annotto Bay and took the narrow Junction Road through Castleton. The road ran parallel to the Wag Water River. Through a massive gorge carved deep into the mountain, the river coiled and rippled its enormous, serpentine body over rocks and silt and sandbars.

The Wag Water River was the doctor's favorite haunt. Whenever he came this way during the daylight hours, he would park and hike down the mountain to the river's banks. There he would sit on the sand and peer into the sluggish, green river undulating silently past. In the daylight, the river

151

was an impenetrable green, thick and soft as a luxuriant moss. It whispered to the doctor as it slithered down the mountain.

But tonight, the gorge was hidden by the blackness of the night, so he drove recklessly through the Junction Road taking corners on two wheels, screeching past country buses and swaying, overloaded trucks that whined down the Junction Road in low gear.

Two hours later, he pulled into a duplex in the suburb of Mona Heights, parked his car under the portico, and walked over the tiled veranda into the small living room of the concrete slab house.

The woman was waiting for him, reclining on the sofa with a sulky look in her eyes. Her black body swelled through a thin, transparent slip.

"Me cook you dinner, but it get cold by now," she said in a scolding voice, sauntering into the kitchen.

The doctor threw his bag on the sofa, made himself a drink and sat down in a stuffed chair with his feet on a hassock.

She came into the living room, raking him sullenly with her stare.

"You don't want you dinner?"

"No."

"All you care about is damn ole country negar. Country negar dat don't even care 'bout himself. All day long you gone to de country — for what? For country negar!" She spat the words out contemptuously.

"Shut up and leave me alone," he said, closing his eyes, listening to the cacophonous cries made by the hordes of nighttime insects. Moths fluttered through the small concrete house, spiralling towards the bright ceiling lights.

"Is none o' me business," she declared, sitting on the couch. "If you want kill yourself over country negar, is none o' me business."

The doctor sipped his drink and stared at her. She

152

reclined against the back of the couch, her slip spilling open at her knees, her female parts bared tauntingly at him.

He drained his drink and walked over to where she lay in a provocative pose, looking peevishly up at him.

"You say to leave you alone," she said sullenly, turning her head away.

"Come here, you black bitch," he said, yanking her off the couch.

"Why you don't leave me in peace, eh?" she whined, her mouth set in a pout.

Nevertheless, she allowed him to lead her into the dark bedroom.

"Move you hand!" The doctor's rough command drifted into the empty, garishly lit living room, now populated only by endlessly swirling moths that fluttered around the ceiling lights.

Seconds later, the woman uttered a piercing squeal.

Chapter 12

The hammerhead followed the canoe throughout the afternoon and into the early evening. Sometimes, when Zachariah became lost in a daydream and forgot about the stalking fish, the black fin would rear out of the water and stalk near the canoe. Zachariah would clutch the gaff and club, and warily watch the movements of the shark.

"I don't love no ugly fish," he mumbled, when the shark persisted in circling the canoe. "Go back to de black bottom o' de sea and leave ole negar alone."

But the shark came back five times during the afternoon. Once, the fin drove straight for the canoe, causing Zachariah's heart to pound and his hands to shake. But the fish dived under the canoe and slid deep beneath its hull.

His body, especially his injured leg, was so afraid of the shark that when the hammerhead swam past, Zachariah felt his skin crawl and his heart beat with terror. He ran his hand soothingly over his bitten leg, as though he were comforting a child, and he told the leg that it had nothing to fear from the shark.

He remembered how his fingers would shake when, as a small boy, he went down to the river to catch the big janga shrimp. The janga lived under the river banks, hiding in the mud and between the roots of water plants. To catch the janga, Zachariah would have to stick his hand deep under the lip of the river bank, where the janga lurked in the rich silt. He would probe under the bank and feel for the janga. When his hand came too close to a janga, the shrimp would fasten its pinchers around his fingers. He would reach quickly under the bank with his other hand and seize the janga behind the head, and pull it out of the water, with the pinchers still biting on his fingers. Sometimes, even after he had killed the shrimp, its claw would still cling to his finger, and he would have to pry it off with a stick.

In those days, when he went down to the river to catch janga, his fingers would quail with fear of being bitten. Zachariah would sink knee deep into the sliding green sheet of water, and tell his fingers not to be afraid. Now that the shark was circling the canoe, his leg was feeling a similar terror.

With the shark circling the canoe, Zachariah pulled in the sail, crawled into the centre thwart and made a weapon to kill the fish with.

First, he cut off the large hook attached to the gaff pole. Against such a big fish as the hammerhead, a gaff was useless. Next, he filed down the blade of the knife until it glittered as bright as light flashing off the sea. Then he cut a length from the old anchor rope and lashed the handle of the knife to the gaff pole. The gaff had been about three feet long, but now it served as a makeshift spear. If the shark swam up to the ide of the canoe, he would try to blind its eye with the knife point.

He sat in the centre thwart holding the spear and looked around the canoe for signs of the approaching shark. But though he would sometimes see the fin rise out of the ocean, the shark never came right under the gunwales of the painted canoe.

"Him look up and see ole negar sit in de boat waiting 'pon him," Zachariah said aloud, "and him say to himself: 'Ole negar hard to kill. Ole negar tough and bony like goat-fish.' "

He did not like this habit he was getting into of talking to himself. He warned himself to be quiet and to keep his eyes on the sea.

Towards the evening, he saw a freighter on the horizon.

155

The ship was so far away that it looked like a child's cut-out pasted against the shining skyline. Attached to a tiny string of black smoke, the freighter moved slowly across the horizon.

At first, Zachariah became excited and hurried to set the sail. But once he calmed down he realized that he would have no chance of reaching the ship. Nevertheless, he hoisted the sail and returned to the rear thwart and sailed the canoe towards where the ship sat motionless on the horizon. But within another hour or two, the freighter had vanished leaving not even a trace of smoke on the skyline.

That night, Zachariah frequently lit the kerosene cresset. On the vastness of the dark ocean, the lantern flickered. A thin membrane of light swelled over the canoe, wavering over the tiny boat. Gathering at the edge of the light, the sinister and enormous darkness shied away. Then the kerosene oil ran out; the blackness reclaimed the canoe. Zachariah drifted to the illumination of the stars and a new, swollen moon.

Because he knew that the sea, the darkness, the heat of the sun and the lurking shark could make him go mad, Zachariah began to arrange the parts of his life he would think about next so that he would never be caught helpless and weak without something to remember. Every night before falling asleep, he collected and arranged the things he intended to think about, presiding over their order and sequence with great care.

The stars came out; the new moon showed its face; the Milky Way appeared like the incandescent web of a spider, weaving a luminous path through the blackness of the heavens. Zachariah ate the kingfish, drank some water, and tried to think about his second son, whose name was Wilfred. As he thought about the boy, Zachariah rested his hand on the shaft of the makeshift spear, alert to the rustling of the dark sea that warned of the approaching shark.

His second son, Wilfred, was like a fish, and Zachariah did not understand him. He stared like a fish. He was silent

156

and withdrawn like a fish. He did not talk unless he was first spoken to; even then he was just as likely to answer in one word. Moreover, he stared at everything with the intensity of a fish: he hovered, he stared, and when he was questioned, he answered in one word.

What had caused the boy to acquire this strange temperament? Zachariah thought he knew the answer. He remembered that when he himself was a boy, his mother had warned him not to eat too much goat. His mother told him that a child's heart and mind formed and grew along with the rest of his body, and took on the character of the animal whose flesh he constantly ate.

"If you eat too much goat," she explained, "you going get goat heart and brain — you going start act and think like goat. Goat flesh going grow in your heart and in you brain. Watch youself!" she added, pointing a cautionary finger at Zachariah.

This is what had happened to Wilfred: as a child, he had eaten too much fish.

By the time Wilfred was born, Zachariah had built the canoe and was earning his livelihood from the sea. The new child was therefore fed mainly fish. Zachariah tried to recall all the different kinds of fish Wilfred had eaten — wrenchman, yellow tail jack, black sam, sprat, butter fish, parrot fish, goatfish, grunt, shad, snapper, mackerel, kingfish, bullhead, and fries. Once in a while, they bought a goat's head and made a soup out of it which they spooned to the child. But most of the time, even the soup they fed Wilfred was made of the cracked heads of fish. And so fish flesh had mixed and grown with Wilfred's heart and brain, causing him to think and act like a fish. Poverty was the cause of it all.

Zachariah shook his head with confusion. He did not understand Wilfred and did not like to think about him. A man likes a little lunacy in his sons — not in his wife. But Carina was more of a lunatic than both his sons put together.

The canoe drifted; the constellations rolled across the

sky. Occasionally, shooting stars darted through the darkness, trailing a glitter of embers.

Zachariah remembered the conversations he had tried to hold with his second son. He remembered the time when he came upon Wilfred sitting by himself on the beach and staring at the sea.

"What you doing?" Zachariah asked.

"Nothing," was the boy's reply.

Zachariah tended to his nets, arranged the calabash bowls and the water bottles in the bottom of the canoe, while Wilfred continued to stare at the sea. Walking casually behind him, Zachariah stooped down to the level of the boy's shoulder and stared past his ear lobe, trying to see what was so engrossing to the boy. Wilfred turned and looked astonished.

"What you doing?" Wilfred asked.

"Nothing," Zachariah replied, looking foolish.

That was the end of the conversation.

Poverty was the cause of his son's peculiar temperament. If Zachariah had been a rich man, he could have fed his sons pork, beef, mutton, goat, chicken, and fish. Perhaps then, Wilfred would have turned out the way he was supposed to, without the influence of the fish dominating his disposition. Poverty was therefore the cause of his son having the temperament of a fish. The white man had everything. The brown man, the Chinaman and the Syrian man — they had everything nourishing to feed their sons. But the black man had little or nothing for his children. The Prime Minister was correct. Socialism was the solution, otherwise the poor breed fish while the rich breed sons.

"Dat must be the correct solution," Zachariah said aloud.

But he did not really understand what socialism meant and he had never understood a speech by the Prime Minister. His thoughts were therefore threatened by an abrupt ending. Fingering the makeshift spear, he reminded himself that he

158

was thinking now about Wilfred — Wilfred who had a peculiar, silent way about him.

Between Wilfred and his mother there was much love. Carina gave to Wilfred the love she had had for the daughter; to George, who was born too soon after the death of the daughter, she gave no love at all, only anger and stubbornness. Even now Carina sometimes stopped what she was doing so she could go to Wilfred, stroke his head and run her fingers down his cheeks. And sometimes at dusk, as the sun fell behind the mountains and the birds flew in from the sea, Carina sat on the doorstep of the shack with Wilfred beside her, and stroked him with love and gentleness.

Zachariah frowned as he recalled the love between Carina and Wilfred. A mother should never favour one child over another. He had said that to Carina many times. When he reached shore he would tell her again. He would tell her first, before he said anything else, just as he clambered out of the canoe and she came running towards him calling his name with joy — and she would be mad with joy at seeing him, too! He would tell her and she would understand how serious a thing it was with him that he should tell her first, before anything else.

"Zach!" he could hear her screaming and see her black body flashing over the sands as she ran towards him, yelling, "Zach! Zachie! You come back! Zach!"

And because she was such a lunatic and would be so overjoyed to see him, she would leap into the air and fly wildly towards him, and he would have to catch her or she would fall on the sand. But he was not sure that he could stand her weight on his injured leg, and even as he imagined their reunion, he felt his leg twinge with pain at the thought of bearing the weight of a flying woman. She would squeeze him and pinch him and knead his flesh as if a man's flesh were bread dough. After that, after she had gurgled, and laughed, and cried, and called his name over and over, and covered his body with welts, then he would say to her,

159

grimly, "A modder must love all sons equal, dat's what me learn at sea." And she would be so startled to hear these as his first words that she would see how seriously he believed that a mother should never favour one son over another.

He came back to himself in the bottom of the canoe, and he was crying. He wiped his eyes but could not stem the crying, so he cried some more then wiped his eyes and said aloud, "You soon reach home." But he quickly reminded himself that madness comes to those who talk to themselves at sea, so he repeated it to himself in his mind, "You soon reach home. You soon reach home. You soon reach home." And saying this quietly to himself, he began to cry again.

After he was through crying, his heart began to hunger because he was alone in the painted canoe and surrounded by the layered immensities of the sea, the darkness, and the stars.

The darkness was so thick that it rolled against his head and purled through his pupils and tried to snuff out the light in his mind. The sea was so somnolent and dreamy, the canoe rolled with such undulative ease, that he wanted to sleep but couldn't because he was afraid of the lurking hammerhead, and of the darkness.

He pulled himself up in the bottom of the canoe, wrapped his arms about his body to shield out the chill, and continued to think about Wilfred. But before he began to think, he chided himself for cruelty, for planning to greet Carina so heartlessly. He decided, instead, that first he would tell her of his love, of how badly he had missed her; then he would tell her that a mother must love all her sons equally. The emphasis would be preserved, but without the cruelty.

He turned his thoughts again to Wilfred. Everyone liked Wilfred, even the Principal. Once, Zachariah was painting his canoe and the Principal, who was driving through Charity Bay, stopped his automobile and parked on the edge of the roadway. He came down to the beach and stood among the canoes, talking to Zachariah about Wilfred.

160

It was a pity, Zachariah thought then, that he did not have his machete with him that day because he still owed the Principal a chop for beating George. However, Zachariah painted the canoe and said little, leaving the Principal to do most of the talking.

First, the Principal asked some foolish questions about fishing, then talked briefly about Socialism, about the Prime Minister, and about the evils of British Colonialism. Zachariah answered politely and painted the canoe, wondering why the Principal didn't drive straight to the rum bar where he was to be found every evening after school.

Then, the Principal began to talk about Wilfred, about how smart the boy was, and how he should attend the University. Zachariah chuckled and said, "University?" in the same cynical tone that a gunman would use to say, "Heaven?"

"When you smart, de University easy, man," the Principal said with a wheeze: "Wilfred could go dere easy."

Trying to seem humble, the Principal added, "University was hard for me. But for a boy like dat, University a simple matter!"

So, the Principal had made his boastful point: he had been to the University. But any man who would force a boy to become the cheese after he had already been the cheese three times the previous week, deserved to be chopped, whether or not he had been to the University. Zachariah therefore scowled and gave the Principal no encouragement to continue talking.

But the Principal would not stop talking about Wilfred. Wilfred, he told Zachariah, could become anything he wanted to become — a doctor, a lawyer, a politician. Even, and here the Principal chuckled, a Principal. Zachariah grunted.

And, rumbled the Principal, Wilfred was so smart that he would get scholarships, win awards, gain distinctions. Zachariah painted the canoe and grunted when it seemed

161

as though politeness required some response.

Finally, the Principal asked, fully intending to answer his own question, "You don't wonder how I know Wilfred so smart?"

Zachariah nodded because he had indeed been wondering.

Then the Principal told him about the test the school used, the test that came all the way from America, and how all the children were given this test to determine how smart each child was. And of all the children at the school, according to the scientific findings of this test, the Principal explained, choosing his words carefully and mixing up some patois expressions with standard English like the Prime Minister did in his speeches, Wilfred was by far the smartest.

"What happen to George? Him don't have brain, too?" Zachariah asked, not looking up from painting the canoe.

"George no bad," the Principal sniffed. "Him smart. But him no nearly as smart as Wilfred. No nearly."

Zachariah thought about this test that had come from America.

"Dis test," he asked, "dat come from America. Dis test dat say Wilfred so smart, it use talking?"

"No, man," the Principal chuckled, "scientific tests don't bother with talking."

Zachariah nodded, his suspicions confirmed. He blew his nose, washed his mouth out with sea water, and went back to painting the canoe. Because the Principal seemed to expect him to say something else, Zachariah said, "De boy eat too much fish when him was little."

The Principal did not understand, but his belly began to gurgle because it was his rum time. He stood near the canoe and tried to explain again how smart Wilfred really was. Zachariah listened without interest.

But, as he was about to give up and go away, the Principal mentioned that Wilfred was smart because one of his parents was secretly very smart, since scientific tests proved

162

that smartness was passed on from parents to children. It began to make sense to Zachariah.

He invited the Principal to sit on the nearby canoe. The Principal sat and looked at his watch because his rum time was passing. Zachariah, knowing that the poor fellow needed some rum, decided to go with him to the rum bar. The two of them drove off in the Principal's automobile.

They had a rum and discussed whether bats could really be used in soup, whether the Prime Minister could talk nonstop for twelve hours, and whether the national character of Jamaicans had been ruined forever by the British. To all of these points, Zachariah presented a series of arguments leaving no doubt from which parent Wilfred had inherited his smartness.

The Principal got drunk. He tried to explain the misunderstanding with the first son, George. Because of the British influence, the Principal explained drunkenly, everyone in Jamaica wants to be the farmer, but no one wants to be the cheese. But Jamaica needs both the farmer and the cheese, just as Jamaica needs both the Principal and the fisherman. Zachariah scowled at the implication that to be a Principal was to be the farmer, while to be a fisherman was to be the cheese, and suddenly wished that he had brought his machete with him. Foolishly, he had not, so he had to be content with scowling and with drinking the Principal's rum.

That night Zachariah did not fish. He got drunk. By the time he got home, Carina had gone to bed and locked him out of his house. He had to pound on her window and beg her for over an hour before she finally consented to let him in.

The next morning, when he was sober again, he did not tell Carina about his conversation with the Principal. She loved Wilfred more than George and it was foolish to give her another reason that would increase her favouritism.

163

As for himself, he did not care how smart the scientific test said Wilfred was. He preferred the company of George; no father can stand the company of a son who simply stares without speaking. "Too much fish," Zachariah found himself saying out loud at sea. He quickly closed his mouth and, instead, thought it, "Too much fish."

What, however, if Wilfred was indeed so smart that he could go to the University? What would he then become? How would he regard his mother and father who lived in a shack on the edge of Charity Bay? What would he say about his father, who went to sea every night in a painted canoe and caught fish for a living?

Zachariah tried to imagine how such an opportunity would alter the character of his second son. He remembered a fisherman from Westmoreland whose son had gone away to the University, his school fees paid for by a government scholarship. The boy became very learned and respected. He married a fair-skinned woman who spoke with an accent. His children were not born black like their father was, but brown like the skin of the naseberry. One of them, a girl, had straight hair and sparkling green eyes. It was said in the village that her hair was so straight and good that a comb could be run freely through it without snagging the teeth.

Zachariah tried to recall the fisherman whose son had achieved this education. The fisherman was called Qubert. All his life he went to sea in a canoe. He could not read or write. He did not know when or where he was born. All he knew was that he had lived in Westmoreland most of his adult life, and that he had always fished for his living.

But his educated son brought no blessings to Qubert. When the son came to visit, he held his nose high in the air as though something smelled in the village that offended him. He refused to call his father "Papa" as he was raised to, but chose instead to say "Father", the way an Englishman does — through his teeth. Moreover, the boy acted as though he were not familiar with the ordinary sights, people, and customs he

164

had grown up around. His favourite questions were, "What's that?" or "Why do you do that?" or "What use does that have to you?" even though he already knew the answers. But by asking such questions he affected airs and showed off his new high position in life. "What do you call 'bullah?' " the boy once asked his father in a crowded shop, causing the father to feel foolish and embarrassed. For the boy had grown up eating 'bullah' — the unleaven brown cake — and very well knew what it was. Another time the boy asked, "What's a Bustamente Backbone?" when not long ago, he would have done anything for the hard, black sweetie known by that name. When Qubert tried to reply to such questions, he looked and felt foolish.

The boy also refused to drink white rum with his father and would eat no food cooked in his father's kitchen. Local food, he said one day, gave him a running stomach. He strutted around the village addressing elders who had seen him running naked as a child in the streets as though they were his familiars, calling them, no matter how old or grey or frail in years, by their plain last names — just the way the backra addresses his domestics. Yet when his father became too old to fish and could hardly find a shilling to buy bread to eat, this same son stayed away or came forward grudgingly with a few pence, bawling about how poor he was and how expensive his household was to maintain.

This was the kind of thing that happened when a poor negar's child rose high in the world. Yet what could a poor negar do but try the best for his children, no matter how they might scorn him once they were successful?

"Bullah?" Zachariah asked aloud, imagining how he would address his Wilfred, if the boy became successful and stuck-up. "You don't know what name bullah? You don't remember all de bullah you used to nyam as pickney? What name bullah? Damn rude boy, asking you Puppa forward question!"

Alone at sea, drifting in the painted canoe, Zachariah

165

rehearsed the answers he would make to an affected, prosperous son.

"You call me Papa," he growled in the dark. "Me name not 'Father'. White pickney call de Papa by dat name. Black man son call him Papa."

And after he had pondered the possibilities for a few more minutes, Zachariah stirred in the bottom of the canoe and said, "Don't use no big word on you Papa, damn rude boy!"

But then he came back to himself, and realized that he had been talking out loud. He was suddenly sleepy, so he lay face down in the bottom of the canoe. He closed his eyes, his arms folded under him because of the chill, his fingertips on the shaft of the spear. Stars floated overhead. The dew fell. Dreams began to come.

He dreamed of the sea, the sky, and the stars. He dreamed of fishing over the brown reef. In his dream, he saw the kerosene lights from the anchored canoes. He saw the stars and the moon; he heard the sea whisper against the hull of the canoe.

And as he dreamed and the canoe drifted, the sea was everywhere. Dark and limitless, it stretched out between unseen horizons, undulating and lunging in coiling, slumberous movements. In the dreams of Zachariah, too, was the sea, swelling and breathing against his brain.

It was everywhere, this sea. Eyeball shattered against it like old bone; voice could not sing it; dreams could not contain it.

Everywhere was this vast, intangible sea.

Chapter 13

After he had been at sea for four days, Zachariah's body became lean and hard. It stretched out and its sinews showed. Tendons and ribs appeared as the sun stropped the blackness of his skin into a bright sheen, drawing the skin hard and tight over bone. Muscles girded against bone, and the bone stiffened and held taut against the muscle.

The wounds in his leg scabbed over and the scabs thickened until they resembled the shiny backs of cockroaches. The feeling in his toes came back; he could almost move his ankle if he tried very hard. Every morning he peeled off the makeshift bandage and examined the teeth marks of the shark in his flesh. And every morning he was satisfied that his leg was healing properly.

Because he had eaten nothing but salted fish and drunk only spoonfuls of water, his stomach began to growl and tremble, then shrank into a lump and settled against his ribs like a tenderness.

In the mornings, while the sun was still under the horizon, Zachariah tried to exercise in the cool greyness of the dawn. He lay flat in the bottom of the canoe and stretched himself, cracking laziness and sleep out of bone. He tried to do sit-ups, hoisting his good leg high into the air, which caused the canoe to rock and dip into the sea. To clean the stale air out of his lungs, he faced the sun and took deep, cleansing breaths. After that, he slapped himself all over his torso to move the blood into every part. Then he massaged his buttocks to prevent sores from the constant sitting against the hard thwart.

167

The early morning heat lugged sluggishly over the canoe, rising off the sea like a warm, curling mist. But by noon, the heat turned into a dry wind that battered the canoe with an invisible and soundless omnipresence. No amount of cool water could slake his body's thirst from such a heat.

During the days, Zachariah cowered from the heat in the bottom of the canoe and dreamed of shade trees. He dreamed of the thick guinep trees whose shadow was luxuriant and rich with coolness. He dreamed of the mango trees with dense, clustering branches and thick, fat leaves that were impenetrable to the sun. He dreamed of the star-apple trees, such as the one under which he had buried his mother, and the spathodia trees, and of the majestic cotton trees from which his own canoe had been hewed. He dreamed of the trees, felt love for the trees, while the heat fell off the sun and the canoe sailed listlessly.

All through the long days, the canoe was battered by the pitiless, soundless heat of the sun. The sea shrivelled and gnashed a tormented white; the sky blew out at its seams, Zachariah dreamed of the shade trees. Sometimes, because there was no place to hide from the heat, he talked to the sun.

"What a way you rough me up," he complained to the sun as he squirmed against the bottom of the canoe, his skin drenched with sweat.

"You trying to kill ole negar," he accused the sun, swallowing a mouthful of water from the dwindling supply in the bottle.

"De sea try to eat me," he told the sun another time, "'now you trying to cook me. Ole negar not worth all dis trouble. You only goin' get skin and bone."

By noon, he could hardly talk. Thick and swollen with thirst, his tongue flickered inside his mouth with rough, reptilian languor. His throat shrivelled and thickened. His lips cracked and thinned.

168

"All dis for de body of a poor negar man," he mused out loud, moving his head from side to side, feeling the moistness of the heat pounding in his temples.

He dreamed of water. He dreamed of the spring flowing in the bush near where the obeah man lived. He dreamed of rain and of the mysterious saliency of dew. He dreamed of water flowing from the standpipe in Charity Bay, and of water held into transparent, conical obedience by the shape of a glass. He dreamed these one after another while his eyes were open, while the sun burned yellow and intense, and light crackled and splintered off the roiling surface of the sea.

Finally, he could bear it no longer and decided to go into the ocean. He took his pants off and was about to slip over the side of the canoe when he remembered the hammerhead. He put back on his pants and huddled closer to the caking skin of the canoe, curled up helplessly against the heat.

This was the conspiracy of the elements against him. He saw it clearly now. First, the hammerhead slunk out of sight, making him think that it had wandered off, while it secretly swam deep under the canoe and waited. Then the sun burned and tormented him with heat, while the sea rolled cool and inviting against the gunwales of the canoe. This was the springe they had set to trap him. He chuckled out loud, now that he understood this trickery.

To escape the heat, he began to think about Lascelles, the boy who had gone mad with the mistaken belief that he was a cow. He remembered the boy well. His skin was brown and shiny; his eyes were blue; his nose was thick and heavy, as were his lips. Deep inside Lascelles a white man slumbered, conferring brown to his skin and blue to his eyes.

It was the sun that had driven Lascelles mad. Zachariah nodded warily, and remembered.

It was the custom of all fishermen to fish only at night. At night the fish fed. Groggy with sleep and with hunger, the fish idled through the dark seas between coral reefs and over stones, searching for food. Drunk on the darkness, the fish followed the scent of bait into the fish traps. But only at night. To fish stupefied by darkness, a kerosene light on the surface burns like the sun. They gather and swirl into its illumination, seeking food. But only at night.

During the day, fish are alert and sensible. In the daylight, fish practice caution. Wrenchmen hide under rocks, peeping out with disciplined suspicion. Butter fish shy into the waving seaweed, take on the colour of the foliage, and disappear. Snappers search out a dark, unreachable bottom and stay there, louring at the jellyfish. Parrot fish nibble on stones and sand pebbles, fussily chewing and spitting out gravel. During the day, fish are cautious and shy, like newly appointed constables.

It was a plan which God had worked out and which all sensible fishermen followed. For the proverb says, 'God Almighty only mek you see star, no matter which way de wind blow.' In the daylight when the fish were shy and clever, the fishermen rested. At night when the fish were stupid and hungry, the fishermen took their catch.

"Fisherman don't belong out in the sunlight, boy. Him just don't belong!" Zachariah said aloud, his lips stinging and cracking as he mouthed the words.

The sail of the canoe flapped and shivered. Zachariah leaned against the paddle and turned the canoe until the sail again filled with wind and the water rippled against the side of her hull.

But Lascelles, on his way to madness, began to fish during the day. When the other boats were running with the wind towards the beach, Lascelles' canoe was beating over the reef and putting out to sea. And at night when the sun was setting and the other fishermen sauntered down to the beach to ready their canoes for the fishing, Lascelles would be coming in from a long day at sea, carrying his nets and lines. He would catch a few lobsters and grunts. Because to everything there is an exception, and while most fish are stupid at night and sensible by day, the grunt is the opposite: wary by night and foolish by day.

"Is so God is, sah," Zachariah mumbled through puffy lips. "Him out to confuse man, mad up man brain."

Reaching over the side, Zachariah scooped some cool water from the ocean and splashed it over his face. His lips burned and stung from the salt. The sea tapped with teasing catpaw strokes against the hull of the painted canoe. Zachariah tried to think some more about Lascelles.

A fisherman cannot live on the money earned from selling grunts. The grunt is bony and tough; higglers disdain to buy it; housewives do not like it. Lascelles began to go hungry. Simultaneously, the sun started to madden him.

One evening, as the fishermen prepared to put out to sea, they heard a low, sinister moo drift in from the bay.

Everyone turned and stared into the darkening bay with astonishment.

"How cow get out dere?" one fisherman asked.

"You hear a cow?"

"Me hear one, but him at sea."

"Me no hear nothing, brother."

"Rass, boy. See here now! Suppose me meet up a cow tonight at sea and him buck a hole in de side of me canoe?"

The fishermen stared out to sea but saw no cow. They saw only Lascelles' canoe punting towards the shore. As the canoe grounded on the beach, one of the fishermen called out to Lascelles, "You see any cow at sea?"

Lascelles threw back his head, cupped his hands over his mouth and gave off a low, mournful moo. The fishermen waited while the moo rolled over the beach and drifted out to sea. They stared at Lascelles with caution.

"What dat moo good for now?" one old man asked suspiciously.

"Me just love a moo!" Lascelles answered gaily. He unloaded his boat, carrying his lines and nets and laying them on the beach along with a few dead grunt and one sad old

171

lobster. Every now and again, for no reason, he suddenly cupped his hands to his mouth and bellowed out a raucous moo.

"Rass, sah!" one fisherman commented gloomily. "See dis now!"

The others went about the business of loading their boats, grimly paying no attention to the mooing Lascelles. The madness had started. The sun was the cause — fishing in the hot sun. More and more Lascelles began to think that he was a cow. In the morning, as his canoe pulled across the harbour reef, moo after moo rolled over the bay. In the evening, his canoe came ashore swarmed by a strident chorus of moos.

If he remained so, Lascelles would have been harmlessly mad, mooing under the sun without giving grievance to anyone. But he changed his ways. He began to sleep during the day and to fish and moo at night. Then, the trouble began.

The fish stopped biting. Already stupefied by the darkness, they were further confused by the mooing. They huddled at the bottom of the ocean and hid under the ledge of the reef. They took no bait and shied away from the fish traps.

It got worse and worse. On a moonless night, the canoes drifted over the brown reef. Lascelles bellowed out, "Mooo-ooooooooooooooooo!"

An unseen fisherman hissed, "Hush, you rass!"

Lascelles bellowed even louder, "Moooooooooooooooo-ooooooooooo!"

An angry chorus of "Shh! You blood!" and "Hush, you rass!" and "Blood!" took to the air, buzzing like angry wasps.

The fishermen met at Zachariah's house to discuss the mooing. Some were angry and wanted to hold Lascelles down on the ground and force grass down his throat since he thought he was a cow. Others wanted to bring a real cow down to the beach and force Lascelles to load the cow in his

172

canoe and carry it out to sea with him. Perhaps, they chortled, the canoe would capsize and Lascelles would drown and that would be the end of that. One fisherman objected that maybe the cow would drown, too, which would be a waste of a good cow. But another replied that cows were excellent swimmers and could swim great distances with ease. A third pointed out that perhaps the canoe would not capsize and Lascelles would find the company of the cow enjoyable at sea, in which case the fishermen would now have to contend with two moos instead of one.

Everyone got drunk. Some of the younger, impious fishermen mooed tunes to hymns like "Rock of Ages," "My Happy Captain," while the older, more sober fishermen gathered in a corner and stared contemptuously at the singers. At the end of the meeting it was decided that Zachariah would speak to Lascelles about the mooing.

A week afterwards, Zachariah got his chance. He met Lascelles on the beach before the other fishermen were there. He did not know what to say because it was plain to him that Lascelles was mad, so he came right out and said bluntly, "Man don't moo."

"Who say so?" Lascelles asked with a sly smile.

"Me say so," Zachariah asserted stubbornly. "Man not supposed to moo. Cow moo. Man must talk. Or sing. But him not supposed to moo."

"How you know you not a cow?"

Mad. The boy was mad. Zachariah looked at him with pity.

"Because me know me is not a cow. Me is a man. Cow is a cow."

"So cow know him is a cow?" Lascelles began to hiss through his teeth.

Zachariah thought about the question because the boy used to be decent before his madness. Finally, he answered, "Of course, cow know him is a cow." Then he added with some afterthought, "That's why cow don't try and talk.

Because him know dat him is a cow and him must moo."

"Suppose him don't have horn and tail. Den what? Him think him is a man?"

Zachariah looked at Lascelles who stood before him staring with wild-eyed earnestness. The mad, Zachariah thought, must be approached with caution and gentleness. He was sorry he did not have his machete with him in case Lascelles became violent.

"You never see cow without horn or tail?" Lascelles asked, looking perplexed and foolish.

"Of course!" Zachariah replied gruffly.

"So how you know you is not a cow?" Lascelles pressed, moving closer to Zachariah.

Zachariah tried to think of a reasonable reply, one that would get through the madness, but he forgot the argument and what had led up to this question and, becoming angry at himself for forgetting, he snapped at Lascelles, "Me is no rass cow!"

In reply, Lascelles threw his head back and moaned out a sorrowful moo. Zachariah watched the moo rise out of Lascelles' throat, drift through the boy's rounded lips and roll across the sky. Dropping his head and puckering his lips, Lascelles stared with wild, mad innocence at Zachariah who could think of nothing else to say so he shrugged and walked away, leaving Lascelles on the beach mooing at the evening star. That same night, the mooing on the ocean was as thick as ever.

"And so, we loose a madman on a mad boy," Zachariah groaned out loud, remembering what the fishermen did next.

They visited the mad English doctor at the clinic and asked him to help with Lascelles. The doctor sat on the bench in the clinic and laughed. No one understood why the doctor was laughing, yet he laughed, and everyone sat and stared at him politely and did not ask him why he was laughing.

A few days later, the English doctor came down to the

174

beach. He and Lascelles sat on the sand and mooed for each other. The fishermen stood dourly away from them, watching the ludicrous spectacle of a white madman mooing on the sand with a brown madboy. First, the doctor bellowed like a cow; then Lascelles shrieked like a lonely heifer. Following that, both of them lowed together like a bull.

Almost everyone from the village stood on the beach and watched them. Drawn by the noise, the village dogs collected in a restless pack and howled. Then the two lunatics stood up and behaved like cows trying playfully to buck one another. They got into the doctor's car and drove off.

"What him do wid de poor boy?" Zachariah asked the sky through thickening lips.

That was the last time anyone in the village saw Lascelles His stepfather came with a truck and carried away Lascelles' canoe; and because the boy slept somewhere in the bush, he did not even leave an empty house behind him.

Some said afterwards that the doctor killed Lascelles and butchered him for meat, which he then sold to a Chinaman to be made into beef patties. Others said that the doctor repatriated Lascelles to Africa, where he was devoured by cannibals who mistook him for a Trinidadian missionary. A few claimed that the mad doctor persuaded Lascelles to be a full-time cow and carried him off to Trelawny and released him into a pasture where, to this day, he can be glimpsed eating grass beside a dwarf Brahman bull.

Lascelles left nothing behind him – no wife, no children, no property. He disappeared from Charity Bay leaving only a ghostly and unreliable remembrance behind him. And when those who remembered Lascelles had died, then he would be lost forever to the earth.

"Even an animal deserve better than dat," Zachariah said, through swollen lips.

This was the way that fish died – simply vanishing from

the sea. But even some kinds of fish left memories behind them.

There was, for instance, an eel that lived in the rocks that jutted into the ocean off St. John's Point in Westmoreland. How long the eel had lived there no one knew, but some fishermen, who were grown and married, could recall trying to catch this eel when they were children.

St. John's Point bores sharp and pointed into the soft underbelly of the sea. The waves roar in white and foaming, shattering into thin green tongues that lick hungrily at the rocky land. Near the edge of the water, where the rock always glistens black and wet with a thin coating of seaweed, the eel lived in a hole.

Zachariah tried many times to catch the eel. He would clamber unsteadily over the sharp rock, wait for the roaring breakers to shatter, and then hurry forward a few more feet, until he reached the hole where the eel lived. Then he would crouch down under the lip of a ledge, and fish for the eel, while the breakers shattered above him, and water trickled down the back of his neck.

But the eel was wary and cautious. It took no bait of any kind. It ignored shrimp and squid and fries. It would not approach a hook baited with snail, or even with the eyeball of a shad. Yet from where Zachariah crouched near the mouth of the hole, he could look down and see the waving, serpent's head of the eel peering through a cranny and staring up at him.

One day, after he had tried for weeks to catch the eel with no success, Zachariah decided that he would try to jig the eel. He went into the swamps and cut some roots from the young tender mangroves. He squeezed and pounded the roots to a pulp, and drained off the green stain from them. Then he soaked his fishing line and hook in a bowl filled with the stain. After three days of soaking in the stain, the line and the hook turned as green as the sea.

Zachariah returned to the hole where the eel lived. As

176

he was clambering unsteadily over the rock, he met a boy coming from the hole. The boy paused and glanced scornfully over his shoulder at the sea.

"Nobody goin' catch dat eel," the boy said, with disgust. "Me Papa fish three years for him and couldn't catch him. Is a rass duppy eel dat."

Zachariah said nothing, but continued over the sharp rock, which pinched his bare feet. Soon he was crouching down over the hole, while the water dripped down his neck, and the sea roared in his ears.

He dropped the line and the bare hook into the hole, waiting for the breakers to shatter, which would cause the water in the hole to rise. When the sea withdrew, the water in the hole gurgled and fell. Zachariah could then glimpse the speckled, shiny head of the eel.

The eel waved its head with the rise and fall of the water like a seaweed. Zachariah let the hook fall onto the ledge of the cranny where the eel lived. Then he sat and waited.

He waited for nearly three hours, while water dripped down his neck and rolled down his spine. His pants and shirt were wet, but still he waited.

Finally, the eel pushed its head out of the cranny, peering around the hole. When the head extended far over the hook, Zachariah jerked the line, embedding the barb of the hook into the soft throat of the eel.

He fought the eel all day. The eel was coiled several times around a rock and would not let go, no matter how Zachariah tugged on the line, no matter how deep the hook sank into its throat. Blood flowed from the throat of the eel. The hook worked its way up from the throat and fastened hard against its skull. Exhausted, Zachariah braced himself under the ledge of the rock and fought to pull the eel out of its hole. Several fishermen, who had come down to the Point to fish, lay on their bellies on the lip of the hole and shouted down advice to him.

177

Finally, after he could no longer bear the strain of bracing himself on the rock, after he was exhausted and cold and shivering from water dripping down his neck, Zachariah landed the eel, pulling the long serpentine form out of the black cranny, its body waving and slithering out of the water. The tail of the eel was almost out of the water, when the eel lunged and snapped at Zachariah's shinbone, nearly sinking its teeth into his flesh. But Zachariah swung the eel away from his leg and battered its head against the sharp point of the ledge.

It was, the fisherman said. the biggest eel anyone had ever taken in Westmoreland. The older fishermen gathered around Zachariah, admiring the sea serpent, which was longer than six feet. Everyone who witnessed the fight with the eel admired Zachariah's persistence. A few of the fishermen, who had tried to catch the eel for years, grumbled that Zachariah was lucky.

That evening, Zachariah coiled the dead eel around a long stick, and was carrying it towards the village when a white man and woman passing in a car stopped and begged him to let them take his picture. The man was very excited and happy, posing beside Zachariah and the dead eel while the woman took a picture. Then the man asked Zachariah if he would allow him to be photographed alone with the eel, and Zachariah said yes. So the man stood alone holding the dead eel on the stick, puffing himself up as though he had caught it. while the woman took his photograph. Before they left, the man gave Zachariah a pound note and thanked him.

So the eel did not die like any other unknown fish. Its memory survives in a photograph, somewhere in America. And even to this day, when fishermen in Westmoreland talk about eels, someone among them mentions the eel that the boy Zachariah caught.

Zachariah began to feel sleepy; but it was not the sleepiness of a tired man. He rubbed his eyes and stirred in

178

the bottom of the canoe. Cupping some water from the sea, he poured it over his injured leg so that his wounds would sting and keep him awake. It was not good to sleep in the hot sun.

But the heat bled the sleep out of his bones, and tried to snuff out his thinking about Charity Bay, about Westmoreland, about the people in his life. And instead of having thoughts, he began to see dreams — daylight dreams brought on by the merciless heat. That was the beginning of madness — when a man sees visions in the empty sky.

He slapped his face and tried to stay alert. The small yellow sail, puffed up with a light breeze, billowed over the mast; the gentle downwind motion of the canoe would give sleep to a frightened bird. But he had to stay awake. When a man slept in the hot sun, he became mad. Moreover, if land was near and he slept, he would sail right past it.

Land was not near. Only the sea was near. And the sky was near. And the vast slakeless heat — that was everywhere. But not inside his mind. As long as he could stay awake, none of these could drift into his mind. Inside his mind were shade trees and water and Carina and the pitiful boy who thought he was a cow and the mad English doctor and the zinc roofs of Charity Bay and his triumph over the eel. Inside his mind were Mrs. Lewis and the cruelty of wives and the son who was like a fish and the other son who would not become the cheese. But there was no sun and there was no sea and there was no shark and no empty horizons.

He had to stay awake to keep these out of his mind. As long as he was awake, they stayed outside and buzzed against his skull like angry insects. The sky stayed there; the sea stayed there; the sun stayed there; and the horizons enclosed all these but did not enclose his mind. To conquer him, the sea would have to kill his mind. The sea could send the shark to eat his flesh and terrify his heart, but as long as his mind was alive he could fight against despair. His mind would not be killed. It would bristle with dreams and memories.

179

It would shine like the sun and glitter like the stars. He would live to be an old man, to see his son attend the University and become learned, and to put his son in his place if he became too vain and boastful about his success. He would live to love and take care of his first son, who was deprived of a mother's love. He would not be killed at sea like a voiceless fish.

His thoughts would make the sun angry. Well, the sun could be angry. And they would make the sea angry. Well, the sea could be angry. And the sky, too, would be angry. Well, that too could be angry.

His mind was swirling with dreams caused by the heat, and even now he had to reach down into the sea and cup water between his fingers and splash it over his face to stay awake.

"You want me to sleep, eh?" he chuckled, his lips cracking.

The sun chuckled with him; the sea tickled against the hull of the canoe; the sky giggled. And he laughed along with them because it was a good joke. He laughed long and loud and, in his madness, did not even hear his own laughter.

"I know how you are," he said to the sun, wagging his finger at it.

It was a very good joke, and he wanted to laugh some more. But when he laughed his lips cracked and bled. He reached under the seat of the canoe and took out the water bottle and stared at the water line, which was near the bottom. He cast a quick glance at the sky to see if there were any rain clouds in it. There were none. Only the scorpion sun, that lover of bone, drifted invincibly there.

Well, his mind was also invincible. The sun was powerful and the sky was vast, and the immensity of the sea could drive a man mad. But all these things were inside his mind, so his mind was larger. And even now, as he flicked a careful glance at the sky, the sky puffed itself up with boastfulness and took in the sea, and the sun, and carried the world

180

in its womb; but still, his mind contained the sky.

He giggled. His lips tore and bled. Dreams appeared everywhere, like cobwebs. But he drove them away with wakefulness and washed his face with sea water.

Carina, Carina, Carina, black as a shadow, with the temper of a mongoose; Carina who brought three children into the world, nurtured two, buried one, and favours her youngest son over the other; Carina who sings in the blackness of the pit toilet; Carina who visits the obeah man in the bush; Carina floated into his mind like a song, and his mind trilled and whistled and sang the melody of Carina. Carina, Carina, Carina loomed in the immensities of his mind, his mind that could enclose even the mighty sky.

He was so glad to see her that he laughed, and when he heard the laugh he realized that he was going mad. He quickly drank from the water bottle, the water stinging his dry, caked lips.

It was time to think. He needed to think again, to think and protect himself from going mad.

He was trying to think when out of the corner of his eyes he saw the black fish sliding under the canoe. Suddenly, he was awake and his heart was racing. The fish sounded deep into the blue, circled and the fin reared out of the ocean off the starboard, then sank, leaving a coiling ripple on a swelling wave.

Shuddering like a frightened animal, the painted canoe yawed away from the wind, sliding awkwardly on her side down the trough of a wave.

He was awake now and the dreams were gone. Under him the sea glittered as hard as steel; overhead, the sky was brittle as bone. The small canoe seemed to shrink. Suddenly, it rode under him fragile and weak.

He spilled the wind out of the sail, reached down under the thwart and found the makeshift spear, and waited Under the canoe, the black fish stalked. Leaning over the gunwales, Zachariah glimpsed the prowling hammerhead.

It was a nightmare passing through the mind of the ocean — this sly, hungry fish — and this was what the sea, for spite, had sent to terrorize him for all his boastful thinking.

"Come, you rass, you," Zachariah invited. "Come. I have something for you."

The shark surfaced off the port side of the canoe and swung wide around the frail craft, the fin wedging apart the surface of the waves, thrusting black and ugly out of the womb of the sea.

"Come, you rass, you," Zachariah whispered.

In his rashness, he even leaned over the canoe and splashed his palm on the water, flashing the white fleshy palm to the stalking shark.

The fin suddenly turned towards the canoe, lunging beneath the roiling green water towards the hull. The shark slammed into the canoe and, leaning over, Zachariah saw the fish arc its body and sink its teeth into the cottonwood, the fin sprouting so close to the gunwales of the canoe that he could have reached out and caressed the ugly humpback limb.

The canoe screamed. Zachariah was sure he heard the canoe scream. It screamed its pain and revulsion as the shark fought to sink its teeth into its hull. Zachariah, his ears ringing from the scream, unaware that the sound was coming from his own throat, reached over the side of the canoe and took aim with the spear. The shark thrashed and lunged, its crooked, jointed head tilted towards the surface, and Zachariah got a glimpse of a dark, malevolent eye peering passionlessly up at him through the thin green lid of the sea.

He struck at the eye. He struck and he drove the point of the knife deep into the eye, feeling the blade burst through the jelly and plunge deep down to the hilt of the knife. A loud bestial grunt rose out of him, as he twisted the knife deep inside the eye of the shark, shattering the blade against bone.

The ocean blew up in his face. The canoe was hurled

sideways with a violent force. Suddenly, Zachariah was alone in the canoe, surrounded by nervous, trembling ripples of the ocean.

"You rass, you," Zachariah exulted, examining the broken blade at the end of the gaff. The blade felt wet and slimy; the end of the blade shone and dripped with a glistening film that stank of fish.

Off the port side of the canoe, the shark surfaced, thrashing violently, shattering the stillness of the ocean. Then the fin suddenly disappeared and Zachariah was alone again with only the sun and sky and the sea.

"Smell for you food, from now on," Zachariah told the shark, his eyes flashing with triumph. "Tap 'gainst reef like a blind man."

A wave rose behind the canoe, swelled, and burst into a delicate, white blossom of foam and spindrift, ripping apart with a tearing sound. It was the sea gnashing its teeth at him, Zachariah thought. But he did not care. He bared his own teeth wolfishly, and looked all around the canoe at the vast, shuddering ocean.

"I blind you pickney today," he whispered. "Negar not so easy to kill."

Chapter 14

And there was new food that night. A flying fish leaped into the canoe and fluttered in the bottom of the boat, waking up Zachariah. He killed the fish, cut it up for bait, and fished in the moonlight.

By the time the moon had crested the sky, he had caught two bonito. He cut them up and salted the flesh. He ate some of the bonito and wanted to drink from the water bottle, but didn't because there was only a single mouthful left, which he would need during the blistering heat of the day.

He curled up for warmth in the bottom of the canoe and tried to sleep, but it was chilly and uncomfortable. The teeth of the hammerhead had raked deep grooves into the rounded cottonwood hull of the canoe, through which the sea slowly bled. No matter how Zachariah lay in the bottom of the canoe, he still got wet. He slept restlessly, waking up frequently to look around at the dark ocean as though he heard a voice calling to him. By morning he had a cough.

He dreamed of the hammerhead. He dreamed that the shark was swimming blindly through the sea, battering its head against sharp reefs and the hulls of sunken ships, the knife blade jabbing out of the empty eye socket like a broken tooth. He woke up feeling pity for the ugly fish. He wished he had killed it cleanly and put it out of its misery, for the shark was only obeying its nature. He went back to sleep thinking about the shark, and this time when he woke up he had a severe pain in his left eye.

The seas were lifting in a freshening wind when he awoke. Zachariah cupped water from the side of the canoe and hurriedly washed his face. Black clouds silently massed on the horizon. In a bad temper, the sea snarled at the sky; the waves bared white teeth and snapped into the air.

Zachariah hurried to the middle of the canoe to man the oars. He turned the canoe around so that her trim bow pointed into the lifting seas. The canoe rolled and swayed. He took time out occasionally to bail the water seeping through her damaged hull.

The sky glowered and the clouds broke free of the horizon and drifted in a pack across the ocean. Hissing and snarling like a cat, the sea swiped at the sky. Caught in the middle, the painted canoe shook and trembled nervously.

"Dem can't harm you," Zachariah whispered to the canoe, holding her tight into the waves.

The sky compressed into a black malevolence that exploded with lightning. Thunder rumbled across the white seas, rolling like a nervous tremor through Zachariah's bones. The wind whistled and the ocean growled and turned a livid green.

"Dem can't harm you," Zachariah screamed encouragingly to the canoe over the wind.

Everywhere around the small canoe enormous waves gathered, swelling and rising to the hysteria in the wind, bursting and shattering white. The canoe leaped and shivered, jumped into the air, slammed down into the troughs of the waves, then scratched her way up again as all around her a wall of malefic green lifted. She scampered to the crest of the waves, hung there with her rotund black bottom showing, then plunged down, taking water. Zachariah clung to the oars and fought to hold her bow into the heavy seas. As she clawed her way up the sides of swelling waves, he bailed with the calabash bowl, all the while screaming, "Dem can't harm you!" over the hissing white water.

In reply, the water fanged white, and the stinging spray

blinded him. The sky howled with a ravenous hunger for the canoe. The waves attacked her with white teeth, trying to tear open her hull.

She took water and rose sluggishly into the lifting waves. Zachariah screamed encouragement at the canoe and tried to hold her nose tight into the wind. The water swirled around his ankles. He bailed and squinted into the blinding spray and looked over his shoulders at the rearing, shuddering waves.

The seas raged and lunged at the canoe. Giving off a maniacal, frenzied shriek, the wind battered her hull. Hurling into the air, the canoe plunged into the white water, and clambered to the crests of mountainous waves.

"Dem can't hurt you!" Zachariah continued to scream, working the oars until his shoulders were numb.

He was so weary and frightened that he almost began to pray. But though he was tempted, he decided that he would only pray if the canoe was broached and capsized. Otherwise, he would depend on the painted canoe to hold her own against the towering seas.

But as soon as he had made this decision, the wind shifted and the water exploded all around the small craft and the seas threatened to broach her. The waves battered her broadside, and she dipped precariously while Zachariah tried to coax her nose into the wind. She wallowed and shook, and she gave off long agonising shivers.

Zachariah's lips began to bleed, the blood running off his mouth and dropping into the bottom of the canoe where it bobbed and danced on top of the water. His arms were numb; his hands were cramped; his injured leg had no feeling in it. Peering half-blinded over his shoulder, he watched the waves rear and shatter hurling spindrift at the boat.

"Dem can't hurt you," Zachariah mumbled, holding the canoe into the wind. "If dem try and hurt you, I goin' pray. But I know dem can't hurt you."

He muttered these words as though he were uttering

threats against the sea.

The rain began to fall. As suddenly as it had erupted, the sea calmed, as all around the painted canoe raindrops pocked the surface of the ocean.

Zachariah bailed and bailed some more and held the trembling canoe hard into the teeth of the wind. The waves rolled with a vicious chop, spilling out under the canoe, causing her to roll and flop awkwardly, then right herself with a confused shudder.

"Rain," he muttered. "Water."

He bailed as fast as he could, throwing water wildly over the sides, trying to clean the boat so he could catch the fresh water.

The wind fell and the seas eased and both now growled their rage low and throaty. Slackening back into a deep blue, the seas occasionally swiped at the hull of the canoe.

Zachariah bailed. The rain fell harder, roaring and buzzing, shattering the surface of the sea.

He bailed until the bottom of the canoe was almost dry. He tasted the water; a salt taste lingered in it. He started to bail again, but he was suddenly too weary. He fought against the sleep, working the calabash bowl mechanically, moving his arms and shoulders in a slow, somnolent rhythm. Finally, he stopped bailing. His head sagged against his chest; he collapsed in the bottom of the canoe. He told himself that he would not sleep and, while saying this to himself, he fell asleep.

When he awoke, the ocean slumbered under a sheen. The sun was sinking into the horizon. The evening star was out. Riding low in the water, the canoe listed helplessly in the calm. Water swirled around his buttocks; a chill spread through his body.

He tasted the water. It had a trace of salt in it, but it could be drunk. He laughed and cupped the water in his hands and rubbed it over his face, letting it trickle over the

187

hairline cuts of his lips. He filled the water bottle to the brim. Then he took off his pants, and splashed in the bottom of the canoe, as though he were taking a bath, and washed the sticky salt off his body.

Now he had water. The sea had tried to kill him but, instead, it gave him water. He laughed. It was such a good joke that he could not stop laughing. He rolled in the water in the bottom of the canoe and laughed and laughed.

Pattering and tinkling with the soundless laughter of the heavens, the stars came out.

Zachariah was laughing so hard that he could hardly breathe. Recognizing the madness, he stopped laughing, and lay instead in the bottom of the canoe, splashing the cool fresh water over his body.

The darkness paraded its own mysteries. The domination of night began.

Chapter 15

On a late Thursday afternoon during the rainy season, the constable rode his Honda from Manchioneal to Charity Bay to visit with the English doctor at the clinic. He took the only road in this part of the island, a road that beads through the hearts of all the seacoast villages. It was a road the constable knew well, having travelled on it countless times. He knew all its twists, tilts and grades; he knew all its villages, all the shops, huts, and houses jostled together under such names as Long Bay, Fair Prospect, Priestman's River, Boston Bay; and he knew all its potholes familiarly enough to have secretly named them.

At the outskirts of San San he mumbled hello to Josephine, a gaping, toothy pothole which the rains of last year had mothered in the middle of the road. Outside of Drapers he greeted a litter of her sisters: Millie, and Chubby, and Miss Meagre, this last so named for her pitiful emaciation that made her look more like a pariah fissure than a respectable pothole. He knew them all and he mumbled his respects to them all as he rode nimbly by, because they helped the lonely ride pass quickly. But he did it secretly because an ignorant public would no doubt consider him mad and request his removal from high office if they knew that he was greeting potholes.

A little outside of Port Antonio, the constable pulled his Honda over to the side of the road, urinated discreetly behind the trunk of a guinep tree, and took grim stock of his new serge uniform. Humidity had loosened the stiff, disciplined creases ridging the legs of his trousers; a mud ring clung tenaciously to the cuffs of his pants. Centred on

189

the peak of his cap, the Official Shield of the Portland Constabulary suffered the presence of a frowsy, disgruntled smudge.

The constable rode a half-mile down the road, turned onto a little used parochial road and parked his Honda behind a leafy cotton tree.

Out of a saddlebag he took a can of polish and a piece of cotton and, sitting down on a pile of white marl stones, inflicted a glittering shine on his shield. Then, making sure that no representative of the public loitered in the vicinity, the constable furtively took off his pants and used spit and a rag to reduce the mud ring on his cuffs to a hairline smudge. After that, he laid his trousers out on the grass, pulling them as taut as possible to restore rigidity to their creases. While he sunned the trousers on a rock, he sat on the white marl and laboured lovingly over the shine in his shoes.

Fifteen minutes later, restored to official resplendence, the constable mounted his Honda and rode through Port Antonio and into St. Margaret's Bay.

All along the route, the constable was required to dispense courtesies to the public loitering by the wayside, all of whom knew the constable well and wished to have him as a friend. Wise to the ways of his people, the constable was therefore polite but not effusive, and cautiously dispensed a well-regulated and measured hierarchy of greetings.

He distinguished between an open palm wave, which extended full and official recognition and friendship to the member of the public deserving it, and the slightly wilted palm wave, which acknowledged presence but did not elaborately welcome it; and the unopened palm wave, which conceded existence but desired no intercourse with it. Immeasurably beneath these, the constable's greetings dwindled to fingers fluttering mildly against the handle bars of the Honda, to a curt nod, or, for those whom he did not wish to greet at all, to the mere prolongation of an official,

190

bemused stare.

The constable was on the edge of Charity Bay when he first looked out to sea and saw the cloud. It sat heavy with discontent on the horizon, wearing firm, trenchant rain edges. It appeared to be swelling and moving laterally to the shore.

Making a note to himself not to allow the mad English doctor to detain him, the constable gave the Honda another spurt of gas and rode into Charity Bay.

He passed Mrs. Wilson on the roadside and awarded her the full open palm wave. Mrs. Lewis, whom he fully expected to one day arrest for husband-beating, was treated to the fluttering finger. Mr. Hemmings, a sufferer, received a sympathetic but firmly unopened palm. A group of loitering youths were buffeted with a stare. One by one the constable rode past the familiar citizens of Charity Bay and greeted each according to his just deserts.

The constable pulled into the backyard of the clinic, standing his motorcycle against the trunk of a lignum vitae tree.

On the horizon, the cloud began to lour. It turned purposefully towards the shore and increased its speed.

The constable lit a cigarette, glanced at his tucked-in shirt and at the crease in his pants, and surveyed the world with a general contentment. Walking past with a fishnet, Mr. Wilson called out to the constable, receiving the open palm for his trouble, along with a rare, contrived grunt.

For there, to the constable's way of thinking, passed a decent citizen, a man whom he would never have occasion to confront officially, the poor fellow's life being sorely taken up with fishing and the nagging of his old wife.

The constable nodded to himself at his astute observation and was momentarily grateful for having a cat, instead of a wife. He inhaled on the cigarette, threw the stub away, and walked into the clinic to find the doctor.

He found the Englishman lying on the bench in the inner room. The nurse bustled around him, packing away the instruments and samples of the day's work, and casting severe glances of disapproval at the doctor's sprawl.

The constable discreetly coughed.

"Hah!" the doctor exclaimed, rising with obvious weariness. "Constable, how are you?"

"Fine, sah! Fine! And you, sah?"

"Good, man. Good! You're not here officially, are you? Nurse, I haven't shot anyone lately, have I?"

"Me don't know, sah," the nurse mumbled gloomily, holding her nose disdainfully away from a vial impacted with human faeces.

"No, sah!" the constable waved official dispensation and reassured the doctor. "Is all right. Semi-officially. But not officially."

"Good! Good!" the doctor barked, lolling back on the bench and closing his eyes.

An awkward pause sprang up between them and, for a moment, it appeared to the constable the doctor had dozed off. The nurse clinked and scratched at the edge of the room, glowering at the two of them. The constable cleared his throat, this time officially.

Startled, the doctor jumped and sat up on the bench, rubbing his eyes and stretching.

"Sorry, Constable," the madman murmured, "bloody exhausted."

"I understand, sah, I understand." The constable answered with sympathy. Then he pointed discreetly at the nurse.

"Nurse," the doctor bellowed, "leave us alone."

"Me don't mind nobody business but me own business," the nurse grumbled.

"All right! All right!" the doctor said impatiently, jumping off the bench.

The nurse gathered her things.

192

"Me no cook nobody chicken, me no mind nobody business," she mumbled defiantly. "Me is a Christian woman." She left, closing the door waspishly after her.

"She is, too, you know, sah," the constable murmured, looking at the closed door.

"What?"

"A Christian woman. Every Sunday I see her in church."

"Yes, yes, I'm sure she is. I'm sure they all are," the doctor said offhandedly, packing his bag.

"A delicate matter, sah," the constable began, officially.

The doctor sent a searching glance into the crammed bag. The constable followed it, spying, in the jumble, vials stuffed with faeces, urine, and blood; gleaming silver instruments; a hypodermic syringe; a stethoscope; brown paper packets of pills; a note pad; and, protruding incongruously among these, the dull blue butt of the doctor's automatic.

The doctor snapped the bag shut and faced the constable.

"A patient of yours, sah," the constable began, "is missing. Lost at sea."

"Who?"

"His name is Pelsie, sah. I know him by his first name, Zachariah."

The doctor stared hard at the constable and nodded.

"Well, sah," the constable gestured reasonably, "him missing now..."

The constable paused for correction and rephrasing, the patois suddenly seeming entirely out of place in official discourse.

"He's been missing now for thirteen, fourteen, fifteen days, one of those numbers."

The doctor sighed, sat down on the edge of the bench, and waited for officialdom to unravel itself.

'I believe, sah, we can reasonably say that the fellow is lost."

The constable squinted at the doctor. The doctor

193

shrugged and offered no opposition.

"I repeat, sah, reasonable men would call him lost. We don't like to give up, sah, but we have to give up this one to the sea."

Another scrutinizing squint floated between them, read and returned by the lunatic with another shrug.

The constable began to pace as he liked to do when he was talking officially.

"Lost, sah. No doubt about it. Lost."

"Constable, would you like to go and have a drink?"

"Sorry, sah," the constable said smartly, "I only drink on the first Thursday of every month."

The doctor shrugged again. He had learned long ago never to pursue these labyrinthine habits of Jamaicans.

"A man must regulate himself, sah. That's my position."

"About Pelsie, Constable . . ."

"Yes, sah. I can see you're tired. I'll get to the point."

The constable scratched his chin and looked quizzically at the doctor from the other end of the room where his pacing had stranded him.

"The man is lost, sah! Lost! We agree on that. Fourteen days at sea; he's gone by now. Shark eat him. Drowning reach him. Storm, winds, high seas, hot sun. Whatever. Finished. Done with that one."

The constable waved past the catalogue of evils and, rubbing his hands together, prepared to veer into his conclusion. The doctor, who by now had learned never to attempt the acceleration of official discourse in Jamaica, waited patiently. But before the constable could proceed, the doctor announced, "He was dead, anyway. Might as well drown at sea than die in a bed."

"What's that, sah?" The constable looked astonished.

"Melanoma, Constable. The man Pelsie had a rather nasty form of cancer, known as multiple melanoma. He came to me for treatment about a month ago. I sent him to Port Antonio for X-rays. It had already spread into his chest

194

cavity, his lungs. He was as good as dead."

"Good God, sah!" the constable exclaimed.

"I quite agree, Constable. But now you understand my reason for saying it was probably just as well that he died at sea."

"For one poor man to be so unlucky, sah," the constable began, fumbling for superlatives.

"Yes, I suppose you're right, Constable," the doctor said coldly, getting off the couch and yawning. "Melanoma is certainly bad luck. But, on the other hand, blowing away when he did was probably a stroke of perverse good luck."

"The poor fellow has a wife, sah, and two pickney," the constable said, looking inconsolably gloomy.

"I haven't told her, by the way," the doctor said, "and I hope you won't, either. No point in making her feel worse than she already does."

"Although, sah, it would probably make her feel better if she knew."

"Assuming, of course, that she believed me. I'm rather little believed around here, you know, Constable. My patients would rather believe the rubbish of an obeah man, or whatever they call that bush creature who stuffs them on stupid herbs and roots, than believe me. I'm really getting quite a complex about it."

The constable chuckled. The unexpected news about Pelsie's illness had badly affected his prepared business with the doctor. Yet there was something so engaging in the madman's manner, that the constable was always ready to joust with him in genial debate.

"Yes, sah," the constable said thoughtfully. "Obeah. Against the law in this country, you know, sah. When we find out for certainty that a man is an obeah man, we prosecute. But, let me tell you a story, sah, about an obeah man, of something I witnessed with these two very eyes."

"A miraculous cure? Really, Constable, I didn't think you believed in such rubbish."

195

"This is a strange world, Dr. Richardson," the constable said in a sonorous voice, doing his utmost to appear inscrutable as though he himself had witnessed an untold number of wonders.

"If you're sick enough, you die. Medicine is good up to a point. Beyond that point, you might as well call a butcher, or a plumber, for all the good a doctor can do. We doctors don't like to admit it, but we're rather a stupid, blundering lot when it comes to some diseases. We can't do a damn thing. Bloody little worms, viruses, bacteria, beat us all the time. Beat us every blasted day. They gobble up men, women, and children right under our noses. And there's not a bloody thing we can do. Why? Because of the prime law of medicine: if you're sick enough, you die."

"Except when God interferes, sah, on the side of health and goodness. Then no matter how sick we be, we live."

The doctor laughed sardonically. He walked to the window and peered idly through the louvres.

"There's no bloody God, Constable," the doctor said harshly, peering out between the crooked louvres. "It's the best kept secret in Jamaica, next to the Prime Minister's economic policy."

The constable sniffed at the blasphemy, and looked very grave.

"Then, sah, where we all come from?"

"From slimy, microscopic cells. Constable, oozing down the Fallopian tubes of our mothers. Then there's copulation, fertizilation, mitosis, gestation, and birth. Sorry to be so technical, but I wouldn't know how else to put it without sounding theatrical."

The constable blinked in the face of this scientific vocabulary, most of which he had not even faintly understood.

"And where we goin' to, sah?" he asked gently, circling to get a look at the madman's eyes.

"Deterioration, death, and decay," the doctor enumer-

196

ated crisply, still peering out of the louvres. "Back to the mud and the slime. No need to be disheartened, however. There's some encouraging news from thermodynamics: matter cannot be destroyed. Oh, the flesh does rot, of course, and the bone does break down to calcium and sundry minerals. Nothing special about it, really, doesn't even make as good a fertilizer as bat droppings. But the point is that nothing is wasted: the molecules are used again and again. Perhaps they'll be used to make a sparrow's rectum, or a rat's throat, or the bowels of a filthy ramgoat. Nature is very, very frugal, rather like a scrap-iron dealer, always collecting and re-using, never simply throwing anything away — the old bitch. There simply is no stopping her ruthless economy."

The doctor turned from the window and peered with amusement at the constable.

The constable shuddered.

"A man mustn't believe such wickedness, sah," he said, looking intently into the doctor's eyes.

"It's the truth, Constable," the doctor said harshly.

"It's a wicked truth, sah," the constable replied firmly. "No man should have to believe such a wicked truth."

The doctor laughed, a harsh shrill sound like glass shattering. He returned to the bench and sat on the edge of it, peering humorously at the constable, who stood in the centre of the room looking rather grave and bewildered.

The constable stared at the madman and felt so much pity for him that he did not trust himself to approach any closer. For a moment, he felt almost impelled to walk over to the doctor and pat him reassuringly on the shoulder, or put his arm around him and hold him comfortingly to his bosom. But it would have been an intolerable insult if he had made such a gesture. Moreover, the doctor might think that the constable was one of those perverted men known on the island as "batty men" — "batty" being the patois word for the rectum.

Yet there was something so sorrowful and empty about

197

the doctor's life that the constable felt as though he had to offer some consolation. He did not know what he could say to console such an intelligent and scientific white man, so he stood in the middle of the room, looking badly out of place while he cast desperately about in his mind for some consoling things to say.

He went to the window and peered out of the louvres at the ragged village of Charity Bay.

"These people here, sah," the constable said, "they love life. Nobody love life more than a poor man."

The doctor shrugged.

"And yet of all men, the poor man has the least to love about life. Yet the poor man love life the most. How you explain such a thing, sah?"

The doctor stood up, stretched and yawned.

"I don't. As a matter of fact, I'm not sure that they love life altogether as much as you say."

"They do, sah. I know. I see it with my own eye. Now for instance, that man Pelsie, sah, what he have to love about life? He uglier than a damn goat. Nobody in the whole parish uglier than him. He poor as a wild dog. He have three pickney, and one already dead. Yet I know this man, sah, he have great heart."

"What do you mean?"

"I mean, sah, that he is the type of man that would never surrender. Yet he as poor as a church mouse. How you explain such a thing, eh, sah?"

"I told you, Constable. I don't. I don't have to. Because I don't believe it. In any event, it doesn't really matter now, does it? If he's not already dead from exposure, he'll soon be dead from cancer. And where cancer's concerned, it doesn't matter how much bloody heart you've got. All that matters is the cancer."

"No, sah," the constable said firmly, "I don't agree. I'm not a scientific man like you, sah. But I took three passes in my Senior Cambridge exam, and I have a little schooling.

What is in a man's heart counts for something."

"It counts for bloody nothing where cancer is concerned," the doctor snapped.

"A man's heart always count for something, sah," the constable said stubbornly. "That is what the poor man believes. What is in a man's heart matters."

The doctor shrugged and looked weary, as though he were tiring of the conversation. Stiffening perceptibly, the constable assumed his official mien.

"But, sah, to the point."

"Yes, Constable, to the point, if you please."

"As I was saying, sah, about this man Pelsie. He blow away. But, sah, the fellow has a wife and two pickney he left behind."

"Yes," the doctor lied. "I believe I remember hearing something about his family."

"A difficult woman, sah, his common-law wife. Tough! Tough, sah! Tougher than rockstone! And unwilling to admit, sah, that her man is lost. Quite unwilling." The constable paused, anticipating some expressions of incredulity from the doctor.

"I know it's difficult to understand, sah," he said soothingly, as though the madman would never comprehend such stubbornness, "but this is how these people are. So they born, so they die. Rockstone not tougher."

A huge sigh exploded from the doctor.

"Now, sah," the constable said, pacing officially up and down between the louvred window and the wooden bench on which the doctor sat. "This is what I propose to do, with your permission. First, I will write a report declaring the circumstances of this man's fate, about how he blow away and is lost at sea. Then, sah, since you are the medical officer for this district, I will ask you to sign a certificate of presumed death."

"I'll be glad to handle it just the way you recommend, Constable," the doctor said obligingly, packing some vials into his bag as though he were about to leave.

"Of course, sah, the purpose of this is for the insurance. The Ministry of Fisheries insure these fishermen for $1,000 each. And if we file the claim now, in the year of our Lord 1975, payment should reach the widow by the year of our Lord 1977."

The doctor nodded as though he understood, which disappointed the constable, for he had expected the Englishman to ask querulous questions about why such a simple matter as an insurance claim should take so long, and he had prepared a long, scolding talk on the inefficiency of the government bureaucracy in reply. But now that the Englishman seemed indifferent to the subject, the constable had to discard his speech, and proceed into a disappointingly anticlimatic summary.

"Well, sah," the constable said feebly, "that was the nature of my business today. First, I will submit the report. Then, we will file a certificate of presumptive death."

"Excellent, Constable," the doctor said crisply, seizing his bag and heading for the door.

"In my official capacity as constable of this district, sah," the constable continued, following the doctor outside, "I sometimes have to give matters a shove, sah, a push, if you take my meaning."

"Indeed, Constable," the doctor said, opening the door of his car, "I take your meaning very well. I've dealt with some of those government buggers, too."

Standing by the opened door of his Volkswagen, the doctor glanced out to sea and murmured, "Rain."

"Rain to rass!" the constable yelped, looking out to sea. "A whole heap of rain."

For there, across the entire horizon, stretching with unmistakable malevolence, loured a vast, impenetrable rain cloud.

They shook hands in the parking lot. On touching the flesh of the doctor's hand, the constable thought of what

200

the doctor had said about slime, and shivered.

"I'll write my report and advise you, sah," the constable said, hiding his revulsion.

"Do that, Constable," the doctor said.

The Englishman started the engine of his car and drove off, taking the road towards Kingston. The constable put on his riding gloves, briefly smoked a cigarette, and rode off on his Honda towards Port Antonio.

On the outskirts of Charity Bay, he passed a ramgoat rooting through a mound of garbage, and it flashed through his mind what the doctor had said about becoming the bowels of a goat.

"Wicked, wicked thought," the constable muttered to himself over the roar of the Honda's engine.

He should have had a drink with the Englishman. He should have explained to the lunatic that a man with such hopeless thoughts on his brain has nothing but darkness and death in his heart. Yet the Englishman was so scientific and learned, that the propositions and arguments would have to be carefully phrased and forcefully put forward, if they were to sway him.

Just outside of St. Margaret's Bay, where the road climbed high above the sea and skirted a dizzying precipice, the constable pulled over and smoked another cigarette. He straddled his motorcycle and stared out at the ruffled green ocean blanketed by the low, gloomy bank of rain clouds. A flock of pelicans skimmed the ragged waves, flying in V-formation towards the shelter of the mangroves where they roosted. The constable watched the sailing pelicans, trying to see them as made of the bits and pieces of soulless dead people whose bodies had rotted and decayed for centuries in the earth. It was such a ludicrous idea that the constable could not help smiling. And to think that the Englishman really believed such foolishness, really took such an idea seriously! Who but a white man would torment himself with such obvious stupidness?

201

The constable shivered with forboding as he smoked the cigarette and stared out at the wind-swept sea. He could not understand how anyone, even a scientific white man, could live with such futility in his heart.

Chapter 16

The rain came. It came to Portland, and it came to St. James, and in the south it came to St. Elizabeth and to St. Thomas, as all the island was suffused by a vast, louring cloud. The gullies filled with water. Every crevice and crack in the earth bloated, suppurating a blood-red, agglutinous ooze. The rivers churned brown and convulsed over their banks, drooling insensibly into the streets. The earth cracked open countless maws, yawned ravenous mouths, and sucked on the cloud with an unquenchable thirst. All across the island, the people spoke, and sang, and dreamed about the sun. But no sun came. Only the rain came. It came like an agent of eternity. It stalked across the island like a sleek, invincible grey beast. It plastered fields and valleys, railing against shingle, clattering against zinc, pounding on concrete. It fell on man and beast, killing cattle, drowning children, destroying grown women and robust men. The earth cloyed with mud; the soil crumbled; mountains groaned and collapsed. Watersheds tore loose like severed tendons. Dams blew out. Bridges fell. All the earth was battered into submission, beaten into servility by the torrential spate of water, by the hideous ravaging of mud.

The people were seized by an hysterical, raging fear. The end of the world had come, the fanatics cried. Men and women huddled together, shrunk with abject helplessness. They prayed with heartfelt fervour. Many went mad and took riotously to the streets before the final bursting of heavens and earth. Parliament met and called out the army.

Camped placidly on the mud-caked pastures of Moneague in St. Ann, the army dispatched drenched troops into the cities to sulk, bad-tempered and wet, under shop awnings and against storefronts, and stare gloomily at the pestilential downpour.

The rain continued; the madness continued. Ghosts and duppies rolled across the island, instilling terror. In St. James, by the asseverations of thousands, the graves opened and the dead slow-marched at midnight through the streets of Montego Bay, lugubriously carrying mud-stained coffins. Three impertinent crows, perched on a motorized casket, swirled through the streets and lanes of Kingston, knocking on doors and taking a house-to-house census of the living. Television crews sped frantically from one small forgotten village to another to try to film macabre occurrences reported by hysterical mayoral telegrams. Indistinguishably mixed, madness and rain shattered the mind and the earth.

The Prime Minister decided to give a speech. He called his cabinet together and requested seven hours' speaking time from the two radio stations. The stations sent technicians to the House of Parliament. The galleries swelled with frightened people.

We are a suffering people, the Prime Minister began. Three hundred and seven years of British Colonialism have we suffered. Three hundred and seven years of Capitalism and Standard English have we suffered. And, growled the Prime Minister, we can suffer three hundred and seven years of rain if we have to, because it couldn't be any worse than three hundred and seven years of Capitalism and Standard English.

Parliament laughed, but the Opposition did not laugh. The Prime Minister's party was so large that when it laughed the laugh roared like the rain itself, and the mirth flowed through the airways of both stations.

The laughter lifted and sang through the grey, seamless rain, reaching the cultivator battened in his drenched, flaking hut; the fisherman marooned on land and, without the fish, starving; the timorous city dweller whose home had been

204

breached by officious spectral crows, and whose loved ones, heartlessly counted; the terrified witnesses who had seen the dead rise up with their coffins and slow-march to a soundless music through the streets of Montego Bay; the laughter reached all the people scattered and dispersed through the innocent loveliness of this green island, and the people laughed.

Vaster than the louring cloud, mightier than the rain, more plentiful than the profusions of wounds and injuries in the earth, the laughter gathered and spread. It roared across drowned canefields, swirled past shattered dams, caressed the punctured, suppurating earth, lilted through rooms drawn lean with grief, and sang the irrepressibility of hope.

Never was there such laughter. Never was rain and mud and trenchant greyness assaulted by such an insatiable human chortling.

And from the loveliness of the laughter, from the gentleness of the laughing, no one would have known that countless grey and lean days had scratched across the island without a dawn song from the birds. No one would have known that the earth was torn and broken, that the dams had burst, that the island was disembowelled and ripped by a weltering desolation.

The Prime Minister held up his hand to stem the laughing, but the laughing did not stop. Under his fingers, a fat speech curdled, filled with execrations against British Colonialism and the Opposition, bloated with patois expressions and country proverbs, and he wished to give it. But his party, the technicians, the galleries, were laughing so hard that he had to pause, and himself pretend to laugh.

He did not understand why they were laughing. He did not see the great joke in what he had said. However, indubitably the populace was maddened by the rain and silly. He fingered the speech, sipped at a glass of aerated water, and waited for the endless babbling to cease.

Laughing did not stop the rain. The drops pelted down and the water seeped, and everywhere the transformation into mud continued. But the rain would soon stop. The cloud would soon burst, scattering its entrails harmlessly through the skies. The sun would soon come out. For this is how the heart of the poor man beats: soon, soon, soon.

"I always knew this country had a streak of lunacy in it," the doctor said, standing by the window of his concrete bungalow in Mona Heights, and staring out morosely at the rain.

He had just finished reading a lurid story in The Daily Gleaner about the duppy crows that had been touring the slums of Kingston and taking a census of the living.

It had been raining now for a week without stop. The bridges had been washed away; the roads were clogged with mud; the Junction Road, which took him to the eastern part of the island where he visited the clinics, was impassable. He had made short trips to the Public Hospital to help with emergencies, but he had been unable to make his regular rounds. All week he had been cooped up because of the torrential rains, and he was restless and bored.

"When rain fall, duppy come out," the woman said pragmatically. She sat cross-legged on the couch, eating a plateful of yellow yam with her fingers.

The doctor stared out at the grey afternoon. He listened to the interminable patter of drops against the concrete roof, and watched the mud puddles shuddering under the window.

He sighed and went into the bedroom that served as a makeshift office, and sat behind his desk. The room, the desk were in a state of slovenly disarray. Papers were scattered over the desk, piling up as thick as a foot in some places. Medical books were strewn across the floor. Stacked in a sagging pile over against a corner were the latest bulletins from the Ministry of Health. Rain had blown through an

206

open window and stained the bulletins, curling their edges brown and stiff.

He swept a place clear on his desk, scattering papers and documents on the floor. Rummaging through a pile of papers, he searched for his latest poetic effort — a long, free verse poem that he had scribbled over ten foolscap pages of a notepad. Two weeks ago, while lunching under a tree on a country road, he had had another attack of the "divine madness", and the poem had gushed out of him. He had set it aside on his desk intending to revise it later. But now, as he rifled through the untidy contents of his desk, he was unable to find the poem.

"What you looking for?" the woman called out to him from the living room.

"I'm looking for something I've been writing." he snapped, kicking the batch of bulletins from the Ministry of Health that were piled on the floor.

Every week, the Ministry of Health dispatched its new amendments and regulations to its physicians. Every time there was a meeting of the Medical Undersecretaries, some fifty or so new pages were added prescribing treatments, payments, use of drugs, anticipating every conceivable situation a physician might encounter and setting down guidelines for coping with it. This was the new modus operandi for all government officers as set down by the Prime Minister himself who, in a recent speech, had excoriated "the impromptu actions of Colonials" and deplored all forms of governmental improvisation as nothing better than "neo-favouritism". At the Prime Minister's behest, therefore, the various Ministries had been scrambling to devise inviolable procedures for dispensing the services of the government. Forms as thick as bricks swirled through the mail every week and landed on the doctor's desk. He never read them, but merely threw them on top of the sagging pile on the floor.

"Me was looking at it de odder day," the woman said,

standing in the doorway.

"I told you never to come in here and interfere with my personal papers," the doctor raged.

The woman slouched into the room, looking frowsy and dishevelled. She flipped through the papers scattered over the doctor's desk. Her hand dived in between the loose sheets and retrieved the foolscap notepad that contained the hand written poem.

"Damn you," the doctor snarled, snatching the poem out of her hand. "Keep your bloody hands off my personal papers!"

"If me hand good enough to hold you hood, it good enough to hold you paper," the woman replied tartly, flouncing out of the room.

There was such an earthy, primal logic to her reply that the doctor, in spite of his pique, had to suppress a laugh. He slammed the door after her. Then he hunched over the cluttered desk to work on revising the poem.

He tinkered with the poem for nearly two hours, scratching out stale lines and phrases, scrawling in marginal emendations, racking his brains for fresh images. Sometimes, he would pause and flick his eyes over the rain-stained window and listen to the staccato of raindrops on the roof, while he thought about what he really wanted to say. Sometimes, he would scribble furiously as though he could hardly write the words down quickly enough.

The poem was one of those long, rambling, imagistic works such as South American poets are fond of writing. Image tumbled after image in the oddest, most illogical combination that suggested a world view convulsed by randomness and chance. The doctor did not write didactic poetry, for he believed in no definite ideology; nor did he write with feeling, for he was from the school that severely damns sentimentality in serious verse. His poetry was therefore entirely algebraic. It bristled with cryptic and profound utterances intending to startle the reader, without, at the same time, personally implicating the writer. It was poetry that seemed to fit every imaginable situation a reader wished to ascribe to it.

When the woman had first discovered the poem and pored over it out of curiosity, she had been astonished to discover that she understood its parts, but not the whole. Though she read English and knew the meanings of the individual words on the page, she could not for the life of her decipher even a single sentence of the poem. She had left the room stricken with a profound sense of awe at the doctor's brilliance.

The more the doctor worked on the poem, the flatter it seemed, and the more enraged he became. He could not admit to himself that perhaps his feelings were neither poetic nor unique and therefore quite untranscribable into poetry for the same reason that some novels cannot be made into movies. Nor could he admit that perhaps he had no talent for translating his unconscious into universal symbols − the very aim of the sort of poetry he had been struggling to write. Instead, he sat at his desk futilely wrestling with words, images, rhythms, and lines. As soon as he had a powerful surge of feeling and tried to pour it out onto the page in words, the feeling would disappear and the words would ring hollow and empty. When the words sprang spontaneously out of him and copiously spilled on the page, they struck him, on a cold rereading, as forced and contrived. He was like an entomologist trying to mount a firefly at the precise moment that it gave off its phosphorescent burst of light.

Uttering a curse, the doctor crumpled the poem into a wad and threw it on the floor. Then he sat morosely at his desk staring angrily into his clenched fists.

A few minutes later, he retrieved the poem, smoothed out the page, and read it once again. He cut out the first thirty lines, spliced together the first and final stanzas, and typed out the new version on his old portable typewriter.

Still dissatisfied, he cut out another ten lines, and edited out the final stanza.

After another hour of being cut and retyped, the ten-page poem had shrunk to the size of a haiku — about fifteen syllables long. This time, when the doctor read the poem aloud, it sounded pompous and overdone, like a midget straining to utter momentous prophecies. He shredded the page and threw the pieces in the trash can, stomping them down with savage thrusts of his foot.

The storm, meanwhile, had gotten worse. He was suddenly conscious of the shattering roar of rain against the roof. Deep, sonorous peals of thunder rumbled over the house, sending shivers through its walls. The rain beat a tinny drumroll against the galvanized gutters lining the eaves. Frustrated and angry, the doctor paced the untidy room, kicking books and papers out of his way.

There was a timid scratching against the door, which slowly opened. The woman entered the room timorously.

"What the devil do you want?" he barked at her.

"You don't hear de thunder?" she whispered, rolling her eyes at the ceiling.

"Leave me alone, damn it!"

"Why you don't come outside and talk to me, eh?" she pleaded, sidling up against him and stroking his arm.

"Get out of here, damn it!"

He shoved her away from him.

A deafening crash of thunder exploded overhead and rumbled throughout the concrete house. She screamed and huddled against him.

"Me don't like thunder!" she quaked.

"You stupid creature;" he said bitterly, "it can't harm you."

"Me don't like it," she whimpered, stroking his organ through his pants. "Come lie abed with me, eh?"

"Is it a fuck you want?" he asked harshly. "Is that it? You're frightened so you want to fuck away your fear?"

"Come lie abed wid me, nuh?" she whined.

He followed her into the bedroom.

"Why don't you bathe some time?" he growled as he was undressing. "You're beginning to stink."

"But me bathe all de time," she protested.

Another roar of thunder shivered through the floor and walls of the concrete house like an electric shock.

"Lawd Jesus!" she whimpered.

The springs creaked as he climbed into bed with her.

"No use me so rough, Archie," she whispered urgently.

"Shut up."

"Lawd Jesus!" she wailed as the bed springs gave off a clamorous squeaking and slammed loudly into the wall.

Then she was whispering and moaning while he lunged and undulated violently on top of her. Her cries rang through the concrete bungalow, rising above the sounds of rain and thunder, until suddenly the spring stopped rattling and a guttural moan burst from the bed.

He rolled off her with a sigh. She sat up and rubbed her crotch, massaging the soreness with her fingertips, glancing slyly at him out of the corners of her eyes.

"You tek me mind off de thunder, boy," she said, stroking him.

"Shut up," he whispered. "Please shut up."

The doctor stared gloomily at the ceiling, ignoring her hand that tapped fondly against his chest and ran playfully down his body.

"I can't believe what's happening to me," he said morosely.

"What you talk 'bout now?"

"I can't believe I'm never going to be able to write down what I feel. I'm never going to be able to express all the things inside my mind, all the things I feel!"

"What you have inside you brain?" She raised herself up on her elbow and stared down at him with interest.

"You don't understand," he said wearily. "You're just

211

a stupid, ignorant woman. You'll never be able to understand."

"Why you always love to call me nasty name, eh?" she
grumbled, curling up beside him.

"Shut up and let me sleep." He closed his eyes.

"Me love you. Me understand you like woman suppose
to understand man."

"You're so stupid," he groaned. "I don't know why I
even bother having you around me."

"When it get big again," she said confidently, snuggling
up beside him, "you goin' want some more."

Curled up beside him on the bed, she listened to the
sounds of the storm against the walls and roof of the house.

"Lawd Jesus," she lamented in a small, suffering voice,
"you see what punishment you put woman on dis earth to
endure from man."

A few minutes later, she fell asleep.

After nine days of torrential rain, the storm blew over
and brilliant sunshine flooded the skies. On the first clear
morning, the doctor eagerly set out for his country rounds.
He was glad to be out of the house and away from the
woman, who had been steadily getting on his nerves.

He took the road through Constant Spring that wound
over the Junction pass through the mountains. He drove
carefully past mud-slides, dead animals, fallen trees, and a
countless number of gaping potholes. At one point, he had
to come to a complete stop because a portion of the road
bed had collapsed down the hillside, leaving a jagged rip in
the asphalt. A van inched past the chasm in the road, hugging
the muddy slopes of the mountain. As the doctor skirted the
fissure, he glanced down the hill and saw a huge chunk of the
asphalt pavement tilted out of the muddy slopes as though
a road had suddenly burst out of the centre of the earth.

A thin blue mist hung over the green countryside. People

212

loitered on the side of the road, glad to be able to stand once again in the sunshine. Naked children ran after the passing traffic. Dogs barked and chased each other up and down the road.

The doctor pulled the car off the road, got out, and hiked down a muddy trail into the gorge through which the Wag Water River ran. The river was in spate, churning over swollen banks with a reptilian hiss. The water was a dark red and littered with every conceivable kind of debris, refuse, and garbage that swirled and spun in the raging current. In the middle of the river was an enormous, upturned tree, its crown caught in a cataract, its muddy roots bristling out of the churning brown water.

The doctor stood on the slope of the hill staring down at the fast-moving river. His shoes were already covered by an inch of mud. He held on to the wet branch of a bush to steady himself.

"Morning, sah," a deep voice whispered behind him.

Startled, the doctor turned and found a black cultivator sitting on the muddy slopes and staring gloomily at the river.

"Good morning," he said crisply, turning his attention back to the river.

"De river mad dis morning," the man said.

"Yes, I can see that."

"She kill me only pig. See how she eat de pig dere."

The doctor turned and looked at the cultivator, and saw where he was pointing.

Against the far muddy bank, wedged between two mud-stained boulders, was a bloated dead pig lying on its back, its stiff, stumpy legs thrusting rigidly into the air. Brown water cascaded in a smooth hump over the head of the pig; across its throat, the muddy water rolled, as taut and smooth as a garrotte.

"Me see de river reach up and grab de pig," the man said dolefully, "but me could do nothin'. De pig was trying to eat on de bank, when de river grab him. Now him eating me

213

pig."

"You mean to say," the doctor said firmly, "that you saw the animal fall in."

"No, sah. Me mean to say dat me see de river grab him and pull him under."

"Bloody nonsense," the doctor muttered. He started up the trail.

"Me see it wid me own two eye, sah," the cultivator grumbled, watching the white man clamber up the trail. "Me no care whether or not white man want believe me. Me see de river drown de pig wid me own two eye."

The doctor hiked up to the road, the hiss of the churning river fading behind him. He got into his car and resumed his journey to St. Thomas.

"Superstitious idiots!" he muttered, honking to pass a whining, swaying truck that crawled up the hill, trailing a billowing cloud of diesel smoke out of its exhaust.

But all through the days, as he mended limbs, treated sores, bandaged wounds, he could not get the sight of the bloated, dead pig out of his mind, nor forget the doleful sound of the cultivator's voice. He had been on this God-forsaken island too long, he told himself grimly. Too damn long.

Chapter 17

The day came to the painted canoe. The night shrank from it. The stars withdrew. The ocean was seized by a deathlike quiescence.

So there was only the painted canoe, and the man, and this day. Zachariah struggled out of the bottom of the canoe, raised his eyes and looked at this twenty-eighth day that he had been at sea. On the horizon the day sat, rakish and mournful as a spider. There was neither love in it, nor joy, nor laughter. There was nothing of the loveliness of the earth in it. It was pinched and grey and starved. The day and the man stared hard at each other.

The man was shrunken and frail. His body was pared down to bone. His lips were shredded with wounds. His ankles were swollen. The teeth marks of the shark in his leg throbbed with pain.

Zachariah was so weak that when he raised himself to look across the ocean at the day, he could barely see because his eyes were close to blindness.

You know the sun, how mighty it is, how incandescent and burning; and you know the sky, boneless and immense, having neither fringe nor edge nor dimension; and you know the sea, vaster than the land itself, more subtle and beguiling than the stars; you know these, how lordly they are: and there, pitted against these, was a weak, hungry black man whose body hung with bone.

But Zachariah was nearly mad. He had been at sea now for twenty-eight days. He had been alone and friendless. The shark had eaten his flesh. The sun had scorched him. The sky had stretched its jointless limbs above him. The ocean had sung to him like a mother. He had eaten nothing but fish. He looked at the day, and he laughed.

But he could not laugh too much because his lips would crack open and bleed. His tongue was swollen with thirst, and could not stand the pain of laughing. He was so weak that he could not even manage the laughter of a young man in Charity Bay. Nevertheless, when he saw the day, he laughed, because he was nearly mad.

He lay in the bottom of the canoe and the boat drifted. He lay and blew heavy with the strain of laughing. He lay and told himself to stay huddled in the bottom of the canoe, to think of the son who would not become the cheese, or of the son who was like a fish, or to think of his woman who had the temper of a lunatic.

But he could no longer bring himself to think, nor to dream, because of his great weariness.

The day watched the man writhing in the bottom of the painted canoe.

When Zachariah moved his limbs, he appeared ludicrous and slow, like a great unshelled snail. His muscles were so sore and stiff that he could barely move. In the bottom of the canoe were the bodies of some dead fish, and the bones of a few eaten fish. And there, too, beside the dead fish and the spines of dead fish, were the dreams that had kept Zachariah alive for these countless days. Now they were lean and wingless, and his mind could no longer fly on them.

The sun came out. It came out slow and songless, this lover of bone. It came out fussily from behind a low cloud, and it hunched suspiciously on the horizon, moving like a sleepy watchman.

The sky cleared and stretched out without a creak, and its great blue unsheathed above the painted canoe.

The sea woke and began to sing, and to rustle her webs against the black hull of the canoe, and she sang of love and joy in the voice of a mother.

The three of them were now waiting. This was the day they would kill the man. In the bottom of the black hulled canoe was the man, sick with longing and weariness.

And as the sun and the sky and the sea waited, Zachariah tried to cry but could not because he was too thirsty, and wanted to dream, but could not because he was too sick, and wanted to think about his son or his woman, but could not because there was no strength for thinking left in him. So he lay there in the bottom of the canoe and endlessly it swung on the face of the ocean, oscillating like a compass needle.

The sun rose higher and the heat spread across the ocean as the sun began to chew on bone. Of love and of memory the ocean sang, inviting the man into its loveless blue. The sky unbeaded its immensity that strikes wonder and fear into every heart.

He did not stir, this man. He lay in the bottom of the canoe and tried to recall past loveliness. He had had a childhood. A mother had loved him.

Out of the sun, the sky, and the sea, childlike and innocent, came the sleep.

Zachariah shook his head and the canoe shivered. He would not sleep. He tried to think. He tried to raise himself. His muscles strained; joints and cartilage snapped. He raised himself and reached over the side of the canoe and washed his face. His lips burned and stung. He shook his head to clear away the sleep. Crawling into the middle of the canoe, he ran out the oars and tried to row.

The oars dipped sluggishly into the water. He leaned against the oars. The small canoe rocked but did not move. His head collapsed against his chest.

He could not row. His strength was gone. Well, then he would sail. He tried to set the sail but he was too weak. He tangled the rope around the center thwart and could not free it. He hung his head and rested.

The canoe waited. The sun waited. The sky and the sea, they too waited. But the sleep did not wait. Waif-like and friendless on this vast ocean, it whimpered longingly to the man.

He could not sleep. Gritting his teeth, he swore he would not sleep. He would stay awake and remember. He would think and stave off the sleep with his thoughts.

But everything begged him to sleep. The sea whispered and moaned of sleep. Her song was lovely and beguiling. The sky arched overhead. The heat weakened him. And so to keep himself from succumbing to the sleep, he began to think of the worst misery he had ever known. He thought about his dead daughter.

The daughter was born first, long before the sons, at a time when he grew crops on the wild land in the bush country. She came into the world weak and small, and with an unquenchable hunger for milk. Moreover, the midwife cut her badly, and out of her stomach a small tube protruded. The cut began to heal and the tube flowered into a thick scab. In those days, only Port Antonio had a doctor.

But the child was too weak to travel such a distance by bus. Carina wrapped her in a blanket and laid the child to her breasts. She sucked with a maddened hunger.

Feeding could not satisfy her. She cried and begged for more. Then the fever came. It stole upon her. With no more than the life of days in her heart, she began to die.

They saw it happening. Carina was weak and exhausted. She was a young woman then and giving life to a child had ripped her insides. She lay helpless on the bed. When she moved, blood spurted out of her.

And he, he did not know what to do. He had no nipple to give the child to suck. He gave her his finger and she mouthed it and sucked it, and when nothing came out of it, she wailed her hunger. So he took her into his arms and sang to her.

He held her, and she quivered against his chest, and she wept, and he sang to her. But she was too young to understand song. All she understood was her mad, desperate hunger. She cried; her limbs shook and trembled.

Death came, fluttering through the waving limbs of the child. Sick and bleeding on the bed, Carina moaned and talked in a delirium. The child shivered with a fever. Great spasms seized her, beating her arms and legs like shattered wings. The zinc roof house trembled and shook with her spasms.

He ran into the night, screaming for the midwife to come. Mrs. Wilson heard and ran to fetch the woman at the other end of the village. He ran back into the house to sit with his daughter, to beg her not to die, to sing songs to her of life and of hope.

He sang to the child. He held her in his arms and huddled her against his bosom to keep the warmth of life in her. He sang the old songs. She cried and shook, and a frail, inconsolable trembling rushed over her. The neighbours came and gathered around him, and the walls of the house twitched with frantic, tumbling shadows.

And he was singing. He was singing of loveliness and of laughter, and singing with all his might and with all his heart, singing and chanting and breaking out into as much song as he was capable of, to sing away death from his daughter. There was such a mad, unbelievable singing coming from him. Everyone in the room drew away from him while he clutched the body of his child and sang to her as her small limbs ticked off the final stiff strokes of death.

He held her, gathered her into his arms as one would gather fragility itself, and sang. She quivered, and her body throbbed of death, and squirmed of death, and wilted to death, while he sang of life, and he sang of hope, and he sang and chanted of love. As he held her, gathered inside his arms as a sorrowing man might cradle the consolations of his life, right there, death came to her and devoured her.

219

The small body leaped, its limbs driven by a convulsive stiffness. Then the child was dead, her lifeless body hardening against his bosom, as he sang.

In the bottom of the painted canoe, Zachariah came back to himself, and he was weeping.

There was the sun, and the sky, and the sea, and the painted canoe; and in its bottom, a black man who wept. But now there was no weakness in him, or sleep.

For the sun had no greater misery to give than he now remembered; and the sea had no stronger love to sing than he had sung to his daughter.

It was an old enemy, this death. It comes as sleep. It passes as the sun. It dances as the sea. It is fringeless as the sky. It has a passionate hatred for man. It has a grievous longing for stone. But he, he would never willingly give in to it. Never.

The man wept for his dead child, and as he wept, an indomitable rage for life burned inside him.

"Me not sleeping," he whispered fiercely through his tears.

He sat upright in the middle of the canoe and began to row. The small painted canoe heeled to the touch of the oars then swung and whispered through the waves.

Untangling the rope from around the centre thwart, Zachariah set the sail, steering towards the horizon. The canoe soughed through the seas. Across its stubby bow, the tip of a blue mountain lumbered on the horizon, crouched there, and waited.

220

Chapter 18

When Zachariah sailed into Charity Bay, men went wild with joy and wept like children; women threw themselves on the beach and kissed the sand; children wailed with fear and clung to their mothers. For it was not one who acted so, or two, or even three, but all who lived in Charity Bay, and some who squatted in the bush, and some who lived in Manchioneal and Hector's River, who heard and came and also went mad with jubilation. Even a passing bus stopped and the passengers went down to the beach to see why the people were so joyful, and when these strangers heard the story, even they swirled and danced around Zachariah and the beached canoe. The bus driver, who lives in the parish of St. Thomas, wept when he heard about the miraculous return of Zachariah, and called on his dead wife to bear witness. Their differences and divisions forgotten, the crowd screamed their joy in such a mighty voice that the fish heard and were downhearted and swam far out into the bottomless sea, and for days afterwards the fishing was bad. How many have seen such a day, when the solemn, the old, the bearded, the drunken, all gambolled and pranced light-heartedly like dogs in the spring?

Even today, a stranger would not believe the stories they tell about that day. For they say that the fisherman Zachariah, lost at sea for innumerable days, bitten by a savage shark, burned by the sun, did not crawl onto land begging mercy and foaming at the mouth like a man with fits; did not tear off his shirt and scream like an infant for the earth that was his mother; did not blubber or talk foolishness as if loneliness

221

had robbed him of his senses — did none of these unmanly things. They say that when he came back, after the misery and loneliness of countless days pitted against the mightiness of the ocean that growls in a voice no man can match; against the pitiless sun that loves only bone; against the husked and empty skies that fill all hearts with terror and wonder; against the beast shark that had nearly severed his limb with its teeth; when he came back from passing days and nights among these enemies of all men, he was ragged and thin and torn and ugly as ever, but his back was stiff, his senses clear, and he had all his manly dignity. He did not even stink from all those days alone in a small canoe with dead fish, for he had washed himself in the ocean just before he sailed into Charity Bay.

Some say he wept when his woman ran to him, and held him, and squeezed his body with all her great strength, nearly toppling him over. Others say that all wept but he, that he was joyful and glad beyond weeping. And some say that he moaned with love and joy for the land of his childhood when his feet touched the shores of Jamaica, and his eyes saw the familiar faces, houses, canoes, trees, and dogs of the village. And still others claim that after the expressions of joy and love exchanged with his woman, his first words were that a mother should never favour one child over another, but no one sensible would believe that a man after such suffering would say such a foolish and well-known thing.

Arm in arm with Carina and his sons, he limped wearily to his small house, for his wounds still troubled him. From inside the house loud crying and wailing could be heard as he was reunited with his own bed.

While he went off to his home with his family, the fishermen gathered curiously around the Lucky P. The small black hulled canoe rested on the beach, the edge of her furled sail rippling in the morning breeze. Fingers touched her gunwales and stroked the wounds in her underbelly made by the teeth of the shark. The fishermen hauled her high on the beach and covered her from bow to stern with coconut fronds so that the sun would not dry her out, causing her painted hull to strip and peel and crack. The yellow sail was hung out to dry, the mast leaned against a coconut tree. Then the fishermen sat on the sand in a circle around the painted canoe, touching the teeth grooves of the shark, wondering aloud about the size of the beast that had tried to eat Zachariah, exchanging stories about the wicked fish of the sea. A few of them drove the dogs away from the house of Zachariah, so that he could sleep undisturbed by barking or growling.

He slept only two hours; then he was up and limping restlessly in the yard, pursued by Carina who scolded him and pushed him back into the house. He fell asleep again and slept this time for twelve hours. He awoke and ate and went outside to look at the lights of the canoes floating over the fishing reef beyond the clutch of the bay's arms.

Carina came out and led him back inside to the bed.

"Woman, you gone mad? Me too weak," he muttered. But she led him inside and they made love as if they were young again. And it did not matter who rode on top of who, for that quarrel was long forgotten in the heat of lovemaking. Indeed, each was so willing to give in to the other, that each insisted that the other one be on top, which nearly led to a new quarrel. After making love, they fell asleep in each other's arms.

Five hours later, he awoke. It was still dark, and Carina was again on top of him, caressing and fondling his body.

"Rass," he grunted, "you don't see me suffering from wounds?"

But they made love again, slept in each other's arms, and were still sleeping when the sons awoke and stole away to school without breakfast.

When he awoke, the village nurse came by to look at the wounds the shark had inflicted on his leg. She touched

223

his leg with her fingers, pressing into the muscle, and asking him questions about pain. Then she scratched his toes to examine his reflexes and made him stand up and extend the leg to see if there was any damage to the muscle. When she was done, she said that she'd never met a tougher negar, and that though the nerves in the foot may have been damaged, causing the numbness, the leg was well on its way to healing itself. She left, shaking her head in wonderment and muttering about how tough a negar Zachariah was, a remark that aroused Carina to anger. But Zachariah did not mind, taking it, instead, as a compliment.

That Saturday, there was a lavish celebration. The fishermen sold fish and bought a fat goat, and it was led bleating and crying into Charity Bay. Early on Saturday morning Mr. Ferguson bound the hind legs of the goat with a rope and hoisted the screaming animal upside down from the limb of a tree. With a deft stroke of his machete he opened a thin red slit in the goat's throat. While the carcass drained, the fishermen sat nearby, drinking white rum and playing dominoes.

Lowering the dead goat, they skinned it with sharp knives. The head and feet were severed and given to the women to boil into a peppery soup known as "mannish water". The remainder of the carcass was hacked into small pieces and placed in a kerosene tin to be curried.

That night, the men and women danced in the village hall to the music of a hired sound system and feasted on the goat. Everyone in the village was there. Mr. Wilson was there, drunk and dancing with Mrs. Wilson and with younger women. Mr. Roper got so drunk that, like his wife, he talked in tongues. Mrs. Roper jumped and leaped to the reggae music and whispered into the ears of a young man on the dance floor. Even Mr. Hemmings got drunk. But Mrs. Hemmings, who said she was reforming, did not get drunk, for she sipped only coconut water and stood near her husband scolding him the way he often used to scold her.

224

Even the constable was there. He came all the way from Port Antonio on his Honda. He was resplendent and shining in his new uniform, and he had polished his holster and gun until they glittered. The young women gathered around the constable and criticized the way his uniform had been ironed and berated him for being a bachelor. The fishermen shook his hand and made him feel welcome. And even when all were drunk no one called the constable "Babylon", which is a name the angry call the police and which the police do not like, for it implies that they are as wicked and sinful as the ancient Babylonians of the Bible. But none called the constable that provoking name.

Zachariah himself got drunk. He did not mean to. He did not like to have his mind confused by rum nor to wake up the following morning and not remember what had gone on the night before. He had intended to eat goat and drink beer and pretend to be as drunk and merry as everyone else. But Carina began to dance with a younger fisherman and Zachariah, who could not dance, became angry and jealous. He sat in a corner watching them dance. Before he knew what he was doing, he was drinking white rum.

Soon he was so drunk that he did not care whom Carina was dancing with. He began to hold a loud, embarrassing conversation with his dead mother as if she sat beside him in a chair. Himself in a stupor, Mr. Wilson came over and Zachariah introduced his mother to the old fisherman. Mr. Wilson bowed to the duppy mother and told her that she had borne a magnificent, though ugly, son. Neglecting his mother, Zachariah and Mr. Wilson then sang ribald songs in a loud chorus. Mrs. Wilson came and took her husband home, leading him, still singing at the top of his voice, past the silent, dark canoes.

Left by himself in a corner, Zachariah sang rude songs in a raucous voice — the sort of songs that Seddie used to sing. His mother got vexed and went away. Zachariah repented and began to weep. He stumbled across the dance floor pleading with the angry duppy mother not to leave him. A crowd of drunken fishermen staggered after him also pleading and shouting at the duppy to stay. Even the constable, who was blind drunk, went with them and offered to shoot his pistol over the duppy's head to bring her back.

Chased through the dark village street, the stubborn duppy would not heed, so the men staggered back towards the hall singing rude songs, trailed by a pack of howling village dogs.

A fight started. Emboldened by his drunkenness, Mr. Lewis went into the corner where his morose, truculent wife sat, grabbed her by the nape of the neck, and beat her. Everyone formed a noisy circle around the grappling couple, pushing and shoving and shouting encouragement to one or the other.

The constable elbowed his way through the screaming throng and tried to pull the couple apart, but the crowd roughly pushed him aside and the fight continued. Bewildered, the constable stood at the edge of the crowd and tried to pull his gun. But in his stupor, he could not free the gun from its holster, so he demonstrated his disapproval by staggering outside and falling asleep beside his Honda.

Meanwhile, Mr. Lewis trounced Mrs. Lewis and drove her bawling from the hall and was borne triumphantly around the room on the shoulders of the crowing, victorious men, while the women hissed and booed and threw goat bones at him.

In the heat of the row, Carina challenged Zachariah to wrestle. Downcast and melancholy about his mother, Zachariah refused, and instead they staggered home and fell asleep in each other's arms.

The party broke up, some couples managing to make it back to their houses, others falling asleep on the beach beside the canoes. Some even dropped in the hall and began to snore immediately.

So drunk had the villagers been that the next morning

the church was only half full. Parson Mortimer, who knew about last night's binge, told a story about a man who had died in a drunken state and whom the Lord immediately delivered to the devil. In turn, the devil immersed the drunken sinner in a cauldron of boiling white rum. For the next hour, the Parson described how the man was boiled by the devil in the bubbling white rum, how his nose boiled off, how his eyes shrivelled and popped out of their sockets, how his skin — originally black — turned lobster red. Mr. Wilson fell asleep during the description of these horrors and snored so loudly that his wife woke him with a sharp kick in the skin.

Subdued and hung-over, the congregation shuffled gloomily out of the church. The Parson ran around to the front door to tell them individually how hideous each would look after being boiled in a cauldron of hellishly hot rum. As Mr. Wilson filed past, the Parson shouted to him that after he had been boiled by the devil for a thousand years, his hair would turn a hundred times whiter than it already was. Mr. Wilson scowled and muttered "rass" several times under his breath.

Chastened and guilty, everyone stayed in his own house that day, sleeping off the effects of the white rum.

A week later, Zachariah went back to sea. During the week, he upended the canoe and applied boiling pitch to the grooves made in her hull by the shark. He melted the pitch and swabbed it over the grooves like an unguent. While the pitch dried in the sun, he went to the village shop and played dominoes and told and retold the story of the hammerhead many times. But after a week of resting, he was ready again to go back to sea.

That first night, the other fishermen drifted near his canoe and kept a watchful eye on the Lucky P, their harpoons ready to fend off sharks. Many of the fishermen were filled with dread, fearing that the sea would be malicious and spiteful because Zachariah had escaped her. So they circled protectively around his canoe at nights, pretending to be fishing in the vicinity, and keeping a sharp lookout for the wiles of the sea.

This continued for a week until Zachariah angrily told them to leave him alone, for he could not fish among such a cluster of canoes. By the following week, he was fishing where he had always fished, near the canoe of Mr. Wilson, and, as always, they kept an eye out for each other.

Three weeks after he had landed in Charity Bay, Zachariah caught a sixty-pound kingfish with his mangrove-dyed line. Men said it was the biggest fish anyone had ever caught with such a thin line. And it was a wonder that the fish had been near the reef, for the kingfish is an ocean-going fish which does not love shallow water. Surely, the men said, Zachariah was the best fisherman in Portland, to have caught such a strong fish with a line that other men use on the foolish goatfish and the devious wrenchman.

After all his years in Charity Bay, Zachariah was finally given a nickname. It was not a belittling nickname, but a name celebrating his strength and prowess. Men began to call him "Kingfish."

And so Zachariah settled back into his customary way of life. Men told and retold his story to strangers who passed through the village. Strangers from other parishes, on seeing Zachariah in the streets, paused and begged him to let them see the wounds the hammerhead had made, and to tell them the story of how he had blinded the ugly shark. Children sometimes followed him from the village shop, or loitered near him on the beach offering to help him ready the canoe for sea, scuffling among themselves for the privilege of holding the ends of the net Zachariah was weaving. Forward young women, who had never before cared the least about him, now hailed him familiarly and tried to draw him into rude conversations. But Zachariah wanted no part of such doings, for he was already in love with one woman and had no desire for any other.

But among all the celebration of his return, there was one in the village who was not glad that Zachariah had come back. When the nurse told the English doctor about the miraculous return of the ugly fisherman, the doctor walked silently to the louvred window, peered out at the sea, and gave off a cynical, bitter laugh, which caused the nurse to stare at him with wonder and astonishment.

Chapter 19

In November, the Christmas breeze wafts down the Gulf of Mexico and soughs across the Greater Antilles, cooling the ragged chain of islands that grows out of the ocean from the Florida Keys to the furrowed brow of South America. Because they blow every year during the Christmas season, these trade winds are known in Jamaica as the "Christmas breeze".

All over the island, people eagerly look forward to the time when the Christmas breeze blows. Children make their bamboo kites during the summer months and wait for the Christmas breeze to fly them. Labourers and cultivators long for the Christmas breeze, which freshens and cools the days, causing the cane fields to sway, the fronds of coconut trees to windmill, the sea to ripple like immense fields of tall grasses blooming between the craggy arms of promontories, bays, and peninsulas.

Old Jamaicans love this time of the year, for the air is brisk and healthful, as an exaltation of freshness and sweet autumnal smells sweeps over the earth. In these cool evenings, the old people sit under the awnings of shops and on the sagging porches of wooden houses, gaze fondly at the antics of their grandchildren, and remember their own long-lost days of childhood innocence. It is as though the breeze blows the spirit of Christmas from across the sea, bringing a sparkle of anticipation and joy to the eyes of children, bringing memories to the minds of the old, bringing excitement and expectation to the hearts of the young. The song of birds, the sounds of music, lilt through the air. Shopkeepers hang streamers across the windows of their shops. The poinciana leaves turn red, bleeding, the villagers say, with the spilled blood of the Saviour.

When the Christmas breeze came this year, the people of Charity Bay were glad. The fishermen love the breeze, for it helps the canoes scud out to sea and beyond the reach of the bay to the shoals where the fish are taken. The women love the breeze because it brings the giddy scents of blossoms to the air. But this year the Christmas breeze brought a cough to Zachariah — now known throughout the village as Kingfish — and it was a cough he could not shake.

It began, Zachariah thought, as a cold, except that he had no fever, his nose did not run, yet he had a persistent cough even at nights when he fished. At first, Zachariah said it was a dry cold that he had picked up from the damp nights at sea. He drank lime juice mixed with wild honey, and sipped on a green bush tea that Carina prepared as a remedy. But nothing seemed to affect this cough. It got worse; moreover, he coughed so much that the other fishermen complained that the constant hacking noise was ruining their fishing. Mr. Wilson suggested to Zachariah in a kindly way that he stay ashore until the cough was cured.

But after he had stayed ashore for four nights, during which he prowled restlessly around the house and walked down to the beach to stare out at the dancing lights of the fishing canoes, the cough got no better; in fact, it got worse. He was coughing so often and so loud that he could hardly sleep. He also began to lose weight. Suddenly, he knew that his sickness was not an ordinary cough. He visited the English doctor on Thursday at the village clinic.

The English doctor looked down his throat with a flashlight and listened to his lungs with the stethoscope. Then he walked across the small concrete room which was so empty that his footfalls made a faint echo, and he stood by the louvres and stared morosely out at the sea.

Zachariah sat on the wooden bench, his shirt off, and waited to be told what his sickness was.

"I'm afraid it's quite serious," the doctor said, his back to Zachariah.

"What, sah?" Zachariah asked, blinking with incomprehension.

"Your cough," the doctor began, waving his hand. He turned and faced Zachariah.

"I may as well be blunt with you, Pelsie," he said, looking into the eyes of the ugly fisherman, "I'm not much good at mincing words. You're very, very sick. There's not much I can do for you. I'm sorry."

Zachariah blinked furiously, and stared at the Englishman, who would not meet his gaze.

"Sick, sah?" Zachariah asked. "How sick? What sick me?"

"Do you remember when you came to see me a few months ago, before you had your mishap at sea?"

"Yes, sah. Me remember."

"Do you remember I sent you to Port Antonio to have an X-ray taken?"

Zachariah nodded. It all flashed through his mind — the long, wearying bus ride to Port Antonio; the interminable wait on the uncomfortable wooden benches crammed between bleeding, moaning, suffering people; the rough mulatto nurse who scolded him for not standing up straight enough before the machine.

"The results of the X-ray came while you were thought to be lost at sea. I'm afraid you have cancer."

Zachariah did not know exactly what the word "cancer" meant, but he knew that it was a word whispered fearfully by old people.

"What you saying to me, sah?"

"I'm trying to tell you that you're terminally ill. I'm sorry. I wish I didn't have to say that. But there's nothing at all I can do for you, except perhaps give you some pain pills."

"You mean," Zachariah stared at the doctor, "that me

232

goin' dead soon?"

"Yes. I'm afraid that's exactly what I mean."

A look of impenetrable obduracy came over Zachariah's face, and right before his eyes, the doctor saw the bony black face stiffen with determination and stubbornness, saw the light blazing in the shrunken black eyes, saw the hard, unyielding lines that bulwarked that swollen, monstrous jawbone, and understood why this nondescript man had survived all those days alone at sea.

"When me blow away," Zachariah growled, his eyes blazing, "everything try kill me. De sea, de sun, de breeze, de shark. All of dem try and kill me."

Now all the Englishman could see were the eyes in front of him, the eyes that raged and burned with a brutal and obdurate lust for life, with the most horrible, insensate determination that the doctor had ever seen; and there was such a wild, fanatical intensity to those eyes that the Englishman almost laughed hysterically when he remembered where he was, and who this pathetic man was, and what a miserable, grovelling life he was fighting to preserve. The doctor felt a sudden flash of rage at this ugly creature's unreasonable will to live. It made no sense at all to him — it was stupidity beyond reasoning.

"All o' dem try to kill me," Zachariah muttered, his eyes smoldering and intense, "but me come back! Me come back!"

The lines in the face tightened and drew taut and, as if it were a physical force, the Englishman saw and felt the brute will of this impossible creature raging in his eyes and stiffening his limbs until his body quivered and shook.

"And wid dis, too," Zachariah declared, "it not goin' beat me. Dis no more powerful dan de sea. No stronger dan de sun. No mightier dan de wind. No wickeder dan de shark. Dem don't beat me. Dis not going beat me."

The doctor averted his head and looked out of the window at the ruffled ocean furled against the ragged coast-

233

line of the bay. He was no longer seeing an ugly fisherman sitting on the bench, expressing his will to survive. Instead, he saw billions and billions of stupid, microscopic, primordial cells, infinitesimally formed into strings of throbbing red organs, muscle, bones, and tissue; and impregnated throughout these moronic, unreasoning billions of slimy cells was the life force of nature — the insatiable drive to keep wriggling, to carry on all the vast and singular idiocy of nature, all the pointless, futile orchestration of nature's blind, irrational, stupid lust for life. And it did not matter whether the cells were formed into the slippery head of a worm, the dirty snout of a sow, or the gangling body of an ugly black fisherman — all that mattered to the greedy, cruel, parsimonious bitch of nature, was the useless prolongation of life into seconds, minutes, hours, days, months, years — all that counted was the pneumatic pulsations of cell membranes, that the heart should pound, and the bowels should churn, and the cells should ply their secretive and idiotic trade with one another forever, blindly, stupidly, incontinently throbbing to the silent rhythms of life.

The doctor grabbed onto the window sill to steady himself, for he was suddenly overwhelmed by such a monstrous vision that he felt giddy. What did poetry matter, or art, or music, to these slimy, microscopic, insensate cells? All they valued was life at all cost, life at any sacrifice, no matter how tawdry, stupid, futile or meaningless — the nasty, mindless objective was the prolongation of life.

Suddenly, for the first time in his life, the doctor was seized by an apocalyptic insight into the nature of God. God was not limbed or visible. God was one of these tiny, noiseless, slimy cells — an infinitesimal drop of protoplasm swirling through the black voids of the body — the master germ cell that slunk away from the rotting carcass of organs and tissue felled by death, stole into the crotch of some unsuspecting woman and burrowed like a parasite into her womb, awaiting fertilization and conception to set into

234

motion again another frenzied explosion of cellular growth, another pointless, inane burst of life.

The doctor moved away from the window and took in the pitifully ugly fisherman who sat before him and followed his every movement with burning black eyes. For a second, he was seized by a wild, insane desire to shoot Zachariah in the head and put him out of his misery.

The doctor sat down, with a loud sigh.

"I suppose you believe in God," he said, staring hard at Zachariah.

Zachariah nodded gravely. "Of course, sah."

He wanted to add, however, that he was not one of those thankless, useless negars who believed in running to God over every little thing. He was about to explain that when he was being stalked by the shark, and scorched by the sun, and terrified by the emptiness and loneliness of the naked ocean, not once did he grovel and beg God to help him. He wanted to tell the Englishman about his idea that God does not like to be bothered by the petty worries of the negar, and that God would not help a really desperate man who had, in the past, run to him over every little trouble. But the doctor was not the sort of man to whom one could confide such personal beliefs, so Zachariah merely nodded, to emphasize that he believed in God, and gave no other information about his special beliefs.

The doctor walked to a plain wooden chest that was hung on the unpainted wall, took some pills from a bottle, and poured them into a brown envelope.

He started to write out instructions for using the pills on the envelopes, when he looked up at Zachariah and asked, "Can you read?"

Zachariah hung his head with shame. "Not too good, sah," he muttered.

"Take one of these pills when the pain becomes unbearable. Try not to take more than four in one day. Do you understand?"

"Me don't need no pill, sah," Zachariah said.

"Don't use them if you don't want to. But take them anyway, just in case you change your mind."

"Me not going use no pill, sah," Zachariah said stubbornly, putting on his shirt.

"Take them anyway!" the doctor snapped, extending he packet.

Zachariah reluctantly took the pills, climbed down off the wooden bench and shuffled out of the room, closing the door carefully behind him.

"You'll be in heaven within three months," the doctor muttered sarcastically after the fisherman had gone. Then he uttered a curse and punched the wooden chest so hard that it fell off the wall with a tremendous crash.

"What happen, sah?" the nurse asked, bursting excitedly into the room.

"Nothing," the doctor replied, rubbing his skinned knuckles. "Get out and close the door. Give me five minutes alone before you send in the next patient."

"Yes, sah," the nurse said, rolling her eyes as though she suspected foul play.

The doctor walked over to the louvred window and stared out at the shining sea.

Zachariah said nothing to Carina about his illness, though she pried constantly and asked many questions about what the doctor had said. He brushed off her concern and went down to the beach where the canoe was hauled up on the sand. Coughing and hacking as loudly as ever, he prepared the canoe for the night's fishing.

That night he fished under the lee of the dark promontory, away from the other fishermen so that he would not disturb their catch with his coughing. When the night breeze blew and he became chilled, he coughed so much that he could hardly concentrate on the fishing. He took only a few scrawny wrenchmen and half a dozen parrot fish. But he

236

had made up his mind that he would no longer fish near the other canoes.

It was, however, impossible for him to hide his sickness. His coughing got progressively worse. The sickness wreaked a terrible ruin on his body. It pared away his muscles, drew harsh lines down his face, feasted on his great strength, and left him helplessly coughing. It uncovered haunting blue shadows under his eyes. His haunch bones showed, bursting flat edges through his shrunken abdomen. He became cadaverous and gaunt, and everyone who saw him knew that death was stalking nearby.

One night he coughed so hard that he became weak and trembling and could not even row the canoe past the tides of the breaking reef. He had to return to shore and be led home on the arm of Carina. The next week Carina went to see the Englishman.

She waited in the bare concrete room, staring fixedly at her feet and speaking to no one. Then she was standing sullenly before the doctor and asking about Zachariah's sickness while behind them the nurse hovered, perpendicularly centred in the doorway.

"Your husband is very ill, Mrs. Pelsie," the doctor said gently.

"Dey not married, doctor," the nurse sniffed.

"Mind your own goddamn business," the doctor said wrathfully, turning to glower at the nurse, who slunk back into the other room where she could be heard in the background, berating a patient.

Turning his attention to Carina, who still stared defiantly at the bare floor, the doctor looked as if he wished to say something else. Then he shrugged and simply said, "I'm afraid your husband is dying of cancer."

"You lie!" Carina hissed.

"No, I'm sorry. It's the truth."

"Him just blow away! Him just come home from de sea!"

237

"He had cancer even before that. Do you remember the lump he had under his neck?" The doctor tapped his own neck ominously with his forefinger.

"Zach not goin' die!" Carina screamed. She turned and ran out of the room.

Wild and frenzied and hysterical, Carina ran into the bush, past the cleared patch of land where she had first met Zachariah, past the pasture where the villagers graze their goats and heifers, past the small stream that trickles down into Charity Bay and empties into the ocean; past all these she ran like a woman gone mad. Finally, she came to the house of Lubeck, the obeah man. On the floor of Lubeck's house she threw herself and sobbed out what the doctor had just said about Zachariah.

Lubeck kissed his teeth with contempt. The Englishman was mad. Everybody knew that. Moreover, the doctor would soon be dead, for Lubeck himself had killed five chickens on this lunatic's behalf. Lubeck had herbs and weeds that could cure any cancer. Tomorrow, he would come and kill a chicken and sprinkle its blood on the transom of her house and say the proper words. Zachariah would be well again. He would fish and become prosperous and live to see his sons grow into manhood.

Carina had stopped weeping. She was grateful and relieved. For this advice she paid Lubeck a dollar in small change which she had carried tied in a knot in a corner of her handkerchief.

Through the bush she went again, clutching the herbs and weeds as if they could give life, and back down the straggly pathway that dribbled through the thick undergrowth and led from the house of Lubeck. The sun shone and the breeze soughed through the trees and the birds sailed past on the wind, and nowhere among this loveliness could she see death.

When she got to her house, Zachariah was sleeping and coughing even in his sleep. She lit the stove and boiled the herbs and weeds then crept into the doorway and peered into the room where he slept. As she stood there staring at the man she loved, he exploded into another savage round of coughing which battered the bedspring against the wooden wall.

He woke up. She brought a mug full of tea to him. Sitting on the bed, he looked warily into the mug.

"From Lubeck?" he asked suspiciously.

She did not answer, pretending to be engrossed with moving the bed so that the spring would not pound a hole into the wall.

"What you give dat man me money for?" he asked crossly.

"Drink de tea!" she scowled.

He placed his feet on the floor and looked dubiously at the sickly green liquid swirling in the mug.

"De Englishman tell you?" He did not look into her eyes as he asked this.

"Him lie!" she hissed.

"Him go to de university to learn to lie?"

"Him lie!" she snarled even louder. There was no arguing with her when she was in such a stubborn mood.

He shuffled his feet and continued to look sideways at the mug and, after a long pause during which she pretended to be interested in the bedspring, he said, almost in a whisper, "Life funny, eh?"

"Drink de rass tea!" she snapped, determined to listen to no childish prattle about the oddness of life.

He shrugged and drank the tea, making faces and muttering that Lubeck would poison him one day with his foolish bush mixes, then got up and went down to the beach to prepare the canoe for the night's fishing, trailing behind him the loud, rasping, devouring cough.

She stood in the doorway and watched him go, stooped over in the shoulders from the many years of rowing the canoe, limping from the wounds the shark had made in his leg. She watched him as he walked with that peculiar, small-stepped gait of a man who had spent many years of his life in a small boat at sea, and she felt such a surge of protective love well up inside her that there were tears in her eyes.

"Zachie not goin' dead," she muttered, to any malign duppy that loitered in the neighborhood, out for mischief.

"My Zachie not goin' dead till he old and grey. Den we goin' dead together, me and him. You hear, duppy? You hear?"

Her eyes flashing, she looked around in every corner of the small, cluttered house, to see if the duppies understood. And when she saw no shadows move, no grey shapes flit through the shafts of sunlight streaming into the tiny living room, she turned her eyes back to Zachariah, and watched as he loped down towards the beached canoes.

Chapter 20

Word spread throughout the village about Zachariah's sickness. Eyes followed him as he limped past the square. Behind his back, people whispered about his grievous luck. To his face, they shrank from his presence, for all could see the ravaging hand of death upon him.

One morning, the villagers awoke to see a terrifying bird perched on the zinc roof of his house, its black, shiny wings outstretched to catch the warmth of the morning sun. It was a carrion bird, a scavenger that smells death from miles away. Eyes stared at the ugly bird; women cried out in shrill voices. Mr. Wilson, who had just rowed in from a night at sea, rushed across the road and threw a stone at the bird, which flew high up in a tree and peered down at him through the leaves. When Carina came out of the house a few moments later, she saw the silent crowd massed on the beach, staring ominously at her house. From inside the bedroom, through the open window, the sounds of Zachariah's cough drifted down to the beach, sending a shudder through the villagers.

It was the shark, people muttered, the duppy of the fish which Zachariah had blinded, that had invaded his body and was eating him from within. Lizards, killed by mischievous schoolboys, have been known to come back as duppies in the dark of night, to goad and torment their murderers. Butchers, after a day's work, often suffer wailing visions of the animals they slaughtered. For as everyone knows, animals have spirits, which sometimes become vengeful against humans who have harmed them in life. So it was muttered in all the living rooms and shops of the village, that Zachariah was being devoured by a duppy shark.

241

In the village, everyone shunned him, for fear of provoking the wrath of the duppy. No one came to visit him in his house. Fishermen, who a few weeks before had hailed him as a companion, now crossed to the opposite side of the street when he approached. Children, who used to gather around the canoe and beg him to tell the story of how he had blinded the hammerhead, now hid behind tree trunks when he came near. Buxom young woman, who used to sidle up to him on the beach and chat all kinds of rudeness to his face while running their eyes up and down his powerful body, now walked quickly past, their eyes fixed determinedly on the asphalt roadway. And when Zachariah and his family went to church on Sundays, none of the villagers would sit immediately next to him. Only Mr. Wilson was the exception. He continued to visit Zachariah. He walked with him openly in the street. He made it known in all the shops that Zachariah was still his friend, no matter that the duppy devoured him from inside.

The Parson had heard the rumours about Zachariah. He heard about the carrion bird on the roof of his house, and he heard the stories about the malign duppy. He could see with his own eyes that death was stalking Zachariah. For when he looked at him, he could see that Zachariah was becoming shrunken and frail, that his hand trembled when once it had been steady, that the cough wracked him constantly.

One evening, when the soft shadows of the mountains and the trees stretched luxuriantly over Charity Bay, the Parson parked his car before Zachariah's house and knocked on the door to his shack. Zachariah came out and sat on the doorstep and talked with the Parson.

The Parson talked about all kinds of preliminary foolishness. He talked about how the roof of the church was leaking; about how the Christmas breeze did not blow as energetically this year as in years past; about how the Prime Minister had promised electrification for Charity Bay before the end of this decade; and about how the youth of Portland was experiencing a general decline in morality. And all the while he was talking, he looked at Zachariah slyly out of the corners of his eyes, as though he was trying to gauge the effects of the sickness on the temperament of the ugly fisherman.

Zachariah was polite. He did his best to answer all the Parson's forward questions and comments in a sensible way. But he knew that the Parson had some specific reason for coming to see him, and he was curious to hear about it.

The Parson had gotten fatter since Zachariah had blown away. His belly was firm and full as the girth of a barrel. He wore pomade on his hair, which was slicked down in greasy waves that glistened with the colours of the sunset. When the Parson smiled, his teeth flashed with the gold fillings he had gotten in America.

But after a while, the Parson looked at Zachariah and said, "Brodder Zachie, dis sickness take you bad. It take you very bad. Brodder Zachie, I don't want to say dis, except that you is of me flock, and is me duty as shepherd to give religious counselling. Brodder Zachie, de time come for repentance, for a softening o' de heart and a looking forward to God for mercy."

Zachariah laughed. The Parson looked stunned, as though the fisherman had said something profane. But all Zachariah had done was to give a soft, throaty chuckle, like the purring of a contented cat. The chuckle, however, provoked him to another spate of coughing, which brought a cruel gleam into the Parson's eyes, as he surveyed the hacking, trembling fisherman, who doubled over on the doorstep and coughed uncontrollably.

When the coughing had subsided, Zachariah looked across the bay to where the harbour beacon stood on the mountain slope among a grove of banana trees, flashing its light to passing ships day and night.

"Me not ready to dead yet, Parson," Zachariah said with another humourless chuckle, "but when me time to dead come, don't fret youself 'bout me. Me goin' be good and ready."

The Parson squirmed restlessly and looked provoked. He had come to Zachariah's house for a cruel, perverse reason — to see his enemy humbled in the face of death. He had come expecting contrition and apologies for past offenses. But instead, Zachariah was laughing as though he were hale and hearty and sitting with the Parson in a rum bar, not a worry on his shoulders.

Feeling as though he were being mocked, the Parson scowled and looked vexed.

"Dis is not de right attitude to approach de Almighty wid, Pelsie," the Parson said severely, brushing a leaf off his shoe, where the soft evening breeze had blown it. "Dis is not de right manner at all. Dis is de vain, boasty attitude of a man who think him goin' live forever. Dis is how young, healthy man go on all de time. But sick man shouldn't act so stubborn when death peeping at him from 'round de corner."

Zachariah shrugged and looked out to sea, and the Parson saw in his eyes a fiery, stubborn glint which told him that the fisherman was still as intemperate and hard-hearted as ever.

"Westmoreland negar don't dead so easy," Zachariah muttered, his eyes roaming over the mountain range that loomed lush and green behind the village, his ugly jaw locked in an obdurate expression. The Parson became overwrought.

"Listen to me now, Pelsie," he began angrily. The door behind them creaked and Carina stepped out into the softness of the evening and sat beside her man.

The Parson blustered and changed the subject. For the next two minutes, he talked aimlessly about some new foolishness. When he saw that the woman did not intend to return to the house, he stiffly said, "Good evening," and walked to his car.

Carina followed him out onto the road, her hands in the pockets of her loose, calico dress. The Parson thought that she

had come to ask him to say prayers for Zachariah. He was
ready to berate her over her man's stubbornness and vanity,
to tell her that his foolish attitude would put his soul into
jeopardy. But as soon as the Parson had gotten into his car
and looked up at Carina, he knew that she had overheard his
conversation with Zachariah. Her hand came out of her dress
pocket and the blade of a shiny knife glittered between her
fingers.

"You no come back and trouble me husband again," she
whispered fiercely. "You come say one more bad thing to
him, and I goin' cut off you hood."

"Woman, you mad?" the Parson gasped, shuddering at
the thought of his hood being severed.

"You hear what me say, sah?" she hissed, waving the
knife blade against the window.

He started the car, rolled up the window, and drove
away quickly.

Two Sundays later, Zachariah walked out in the middle
of a sermon that he disagreed with. The Parson, on seeing
him tiptoe out of the church, ranted and shrieked and
pounded his fist against the pulpit, becoming so vexed that he
could hardly catch his breath.

Zachariah was so weak now that he could not fish every
night, for he required as much sleep as an infant. He stopped
going to sea every night, and went out instead three nights
a week, always fishing near the lee shore of the promontory
where he could hear the crack of the surf against the rugged
outcropping rocks that thrust deep into the sea, far away
from where the lights of the other fishing canoes drifted.

But he had lost so much weight and had become so weak
that sometimes he could barely row the painted canoe
against the tide that surged through the breaking reef in the
middle of the bay. Carina decided that she would go to sea
with him from now on. When he protested, citing all sorts
of superstitions against women being at sea, she refused to
listen. In the end, she had her way, and he took her out for

a night of fishing.

She took the oars and easily propelled the canoe through the surging current of the breakwater. Zachariah sat in the rear thwart and steered. Soon the canoe was clear of the breakwater and driving down the shoreline towards the craggy arm of the promontory where Zachariah usually fished.

But it was not a successful night of fishing, for Carina was constantly fretting about the two sons, wondering what sort of mischief they would get into. She talked constantly about the strange noises the sea made against the hull of the canoe. Towards morning, after the sliver of the moon had sunk into the sea and the lights of the village had gone out, a large black fin slunk past the wavering glow of light thrown off the bow of the canoe, and she uttered a piercing scream. Zachariah jumped so hard that he nearly fell out of the canoe.

"De shark!" she quailed, pointing to the rippling track the fish had made in the becalmed sea.

"Hush you mouth!" Zachariah scolded.

"But me see de fin!" she said, clinging to the gunwales of the canoe.

Zachariah comforted her as well as he could and determined that he would never again take her out to sea with him. For she was too accustomed to the firmness of the land to get used to the dark, lunging sea, and to the creatures that prowled around the canoe. He told her that no man on the island had a better, more loving woman. He spoke to her as though they were lovers meeting for the first time. But after she had calmed down and no longer flashed her eyes fearfully at every whisper the sea made against the hull of the canoe, he explained to her that he could not go to sea with a woman who made such a fuss over the passing of a harmless shark, that from now on he would fish only two or three times a week to conserve his strength, but he would fish alone.

She argued futilely against his going alone to sea with the

246

sickness upon him, but she saw his eyes in the flickering glare of the kerosene cresset mounted on the bow of the canoe and knew that he had made up his mind. It was just as well, she sighed inwardly. She did not like to be at sea. She was nervous at the sighs and whispers of the ocean, and she was squeamish about the way he drove the knife point through the eyes of the fish, or the way he battered the wriggling fish against the thwart of the canoe. She was not used to seeing the fish wriggling and gasping for life. So after that first night, she never went to sea with him again, although she often made the offer. Her heart, however, was never in it.

Christmas came and still Zachariah had taken none of the pills that the doctor had given him. He was in agony. He made no outcry when he was awake, and no one could read pain in his horrible, shrunken ugliness. But in the nights he whimpered in his sleep, and Carina heard and sat beside him in the darkness, going mad with helplessness and grief. Sometimes she caught a glimpse of his face twisted in a grimace of agony, but if he saw her looking at him, he would immediately begin to whistle or pretend to be staring nonchalantly about him.

Again and again Carina ran through the bush path to Lubeck, coming back with more herbs and weeds and chicken blood. She made soup. She boiled teas. She smeared blood on the transom of their bedroom door. He suffered excruciatingly, but always in a stubborn, determined silence.

Alone at sea, he would sometimes groan out loud when the pain struck with an especial fury. Sometimes he would give off a tremor and double over as though to hold the pain in and stop it from spreading. But when he was in the streets, or when he was where people could see him, no matter how severe the pain was, no matter how much he felt like screaming, he made no outcry, he gave no sign, but continued as always -- stubborn, sluggish, and ugly. No one could tell how much he was suffering.

But there was one in the village who knew — the doctor. When Zachariah no longer came to see him at the clinic, the doctor began to make it a practice of stopping by Zachariah's house at the end of the day. Carina would greet the Englishman with a scowl — for she did not like or trust him — and would sullenly call Zachariah to come into the living room, where the Englishman would be waiting to examine him.

When the Englishman placed the stethoscope against the chest of the fisherman, he heard the cancer hissing inside him like a wrathful snake. He would sit and listen to him breathe and look down his throat and then ask questions about how he felt and whether or not he had taken any of the pills. To all these questions, Zachariah gave polite, perfunctory replies. He did not explain that he was suffering excruciating pain. He did not mention that yesterday he had spat up an ugly, curdled lump of blood. He did not say that last night at sea he had coughed so loud that he had been paralyzed afterwards with breathlessness and had not even the strength to tend to the line on which there was a dancing fish. None of these occurrences did Zachariah confide in the doctor.

But the Englishman knew what he was suffering, for he had had experience with other patients who had died from this kind of cancer. After each examination, the doctor would leave thinking to himself that the fisherman could not last much longer. It was only a matter of time. Sooner or later a blood vessel in his lung would rupture, and he would haemorrhage internally.

At first, the doctor thought it would only be a matter of months. Then, as the fisherman's condition steadily worsened, the doctor thought it would only be a few weeks. And after a couple of weeks, the doctor was sure that the fisherman would only last a few more days. No one, the doctor told himself grimly, could survive with that much cancer growing inside him.

But every week, when the doctor returned to Charity

Bay expecting to hear that the ugly fisherman had died after a violent coughing spell, he would find Zachariah at home resting in preparation for the night's fishing, and the Englishman would be astounded to learn that he was still going to sea. For it was only a matter of days now, the doctor told himself, listening again to the harsh hiss of the cancer inside Zachariah's lungs. He could not last much longer. Next week, the Englishman told himself, as he left the house after another of his already countless visits.

But next week Zachariah would still be there in the dark room resting for the night's fishing, and the woman would still be sullen and gloomy, and the two sons would still be timorous around the strange white man who sat in their house and listened to their father's breathing with a strange instrument. The younger son, Wilfred, came close to the doctor on one of his many visits, and asked questions about how the stethoscope worked, until his mother came and shooed him away from the Englishman.

"Him have a whole heap of brain," Zachariah told the doctor with an apologetic smile.

"I can see that," the doctor said, trying to sound cheerful as he listened to the ominous rattle of cancer inside the fisherman's chest.

Zachariah wanted to tell the doctor about what the Principal had said, but he did not wish to sound too boastful to this white man, who came to his house for nothing and tried to care for his health, for not every man could have an intelligent son. So he said nothing about what the Principal had said, but talked instead to the doctor about many other things, such as his experience with sharks, and how his bitten leg felt, and how good the fishing was in the new spot under the lee shore of the promontory.

Sometimes the doctor would offer to give Zachariah an injection, for he could tell from the hiss of the cancer that the fisherman suffered excruciating pain, but Zachariah would always refuse as though he felt nothing.

249

After each visit, the doctor would be frustrated and angry at the fisherman's stubbornness, which always put him in a perverse, cruel mood, and he would tell himself grimly, "He'll be dead by next week."

But the following week, he would arrive at the small house and be amazed to find Zachariah resting again for another night of fishing as though inside his chest, deep within the catacombs of his lungs, the cancer did not eat away at him.

Then the doctor would leave telling himself, as he drove through the chasmic darkness of the Junction pass, that Zachariah would be dead for sure within the week, and would come back once again to find the ugly fisherman as obdurate and serene as ever, even though the cancer inside him would snarl through the stethoscope, making a bestial sound like an animal disturbed in its lair.

As the months passed, with the fisherman struggling obdurately against the agony of cancer, the doctor got madder and madder at his implacable, unbending attitude in the face of death, at his unyielding stubbornness, his inflexible will to survive, to drag on through the pain that would make ten other men howl for their mothers, that would cause even a saint to whimper and beg for mercy. But even with this excruciating pain that Zachariah was suffering, still he persisted in acting as though he would live to be an old man, still he ventured out three times a week to fish and bring home food for his family, still he had not even cracked open the brown packet of pills that the doctor had given him. It was a senseless stupidity that drove this ugly brute to act so, the doctor told himself with an unreasoning fury as he drove once again through the Junction Road after having just listened to the cancer gurgling noisily inside Zachariah's chest.

"The sonofabitch must die soon!" the doctor growled to his woman, who rolled her eyes in contempt over his

250

worrying about country negar.

"Ole negar hard to dead!" she said scornfully. "Dem love de earth too much."

"But you should hear the cancer inside his lungs!" the doctor said, pacing agitatedly through the drawing room of the small bungalow. "My God, if you could hear it as I do! If you only knew what it meant! He must be suffering unbelievable pain! Yet he acts as though he's going to live for another fifty years."

"What you bodder yourself so 'bout ole negar, eh?" the woman scowled, wriggling on the sofa where she had been reading a comic. "Me tell you, ole negar don't have de decency to dead when dem time come. Is so him make, to cling to life like weed."

So it was a paradox and a mystery that as the days and weeks and months slipped by; as Zachariah inched himself agonizingly through every excruciating second of the time he had lived since coming back from the sea; as the doctor went to see him every week and listened to the cancer; slowly, surely, over the passage of time, the doctor came to be on the side of death. For the doctor did not believe in God, and he did not believe that the human heart through its own strength of volition could make a difference, and he did not believe that there was anything before the coming of man, or that there would be anything left after the carcass of man was putrefying in the grave. But the one thing the doctor believed in, and worshipped as though it were a God-head, was inevitable death.

So as the weeks passed and Zachariah struggled and fought against the cancer with sheer willpower, the doctor found himself becoming more and more enraged at the temerity of this stupid, ignorant, illiterate fisherman, who thought that by force of will, by nothing more than a stubborn, insatiable love of life, he could deter the inevitability of his own disintegration. There was nothing courageous or admirable in the waging of such a stupid, senseless fight,

251

as far as the doctor could see. It only prolonged the misery, and made matters worse. With every passing week, the hissing of the cancer resonated louder and louder in the doctor's stethoscope.

And what made the ugly brute so stubborn, anyway, the doctor asked himself often and angrily? What about his worthless life was worth saving? He had spawned two healthy sons who would carry on his name; already, he was well into his middle years. Ahead of him stretched years of wretched poverty; countless, perilous nights at sea; a life as drab and unrewarding as it was meaningless. Yet the misshapen, ugly brute fought savagely and implacably for his life, as though his passing would be mourned by millions, as though his name was destined to go down in the history books. There was something gratuitous and unreasonable and futile about the fisherman's pointless, stupid, insensate defiance that drove the doctor into a perverse rage.

"What you hear, sah?" Zachariah asked the doctor one evening. The fisherman had nearly hyperventilated from taking the deep breaths the doctor had asked him to.

"I hear a hissing sound," the doctor said, putting away his stethoscope.

"What dat sound tell you, sah?"

The doctor shrugged. He could not explain any of what he really thought to such a stubborn, ugly fool. So he merely shrugged and made some offhanded remark about the cancer.

"It must sound like de sea at night, when she beg ole negar to jump in," Zachariah said wistfully, staring through the open front door of his house at the shimmering green sea.

The doctor was startled. He peered into the mouth of the fisherman and saw a fresh spread of black polyps stalking determinedly out of the cavernous black throat towards the red defenseless tongue.

"Dat how she get negar to drown," Zachariah said with the chuckle of one who had struggled so long against the sea that he had come to admire and love her. "When fisherman

252

first put out to sea, dat's when he drown de most. For she talk to him at night and confuse him brain so him don't know where him is."

The doctor picked up his bag, asked whether he had taken the pills, winced at the negative reply, and walked determinedly to his car.

"The sonofabitch can't last another month!" the doctor grated as he careened recklessly down the tortuous Junction Road, the gorge of the Wag Water River yawning against the side of the road like a fissured wound in the earth.

"Why you troubling you brain wid dis ole negar, eh?" the woman protested, when the doctor tried to tell her the latest episode about Zachariah that night.

"You go on like you love dat ole negar," she said sulkily, wriggling towards the bathroom.

"I don't love him," the doctor snapped, "I hate him! I hate his filthy, stupid ideas! I despise his ignorant, senseless, worthless, ridiculous life! I detest him! I loathe him!"

He had screamed this so piercingly loud that the moths and bugs that had been hovering contentedly around the ceiling light fixtures, took to the air and fluttered around the room in erratic, tumbling patterns of flight.

The woman turned in the doorway and stared at the doctor, who was quivering and white-faced with anger.

"Dat's what me tell you long ago 'bout ole negar," she said triumphantly. "Dem worse dan dirty dog. Nobody love ole negar!"

Then, with a haughty swish of her loose, calico frock, she disappeared into the bathroom, leaving the doctor standing in the stark glow of the overhead light, his eyes burning with rage.

Chapter 21

So now it was Christmas time, and the festivities of the season had begun. Children whispered their joys to one another; young men and women strolled arm in arm through the village square, dressed in their Sunday finery; Christmas songs were heard over the radio and over the speakers wired to the porches of the village shops. Those villagers who could afford it placed colourful paper bells over the doorways of their houses. Mr. Lewis ran a string of pepper lights over the awning of his shop, and everyone passing through Charity Bay marvelled at how festive and joyful the colours of the lights were. As Christmas Day approached, there were dances in the village. Fairs were held in the pasture land behind Charity Bay to which craftsmen came selling their Christmas wares — their whirligigs and kites and plexiglass rings, which parents bought as presents for their children.

The John Canoe dancers began to rehearse their Christmas dances in the bushlands. Everyone could hear the throbbing sounds of the drums coming from somewhere at the base of the mountains behind Charity Bay. The dancers worked on the costumes they would wear. Some would be garbed in animal costumes; others would masquerade in the gloomy colours attributed to the duppies. And when the time for the dancing came, the dancers would stream into the street wearing the costumes of outlandish creatures, whirling and prancing to the sounds of the tom-toms, and to the high, shrill notes of the reed flutes.

Last year, Zachariah had played the part of the horse-head in the John Canoe dances. He had made the head of a horse from scraps of wood and pieces of tin, and he had cleverly painted his mask to make it look frighteningly real, causing small children to run screaming away from him when he danced near them. But this year he was too weak and sick to join the dancers. He offered his horse-head costume to Mr. Lewis, but the shopkeeper refused, saying that he had had a new one made by a carpenter in Port Antonio. But Zachariah knew that the real reason for the refusal was that Mr. Lewis did not wish to wear anything which Zachariah had once worn, for fear that he would catch bad luck from the ugly fisherman.

This year, Christmas was not the same as ever for Zachariah and his family. Usually, Zachariah would fish especially hard during the weeks before Christmas and accumulate some Christmas money, which Carina would use in Port Antonio to buy gifts for the sons. But this year there was little money, because Zachariah had been too weak to do any strenuous fishing.

So one night, after Zachariah had put out to sea, Carina assembled the sons in the living room and explained to them that there could be no special gifts this Christmas. She was especially gentle with them because she remembered how eagerly she herself had looked forward to Christmas when she was a child. But, as she tried to tell the sons, their father was unwell this year and could not work as hard as he usually did at the Christmas season. The sons looked crestfallen and gloomy, but they nodded and said that they understood. George, the older son, showed his mother a slingshot he had made from the crook of a tree, the tongue of a worn-out shoe, and the rubber of an inner tube.

"Me goin' go in de bush, Mama, and shoot one peadove for we Christmas dinner."

The younger son, Wilfred, asked questions about Zachariah, wondering how sick his father was and whether he might die. Carina stiffened when she heard her favourite son say that word.

"You Papa not goin' dead!" she hissed. "No make me hear dat word in you mouth again."

But she said this so vehemently that Wilfred looked away, tears welling into his eyes, and understood.

On Christmas Eve, the popping sounds of firecrackers rolled across the village as the children began to celebrate. The John Canoe dancers came out of the bush and danced through the village. Prancing, squealing children followed the torchlight procession and dancers. Fishermen masquerading as animals and duppies, acting out the movements of the mongoose, the donkey, the green ground lizard, their faces hidden behind painted masks, their bodies covered by long, tattered robes, whirled and howled to the thumping rhythms of the music, as the John Canoe procession moved from house to house, begging alms for the dancers. Villagers came out of their shacks and stood in their yards, applauding the antics of the shrieking dancers, paying them a few pence, some fish or fruit, for their efforts.

From one shack to another the torchlight procession went, the dancers pausing before each house to leap and whirl to the reedy trill of the flutes and the pounding of the goatskin drums. But when the procession came to Zachariah's house, it did not stop, but danced right past to linger briefly before the house of the Wilsons, who lived right next door.

Nevertheless, Zachariah and Carina sat on their doorstep, the squealing, excited sons at their feet, and watched the torchlight procession swirl past, followed by a ragged, romping pack of village dogs.

"Brute dem!" Carina muttered as the dancers passed without stopping. "When bad luck reach a man, him can't call nobody him friend."

"Pshaw." Zachariah said, after a fit of coughing, "no mind dem fool-fool people."

That night, in the church service, the Parson used the occasion to boast about how travelled and sophisticated he was. He told the story about the birth of Jesus as he did every year, and as always he included a vivid description of the snow storm which Mary and Joseph had tramped through, looking for a place to lodge. Every year the Parson elaborated a little more on this snow storm, for by doing so he had a chance to impress the villagers with the exotic story of snow. No one else in the village had ever seen snow, and only a few schoolchildren had even seen pictures of it. So when the Parson talked about the great, cold, whirling white flakes filling the air, layered like thick cream on the ground, clinging to the branches so that the greenest tree turned white like the hair of an ancient granny, everyone sat very still and was greatly impressed. According to the Parson, the reason why Mary and Joseph so desperately needed lodging was because of the terrible blizzard that had been blowing through Jerusalem that first Christmas Eve. Thus, the Parson was able to brag about how many blizzards he had lived through during his schooling at the American university.

"Every year de same snow storm blow through Charity Bay," Zachariah grunted as he filed out of the church and walked with his family down the dark street beside the sea.

"Dat man mouth bigger dan goat's," Carina replied.

Villagers strolled down the street wishing one another Happy Christmas. Occasionally, the sound of firecrackers rolled over the village. Dogs howled and barked, sometimes wailing in packs, their eerie cry mingling with the sounds of human revelry. The soft Christmas breeze soughed off the sea and down the street, fluttering the dress clothes of the worshippers walking towards their homes.

The two sons did not pass the Christmas empty-handed as they had expected, for Zachariah had carved two gigs from the wood of a lignum vitae tree, and when the family arrived home, he presented these to his children. The gigs were smooth and round and sanded so finely that the wavy veneer of the wood showed through the shellac. Each gig was artfully notched so that the string could be wound firmly around its circumference, and each was pointed with the sharp end of a thick nail. The sons wanted to spin the gigs in the house, but Carina forbade it, saying that they

257

would only bore holes in the wooden floor. So the sons crept away excitedly to their beds, stroking their new toys and eagerly anticipating the coming of morning when they could go into the street and spin their gigs.

Anyone passing the Pelsie house that night would have seen only a darkened shack, its shabby curtains drawn, and would have heard the incessant coughing of the stricken fisherman pealing out into the dark night like the tolling of a death knell, and would have thought that inside, the inhabitants were huddled and beaten, cowed by the bad luck that stalked Zachariah. This, indeed, was what a young fisherman, a newcomer to Charity Bay, told his woman as they walked arm in arm past Zachariah's house and heard the sounds of a hacking cough coming from the dark interior. The young man shook his head and wondered what anyone could do when life brought such crosses down on his head. And as he made this heartfelt comment, the young man shuddered as though something dreadful might strike him too, and wondered whether he could bear it.

But neither the young fisherman or his woman could see inside the small house; could see the sons curled up in their beds, their fingers clutching their new whirligigs; could see Zachariah and Carina wrapped in each other's arms so tightly, that when the fisherman coughed, both bodies twitched and trembled on the bed, as though they had become one stricken person.

"Another bloody Christmas!" the doctor said sourly, grimacing as he emptied a shot glass of white rum.

He was having a drink with the constable in a dingy Port Antonio bar. Loud, ear-shattering music boomed out of the speaker mounted above the bar. Shadowy couples rocked and swayed on the dance floor. The air was filled with smoke, the smell of rum, and the discordant jabber of a large throng of merrymakers.

258

"Yes, sah!" the constable said enthusiastically. "A wonderful season! A joyful time in the West Indies!"

"What'd you say?" the doctor asked loudly over the piercing music.

The constable shouted what he had just said.

"Why d'you keep calling me that bloody word?" the doctor demanded a little belligerently, peering through the swirling smoke at the constable.

"What word, sah?" the constable asked affably.

"Sah! Sir! However you say it! What don't you call me by my blasted name? Do you know my bloody name, Constable?"

"Oh yes, sah," the constable grinned. "I write it up enough in my report to know it well. Archibald Richardson."

"Call me Archie. I rather like my name, even if it is a little stuffy. Don't use the bloody word on me any more."

"As you say, sah. I mean, Archie."

"Bloody good, Constable," the doctor said with the bravura heartiness of a drunken man. He slapped the constable on the back. "Let's have another drink, Constable, shall we?"

The doctor beckoned to the barmaid loitering at the far end of the bar, where she was smoking a cigarette and flirting with an American sailor.

"By the way," the doctor asked, when the drinks were ordered, "what the devil is your real name? Surely, your mother didn't christen you 'Constable'?"

The constable chuckled and shook his head over the rum-inspired mirth of the Englishman, a fine, hearty, wonderful fellow, the best white man in the world, a doctor who was enough of an unassuming, regular chap to actually come with the constable for a drink in this common, countryside bar. Shaking his head in amazement at what a fine fellow the doctor was, the constable said, "My name, sah? I'm sorry, man! Archie! I don't usually give out my name for it is not a name a man can love. Anyway, my given name is Marion."

259

"Marion?" the doctor guffawed, nearly spilling his drink. "Good God! Marion?"

"Yes, Marion," the constable said dourly.

"I think it's a bloody fine name! There's not a damn thing wrong with it. Anybody who says anything different'll have to answer to me!"

"Thank you, Archie," the constable muttered. "You're truly a good friend."

The music rose to a bellowing crescendo and abruptly died. Voices, raised in boisterous chatter, suddenly seemed loud, shrill and discordant, making a nearly unbearable din.

They had been drinking now for the past hour and the doctor had been steadily getting drunker and drunker. Twice already during the evening, he had nearly gotten into a fist fight with some merrymaker who had jostled him. The second time the fight was prevented only by the forceful intervention of the constable, who had identified himself as a police officer and had warned off the other belligerent. The doctor was no doubt saddened over some private misfortune, the constable reasoned, to be in such a foul mood at Christmas. But as the night wore on, the constable learned that the doctor hated Christmas with a passion, and that he always got into some mischief or another at Christmas time because the season always put him in a bad temper.

"Christmas!" the doctor had scoffed. "It's a bloody lie."

The constable had not understood how Christmas could be thought of as a lie. Nevertheless, he replied, "However, sah, it's a good and necessary lie," which drew a scathing rebuke from the doctor.

"You must believe in something, sah," the constable had insisted.

The doctor pondered the point.

"Birth, death, and disease," he replied.

"Nothing more?"

"I used to believe in poetry."

The constable was truly mystified by this revelation,

260

for he did not understand how anyone could believe in such a foolish thing as poetry, which was nothing more than an exercise book activity assigned to schoolchildren.

"But I don't believe in it any more," the doctor had added.

"What about some of the higher things in life, sah? Don't you believe in any of them?"

"Like what?"

"Love. Happiness. The Almighty."

"Delusions of grandeur," the doctor said smartly.

The constable had snickered at this, knowing in his heart that the doctor must have been joking. But when he looked into the eyes of the white man, he saw to his horror that he was dead serious.

"A man must believe in something," the constable said firmly. "It doesn't have to be true. Maybe the thing he believes in most is even an untruth. But he must believe in something."

"Birth, disease, and death," the doctor had replied, calling for yet another round of drinks.

Who could understand such a man, the constable wondered as they bar-hopped, riding around in the doctor's new Volkswagen which he drove with such reckless abandon that the constable, at one point, was on the verge of stepping on the brake, wresting control of the steering wheel, and getting out on the spot. Truly, Christmas had put the madman in a ferocious mood. Nevertheless, they made their way from one crowded, smelly bar to another, talking of various things, the constable proud and boastful of having the white doctor as his friend, the doctor bent on getting so insensibly besotted that he would forget about the misery that Christmas brought to his mind.

Now they were at their fourth bar and had been there for over an hour. They were on such intimate terms that the constable, curious about the living habits of the strange

261

Englishman, had been asking personal questions he would never have dared ask even three hours ago.

"You live with a woman, Archie?" the constable asked at one point.

The doctor shook his head drunkenly. "A pussy," he replied, "not a woman."

"A pussy? Why you say that?" the constable chuckled.

"Because that's all she is to me — a convenient, juicy pussy. Do you know, Marion, that the best pussy in the world is to be found right here in Jamaica? They should export it, like rum, sugar, and bauxite. It'd sell like mad in England. We haven't grown a good crop of pussy there since the bloody eighteenth century."

"So you live with a local woman, den?" the constable asked inquisitively.

He had wanted to ask whether the doctor was living with a black woman, but he couldn't decide on how to frame such a question without seeming impertinent.

"Blacker than coal," the doctor said, as though reading his mind. He turned and looked misty-eyed at the teeming throng of couples swaying on the dance floor behind him.

The doctor went on to talk animatedly about pussy, dragging the constable into a rude conversation. The constable admitted to having had a limited experience. But he repeated the axioms he had learned as a schoolboy — coolie pussy was dry; mulatto pussy was hairy; Chinese pussy was badly positioned, "not between the leg like regular woman, but up front on a belly bone." The doctor guffawed and said that this description was anatomically inaccurate. Chinese pussy, he declaimed with an exaggerated flourish of his shot glass, was where all pussy was, but it had never really appealed to him.

"Too bloody chinky," the doctor explained.

"I'm in nine hundred percent agreement wid you, Archie," the constable said, doing his best at the pretence of seeming a connoisseur.

262

Indeed, the doctor said gravely, there was not the slightest doubt in his mind that in another hundred years or so, a man would be able to go into a shop and buy an artificial pussy, as small and portable as a little kitty cat. And it would be a wonderful invention too, the doctor went on to drunkenly explain, because nowadays if a man wanted just a little pussy to keep himself happy, there was no way he could get it unless he was willing to put up with the bloody woman who walked around with it wedged between her legs. And that could be a bloody nuisance, to have to put up with the constant prattle of a foolish woman when all the man wanted was some pussy once in a while.

The constable had become progressively more scandalized at this rush of obscene, slack opinion from the doctor, and he would not have endured such talk from anyone else on Christmas Eve. But because he held such a high opinion of the doctor, he listened solemnly and even tried to match the Englishman's lewdness.

"Viscosity," the doctor said, sipping on yet another white rum. "That's the principal problem. Viscosity."

"Of course it is," the constable said heartily, even though he hadn't the slightest idea what the doctor was talking about.

"That'll be the major medical problem with the artificial pussy," the doctor said darkly, as though he were expounding on some profound secret.

"Viscosity," the constable repeated, looking sagely at the doctor.

The doctor went on with his theories of how proper viscosity in an artificial pussy could be achieved. No doubt, he said, there would be a bloody hue and cry from the stupid moralists once the first artificial pussy was marketed in America. "The Americans will invent it first, of course!"

"Of course!" nodded the constable, as though the point were perfectly obvious.

But in the end, the doctor explained, the practical appeal

of the artificial pussy would overcome the moral objections.

And so the evening dragged on from bar to bar. By midnight, the mood of the doctor had changed for the worse. He became morose and gloomy and sat at the crowded bars swilling down one rum after another, engaging in none of the lighthearted banter of earlier in the evening. The constable did his best to coax the Englishman into a better mood, but the doctor remained implacably gloomy.

"The bloody fool," he said harshly.

"Who, sah?"

With the worsening of the doctor's mood, the constable had revived the formal mode of address.

"Pelsie! That ugly bugger in Charity Bay."

The constable was taken aback at his vehemence.

"He's a very bad lucky man," the constable said solemnly.

"Bloody stubborn. You should see the cancer in the back of his throat. Looks like bloody mushrooms. Black mushrooms. You should hear it in his chest. He's suffering incredible agony. Yet the bloody fool acts as though he's going to live forever."

The constable sighed and rubbed his weary, bloodshot eyes that stung from the smoke coiling through the dingy bar. There was one thing he didn't understand about this white man, something that had been puzzling him ever since he had first met the doctor. He decided to take the bull by the horns, in spite of the other's moodiness.

"You know, sah." the constable said, "I don't understand the way you mind work."

"Oh, really? What don't you understand?"

"This man Pelsie. You give him medicine. You visit him home for treatment. You take care of him as though he's your best friend."

"Yet the bloody fool won't even take the pain pills I gave him," the doctor muttered.

"And yet everytime I hear you talk about dis man, I

264

get de feeling you want him to die."

The doctor stared at the constable, and it seemed to the constable that the white face before him had suddenly become drawn and weary looking.

"You know what I'd have done weeks ago, if I'd been in his shoes?" the doctor asked, looking the constable squarely in the eye. "I'd have blown my bloody brains out."

The doctor said this in a flat, unemotional voice. Such finality, such intensity shone in the eyes of the Englishman that the constable shuddered.

"But this is what I don't understand even more dan anything else," the constable continued, looking away from the flat, piercing gaze of the Englishman.

The doctor stared at the filthy, grimy counter, cracked and fissured and gouged by anonymous fingernails, burned and charred by countless cigarettes and cigars, stained by beer and stout, and tried to read in the random distribution of grime and dirt, some discernible pattern, some logic that connected one smudge with another, that united one ugly smear with the speckled blotches surrounding it on all sides.

"You try to do goodness in you own way. I don't believe you would do a wickedness to anyone. Even though somebody else might think that what you did was wicked, in you heart I think you would mean to do a goodness. And so I am puzzled, sah, very puzzled about dis."

"You're getting too damn analytical," the doctor growled.

"No! Just one more thing, if you bear me out, sah! You don't believe in God. And you don't think you have a soul. So why? Why, sah?"

"Why what?"

"Why you try to do any goodness at all? Why you come to dis poor island? Why you don't stay in Kingston and treat white people who can afford to pay?"

"Because of my bloody toilet training, that's why " the doctor said harshly, slipping off the bar stool and draining

265

the shot glass with one gulp.

"I didn't mean to be inquisitive," the constable said apologetically, standing beside the bar stool.

"Quite all right, I assure you. But remember this, Constable, and I don't care what you were taught to the contrary in Sunday school. Goodness has nothing to do with the heart or the mind. It only has to do with the bowels."

The constable blinked furiously in the face of such blasphemy on Christmas Eve.

"The bowels, sah?" he asked sceptically.

"That's right. The English discovered this trick years ago. Concientious toilet training produces idealists. I believe the Catholics are on to this, too, although I can't really be sure. But something's got to account for all those bloody Popes."

"Good Lord, sah!" the constable protested.

"Never thought of that, did you? That perhaps a man does a little good not because of what he believes, but because of what he is. That perhaps good hasn't a blasted thing to do with belief or ideology. Perhaps it's a bloody learned trait."

The constable looked sadly perplexed.

"You don't understand, do you, Constable? Someone's played a rotten trick on us atheists. We don't believe in God, we don't think that there's anything waiting for us at the end of life except a bloody worm. Now, you'd think that with this sort of bleaky outlook, we'd become wild pleasure seekers, wouldn't you? That we'd be out for nothing but sheer pleasure; that we'd go stark raving mad for anything different, anything new, illicit, exciting. You'd think that we'd want to do nothing except rape and plunder and sin until every bloody pore of our destructible bodies tingled with absolute pleasure. Well, you're quite right! We're certainly the most lustful, craving, greedy, gluttonous crew you're ever likely to meet. The only trouble is that we never do anything about it. Why? Because we can't, that's why. We're so bloody moral, so stuffily right, that we make ourselves sick. Blast it, anyway! A whole life of opportunity for sin wasted! Ruined! Down the bloody drain! And how did we get to be so wretched? Well, there's got to be an explanation, hasn't there?"

"Well, sah," the constable said, looking bewilderedly about him, "I admit I'm confused."

The doctor's eyes had become quite piercing, reminding the constable of a movie he had once seen about a mad monk.

"Motiveless benignity, Constable," the doctor said sotto voce, as though he were sharing a priceless secret. "That's the reason. You've got your motiveless malignancy — that's when a very bad man commits dreadful crimes for no reason at all. And then you've got your motiveless benignity. That's when an atheist waddles about being moral and good in spite of his disbelief. My own theory is that it's all related to toilet training."

The constable hadn't really followed the drift of this speculation, for he sat squirming beside the doctor wearing an expression of almost bovine mystification as he puzzled about what the other had said. But even as the constable frowned and tried to understand these startling and new ideas, the Englishman threw back his head and laughed so boisterously that the constable wondered if he was being mocked. He was getting a little vexed at the other's antics, when the doctor abruptly shook his hand, muttered some felicities of the season, and left him stranded alone at the dirty bar, which suddenly seemed a place of unaccountable human frenzy. Shuddering with distaste at the blaring music, the din of jovial merrymaking, the swirling smoke, the constable walked out of the bar just in time to glimpse the tail-lights of the doctor's car vanish around a corner.

The constable walked through the darkened streets of

267

Port Antonio, making his way unsteadily up the hill where he had lived for the past twenty years, ever since leaving the home of his old mother.

The small houses that stood in neat rows were dark and silent. Paper bells fluttered over the doorways here and there. From somewhere deep in the heart of the sleeping town, came the throbbing, pulsing rhythms of a sound system. Occasionally, the rapping sound of firecrackers rattled through the night air.

The constable was in a pensive, repentant mood, which he always suffered following over-indulgence of any kind. He was especially cross with himself for getting so drunk on Christmas Eve, a holiday he always tried to observe with temperance. A drink or two, a hearty handshake with a comrade, and some friendly conversation about the affairs of the world — that had been the usual fare of his past Christmas Eve celebrations. But tonight, as luck would have it, he had been so swayed by the presence of the white man that he had followed him from one dirty bar to another, in an orgy of senseless drinking. His footsteps clicking on the pavement of the dark, narrow street, the constable climbed the hillside lane on which he lived, lost in remorse over his own intemperate behaviour.

He did not like the ideas he had heard from the Englishman tonight. Moreover, he did not like the influence the other seemed to exert over him, and which had caused him to depart from his usual, abstemious ways. The constable was especially vexed with himself for taking part in the lewd discussion about the female private parts. He was a bachelor and had had only one woman in his life, a gangling schoolgirl with whom he had copulated one evening after a cricket match. They sneaked off into the bush together, where they made love furtively behind the trunk of a tree. It had been a badly mismanaged affair, awkward, clumsy, and mutually painful. Afterwards, both he and the girl had wept over what they had done. For weeks, he worried that she would become pregnant and that he would be saddled with supporting a child even before he was out of school. He had suffered horrible nightmares about being banished from the cricket team and expelled from school.

Fortunately, however, the girl did not become pregnant. Indeed, the experience seemed to have affected him more than it did her, for she was able afterwards to laugh and joke about it, while he himself was never able to see anything amusing in the whole affair. She went on to get a bad reputation as a slack girl who would drop her drawers for any boy she liked. The constable went on to become what he was today — a rather contented bachelor who lived a peaceful life with his cat.

Berating himself, the constable trudged up the narrow lane to the brow of the hill. At the top of the hill, he turned and looked down at the lights of Port Antonio clinging in small clusters against the shoreline like the bloom of exotic clumps of berries, and gradually thinning out as the land veered away from the outskirts of the town and turned dark and lonely where it thrust a sharp jagged mass into the ocean.

He could even see the dark, brooding mass of Flynn's Island, and even make out the lights of the American frigate that had nosed her way into the channel this evening, releasing a horde of sailors who streamed through the streets of the town and glutted the insides of the bars. As he ran his eyes over the familiar, darkened terrain of the town, the constable could glimpse the vestige of another white man's stay in Jamaica — the hulk of a crumbling mansion built on a sandy spur of land that overlooked the harbour of Port Antonio. "Folly" was the name the locals had given to this white man's house which, according to the legend, had been built of cement mixed with sea water.

The rich white man had come to Jamaica from Scotland with his new bride, and had decided to build her a mansion on the seashore. But shortly after it had been built, it was

269

said, the house began to crumble and sink because of the sea water in its foundation. Within months of being built, it had become uninhabitable. Now it stood abandoned and ruined on the peninsula, its walls sinking into the sand, its foundation tilted giddily into the air. Vagrants used the hulk as a place of shelter. Trysting couples fornicated in the shadows of its walls. A stench of urine rose off the white stone of the abandoned building. Schoolboys scribbled obscene verses on the walls of its spacious bedrooms. Even as the constable looked down from the brow of the hill, he could make out the desolate ruins standing forlorn and stark on the beach like the abandoned shell of some monstrous sea crab.

Folly House. It reminded the constable of the vast, dreary emptiness inside the doctor's heart. Such a scientific man to believe in such lunatic ideas: to believe in the invention of the portable replica of a woman's private parts; to believe that death shattered every inch of a man's identity, dispersing him into anonymous particles that came together as the parts of plants and beasts; to say that he lived with a "pussy", and to talk so coarsely about the woman he shared a bed with; worst of all, to hold such foolish, perplexing notions about toilet training!

The constable blew a loud, mournful sigh, for he was thinking that, in spite of his faults, the Englishman had genuine goodness in his heart to work so hard at the clinics in the countryside which even the Jamaican black doctors shunned, preferring, instead, to live and practice in the metropolitan sections of the island where the rich white and mulatto families lived and could afford to pay expensive fees. Truly the doctor was a mystery, the constable thought with another mournful sigh.

A bell began to toll somewhere in the heart of the dark town, the sound drifting thin and clear on the night air. A soft, stirring breeze moved through the darkened lane, and the constable smelled the distinct pungency of the ocean. Slowly, imperceptibly, the quiet and beauty of the night was working its magic on him. He felt relaxed and at peace with himself. Sucking deeply on the night breeze, the constable started down the hillside, humming a Christmas carol under his breath, thinking how his cat would come to the door and greet him, imagining how smooth and cool the sheets of his bed would feel to his weary body.

On the way to his house, he passed a small, dark church and paused to look at the graveyard. The tombstones looked soft and fuzzy under the gloom of a towering Flame Heart tree. His fingers tapping quietly against the pointed tip of a wrought-iron fleur-de-lis on the ornamental fence, the constable stared thoughtfully at the shimmering grave markers. Then he opened the gate and went inside the church. Tiptoeing into the dark, cavernous interior, he fumbled for a bench, knelt down and prayed.

Fifteen minutes later, he emerged from the church feeling refreshed and pleased with himself, as though he had just done something wonderful and good. He was humming "Silent Night" as he ambled down the dark, narrow lane towards his house.

The doctor, meanwhile, had arrived home safely by the skin of his teeth. He had driven down the Junction Road like a veritable lunatic. Twice he had almost skidded over the precipice and into the gaping maw of the Wag Water River gorge. Once, he missed a slow, trundling dray by inches, veering around it at the last second. He knew that he was drunk and that his reflexes were affected, but he drove as fast as ever, laughing maniacally over each narrow miss. When he finally arrived home, he was so breathless and excited that he could barely stumble out of the car and into the drawing room, where the woman was curled up on the couch sleeping.

On hearing the car pull under the portico, she jumped up and scolded him loudly in a screeching voice. She followed him into the bedroom, where he pawed at her body and tore off the front flap of her panties. But when she indulgently lay down to give him what he wanted, he could manage only a feeble erection before falling into a stupored sleep. She tried coaxing him to further vigour by fondling him and wriggling her tongue in his ear, but he was dead to the world and snoring raucously, his arm dangling over the side of the bed. She covered him with a thin blanket and sat on the bed with her knees drawn up under her chin. Staring gloomily out of the burglar-barred window, she listened to the singing of the crickets.

Chapter 22

Christmas passed off the calendar and into the memories of children. Then came Boxing Day with its merry fairs and garden parties, followed by New Year's Eve, which the villagers of Charity Bay celebrated with a roisterous dance held in the public square. Then it was the New Year puffing thick and full of promise on the wall calendars.

Zachariah was now so weak that he could no longer go to sea unless there was a prevailing land breeze to carry him through the breakwater. When such a breeze blew, he would hobble determinedly down to the beach and set sail in the painted canoe, and the breeze would waft him through the harbour and blow him down to the lee shore of the promontory which the fishermen now called "Kingfish place". At nights, Carina could see his solitary light drifting against the dark shoreline of the promontory, miles away from the clustering lanterns of the other canoes. When day broke, it sometimes took him five hours to make his way to shore because he could no longer manage the heavy oars and had to wait on a favourable wind.

He continued, in spite of these hardships, to bring home a catch. But he was such a sorry-looking, wrecked shell of a man that even the higglers shunned his catch, saying that the hand of death was upon his fish. Carina had to take the bus to Port Antonio where she could sell the fish to strangers in the market, who knew nothing about the health of the fisherman who had hauled the fish out of the sea.

Bones sprouted out of him, jutting from every soft pouch of flesh, bones so conspicuous and visible that even a child

273

could count them. His rib bones showed against his chest; his haunch bones lifted out of his abdomen; his shin bones hung off his legs. He had lost so much weight that the shape and contours of his face had changed, making him look even uglier. His jawbone, which childhood disease had twisted and enlarged, now protruded so prominently off his skull that passing strangers who saw him flinched at his grotesque ugliness. All over his emaciated body, the skin hung in slack, reptilian folds over jutting bone.

Yet he persisted in going to sea. Carina pleaded with him every night not to go to sea until he was well again, and even as she said this, she would cast her eyes into a corner as though she had uttered a lie. His sons offered to go to sea with him. George showed his muscles and boasted that he could row the canoe as well as any boy his age. Wilfred, the silent one, came to him one evening and stood diffidently at his side, tugging at his great, gnarled hand. And when Zachariah looked down at him, the boy whispered that tonight he wished to go to sea and learn the trade of the fisherman.

But Zachariah would carry no one to sea with him. He persisted as obdurately as ever in following his old habits. He even went down to the village shops in the hope of playing a game or two of dominoes. But when the other fishermen saw him coming they would put away the bone cards and pretend to be engrossed in some private affair. So Zachariah learned that none of the men would play dominoes with him any longer, and he kept to himself during the daytime hours.

Once, weary and dispirited, after it had taken him the whole morning to return from the sea, he told Carina that he intended to sell the canoe and use the money to live on until he was well again. For they always said those words as though repetition would make them come true — every plan they made was "until he was well again". Carina objected that without the canoe they would have no source of food, but as soon as she had had a chance to think it over, she willingly agreed that they should sell the canoe and use the money to live on "until he was well again".

One day, therefore, a young fisherman and his uncle made a journey from Manchioneal in the uncle's truck, to buy the painted canoe. The fisherman had heard all about the adventures of the sturdy craft, about how it had survived the teeth of the shark, the rains at sea, about how it had clawed its way back to shore after being blown into the immensities of the ocean, and his heart was set on acquiring such a famous boat for his own. He came one morning and sat on the beach cross-legged with Zachariah, and counted out fifty dollars in fifty cent coins and one dollar notes, handling the wrinkled, grimy bills with care, laying them out in the outstretched palms of Zachariah. When the money was counted, Zachariah asked the young man to leave him alone for a few moments with the canoe. The young fisherman agreed. He withdrew to the road where he sat on the fender of the truck and waited with his uncle.

But once Zachariah was alone with the painted canoe, he was so torn with sorrow and memory that he knew he could not deliver her into the hands of a stranger. For as he stood beside the canoe and ran his fingers over her gunwales and remembered how he had hewed her out of a tree; how she had borne him safely through the storms, winds, heavy seas; how she had protected him from the jaws of the hammerhead; how she had clothed and fed his family all through the years; when he thought of all these things, he realized that he had made a dreadful mistake to think that he could give her up to a stranger. It would have been like selling one of his own children.

He made up his mind. He walked resolutely to the truck and returned the money to the young fisherman and told him that he had had a change of heart and could not sell the canoe. The young fisherman became vexed. He raised his voice at Zachariah, uttering all sorts of threats and curses in his ear. He howled that he had rented his uncle's truck to carry the canoe to Port Antonio, and that because of Zachariah's indecision he would lose that money. He followed Zachariah down the street, yelling curses and imprecations at him, threatening to thump him down on the asphalt roadway. Zachariah, who knew he was in the wrong, offered no replies to the young fisherman's taunting insults. Instead, he walked wearily down the road, ignoring the screaming fisherman, and went into his house. The young fisherman stood before the house, bellowing oaths and threats against Zachariah. The uncle pulled the truck up before the house, and added his voice to his nephew's. A crowd gathered, listening solemnly to the recital of grievances.

Finally, Carina could not bear to hear Zachariah insulted in such a riotous, shameful way. She took up a sharp machete and went into the street and faced the young fisherman and dared him to say one more threatening word against her man. The uncle picked up an ugly rock and clenched it between his fist. But when he looked into her eyes, he saw murder shining there, so he blustered and backed down, throwing the rock away. The truck roared off, and the young fisherman hurled one final curse when he was safely out of reach. For days afterwards, the villagers gossiped about this unseemly row and about what might have happened had the young man and his uncle not backed down.

So the canoe was not sold and there was no money to be had from it, and still Zachariah was so weak that he could hardly fish. Carina scolded him over his mishandling of the sale of the canoe, but because he readily admitted that he had been wrong, she did not say too many biting things. In her heart she had known all along that he would not be able to sell the canoe which he had named after his mother and which, next to his woman and his sons, he loved more than anything else in the world. So she only said a cross word or two and then she dropped the matter entirely and it was soon forgotten.

The doctor continued to visit Zachariah every week for examination. And though Zachariah was now mainly skin and bones, suffering such excruciating pain that he could hardly breathe, yet he still had not even opened the packet of pills. With each visit, the doctor found him weaker and weaker until it was plain that death was only days away, and that death would have cut him down months ago except for his implacable obduracy, except for his indomitable will to live.

"The pain!" the doctor exclaimed to his woman. "The pain he must be suffering!"

"Me don't want hear nothing' 'bout no damn ole country negar," the woman scowled, flouncing out of the drawing room. Lately, the doctor had not approached her as a woman and she was feeling neglected and abandoned. For all he had on his mind, and all he talked about morning, noon, and night, was some rass ugly negar who didn't have the decency to dead when his time came. She would not put up with his foolish obsession.

The doctor had driven Zachariah to the Port Antonio hospital, where he had arranged for him to take an X-ray. When he looked at the X-ray film, the doctor saw cancer, dark, malign, sinister, spreading in slashing strokes over the lungs, through the internal organs. When he palpated the abdomen of the fisherman, the doctor felt cancer bristling under his fingertips, knobby and stiff like the tops of fresh mushrooms. And when the doctor looked down Zachariah's throat, he saw that the black polyps had taken root at the base of the tongue growing so thick and furiously that there was little opening left in the throat for food to pass through. So exhausted and weak was Zachariah that on the drive back from Port Antonio he fell asleep beside the doctor, snoring loudly, hacking and coughing until he was breathless.

The doctor slowed the car at the top of a precipitous embankment, and for one wild, giddy moment he thought of driving the car over the cliff while the fisherman was still asleep, putting him out of his misery once and for all. He even thought of shooting him in the head, as he would a suffering animal.

The car stood poised on the shoulder of the road overlooking a perilous fall to the ruffled edge of the sea. Breakers wreathed and coiled around glistening black rocks, and the doctor was staring intensely at Zachariah, wondering how he could kill him cleanly and mercifully, when the fisherman suddenly coughed and stirred, opening his eyes to peer groggily around him.

"We reach yet, sah?" Zachariah asked, rubbing a gnarled knuckle over his shrunken eyes.

The doctor started the car and pulled gently onto the road.

"No," he said soothingly. "I just stopped to rest a bit."

"Is a long drive, sah," Zachariah muttered, resting the back of his head against the seat. He closed his eyes and was instantly snoring again, while the doctor negotiated the hairpin curves cautiously, thinking about a merciful way to end the life of the stubborn, ugly fisherman.

One whole week, Zachariah did not go out to sea. The family would have gone hungry except that Mr. Wilson shared his catch with them. But for one whole week, Zachariah was laid up in bed, muttering like a delirious man, coughing up blood. When he was awake, he was so feverish and sick that he could hardly even swallow water.

Death was everywhere about the house. Carina saw it flit through the rooms like a shadow. She heard bats rustling against the windows. She heard the restless sounds of prowling, scurrying rats. She heard the whimpers of unseen nocturnal animals. She saw duppies and spectres gathering formally in her bedroom. She went to Lubeck, collected talismans, herbs, and potions, which she smeared and hung everywhere throughout the house, to protect her frail, rasping husband from the stroke of death. Dogs, passing her house at night, would suddenly sit on their haunches and howl. Black carrion birds seemed to hover constantly above the house, drifting stealthily through the pale, thin sky. And everywhere she looked in the darkness of night, she saw lizards, and she heard spiders, and she witnessed unmentionable presences craning over the bed and breathing on the cheeks of her dying husband.

She could not sleep. Starting at every whisper, at the crack of a twig, at the rustle of the writhing sea, she would jump up and light the kerosene lantern and search the house, carrying in one hand a talisman, and in the other, her sharp machete. Night after night, she kept watch over her sleeping husband, trying to ward away the evil presences that hovered over his bed.

It was now Easter week, a time the villagers celebrate by eating fruit buns and hard cheese. A flurry of new frocks and home-made hats had appeared throughout the village. Men went into Port Antonio and bought new, Easter shoes. Among the children, the marble season was in full swing. Groups of boys could be seen gathered at the sides of the village shops, playing "bounce back" marbles against the pitted walls. The young men played village cricket on the greens of the pasture-land, applauded and criticized by their elders. Last week, the tarpon had run into the harbour, and the fishermen had netted some of these tremendous fish, selling them for a fat profit. The time was joyful and festive for all, except Zachariah and his family. For it appeared that the ugly fisherman was on his deathbed.

On Holy Thursday, the doctor stopped by in the afternoon to conduct his weekly examination. Carina slunk into the living room, sat down wearily and peered suspiciously through the opened door as the Englishman examined Zachariah. The doctor listened to his breathing, and peered down his throat. What he heard and saw made the Englishman grimace. Then he felt Zachariah's abdomen and what he touched made his fingers flinch.

279

Zachariah was in such severe, unbearable pain, that he had almost taken a pill this morning, but had fought down the impulse with his immense will. Now he lay crumpled on the bed, breathing with a hissing wheeze that was audible even where Carina sat.

The doctor had made up his mind. He reached into his black bag and he took out a syringe and a thin, silver needle, and he filled the syringe with a cloudy liquid. Racked by a bout of coughing, Zachariah was huddled against the wall. The doctor glanced through the ajar door to where the woman sat in the dimly lit living room, her head bowed with weariness. Then he took out a piece of cotton, dipped in alcohol, and wiped it on the arm of the coughing fisherman. Zachariah sprang up at the doctor's touch, and saw the shining needle.

"I'm going to give you a shot," the doctor said crisply, squeezing a tiny drop of liquid through the inverted needle.

"For what, sah?" Zachariah stared at the needle held between the doctor's fingers.

"This is to clear your lungs," the doctor said, "to help you breathe more freely."

Weary, racked by pain, Zachariah shrugged and made no move to resist. The doctor reached down, seized the black arm between his fingers, and aimed the needle. But just as he was about to thrust the tip of the needle into the fleshy part of the arm, Zachariah looked into the green, glittering eyes of the doctor, and saw something shuddering there, some shadow in the room that shimmered deep inside the watery pupils of the doctor's eyes, and he recognized something he had once seen when he had peered into the malign intensity of the sea.

With a cry, Zachariah yanked his arm away and jumped against the wall, shrinking away from the other's touch. The door burst open and Carina stood glowering over the bed, peering suspiciously at the doctor.

"What you do?" she hissed at him.

280

"Nothing, yet," the doctor said coolly. "But I was about to give him a shot before you came barging in."

"I don't want dat kind o' shot," Zachariah growled, cringing next to the wall.

"He don't want no injection!" Carina said. She held her ground against the advancing doctor.

"Listen, you ignorant, stupid woman!" the doctor began, his face red with anger.

Zachariah pulled himself out of bed and stood unsteadily over the Englishman.

"Don't call me woman no name," he growled, glaring at the white doctor, who still held the needle between his fingers.

The doctor shrugged and put away the syringe. He gathered his bag and stepped out of the room. But when he reached the front door, he turned and roared like a man driven mad by frustration.

"You're a bloody fool, Pelsie! A stupid, bloody fool!"

Then his car was screeching away from the house and hurtling through the narrow street of the village, while pedestrians and bystanders gawked at the recklessness of the English lunatic.

Zachariah hobbled to the window and looked out at the sea and saw that a land breeze was blowing so hard that the harbour waters were flecked with whitecaps.

"I goin' to sea!" he muttered with decision.

Carina screamed at him and begged him to return to his bed, but his mind was made up and he was in the grip of his obdurate nature. No matter how she scolded and raged, he moved implacably through the house, preparing himself for a long voyage at sea. She saw how he filled the blackened cresset with oil and she saw with horror how he filled two bottles of water, and she saw how he packed some crusts of hard dough bread into a paper bag and she bawled with grief and begged him not to leave her. But he reached down and stroked her hair gently, rubbing his bony hands

281

over her cheeks with a touch as soft as the summer wind. Then he was gone through the front door and she was running after him, screaming for him to come back.

The Wilsons, hearing her cries, stood on their own doorstep and raised their voices after Zachariah, begging him to remain. And a few loitering fishermen who were passing by, or who were labouring on the beach, gathered solemnly to watch as the sickly, bony fisherman tried to shove his canoe into the sea. They saw how he fought against the grip of the sand against the hull of the canoe; they saw how he clenched his teeth and they heard mighty groans of effort come from his throat, heard how his struggle was cut short by bouts of coughing, and no one lifted a finger to help him; for his woman was screaming from the doorstep of her house, pleading with him to return to bed; and his neighbours were crying forlornly out to him; and even those fishermen who had shunned him because of his bad luck added their voices to the outcry and begged him to stay.

Slowly, in inches, in infinitesimal surges over the gritty sand, Zachariah pushed the canoe into the water. He clambered over her stern, nearly capsizing her, for the land breeze was blowing and the surf was rising, and the canoe reared and tossed as though she would not willingly leave the harbour. And with the sound of voices wailing after him over the cry of the wind, Zachariah broke out the yellow sail, and the painted canoe immediately surged ahead under the stiff land breeze, and danced with the wind abeam as she soughed through the chop and drove towards the harbour breakwater.

The voices rose so clamorously after him that if sound could break a heart, his heart would have been broken to hear them. For everyone ashore who saw the canoe slip through the breakwater thought that Zachariah had gone to sea to die. But they were wrong. He had gone out onto the deep not to die, but to pray.

The Englishman, meanwhile, drove like a raging lunatic

through the Junction Road. He squealed around tortuous corners and roared through sleepy fishing villages. Just outside of Golden Grove he hit a pig at such high speed that the animal was tossed shrieking and spinning into the air. But even then, he did not stop, though the owner of the pig ran after the car and hurled rocks at it. He was weeping as he drove, and he could see the road only dimly. Nevertheless, he raced through the pass with squealing tires. At the mouth of the trail that led into the gorge of the Wag Water River, he pulled over, locked his car, and hiked down the steep hillside.

Standing on the silted banks, staring as the river slithered over rocks and stumps, its waters shining with a smooth, iridescent sheen, the doctor wept, his heart filled with rage and self-revulsion. The river rolled past the weeping white man, licking at the walls of the immense mountain on which it had fed for centuries, shining in the bright afternoon sunshine as though it had just preened itself clean for a lover. The afternoon sun threw spiny shadows of bamboo over the river, where they lay, impalpably shuddering on the gleaming stillness. High overhead, a john crow wheeled, no more than a distant speck in the glistening sky.

But it was the smooth, purling river that drew the gaze of the weeping doctor. For it was as green as the eye of a cat, and it rolled so softly through the gorge that it scarcely made a whisper. Through his tears, the doctor stared at the coiling river, and thought he heard it hum as it fed on the sheer rock walls of the gorge, and thought he heard it chuckle as it wrinkled against smooth white stone on the far bank. He stood on the bank of the river, his shoes sinking into the mud, and the river reached out and touched him, pawing him softly, persistently, like a wooing lover. The doctor gasped and stared down at his shoe, and saw how the water rolled over his instep and lapped like a green tongue at his ankle bone.

He stepped away from its touch and retreated behind a

283

huge white boulder, where he slowly undressed, shedding first his shoes and his socks, and then his shirt, and finally his pants and his underwear, arranging his clothes in a neat pile on the marbleized face of the rock, until he was standing on the black, silted bank, naked and shivering, as a soft breeze wafted coolly over his nakedness.

Then he stepped into the river, approaching coyly at first, sinking down to his ankles. Little mushroom puffs of mud swirled in his footsteps, giving off a sour, intestinal stench.

Chapter 23

The new doctor was a brown man from Mocho, a tiny village in the parish of St. James, no more than a smudge on the Jamaica map. He had been trained in medicine at the University of the West Indies, and in return for his education, he was bound to work for the Ministry of Health for not less than five years. Like many of the young Jamaican doctors who had been entrapped by the government through this arrangement, he was eager to serve his sentence (for so he laughingly termed it to his sophisticated university friends in Kingston) in Siberia (another of his metaphors). But in the meantime, he was impatient with the uncouthness of these country people, and he treated them roughly and unkindly, addressing them in the haughty tones that brown men use so successfully to put their black countrymen in their place.

Mainly, these people were shirkers, parasites, and blowhards, the doctor knew, as he had learned so well from his long experience with them. In fact, the doctor had grown up under rather similar and humble circumstances, in a village very much like Charity Bay, but he had now attained such a high place in the world that the very thought of his origins made him feel squeamish and revolted. He wrote to none of his childhood friends from his village, and he could barely find time to send a letter a year to his mother, who badgered him weekly with long, semi-literate epistles filled with idiotic village gossip and much motherly grovelling. If he had any gumption at all, the doctor told himself severely over and over, he would write his mother a strong letter couched in the imperious grammar of a learned man, telling her once and for all to stop filling his mailbox with such trivial rubbish as she put in her letters. But he was still somewhat cowed by his strong-minded, pious old mother, and was reduced to combatting her insular nature by writing only at Christmas, and then only a short, pompous letter filled with lies about his academic glories. Sometimes, just to remind her of how far he had come in the world, he would even throw in a medical term or two, which she would no doubt show to all the villagers, who would read over her shoulder trying, with awe, to mutter the unsayable jargon of his esoteric profession.

Immediately after he had been assigned to the Charity Bay clinic, enmity had sprung up between the new doctor and his patients. For he made it quite clear that he cared nothing about them or their worthless lives, and that he was only at the clinic every week because the socialist government had duped him into a specious unfair bargain, which he was now obliged to pay off. But even though he had to show up at the clinic, and had to deal with a procession of shirking illiterates, had to put up with their home-grown remedies, with their superstitious beliefs in obeah and miracles; even though he had to lance their filthy boils and stitch the lacerations they inflicted in each other's flesh, and medicate their nasty scabrous sores that they caught from living in excrement and filth, and look into their stinking mouths filled with rotted stumps of teeth; even though he had to endure all this misery and uncleanliness from these wretched people, yet there was nothing in his contract with the Ministry of Health that said he had to like them or their dirty way of life. He did not have to endure their superstitious prattle and he did not have to become embroiled in their pointless feuds. He did not have to pretend that they were civilized, nor did he have to exert himself in any supererogatory effort at patching up and mending their miserable bodies.

For their part, when the villagers saw that the new doctor was a brown man, they took an instant dislike to him, going to the clinic only if they were at death's door. For it was well known throughout Jamaica that no man is more implacable and hard-hearted against the negar than a brown man. The Prime Minister had vehemently denied this stereotype in numerous speeches before Parliament, claiming that it was a myth spread by the British to divide the people. Nevertheless, the people continued to believe that the brown man is wickedness itself in his dealings with the negar. The white man will at least talk out of both sides of his mouth and put on a good face for show, even if he secretly hates you behind your back. But the brown man scorns the black man both publicly and privately, abusing him at every opportunity over every little foolishness. For the brown man aspires to become white, and loathes anyone who reminds him of where he came from. Even a schoolboy without any sense knows that it is better to have either a white teacher or a black teacher than a brown teacher.

The new doctor, moreover, lived up to the reputation of his colour. He acted as though he didn't care which patient lived or which one died. He scolded all over their ignorance, raising his voice loudly in the small examination room of the clinic. If anyone dared to answer him, he would fly into a rage and order them out of his office. And it did not matter if the patient's hair was as grey as a grandmother's, or if his limbs were shrivelled up with age. Everyone in the village came in for the same coarse, abusive treatment from the new doctor.

Except, of course, the slack young women, especially the plump and shapely ones. For it was soon whispered in the village that the brown doctor was as lecherous as a goat, and that he was especially fond of fat young women. When such women came to see him, even if they complained of a broken toe, the doctor would make them undress completely and devise some pretext for rude fondling. One slack young woman openly boasted that when she had gone to see the doctor about a cut behind her ear, he had taken off her drawers and given her a good grind right on the examination table. She lewdly bragged about the doctor's "injection", and made jokes about the size of his "needle". Husbands, on hearing these stories, refused to let their wives and daughters attend the clinic alone, but would accompany them and stand listening outside the examination door, determined to break in if they heard any foolishness going on.

Six months passed under this new doctor, months that seemed interminable to him, months that hung malevolently thick on the calendar. Many times he had plotted his escape, scheming about slipping away from Jamaica and migrating to another island where he could start a prosperous practice in some big city. But he was afraid that the government would revoke his degree if he did that, for the Prime Minister had gotten severe lately about doctors breaking their contracts with the government and had proposed a new law to Parliament that threatened to exact stern reprisals for such breaches. No doubt about it, the doctor told himself with a sigh, he was doomed to mingle with these filthy, stupid people for the next five years, and all because he had had the ambition and brains to want to better himself instead of living out his years in some stinkhole like Charity Bay frittering away his life, dragging fish out of the sea. He saw himself as a victim of the idiotic policies of socialism. Yet there was some smidgen of self-aggrandizement in his suffering, he told himself with martyred self-indulgence, for men of ambition and principle are always persecuted by visionless socialists. He wrote something to this effect to his mother, who became so aroused that she sent a stinging telegram to the Prime Minister, demanding the release of her son.

The new doctor, however, got along well with the crusty nurse in Charity Bay, for he treated the patients exactly the way she had known all along that they should be treated. It was the insane Englishman who had brought a different. foreign mode of behaviour to Charity Bay, pretending that

288

inferiors are equals, listening attentively to all the prattling foolishness of an ignorant people who had nothing important to say. And what had he gotten for all his trouble? Death in the Wag Water River; drowning like some wayward schoolboy who had skulled time off from his lessons to steal a swim. And drowning under perplexing circumstances, too, for witnesses said that before dragging him under, the river had stripped off the white man's clothes and folded them neatly on a rock and taken his naked white body into her belly where she held him for some five days, before tossing his ravaged corpse against the pylon of a bridge. Now, when the nurse raised her voice and scolded the foolishness of a patient, she did not have to endure the wrathful reproach of the white foreigner, who was always meddling and interfering and ruining discipline and making matters infinitely worse. After all, the nurse told herself, did she not live among these people? Did she not know how they should be treated? Did she not fully understand their slack and rude ways, their slovenly habits, their wild indiscipline?

So the new doctor and the nurse saw eye to eye on the way patients should be treated. She was respectful and proper in his presence because he was a learned doctor and she was only a country nurse. But when it came to patient discipline, he deferred to her superior experience. When she berated some whining scoundrel who came running into the clinic over every little thing, the doctor would either leave her alone, or would come out of his room and add his voice to hers, lending sting to her authority. With this side of the new doctor, the nurse was very well pleased.

But there was another side to him, one that she bitterly resented. Ordinarily, she did not care to work for brown men, for she found them to be very forward people who always put on high and mighty airs for themselves. But what was even worse was the reputation that the doctor was getting among the rude, vulgar women of the village. Once, when the nurse was walking past a bar, behaving quite

289

respectably and proper, one of the rude girls had bawled out and asked whether her "boyfriend" — meaning the brown doctor — had come to the clinic yet, shouting out lewdly that she needed a "grind", which had drawn loud, raucous laughter from a few slackers who loitered in the vicinity with nothing better to do. And indeed, the nurse had begun to suspect that there was some truth to these rumours. More than once when the doctor was examining some buxom young woman, the nurse had tried to open the door on some pretext of needing to see the doctor and had found it locked. And when she had pounded determinedly on it, the doctor would either yell at her to go away, or he would open the door much later, looking winded and dishevelled as though he had been up to no good. The nurse knew from grim experience that slatternly young women who hold themselves and their bodies cheaply are common even in as staid a community as Charity Bay. Moreover, such women are quick to crack open their legs for any young man with good prospects — such as the brown doctor — in the hope of breeding a pickney for him and being supported for the rest of their lives. It was therefore her bounden duty, the nurse often and sternly reminded herself, to save the doctor from the wiles of such creatures, and to preserve the moral standing of Charity Bay.

Secretly, in her own prim way, the nurse was conducting a campaign of saving the brown doctor. For instance, she had already broken the lock to the examination room, so that the doctor could not shut her out when he was about to fall victim to some guileful slut. Not knowing what was good for him, the doctor had repeatedly asked the nurse to have the lock fixed, but she always conveniently forgot. Finally, one day he showed up with a new deadbolt lock, which he installed himself, taking the only key. But no sooner had he driven off than she set to work with a hammer and chisel and battered the lock to a twisted pulp, lying to the doctor that the damage had been inflicted by burglars. By such devious means, the nurse strove to maintain the moral standing of her community. Her mind was quite made up; no matter how many new locks the doctor put on the door of the examination room, she would break them all.

The other side of the brown doctor that the nurse disliked was his aloof, superior air, as though he knew all the answers to every one of God's mysteries. This, too, had been the attitude of the Englishman, and indeed, of every doctor ever assigned to Charity Bay, with the exception of old Dr. Morrison, a black Jamaican who had not forgotten where he had come from. When the nurse tried to explain to the brown doctor some of the marvels and wonders she had been privy to witness in her short lifetime, he assumed a manner very much like the dead Englishman's, and openly scoffed. For instance, when she tried to tell him the miraculous story of Zachariah Pelsie, who had been stricken by wasting, terminal cancer, who had been living for months at death's door, and who had gone to sea on the afternoon of Holy Thursday and returned three days later, his hacking cough lessened, the doctor had tauntingly laughed right in her face. Agitated and angry, she had sworn on her mother's grave that the story was true. She had uttered the first oaths she had used since the man she had once loved had absconded to America with all her money and never come back. She swore to the snickering doctor that after the fisherman came back from the sea, the cancer unexpectedly and mysteriously began to heal, that his body gradually recovered its colour and strength, and that even today his cough was completely gone and he was walking and talking like any healthy fisherman who goes to sea every night to catch fish. As God was her witness, the story was the blessed truth, and anyone who lived in Charity Bay could vouch for it, she said as fervently as she could, while the brown doctor leaned back in his chair and peered at her with a most annoying look of superiority.

"Remission!" he said airily, as though he knew it all.

"A miracle, sah!" she maintained stoutly.

"Remission, Nurse, that's all. Remission," the doctor said with a knowing snigger. "It's probably going to come back someday. So cancer go sometime. We don't know why. But I see better, more dramatic remission than that with my own two eyes when I was practicing medicine at the University."

"But, sah!" the nurse sputtered angrily. "Why it happen after him put out to sea to beg de help of God? Why should it happen just at dat direct time except that de hand of God touch him at sea?"

And this attitude of his, this condescending, frivolous, haughty manner, was what the nurse had despised the most about the foreigner — yet now she was bound to endure it from his brown-skinned successor. Under the circumstances, what had she done but swap "black dog for monkey" as the proverb warns every sensible soul not to do? For now the same arrogance was shining in the brown doctor's eyes, as he tolerantly explained to her the twin principles of coincidence and remission, while she squirmed peevishly and suffered through being talked down to as though she were some ignorant schoolgirl. Moreover, the brown man, when he expatiated on such obvious lies, had a disgusting habit of wrinkling his nose as though he was constantly smelling some odour that offended him. It was all a matter of immunology, the brown doctor lectured her, something that nobody understood about cancer. The nurse, unable to bear it any longer, raised her voice to protest, but the brown doctor silenced her by chiding, "Shame on you, Nurse, to believe in such country rubbish! You should know better than that!" Which was such a scathing, stinging rebuff that she was speechless with vexation and had to go quickly into the other room and pretend to be engrossed in some task before she burst into tears.

Had the brown doctor not been such a scoffer, the nurse could have told him other, more mysterious happenings, things that would have made his eyes pop open. She could

292

have, for instance, told him about the numerous times she had seen the duppy of the dead Englishman standing over her bed, peering down at her, as naked as the day his mother had borne him. Up to last week, she had seen this duppy in her very bedroom. When she had called out in a frightened voice and reached under her pillow for the talisman Lubeck had given her to ward off malevolent presences, the duppy had uttered a mournful sigh and disappeared. It was the Englishman come back to haunt her for all the times she had opposed him — Lubeck himself made this diagnosis. Moreover, and this she told no one, not even Lubeck, she suspected that the English duppy had evil designs against her body, for the last time he had appeared to her he had tried to get her to touch his big, erect manhood. Even death had not abated the foreigner's slack nature, the nurse thought with a pious shudder.

The brown doctor, however, knew it all. He knew all about duppies, and he knew all about obeah, talismans, and miracles. To this day, when the doctor's own mother was sick, she first went into the bush to consult the obeah man and be treated with his herbs, before she would go into town and see a physician. And though the doctor was too ashamed to admit this to anyone, when he was a child he himself had seen a rash of duppies. He had seen the duppy of a fisherman who had been killed by a shark. He had seen the duppy of a draycart driver who had died from being kicked on the head by his donkey. And once, too — though he could only dimly remember the time — he himself had quailed and shivered with fear over stories of obeah, duppies, and miracles. But today, with his new high position in life, he was more scornful and bitter about such stories than any American-educated priest.

It was a steaming summer day. The brown doctor was done with his patients and was packing up the specimens he intended to carry to Kingston. All in all, he was pleased with the·day's work. He had treated some twenty-six patients,

293

including one man suffering from a nervous affliction he claimed to have contracted from a duppy bite. The doctor had heaped scorn and ignominy on the man and driven him out of the clinic.

What especially pleased the doctor today was his overall general demeanour, for he lived in constant fear of shaming himself with some throwback, bumpkin behaviour from his childhood. But today he was well pleased with his manner, his forcefulness, his presence, all of which had been impeccable. No doubt, he had duly impressed his patients with his learning and his bearing. He had scolded them in a firm, authoritarian voice, and had talked to them about their ills and afflictions in a manner that they could understand. Because he himself was a Jamaican, the doctor could listen to a patient complaining about "water on me brain", or "pain in me navel root" and understand what was meant; and when he suggested treatment, he could address the sufferer in a polyglot of folk remedies and medical prescriptions that was highly appealing to the simple mentality of these people.

The doctor lit a cigarette, walked to the louvred window, and thought about the day's work with a sigh of satisfaction. Against the wall was a glossy calendar on which he ticked off with a red X each served day of his indenture to the wily Jamaican government. He walked over to the calendar and scratched another X on the page, and blew a lugubrious sigh at how thick and fat the calendar was.

Returning to the louvred window, the doctor daydreamed about his future life. When he was done, he told himself, he would leave the West Indies altogether. A man with brains and initiative had no future in such a place. He would migrate to America, have a successful practice, live in a mansion, and drive a big car. Perhaps, someday in the distant future, he would even pay his mother's fare so she could come and visit and be boggled beyond belief by his success. He could hear her now, extolling in patois superlatives the opulence of his home, the luxuriousness of his car, the splendour of his clothes. The villagers, their eyes popping out with wonder, would crane forward to absorb every word, shaking their heads with disbelief that one of their own sons, a boy who used to run naked and barefoot through this humble village, could have risen so high in the world. A faint smile of anticipation creased the doctor's lips, as he thought about how his reputation would spread throughout his home village. Perhaps he would even visit it someday, taking his children to see the birthplace of their father. He had no children yet. Indeed, he was not even married. But all that would come later, once he had served out his sentence to socialism. He tried to imagine what his future wife would be like, but couldn't. The only thing he knew for certain was that she would not, under any circumstances, be a West Indian. Perhaps he would marry a rich American girl. There was simply no end to what a man of persistence and brains could achieve in this world.

The doctor was peering dreamily out of the window, past the hibiscus bush whose summer flowers were tossed by a sea breeze, when the ambling figure of an incredibly ugly man carrying a sail pole came into view. Squinting through the column of smoke spiralling off his cigarette, the doctor recognized the fisherman Pelsie who was supposed to have been miraculously cured of his cancer. The fellow was monstrously ugly, his face disfigured by a swollen, elongated jawbone. Huge, gnarled hands dangled at his side, as he shuffled across the street with the sail pole slung over his shoulder, walking with the peculiar, rolling gait of a seafarer.

"Acromegaly," the doctor muttered, recognizing the twisted bone structure caused by a malfunctioning pituitary.

The hand of God on such an ugly, bestial-looking creature? the doctor asked himself sardonically, watching the gangling fisherman disappear down the pathway that led to the beach. Where was the miracle among all this nightmarish ugliness?

No doubt, when the wretch had contracted acromegaly, people had thought him obeahed or touched by a malevolent duppy. All along, the brute had had only a stupid, clinical condition that was treatable by surgery.

The doctor shook his head in amazement to think that a man as learned and gifted as himself — a doctor! — could have risen out of the same abyss of superstition in which that monstrous-looking brute now wallowed.

"Now, that's the real miracle!" the doctor muttered in a heartfelt voice, stubbing out his cigarette on the cobwebbed window sill.